Tales from Two Cities

Dervla Murphy

Tales from Two Cities

Travel of Another Sort

*It is always an impertinence for a man to claim
to write about a community of men, whether
his own or another. He cannot avoid talking
about them as if they were objects under a
microscope, and this denies them their
subjectivity and dignity. Further, he cannot
avoid making general observations about
them, and that involves denying them their
uniqueness. Such general observations again
have an air of unreality about them. While they
might describe some members of a society
accurately, they never fit all*
BHIKHU PAREKH

JOHN MURRAY

First published 1987
by John Murray (Publishers) Ltd
50 Albemarle Street, London W1X 4BD

Typeset by Inforum Ltd, Portsmouth
Printed and bound in Great Britain
by Butler & Tanner Ltd, Frome

British Library Cataloguing in Publication Data

Murphy, Dervla
  Tales from two cities : travel of another
  sort.
  1. Minorities — England 2. Cities and
  towns. — England
  I. Title
  305.8'00942   DA125.A1

ISBN 0–7195–4435–1

Contents

Acknowledgements   vi

Prologue   1

PART ONE

MANNINGHAM IN BRADFORD

1	Among the Mirpuris	5
2	Poor Britain	34
3	Domestic Dramas	51
4	Races Apart	67
5	How Anti-Racism Came to Britain	87
6	The Honeyford Affair	103

PART TWO

HANDSWORTH IN BIRMINGHAM

7	A Bed-sit in Handsworth	145
8	Singing on Sundays	160
9	Black, White and Browned-off	174
10	Black Talk	193
11	In and Around the Villa Cross	214
12	Liming Rastas and the Law	232
13	Action	255
14	Post-Riot	292

Epilogue   308

Acknowledgements

Many people have contributed in diverse ways to this book. Some, who will violently disagree with certain passages, would prefer not to be named. But my gratitude goes to them no less than to: Diana, Jock and John Murray, Jim Rose, Brenda and Keith Thomson, Jenny Woodward – and my neighbours in Manningham and Handsworth who appear in these pages *not* under their real names but without whose friendship, trust and guidance this book could never have been written.

The Joseph Rowntree Charitable Trust made it possible for me to devote more than two years to this project but are in no way responsible for the views expressed or for any inadvertent factual errors.

For Margaret Fogarty

without whose practical help, moral support and
many clarifying words of wisdom this book could
not have been written.

Prologue

The seed of this book was sown in the autumn of 1966. While cycling from London to Edinburgh I met many representatives of ethnic minorities, the majority then comparative newcomers to Britain. From Scotland I wrote to my publisher, describing this journey, and in response he suggested a book on Brown and Black immigrants. Although the subject tempted me, I doubted my ability to tackle it and not until 1983 did I find enough courage to accept the challenge. But my 1984 activities were curtailed first by a peculiarly debilitating form of hepatitis, acquired in Madagascar, and then by a frolicsome bullock who broke my back on a riverbank in Ireland. So the project was not begun until January 1985.

Nothing in my life had prepared me for *residence* in deprived urban areas, as distinct from reading about them or discussing them with involved friends. After a few months I began to feel slightly peculiar – on edge, restless, in an odd way under stress despite the increasing fascination of my work. Only then did I realise that never before had I been confined for so long to a city, or even a big town. As a truly rural animal, this new experience in middle-age almost over-taxed my adaptability. Curiously enough, the obvious horrors of urban life – traffic noise, crowds, polluted air, over-heated shops and offices – bothered me no more than the many unnatural minutiae. Like taking clothes to a laundrette, full of baffling machines, instead of washing them in a tub and hanging them on a line between apple-trees. And swimming in a chlorine-flavoured indoor pool instead of a river. And using fire-lighters instead of kindling gathered in a wood. And never seeing the night-sky or being able to enjoy the weather. In the country, every sort of weather is pleasurable: gales, frost, heat, rain, snow. In cities, each weather mood merely exacerbates some nuisance – litter blown in one's face, burst pipes, effluvia from rotting garbage, sprays of oily water, treacherous piles of dingy snow. At the end of my exile I was no longer puzzled by youthful vandalism, drug-addiction and despair.

As a newcomer in Manningham and Handsworth, I had to explain to some of my neighbours, and to local community leaders and Race Relations Industry (R R I) workers, that I am neither a journalist nor an academic, that I belong to no political party or pressure group and have no religious affiliations. This thumb-nail self-portrait baffled many. For some thirty years, race relations have been providing much grist for the mills of academics, journalists and politicians. Such people are familiar figures in multi-racial districts, but a pen-wielder belonging to none of those categories (and who chose to *live* in inner-city areas!) had a disconcerting effect. Among Browns and Blacks, my scribbling presence in their neighbourhoods provoked varied reactions. There was much uncomprehending indifference. There was an amount of explicit hostility – "We don't need any more *studies* of our problems, we need *action!*" And there was occasional faint optimism – "Maybe your book can help us."

Many Whites imagine Britain's ethnic minorities to be far more numerous, and therefore 'threatening', than they are; 'ten or fifteen per cent' is a usual guesstimate. Yet the 1985 figure for the entire non-White population, including Chinese, was 2,376,000 – 4.4 per cent. It is therefore ridiculous to describe *Britain* as a multi-racial society; that description applies only to certain urban areas. Ironically, racists and anti-racists reinforce each other's positions by over-emphasising the significance of the Brown and Black elements in contemporary Britain.

Despite the above figures, this is not a book for those in search of statistics, graphs and percentages. It is a personal record of daily life in multi-racial areas and those academics and race relations experts who dismiss it as 'anecdotal', 'impressionistic' or 'subjective' will be right. Much of it deals with perceptions – with how people feel, and why.

PART ONE

MANNINGHAM
IN
BRADFORD

The Council's race relations policies must make more progress if we are to meet the expectations of young Black Bradfordians. Some 62,000 in the District (out of 464,000) have their family origins in the New Commonwealth and Pakistan . . . In two areas there will be a large measure of agreement among all three political parties on the Council. Firstly, there is the unique nature of Bradford's problems, facing the largest increase in population of any Metropolitan District in the country – and facing it in the inner-city areas where our resources and land are already under severe pressure. Secondly, the changing face of Bradford will call for new ideas, new attitudes and ways of working, and new relationships from all of us, members as well as officers. In ten years the District has moved from full employment, a superficially healthy-looking economy and relative prosperity for virtually everyone, to massive factory closures, some 12,500 people who have been out of work for more than a year, 7000 of whom have been jobless for more than two years. Nearly 50,000 people in the District are drawing Supplementary Benefit, and more than a third of all families rely on some kind of State benefit . . . Only 7 per cent of black school-leavers are finding work, compared with 37 per cent of white school-leavers. One in six of all unemployed people come from the black communities, though they make up only a tenth of the workforce . . .

District Trends 1984: The Changing Face of Bradford

It is human, when we do not understand another human being, and cannot ignore him, to exert an unconscious pressure on that person to turn him into something that we *can* understand. The effect on the person so influenced is liable to be the repression and distortion, rather than the improvement, of the personality; and no man is good enough to have the right to make another over in his own image.

T.S. ELIOT: *Notes Towards The Definition of Culture* (Faber)

1 · Among the Mirpuri

It was 8.30 on a January evening: very wet, very cold, very dark. Outside Bradford's Interchange the passengers off the London train scrambled for taxis, bent against a squally sleet-laden wind. An elderly couple asked where I was going and offered to share their taxi. It seemed the White driver was an acquaintance, which probably explained why they had deliberately missed their turn in the queue, allowing someone else to take a Brown-driven taxi. (Few Bradford taxi-drivers are White.)

Almost opposite the Interchange a floodlit neo-classical building – St George's concert-hall – magnificently contradicted my expectations of universal urban decay. But the rest of that taxi-ride was as expected, along a wide dark street – Thornton Road, where Bradford's first mill was opened in 1798 – with blank industrial ruins looming cliff-like on either side, followed by black voids where other mills or factories had recently been demolished. The street lights were very dim. There was almost no traffic. There wasn't a human in sight. I was reminded of travel in Madagascar, where one always seems to arrive after dark in unimaginable, unlit towns. Yet already, most oddly, I found myself falling in love with Bradford – perhaps partly because of the welcoming atmosphere created by my three companions, with their direct, warm-hearted interest in the newcomer. But of course it was more than that; places have energies that are instantly apprehended, regardless of the manner or moment of one's arrival.

My companions' warm-heartedness did not extend to Browns and Blacks. When I divulged my Bradford purpose their feelings were at once revealed.

"I hope you'll tell it like it is," said the driver. "How they've messed up this city – and worse to come, the way they're breeding."

"Back in the sixties," said the wife, "we were told they'd not settle, they'd be gone after a few years. I never believed that. Why should they go back to their jungle when they can live off the tax-payers here?"

"They've destroyed us both ways," said the husband. "Our industry's been killed by cheap imports from Asia – and why? Because out there they still pay slave-wages. It's O K if they exploit each other, but sack one of them here, for good reasons, and we've a court case about discrimination! No wonder people don't want to employ them. Once you've got them you can't get rid of them – *I* know! I've had my problems. It's *intimidation* of Englishmen we have now – not *discrimination* against blacks . . ."

I was soon to become familiar with these half-truths, suspicions, exaggerations and distortions: symptoms of fear, ignorance and angry frustration. If something has gone dreadfully wrong with the management of your own society, it's some comfort to feel that 'They' are really to blame.

Turning right off the Thornton Road, we zig-zagged through a maze of little one-way streets. "Paki kids have no road-sense," explained the driver. "They fool around all over like they never saw a car. So the Council blocked one end of half the roads – never mind *us* being inconvenienced!"

"You're wrong," said the husband. "The *police* had them blocked! Makes it easier to deal with riots. And riots we'll have, sooner or later."

The driver evidently knew Boston Street well and despite the slashing rain insisted on carrying my luggage through a dark covered passageway to what seemed to be someone's back-door. As a stranger to the North of England and its architectural idiosyncrasies, I could never have found my destination unaided; it wouldn't have occurred to me to look for a hall-door in what appeared to be a backyard.

A chain of friends and friends' friends had led me to Boston Street, in the heart of an area described by some locals as Bradistan or Pakiford. The luxury of my small, square ground-floor bed-sitter took me aback. It had a writing-table by the window, books about all aspects of race relations lining one wall from floor to ceiling, a dual-purpose divan and wall-to-wall carpeting – *not* my idea of slumming it. In the tiny hallway I found a sink and electric kettle; at the top of the narrow stairs was a bathroom, to be shared with a young White couple – among the few Whites on Boston Street – who soon became good friends. Later I discovered that during vacations this luxury apartment serves as an academic's refuge, to which my friend Kate retreats from family distractions to write about race relations learnedly and sensibly (the two, alas! don't always go together).

I awoke before dawn and for an instant fancied myself back on the Indian sub-continent. Small sounds, like fleeting scents, can have powerful associations; and a yard or so from my head, on the other side of the wall, a woman (or child) was rhythmically pounding spices.

Joseph Fieldhouse's *Bradford*, read over breakfast, told me that during the second half of the nineteenth century six mill-worker families sometimes occupied two back-to-back dwellings and it was not uncommon for forty people to share one earth-closet. The Boston Street area then included some of Bradford's most congested and poorest housing, where the highest death-rates from infectious diseases were recorded annually and infant mortality was one in five. (In 1985 Manningham was one of two inner-city areas where seventeen out of every thousand babies died before their first birthday, compared with ten in other areas.) The building of back-to-backs was made illegal in 1900. Earlier attempts to ban them had been thwarted by the mill-owners, who liked the idea of being able to squeeze forty-two houses onto one acre. Before the passing of an 1860 bye-law, the density was *sixty-five* dwellings to an acre; but none of those older back-to-backs remains.

I drew the curtains on a reluctant dawn: cold grey light seeping through low clouds. The squally north wind carried a red and blue sliced-pan wrapper past my window; it swooped and soared like a stringless kite, trapped in the narrow area between my row of back-to-backs and the row opposite – twenty yards away, beyond a rough wall of concrete blocks. Some houses had been expanded by the addition of attic rooms and brightly painted dormer windows broke the symmetry of a long dark line of slate roofs.

Eager to explore, I hastened out. A cheerful milkman greeted me, then asked a question. He repeated it twice but to his huge amusement I couldn't understand a word he said. It seemed my local language problems would not be confined to the Browns; West Yorkshire's accents are attractive, but you do have to work hard at some of them.

Beyond the covered passage (six foot six inches wide and eight foot high, in obedience to an 1860 bye-law) I was on the dog-shitty pavement, surrounded by frozen mounds of soiled snow and looking up a long steep street of back-to-backs in varying states of disrepair. Opposite my pad a dozen new brick bungalows for O A Ps overlooked a humpy patch of wasteland. Near-by, at the foot of the hill, several houses had recently been demolished and the quarter-acre of rubble was strewn with squashed tins, broken bottles, old shoes, battered saucepans, two dead television sets and a stained mattress.

I walked uphill – as yet no one else was astir – pausing occasionally to look down at an uninspiring city-scape of gawky mill-chimneys dominating colossal factories and warehouses, the majority now disused. On the far side of the valley a sprawl of buildings, old and new, covered the lower slopes of a long, high ridge. Above them were snow-flecked fields; Bradford is a small city.

Half-way up Boston Street two young Sikhs, wearing mufflers and mittens, were opening a poorly stocked greengrocery opposite a dour, dark-stoned Nonconformist church with broken windows. I bought a pound of apples and introduced myself by way of letting the neighbourhood know my purpose in Manningham. One young man said crisply, "You'll find no race problems here unless you're looking for them. People who want trouble make it." I felt they were not going to be allies.

Twenty minutes later, among the little streets off Carlisle Road, the scene suddenly became animated as children of all ages made their way towards various schools – including Drummond Middle School, then at the centre of the Honeyford Affair. A parent or grandparent escorted the smaller ones. Those habitually escorted by males came, I later discovered, from ultra-orthodox purdah households. However decrepit or neglected-looking a house or garden might be, the children emerging from it were well-groomed and neatly dressed. One needs to remind oneself at intervals how much living standards have improved, for even the most deprived of inner-city residents. In 1899 Bradford pioneered school medical inspections, organised by the celebrated educational reformer, Margaret McMillan. The first inspection revealed that over one hundred Manningham children had not taken their clothes off for several months.

I wandered around Manningham all day, occasionally relaxing in pubs or what I spontaneously thought of as *chai-khanas* – Mirpuri cafés, where one could enjoy, very cheaply, those freshly cooked savoury tidbits which most Browns still prefer to the packaged horrors foisted upon us gullible Whites by the food industry. Within that small area the range of Brown enterprises was astonishing: drapers, grocers, halal butchers, insurance and travel agencies, electrical and video shops, newsagents and tobacconists, shoe-shops, tailors' workshops, doctors' and dentists' surgeries, new and second-hand furniture stores. But it was evident that this is an area in deep economic trouble. The shops were sparsely stocked and many shabby premises looked as though they might close at any moment – which several did, during my time in Bradford.

The Mirpuris' self-servicing philosophy partly explains why so many speak little or no English though it may be twenty or even thirty years since they left Azad Kashmir. Even some who attended local schools have only a sketchy knowledge of the language: a serious handicap when job-hunting in the 1980s. (Their fathers and grandfathers needed no English to work in the mills and factories, but few such jobs remain.) A remarkable number of Brown bus-drivers are incapable of holding a conversation in English, yet are often to be seen absorbed in an Urdu book as they sit in buses during breaks – while their White colleagues discuss football and racing.

Conversationally my first Manningham day was not very fruitful; only one casual acquaintance seemed likely to become a friend. But I had known that encountering Mirpuris in Manningham would be quite unlike encountering them in Azad Kashmir. As a solitary White woman, cycling through their territory, I had provoked excited curiosity, some initial distrust or apprehension and a great deal of hospitality. As a White in Britain, I was just another of those people with whom the average Mirpuri chooses to have minimal contact, partly (but only partly) because most Whites have never shown most Mirpuris an alternative course.

As I returned to Boston Street, hundreds of schoolchildren were also returning home. Observing their adult companions, I marvelled at how little exile has changed these people – at least externally. The way the women walk and dress and gesture and speak to their children and carry their babies makes the 1960s notion of 'assimilation' seem laughable. Many of the older men, and a few of the younger generation, still wear loose shirts and baggy trousers and skull-caps or warm Gilgiti hats; and some have carefully hennaed hair and beards. Already I could recognise a few faces, seen earlier in the café or offices. These also serve as clubs where men discuss news from the villages, marriage contracts, business deals or details of the latest faction fight about funding for Bradford's new mosques – and where in emergencies interest-free loans may be obtained for an urgent journey home or the purchase of a bargain-offer house.

I felt then a stab of nostalgia for the Mirpuris' homeland. Momentarily, the hills and chimneys and laneways of Bradford were replaced, with the vividness of an hallucination rather than a memory, by the wondrous beauty of Azad Kashmir as I first knew it in 1963 – before migrants' remittances brought some prosperity to their villages. The area was then a 'restricted zone', being part of the territory to which India and Parkistan both laid claim after Partition, and foreign travellers required a military permit. The stony dirt tracks carried no motor-traffic and in deep gorges, between red and silver cliffs, rope-pulley 'bridges' spanned swift snow-fed rivers. Ancient pine-forests darkened the higher ridges and on steep sunny slopes vivid butterflies, big as bats, hovered over white and bronze heather. Where the slopes became gentler, groups of mud-walled thatched dwellings were scattered between neat irrigated terraces. On level ground stood grey villages of dry-stone houses, the majority single-storeyed, where grain was winnowed on mud threshing-floors. Every day the women and girls had to walk at least three miles to fetch water, or firewood, or grass for the buffalo. And always, away in the distance, rose the foothills of the Himalayas, massive and rough and forever snowy.

Coming back to Manningham, I wondered if my new neighbours ever longed to exchange Bradford's monochrome streets and low grey skies for their own bright land of blue and golden spaces. But mine was the romantic traveller's image. Most Mirpuris no doubt see Azad Kashmir not as one of this world's loveliest regions but as one of Pakistan's poorest districts.

In 1963 the pattern of migration to Britain was already well established, though it had not yet visibly marked those areas I explored. Badr Dahya, a distinguished Pakistani anthropologist (to whom I am much indebted), found that:

> The first Indo-Pakistanis to settle in Bradford were former seamen who, during 1941, were directed from seaports such as Liverpool, Middlesborough and Hull to munition factories and essential wartime industries in the Bradford and Leeds areas. These were the pioneers whose arrival in the city, and whose economic success there, led to the subsequent emergence and development of the immigrant communities.

That economic success was based on the purchase of shabby back-to-backs or terrace houses which no one else wanted. These were in city-centre areas from which prospering earlier immigrants (Central and Eastern Europeans) had recently moved, or in once-middle-class districts long since deserted in favour of suburbia. Prices were low: from £45 for a beat-up back-to-back to £250 or so for a spacious if decayed Victorian or Edwardian residence. Thus no building society loans were needed; buyers only had to put down deposits of £10 or £12 and pay 75 pence or £1 weekly to the seller. Meanwhile the new owner was in a position at once to make money by taking in lodgers, usually his compatriots.

Until 1950 or thereabouts, most of these were seamen who had jumped ship in a British port and made for Bradford, where they knew kinsmen would help them to find work. In those days British manufacturers were putting advertisements in Pakistani newspapers, seeking a malleable labour-force to do nasty jobs disdained by the British. There was nothing haphazard about Pakistani migration, even in the days of jumping ship, and a sophisti-cated sponsorship system evolved – which is responsible for the cohesiveness of Bradford's present-day Mirpuri community. As Badr Dahya discovered:

> From the early days of settlement, the migration of Pakistanis has been selective in terms of specific areas and specific families of origin . . . This has affected the growth of the community in Britain generally and enabled the immigrants to create small-scale units based on village-kin ties.

Few women migrated during the 1950s; in 1961 there were only eighty-one in Bradford – and 3376 men. The early immigrants planned to return home after five or ten years, having sponsored a son, brother, nephew or cousin to replace them and maintain the eastward flow of cash. Then in 1960 it was realised that imminent immigration controls would restrict the free move-ment of adult males and prohibit children from entering Britain unless both parents were already resident.

In the eighteen months before the 1962 Immigration Act became law – the 'Beat the Ban' period – thousands of women and children arrived to join their menfolk. Several Mirpuris told me that this Act is responsible for contempor-ary Britain's rapidly increasing Brown population. Had the menfolk been able to return to their families for a year every four or five years, or to remain back in Mirpur while younger men replaced them as migrant workers, many would have sought jobs in the Middle East when the recession came to Britian. "But", as one man put it, "you can't take a family to those countries. And you can't leave your wife and children here unprotected – it's not like leaving them in the village. So now for us there is no escape from Britain." The Mirpuris, contrary to popular White opinion, are not the sort of people who enjoy being on the dole.

Most of Bradford's (and Britain's) Pakistanis come from Mirpur, but there are also many thousand improbably named Campbellpuris. (It is hard to get exact figures for this sort of breakdown.) Their cultural background, and the history of their migration and settlement, are similar to the Mirpuris' yet the groups rarely mix. Most Campbellpuris come from the Chhachh area in a sub-district of Campbellpur – a corner of the world so obscure that it doesn't show up even in the *Times Atlas*. It has been unkindly suggested that post-Raj no one immediately gave Campbellpur a more appropriate name because officialdom had forgotten (or never knew) it was there. Being on the borderland between the Punjab and the North West Frontier Province (NWFP), it was often crossed and plundered by Sikh – and, later, British – troops, en route for a show-down with Afridis or Mahsuds. The town of Campbellpur (recently renamed Attock) is about midway between Peshawar and Pindi, just south of the GTR and not far from the Attock Bridge and Emperor Akbar's mighty Fort. The District's terrain is bleak and begrudging and for generations its menfolk have been migrant workers. In winter Campbellpur is too cold, in summer too hot. When I cycled through at the end of May 1963 I wrote in my diary:

> It feels like my very lungs are being blistered by the hot air. There are few trees, little greenery: on every side stretch bare stubble fields and arid wastes of rock and stony soil. One of the most appalling local sights is a cow in calf; so underfed you can plainly see the whole shape of the calf in the womb. Most humans also look underfed. In a local hospital the woman-doctor told me she does an average of twenty caesarean operations a week without one nurse or anaesthetist to help her. As a result of malnutrition, the mother's pelvic (and other) bones weaken during pregnancy, when her calcium is going to the baby, so she can't give birth normally. Some time ago, having tried to push birth control and failed, the government in despair put a tax on every new-born baby; but that didn't work either and has now been dropped. Eighty per cent of the girls still marry as soon as they reach puberty and produce ten, twelve, quite often fifteen children, seventy per cent of whom are born diseased – but fated to live on as semi-invalids because epidemics are coming under control.

It's surprising that many more Campbellpuris didn't migrate to Britain in the 1950s and early 1960s when the going was good; Mirpuris attribute this to a lack of initiative and energy. Yet as far back as 1907 the Punjab District Gazetteer (quoted by Badr Dahya in *Urban Ethnicity*) reported: 'From the northeast corner of the Chhachh very large numbers of men go out as stokers on the P&O and British India boats and come back shattered in health but full of money.' The Campbellpuris did not of course have a Mangla Dam equivalent in their lives. The creation of this hydro-electric scheme in the 1960s (it was inaugurated by President Ayub Khan in 1967) submerged some 250 Mirpuri villages and displaced over 100,000 people. Many used their lump-sum compensation money to move to Britain, though the notion that the dam was the *main* cause of Mirpuri mass-migration is quite false. Years before Mangla had been decided on, thousands were working in Britain and the sponsorship system had been firmly established. It might be truer to say that migration was stimulated by Partition, which caused an influx of

newcomers into Azad Kashmir from the Indian side of the Cease-Fire line.
This stimulus was lacking in Campbellpur, which remained comparatively
unaffected by the tragedy of 1947.

It is significant that the main Pakistani and Bangladeshi communities in
Britain – the Mirpuris, Campbellpuris and Sylhetis – all had a long tradition
of service as seamen which enabled the pioneer settlers to travel to Britain.
Their kinsmen joined them by (sometimes) more orthodox means. But
unorthodox means were needed during certain periods and in *Colour and
Citizenship*, published for the Institute of Race Relations in 1969, we read:

> Travel agents began to be active at an early stage (of the post-war migrations) in the
> ports and large towns . . . Pakistani agents established offices in Mirpur town in
> 1956-57 . . . and helped intending migrants to evade restrictions . . . All the various
> systems of control tended to work in an arbitrary and unsatisfactory way. The
> illegal practices employed by the travel agents to get their clients to Britain
> developed essentially as a black market to get round restrictions imposed at first not
> by Britain but by their home governments . . . Sometimes ingenious methods were
> used by travel agents: legitimate passports would be obtained for travel from India
> to Mauritius or Singapore, and migrants would go by that route to Britain. In
> Pakistan, passports were obtained for journeys for Muslims to visit holy places and
> migrants would go via the Middle East. Punjabi Sikhs were even disguised as
> Pakistani Muslims and smuggled through in the same way. Illiterate East Pakistani
> peasants sometimes arrived in Britain as 'students' – they travelled to Karachi,
> where an agent wrote on their behalf for a place in an educational institution in
> Britain. Upon acceptance, the necessary documents could be obtained. The most
> common illegal method was, however, forged passports endorsed for Britain.
> Passports were obtained from those already in Britain and a new photograph
> substituted. This practice reached such a pitch in the Indian community in Britain
> that Pandit Nehru was directly approached and asked for the substitution of
> genuine for forged passports in cases where the latter had been obtained in good
> faith. The request was eventually granted.

Those wheelings and dealings went on twenty-five to thirty years ago and
by now few Whites remember that they were meant not to deceive the *British*
government, which was then longing for more and more foreign labour, but
to outwit Indian and Pakistani restrictions on emigration. The caricature
image of 'sly Pakis', who wormed their way through all British legal barriers
to steal the jobs of decent Englishmen, is depressingly prevalent in Britain
today. Yet as *Colour and Citizenship* points out, quoting from a 1968 study
of the wool industry by B. Cohen and P. Jenner:

> The degree to which new capital investment and the employment of immigrants go
> together is surprising, and it would be fair to conclude that the employment of
> immigrants has facilitated new capital investment in the sample of firms under
> study. This is because new machinery is too expensive to be worked only forty or
> forty-eight hours a week and must be employed as intensively as possible, thus
> necessitating shift work. This is a trend not confined to the wool industry . . . It is
> well recognized that there is a general disinclination to work nights or changing
> shifts, and higher rates of pay are the general rule. The Pakistani workers are usually
> more willing to take this work than local labour.

Few Pakistanis ever returned home permanently, yet during the 1950s and '60s that curious psychological phenomenon known as 'the myth of return' was almost universal among them. Writing about the migrants' housing, as late as 1974, Badr Dahya observed:

> The immigrants' preference for a particular type of housing is a form of response to their immediate needs and interests, and an expression of their non-committal to Britain. In keeping with their myth of return, the immigrants do not regard the house in Britain as a 'home' but as a short-term expediency related to a particular goal or goals. It cannot be over-emphasized that the immigrants came to Britain with the firm intention of earning and saving money and eventually returning to their homeland. They did not come in order to enjoy a comfortable life here.

To some Whites, the myth of return seemed one more undesirable 'Paki' trait, a pretence designed to soothe White fears. Yet it is common among migrant communities, including the Irish, who did return to Ireland in considerable numbers during our brief economic boom in the late 1970s. However, the Pakistanis' situation was and is very different. Although their standard of living remains lower than the White working-class norm, the extreme contrast between the conveniences and facilities available in Britain and in Pakistan quite simply unfitted them for a return. Yet among the original settlers one meets some who still talk of going home; for them the myth has become a near-neurotic form of self-deception. They need it to comfort themselves, especially when the going gets rough on the domestic scene, with conflict between children and grandchildren posing problems that anger and frighten them.

Meanwhile, back in the villages, those family heads who have long ruled their migrant dependants by remote control are taking off for Paradise. And, as they depart, the old *biraderi* structure is weakening. Some young Mirpuris (and Campbellpuris) complain about money flowing away east, but it seems the flow is now lessening and may quite soon be reduced to a trickle.

* * *

Within days of arriving in Bradford I realised that terminology is the first and not the lowest hurdle for any writer on race relations in Britain. If you are 'politically aware' there is of course no problem; everyone who is not White is Black, matter-a-damn if they are magnolia-coloured Vietnamese or fairer-than-Italian Pakistanis with green eyes and brown hair. But writers are by nature distrustful of usages that tend to muffle thought or conceal facts. In Britain there is quite enough ignorance and confusion about Browns and Blacks without increasing it by applying the same label to two totally different branches of the human race. Moreover, most Asians are proud of their distinctive cultures and resent being described as 'Blacks'.

Several anti-racists warned me that if I did not use 'Black' as a political statement I would be signalling a lack of support for their cause. Since I do not see myself as an anti-racist warrior, this left me unmoved. However, my choice of 'Black' to describe West Indians is itself imprecise. Because of genetic contributions from Europe, and to a lesser extent from India and China, most West Indians are not African black. Yet among the younger generation many who are almost White choose to be described as Black – this is *their* choice, which celebrates the fact that the Caribbean's dominant genes are *African*.

In Britain, 'Asian' is popularly used to describe Indians, Pakistanis and Bangladeshis. Yet many other Asians are also present in varying numbers – for example, there are some 122,000 Chinese, as compared to 99,000 Bangladeshis. Therefore I refer to people from the Indian sub-continent as 'Browns', while aware that this too is imprecise because they range in colour from White Pathans to Black Madrassis. Finally, I was told that 'immigrants' can no longer be used, since by now some fifty per cent of Britain's Black and Brown communities are British-born.

More snow fell – quickly became grey – froze in untidily shovelled heaps. The wind was the coldest I could remember since Baltistan a decade earlier at the same season: and Baltistan is in the High Himalayas. Perversely, the Brad-fordians seem quite proud of their vile climate. "It's the Pennines," they say affectionately, as the days and the weeks pass without the sun ever once penetrating the city's lid of pewter cloud. What must their life have been like before the Clean Air campaign of the 1960s? In 1844 the Health of Towns Commissioners condemned Bradford as 'one of the dirtiest and worst regulated towns in the country'.

One morning towards the end of January I donned my ex-Himalayan gear and went out to catch the early post. I didn't expect to meet anyone – only mad dogs and Irishwomen go out in the January dawn – but hurrying round a corner I almost collided with a young Mirpuri woman. She was standing on the pavement, banging her fists on the blank gable-end of a terrace house and sobbing semi-hysterically. When I stopped beside her she stared at me with a strange blend of fear, resentment and hope. She wore an anorak over her *shalwar-kameez* and her left cheek-bone was badly bruised. "Go away!" she said. "Go away and leave me alone! Go away and stop interfering!" But the shock of my appearing had checked her near-hysteria. Within moments hope had conquered fear and soon we were standing at the bus-stop on the Thornton Road, en route for Naseem's flat in Leeds.

It took me several hours to get the story straight. At her comprehensive school, Bradford-born Naseem had fallen in love with a Mirpuri fellow-student, also Bradford-born, whose respectable family lived only two streets away from her own equally respectable family. By our standards, no complications; by Mirpuri standards, many . . . Both families had long since decided on suitable spouses, to be imported from Pakistan, for their children; and in Naseem's case the planned marriage involved long-term economic arrangements to do with village farmland.

Almost from their first meeting, at the respective ages of fourteen and fifteen, Naseem and Jahan had formed an unusually strong bond; there was more than adolescent passion between them. Both had been excited by the wide intellectual horizons opened up for them at school, where two teachers had recognised their potential and encouraged them to 'develop their individuality' – not a feature of traditional Islamic education, especially for girls. Neither was willing to accept a non-English-speaking spouse, already moulded, mentally and emotionally, by traditions which in their view needed considerable adaptation to modern life – though not outright rejection. So in October 1984, after a year of futile pleading and infrequent clandestine meetings, they eloped to Leeds – aged nineteen and twenty – believing that their future happiness justified this desperate move. Yet neither felt much immediate happiness because of the grief they were causing to those who loved them and would never be able to understand their betrayal.

This elopement brought dishonour on both families to an extent beyond our imagining. There is no parallel in Western society; the most spectacular European *mésalliance* would be trivial in comparison. King Edward VIII's choice of Mrs Simpson in preference to the throne of England might come closest in terms of treachery, an abdication of responsibility, an attack on the structures that uphold moral decency and social stability, an insult to tradition, an unforgivably selfish giving in to a personal whim. Naseem and Jahan had devastated their families, in both Britain and Pakistan, while jeopardising their younger siblings' marriage prospects and cutting themselves off, perhaps permanently, from the emotional support of their own tight-knit community – an immensely important factor in the lives of young Browns. (Sadly, inner-city White youngsters are no longer aware of belonging to a community.)

Jahan was studying in Leeds for an arts degree. Despite Naseem's two As and a B at A Level, her father forbade her to go to university; but in Leeds she began an Open University Science course. Both she and Jahan hoped to become teachers. They lived in a damp basement flat with a shared outside lavatory in a street of three-storey, rather elegant Edwardian houses not far from the university.

Naseem and I had to put our shoulders to the new door to force it open. "My husband made it," explained Naseem, "after the old one fell apart. But he didn't get the size right." The large bed-sitter – simply furnished, neat and clean – was ill-lit with an icy chill in the air. Using one continuous movement, Naseem switched on an electric lamp, a one-bar electric fire and an antique television set. It seemed that to her, as to too many of her generation of all colours, an active though disregarded television set was as essential as light or heat.

Two days previously, Jahan had been called to Pakistan following the death of his paternal grandfather. For health reasons his father could not fly so this was an inescapable duty, despite the family rift. In true Mirpuri fashion he had borrowed his fare within three hours and Naseem assured him that she would be fine – could easily cope for a fortnight – he mustn't worry. He left the flat at 6.00 p.m. and for the first time in her life she spent a night alone. She couldn't sleep; it didn't help that amidst all the shock and bustle Jahan had forgotten to leave her any housekeeping money. Next day her nerve broke; she had no close friends in Leeds and none of the kin-network back-up that would normally have been available. She and Jahan had often discussed the possibility of attempting reconciliations with their families; the chief deterrent was Naseem's father, a man notoriously unforgiving. However, she and her mother had always been exceptionally close and now, in her panic and loneliness, she persuaded herself that all would be well if she appeared unexpectedly on the doorstep.

Twenty-four hours after Jahan's departure she took a bus to Bradford Interchange and a taxi to her home, two streets away from my pad. The taxi fare emptied her purse but she lacked the courage to walk alone from the Thornton Road bus-stop. Her youngest brother, aged ten, answered her knock and shouted in astonishment. Father at once appeared – abused her verbally – then struck her on the face before trying to throw her out of the house. Mother intervened and was herself beaten up but somehow succeeded in persuading Father that Naseem must at least be allowed to stay the night; it was Siberian cold and the dark streets of Manningham were deserted. She was not allowed to speak to her mother but locked alone in the kitchen, without any bedding. Then at first light, five minutes before we met, Father pushed her onto the street warning her that if she didn't quickly leave the neighbourhood she and her mother would both regret it . . .

It was almost noon when Naseem finished her story; there had been several interludes of tearful incoherence. We went out then, to lunch in a small Sikh restaurant, and discussed what to do next. Naseem had half a dozen relatives in other cities but only one on whom she could depend in this crisis: her mother's sister, who had moved from Bradford to Glasgow four years previously, after her husband's death, and was living with a married son. She worked as a seamstress and within a week of the elopement had secretly sent Naseem a £20 wedding-present money-order. "She hates my father," said Naseem, who under the influence of curry was regaining her poise and what I judged to be a natural cheerfulness. "I think she liked us going against him. She'd be a rebel too if she was younger!"

Three hours later Naseem was on a Glasgow-bound bus and I was on my way back to Bradford. Soon she wrote, assuring me that all was well. At the end of February she wrote again, from Leeds. Jahan was home and anxious to meet me – would I come to eat curry? I did. And Jahan insisted on reimbursing me for that bus-ticket to Glasgow.

Even the most fervent White anti-racist, who repeatedly proclaims the need for 'parity of esteem in a multi-cultural society', finds it hard to feel equal esteem for Brown and White marriage customs. And many will admit, if they are honest, that they can only *pretend* to regard arranged marriages as OK for some (Brown) people. It's all in the conditioning. Everything that marks us as modern Europeans is affronted by the very thought of a young couple being told by their elders that now they are to marry – and like it! The institution of the arranged marriage, as we perceive it, makes a full frontal attack on some of our most revered concepts.

It seems odd that we now take for granted, as a basic human right, complete freedom to choose a marriage partner; parental consent, and sometimes parental pressure, was until recently part of our own tradition. However, we do now value this 'human right' – excessively, most Browns think, deducing from Europe's divorce statistics that 'love marriages', unbuttressed by social and religious expectations of permanence, are a shockingly bad idea.

Among Browns there are 'arranged' marriages, 'approved' marriages and 'forced' marriages. It is not always easy for the families concerned – never mind outsiders – to be sure into which category a particular marriage fits. Dutiful offspring may go through the required matrimonial hoops without complaint while feeling so inwardly rebellious that their marriage really belongs to the 'forced' category. But blatantly forced marriages are rare and their victims usually come of very rich or very poor families. It may however be true, as a few middle-class Pakistanis suggested to me, that forced marriages are now increasing in Britain, especially among Mirpuris, because of the reluctance of British-born youngsters to accept Pakistani-born partners.

Arranged marrriages – the norm – take place after both sets of parents have consulted about the temperaments and predilections of their children and decided that the couple are well suited and likely to develop a genuine mutual affection and create a secure home for the next generation. Usually both youngsters are content with their parents' choice. In the average Brown family, as in any other, parents love their children and wish 'to do the best they can' for them. The children know this and have been brought up to see it as their parents' duty – and one manifestation of parental love – to find them suitable mates. The majority, even now in Britain, do not envy their White contemporaries who are left to cope unaided with the awesome responsibility of selecting a congenial partner for a life-long relationship. They often blame White parents for our high divorce rate, arguing that unhappy marriages are only to be expected if parents shirk their duty.

Approved marriages seem to be mainly confined to the educated, semi-Anglicised middle class. If the changed circumstances of life in Britain make it difficult for parents to play their traditional part they sometimes trust their children to choose for themselves, while retaining the right of veto. I met several 'approved' couples in Birmingham; all were Hindu or Sikh, which was probably no coincidence. Islam is much less flexible, especially where women are concerned. Abdelwahab Bouhdiba states it starkly in *Sexuality in Islam*:

> The primacy of man over woman is total and absolute. Woman proceeds from man. Woman is chronologically secondary. She finds her finality in man. She is made for his pleasure, his repose, his fulfilment . . . Male supremacy is fundamental in Islam . . . The Qur'an speaks of a gap 'of a single degree between the sexes, in favour of men . . .'

Islam's downgrading of women is however another problem, to which I shall shortly return. My own observations of arranged marriages, in Afghanistan, Pakistan, India and Nepal, long ago broke down my inherent prejudice against them. I have stayed in households both rich and poor where the husband and wife – who in some cases had not even seen each other before their wedding-day – were as devoted and mutually considerate as any White couple of my acquaintance. There were of course other households where irritation, boredom or positive dislike marred the relationship between the parents – a regrettable state of affairs, but one not unknown in the West.

The widespread fallacy that all arranged marriages are forced marriages – the gateway to a life of misery – is reinforced by the British media, which sensationalise and over-simplify exceptional cases of suffering, conflict and tragedy. 'Arranged marriages' have become a popular stick with which to beat the Browns – not surprisingly, when even some anti-racists, predisposed to see only good in other cultures, find them hard to take. This is one of many areas in which well-informed and responsible media reporting could do more than all the commissions, committees and councils of the RRI to improve race relations in Britain.

During my evening in Leeds with Naseem and Jahan, I wondered how soon they would regret (if they weren't already regretting) their defiant gesture of 'self-determination'. Although in many ways a remarkable pair, one could detect certain stresses and strains within their relationship after less than five months of marriage. It seemed Jahan was finding it hard, in practice, to abandon that belief in male supremacy which had regulated every male–female relationship in his experience. And Naseem was constantly poised to defend her female equality, without being sufficiently sure of it to do so effectively. It cannot be possible suddenly to discard one's conditioning and switch to thinking, feeling and *being* on a new plane for which nothing – except a superficial school acquaintance with another culture – has prepared one.

In some 'runaway marriage' cases, free of super-scandals like pre-marital 'living in sin' or having 'a little accident', reconciliations do take place after the first baby's arrival, grandchildren being famed as bridge-builders in all societies. But Mirpuri men are more reluctant than most to cross such bridges, however their wives may feel, unless an only son is involved; and Jahan had three younger brothers. Moreover, during our first meeting Naseem had told me of her determination not to have a child until Jahan could afford "a healthy home for it". She admitted that this unilateral decision was not only severely testing Jahan's commitment to 'a marriage of equals' but was causing him some anxiety about his manhood, for how could he be sure of it until he saw his first child? On meeting Jahan I got the impression that he was readier than she for a return to the fold, despite her impulsive dash home when demoralised by solitude. As a woman, she stood to gain as well as lose by maintaining the status quo. For Jahan the peripheral losses, apart from the central gain of marriage to a woman he obviously loved deeply, were humiliating by his standards and not counterbalanced by peripheral gains.

Naseem and Jahan as a couple are at once victims and pioneers: victims of a 'multi-cultural' situation that they personally found intolerable; pioneers whose experiment has to be made since Britain's Mirpuri community must become more loosely knit. They are not of course unique; their generation is producing, of necessity, many such victim-pioneers.

It is extra hard for me – by nature an arch-loner – to comprehend the emotional, mental and material inter-dependence of Brown community members. The Mirpuris are an extreme example of this inter-dependence, which partly explains – without excusing – the harshness of men like Naseem's father towards aberrant children (especially daughters). The stakes involved are very high; not only the honour and prestige (*izzat*) of an extended family but also that of an entire *biraderi* – a kinship group descended from the same male ancestor of which the extended family forms one component. A White family afflicted by a *mésalliance* (which nowadays might be in or out of wedlock) would perhaps refer to being 'disgraced' but their misfortune would not be *felt* as a disgrace in at all the same way. The parents might experience sadness, disappointment and worry about their child's future; but an adult son or daughter, being regarded as a separate automous individual, simply doesn't have the power to spread the contagion of disgrace throughout even their immediate family – never mind an extended family, or a whole community. They might be thought to have disgraced *themselves*, but that's another matter. Urban Britain has no *izzat* equivalent; the Mirpuris would have found themselves much more at home had they migrated to rural Ireland thirty years ago. We did then have something similar: the deep shame felt when a daughter had an illegitimate baby, which prompted many parents to reject such girls in an attempt to conceal the loss of family honour. Even that, however, was not quite the same thing; only the honour of the immediate family was involved so the pressures on all concerned were proportionately less.

The submergence of people's individuality within their group – or rather, the prevention by the group of the emergence of individuality – forms as high a barrier as colour, caste or creed to mutual understanding between Whites and Browns. We manage our relationships on a one-to-one basis, whether with a pub acquaintance, an employer, a lover, a friend, a child, a business colleague. But with most Browns a relationship cannot be one-to-one; *you* are one, *they* are many. Their 'many-ness' gives them an inner strength, security and calm you don't have; they know they can rely on an emotional and practical back-up system that will never let them down as long as they keep the rules. But they lack what 'one-ness' provides: a clearly defined separate mental existence, a fenced-off personal space in which as an individual you are self-regulatory, frequently making independent decisions (for better or worse) and taking up attitudes (right or wrong) that do not necessarily conform to those held by the community into which you happen to have been born.

I remember (in as it happens Kotli, though it might have been anywhere on the sub-continent) talking at length one evening to a dear Pakistani friend, a woman of about my own age who had read history with spectacular success at Cambridge and was then doing research on some esoteric aspect of the Gupta dynasty. There came a turn in the conversation which suddenly revealed her many-ness and I had an absurd yet not insignificant reaction. To me that revelation seemed to make her inaccessible as the sort of friend I wanted her to be; our terms of reference were fundamentally different and must forever remain so. At that time I had not long left Europe; later I learned how to cope with the unexpected appearance of cultural chasms.

I also learned (which proved useful in Manningham) to view those chasms from the other side, trying to get a glimpse of how White one-ness impinges on a Brown – especially an unsophisticated Brown. In everyday life it can be even more disconcerting than Brown many-ness is to us. It makes for unpredictability and therefore undependability; when everyone seems free to do their own thing you can't ever be quite sure of anyone's reaction in a given situation – so how can you *trust* anyone? Evidently there is no book of rules: or if there is it allows so many unwritten exceptions it's not worth studying.

One-ness also appears to condone an extremity of selfishness which Browns find quite barbarous. The most quoted example is our neglect of ageing relatives. It is almost impossible to convince a Brown that many old White people – because of their one-ness – prefer to be independent of children, grandchildren, nephews, nieces, *et al.* But White selfishness is detected too in other spheres. The notion of one brother going bankrupt while another continues to prosper, ignoring the need for fraternal assistance, is abhorrent to Mirpuris. (There are of course some urbanised Browns who have adopted the White way of business and regard such callousness as inevitable though regrettable; but to be guilty of it would still make them feel ashamed.) Again, the White failure to rally round *en masse* during family crises – serious illness, death, a house-fire, a family member in trouble with the police – is deplored and derided. As is our apparent reluctance to share good fortune. Browns are scandalised by the bright son of poor parents becoming upwardly mobile, marrying a posh girl, buying a smart house in the suburbs, driving a fine car, flying off to Miami for his holidays – but leaving his parents in their high-rise council flat or back-to-back, still dependent on public transport. *Izzat* would not permit such arrant selfishness and disrespect for elders. Like most tools of social control, it has its advantages and its disadvantages.

Unfortunately the advantages of Islam's attitude to women are largely confined to Muslim men, with occasional spin-offs for non-Muslim women. I have often benefited from Islamic chivalry; in Muslim countries I was assiduously protected, as a woman, by tribesmen and villagers whose hostility might well have been aroused by a solitary White male traveller. In remote places I have several times shared sleeping accommodation with an unknown Muslim man, rightly confident that Islamic chivalry was a sure guarantee of no hassle. (Exceptional regions, where Islamic chivalry seems defunct, are eastern Turkey and north-eastern Persia. In my experience both areas are infested by sex maniacs, male *and* female. On five separate occasions, when I thought I was safe for the night in a harem, lesbians tried to seduce me.)

However, those who matter in this context are Muslim women and their continuing oppression seems an indefensible anachronism near the end of the twentieth century. Apologists for Islam protest that the Prophet is not to blame, that over the centuries his teachings – like Christ's – have taken a hammering from his followers. Yet the degree of male chauvinist piggery sanctioned by the Qur'an is considerable. While emphasising what Christians describe as the sacramental quality of human love, it also emphasises that the Islamic family should be a male-worshipping institution and gives men the right to beat their wives (a right still regularly exercised in some communities) if they also work hard to maintain them. The fact that all over the world there are millions of loved and respected Muslim wives, and adored and pampered Muslim daughters, owes more to mankind's good instincts than to the wisdom of the Prophet.

The Qur'an 'directives' about the status and function of women were deleterious enough, but worse was to follow. In Arabia the mystical element in the Qur'anic view of sexuality was soon being distorted, originally for complex socio-economic reasons. From this distortion there evolved a system of unrestrained sexual licence for men, based on concubinage. In many regions where Islam prevailed, this led to the virtual imprisonment of 'respectable' women – to that barbed-wire-entanglement of restrictions which long outlasted the 'concubinage era' and even today prevents most Muslim women from becoming anything more than the property of fathers and husbands.

In Britain it is still quite common (though there are fewer cases than previously) for girls to be withdrawn from school at puberty and sent to stay with relatives or friends in another city until marriage-time – the education authorities being told that they have 'gone to the village' in Pakistan. Even harsher is the treatment of girls who have been offered university places and are eager to take them up but won't be allowed to leave home. Within a few months I met nine such thwarted daughters and heard of a dozen more, which made me revise an opinion formed in 1963 as I cycled through Azad Kashmir. One evening I noted in my diary: 'These people are in general the most moronic I've met since Persia.' (In those days one was blithely unselfconscious about racial remarks.) There is however little evidence of dull-wittedness among Bradford's Mirpuri pupils – perhaps by 1963 many of the more intelligent and enterprising villagers had already emigrated?

Some Bradford teachers, who take seriously their responsibilities towards Brown pupils, endure torments of conscience because of the Mirpuris' opposition to the workings of sex-equality in everyday school life. How should a headmaster deal with a sixteen-year-old Muslim girl who is regularly meeting a boyfriend during the lunch-hour – in a public place, and merely to *talk*? Should he act *in loco parentis* and forbid the meetings – with the probable result that they would continue to take place, but furtively – or should he tell the father, who trusts a headmaster to protect his daughter, with the certain result that the girl would be removed from school before doing O Levels? Or should he react as though the girl were White and do nothing? Most teachers' natural inclination is to treat Browns like Whites by way of 'developing their individuality'. But if this leads to friction within families is it the right approach? Should teachers not give Brown girls special treatment to back up parental training and help them to become the sort of young adults who will meekly fulfil parental expectations? Is it fair or wise to nurture independent thinking in girls who cannot hope to enjoy any freedom on leaving school?

One case still haunts me. An intelligent and attractive sixteen-year-old girl had a Mirpuri boyfriend who came every day from a neighbouring school to chat with her during the lunch-hour; they always sat openly on a bench across the road in full view of the playing-fields. The headmaster chose to ignore the situation, though in that particular school a general rule – to placate Mirpuri parents – forbade Brown girls to leave the school grounds during break-times. His leniency was based on the girl's reputation for sound sense; she was a hard worker with a good chance of a university place (father permitting). However, the *biraderi* grapevine eventually relays most of what each Mirpuri does in Bradford and one day Father took time off from bus-driving to catch his daughter in the act. He refused to listen to the headmaster's pleas for mercy and withdrew her from school. Next day he took more time off – just enough to parade his daughter once around the school grounds during the lunch-hour, so that all her school-mates could see her clean-shaven scalp.

Oddly enough, while living in Manningham my feelings about 'women and Islam' remained under control: perhaps partly because of the influence (subliminal!) of local pressure requiring deference to 'multi-culturalism', and partly because one instinctively tolerates taboos that seem an integral part of one's neighbours' religious life. However, when I moved to Handsworth a tiny incident lit the fuse of my rage and I realised that for months I'd been sitting on an emotional time-bomb.

The incident happened in the course of my pad-hunt. I had promised to call back to a certain house, in a street largely inhabited by Pakistanis, to tell the Mirpuri owner whether or not I wanted to rent his flat. I didn't, having found a more suitable base in a Black area, and therefore I brought a box of Punjabi sweetmeats for his invisible wife and numerous children, since he had gone to some trouble to help me. His eldest daughter, with whom I had already had two conversations, opened the door; she was a good-looking nineteen-year-old, timid and rather gauche with the White visitor, but obviously intelligent. Her father was out and when I tried to give her my verbal message and present her with the box she retreated in confusion. I could hear her calling her nine-year-old brother from the back-garden. Following her into the living-room, which opened onto the garden, I again tried to give her my message and the sweetmeats. "No – wait, please!" she said, backing away from me. "My brother is coming – tell him – give it to him!" He arrived a moment later – two foot over a jampot, with poor English, but cheerful and confident and very much in command of the situation. He listened carefully to my message, took the box and thanked me politely, offered me tea and when I declined ushered me to the door. Meanwhile his sister had been standing silent and motionless in a corner of the living-room.

Although this was such a tiny incident, it said it all. If you are grown-up, a fluent English-speaker and potentially competent *but female* you automatically play second fiddle to a scruffy little primary-schoolboy with halting English who *because he is male* is assumed to be already better able to handle 'responsibility' than you could ever be.

Previous talks had revealed that young woman's latent possibilities; otherwise my time-bomb might not have gone off when it did. I felt an almost personal sense of outrage as I walked away from the house, up a street where lots of happy little Brown girls (pre-puberty so free) were playing boisterously with lots of happy little Brown boys. For days afterwards I flinched at each remembering of that brief symbolic scene. Its very brevity and simplicity perhaps explained why it had so devastated me. My Manningham experiences had included a few long-drawn-out women's dramas, to be related in due course. But though the suffering involved was considerable, and draining for all concerned, the complexities of those cases lessened their immediate emotional impact. They required detached thought; to have allowed oneself to *feel* too much could have led to some foolish words or impulsive deeds. In the brother–sister incident there was no such constraint. Therefore I *felt* – and for some days continued to feel, intensely. Then I cooled down and began to re-think my stance on 'women and Islam'; or, more specifically, Pakistani women living in Britain and Islam.

There is nothing monolithic about Islam, with its 500 million or so adherents, and I have so far been using the word far too loosely. 'Islam' is as general a term as 'Christianity' and there are significant differences not only between Sunnis, Shi'ahs and Ismailis but between the Muslims of Africa, Malaysia, Arabia, Persia – and Indo-Pakistan. Moreover, within Pakistan itself the Mirpuri Muslims are often referred to as 'conservative', 'obscurantist', 'bigoted' – even 'fanatical'. Soon after arriving in Manningham I realised that these people are quite extraordinarily like Irish Roman Catholics; between them they create an intangible yet powerful *something* in the atmosphere that is still to be found in rural Ireland. Whether the starting point is Islam or Christianity, it seems the experience of having been for centuries an impoverished, backward agricultural region/country, dominated by tough neighbours and dependent on religious consolations and certainties, fosters the same type of rigid, fervent faith, with much emphasis on traditional taboos, ritual devotional practices and superstitious customs.

How Muslims conduct their religious/social/family affairs in their own countries is their own business. But by now there is a strong case to be made for legal interference in their domestic affairs when they are citizens of Britain, able to avail themselves of all the advantages of being British. Given their continuing reluctance to come to terms voluntarily with some of the laws of their adoptive country, someone some time is going to have to take action about the problems of British female Muslims. This will mean confronting the wrath of British male Muslims, and being accused of religious intolerance, racialism and so on. The first essential, then, will be to move the controversy from the area of religion and race to the area of human rights, where it belongs.

The notion that there can be no interference with Muslim family life because it is so bound up with religious beliefs must be closely examined. For many male Muslims the name of the game is not religion but power. Men everywhere have resisted sex-equality and Muslims are more resistant than most, having enjoyed more power over women, for more centuries, than anyone else. Evidence of this may be found every day among young British-born men who are pleased to think of *themselves* as 'emancipated' Bradfordians or Brummies.

One day in Bradford I was shown around a new Council-funded Asian youth club by Rustam – handsome, energetic, articulate, with a good job in his father's small business. He had come to Britain in 1965, aged five, and never been back to Mirpur. "We could afford it, but why waste money on fares? Our future is *here* – we called my grandparents instead of all that flying back to see them."

Reconstruction work was still going on and Rustam proudly pointed out the area that was being converted into a bar. "But doesn't Islam forbid alcohol?" said I, tongue-in-cheek. Rustam laughed. "Yes, but we are now British – we are forward-looking!" Next we visited the recreation room, where young men and boys were playing darts and pool, and then the gymnasium, where athletic types were taking healthy exercise. "Is this a 'Men Only' club?" I asked, "No, no!" said Rustam. "When work is finished we'll set aside one evening a week for girls. That is enough – not many will come. And those who do will have to pretend they're going somewhere else, like to an evening class!" He obviously found that situation amusing. But he was less amused when I asked why it should be easier to break the alcohol taboo than to be 'forward-looking' about sex-equality.

"That is another sort of thing," he said severely. "If we want to take a drink – well, why not? Times change, people in different countries have different habits. Millions of good Muslims drink. The problem with our women is not the same – it is *important*. You can't be in a hurry about changing old customs or a lot of people will get upset. Most of our women don't want your sort of independence. They're used to security and they . . ."

I interrupted to ask if those few girls who will use the club wouldn't like just enough independence to be able to use it openly, without having to pretend they were going somewhere else. This time Rustam's laugh was slightly strained. "You take it all too seriously! Our girls *enjoy* that game of fooling their parents, for them it makes more fun! You Whites – you try to meddle with our ways but you don't really understand us – everything must be measured by *your* ideas. One day that sort of meddling could make big trouble . . . Just leave it to us. Slowly, slowly we are giving our girls more freedom – but never *too much*! They don't want to have to take decisions – we don't bring them up that way. The head of the family makes *all* our decisions – it's his responsibility and he knows how to judge. What you don't see is how we want to protect our women from worry and stress – then they are better able to look after us and our children."

As we salaam'd on the doorstep I wondered about the attitudes of young Mirpuri men who are not 'forward looking . . .'

Obviously most of Britain's Muslim women would be totally bemused by 'liberation'. Also, thousands of them are perfectly content with their present lot and would oppose, as irreligious, any change in their status. (Just as thousands of Irish Catholic women opposed the legalising of divorce in 1986, despite the fact that so many of their fellow-Irishwomen are suffering intensely for lack of it.) However, these attitudes do not weaken the case for making 'self-determination' possible as an option, which is not the same thing as saying, "Now you're liberated, so get on with it! No more relying on your menfolk!" Given their conditioning, that approach would probably drive even more women to suicide than are now being driven to it by male domination.

The absence of a respectable option compels many women to reinforce their own prison walls; they must seem to remain submissive, and train their daughters to be submissive, because the only alternatives are prostitution, suicide or the isolating disgrace endured by Naseem in her Leeds bed-sit. The girls I met* who longed to go to university or get a job, but had been forbidden to do so, did not want to break with their families; nor did the majority want to choose their own husbands. They only wanted a reasonable compromise between the tight restrictions of their inherited culture and the freedom of opportunity offered by the new culture in which they had been educated.

A minority of Muslim men in Britain are concerned about this situation and would like to see the law changed. If seeking the protection of the courts did not entail widespread publicity many Muslim women now suffering in silence would at least know that they were not hopelessly trapped. Part of the problem is that no one can provide the authorities with the sort of statistics they like as a springboard for action. Most of the evidence is anecdotal and likely to remain so; certainly none of the victims who talked to me would be willing to become an 'official statistic'. Anyone who *was* willing would not, *ipso facto*, be a victim. That is the trap.

One Pakistani academic – who, significantly, did not wish to be named – assured me that it would be possible to bring together a group of reputable British-based Islamic scholars to testify that the Qur'an provides no justification for the restrictions imposed on many Muslim women in Britain. Theoretically this should remove the controversy from the religious plane, but in practice imams ('guardians of the faithful') wield far more authority than reform-inclined Islamic intellectuals. (Again there is an Irish parallel: when it comes to a divorce referendum, reactionary rural parish priests wield more authority than world-famous liberal theologians.) All over the world, imams have fought successfully against modern reinterpretations of the Qur'an.

The fact that Islam recognises no distinction between religious and secular law provokes much mental and emotional confusion among British Muslims. This is one of the fundamentals of their religion; written into the constitutions of most Islamic states is the clause – 'Islamic Shari'a is the source of all laws'. It may be in very small print, if a state wishes to seem 'forward-looking', but it is there somewhere and on women's rights issues the imams make full use of it. Here British schools could help, by incorporating into their multi-cultural education programmes clear information about the legal rights of the individual in Britain. Muslim girls would then realise that as British citizens they were no longer subject to Shari's law, if they didn't choose to be, but *despite being Muslims* were entitled to the full protection of the secular laws of the land.

Any such attempt to help Muslim women would provoke howls of protest about 'racist' interference with another culture. But where do you draw the line? Supposing – as might just conceivably have happened, given Britain's far-flung empire – supposing two tribes of head-hunters had come to work in Bradford's mills and by way of maintaining their religious traditions and cultural integrity had head-hunted once a year and happily returned to their

---

* One of them, aged fifteen, hanged herself in March 1986.

back-to-backs to hang a few of the other tribe's heads over the gas-fire to dry out . . . How would the West Yorkshire police have reacted? Would they have decided that this was all part of the richness of a multi-cultural society? Or would they have sent their murder squad zooming into Manningham to arrest the tribesmen? One assumes the latter, regardless of that ethnic minority's entitlement to 'cultural self-determination' and 'parity of esteem'.

The analogy is not as far-fetched as it may seem. Granted, murder is pretty extreme. But then head-hunters don't think of head-hunting as *murder*; the selective ritual collecting of heads is very much part of their spiritual tradition – they don't roam the jungles every day indiscriminately killing people.

The Islamic oppression of women, ostensibly as part of a religious tradition, is also pretty extreme. Public indignation would engulf Britain if it were revealed that in certain areas it was not uncommon for intelligent, ambitious thirteen-year-old White girls to be withdrawn from school and hidden from the authorities; and for White eighteen-year-old girls who had been offered university places to be forcibly restrained from leaving home; and for sophisticated young White women to be compelled to marry unknown, uneducated imported husbands who couldn't speak English. I have heard several British feminists arguing that it is reprehensibly racialist to operate one law for the Whites and another for the Browns, allegedly because 'all cultures must be given equal respect'.

Many people – teachers, social workers, anthropologists, psychiatrists – have been worrying for years about Britain's Muslim women. Some believe that it would be rash suddenly to modify the rigid framework of Muslim family life; they rely on *time* to solve the problem. Their caution may spring from an understandable fear of an orthodox Islamic backlash. But is this passive approach correct when thousands of young women are *now* being denied natural justice? Must all those individuals be sacrificed while we wait patiently for a *gradual* – and by no means guaranteed – dismantling of prison walls?

Some people quote Mohammed Ajeeb, Bradford's first Mirpuri Lord Mayor, in support of the give-it-time policy. On a 1982 wireless programme he said:

> Since we are living in a society where individualism is very important, our children are bound to be influenced by the values of their British counterparts . . . My own marriage was arranged and I'm living a very happy life, but I think it's the Western values and culture which our youngsters may not be able to withstand. And I think this is bound to happen. Probably after the second or third generation the whole concept of arranged marriage might undergo radical changes.

However, arranged (as distinct from forced) marriages are not part of the problem. And the British cultural environment has the potential for strengthening rather than eroding hardline attitudes. I shall never forget sitting one afternoon in a bus at Bradford's Interchange, waiting to return to Manningham. The window seat beside me was occupied by a Mirpuri grand-dad: small and wiry, with a short beard, a hooked nose and that aura of dignified resignation common to many of his exiled generation. He wore baggy pantaloons and a flowing shirt and spoke no English – or if he did was not disposed to converse with an unknown woman. I was opening my newspaper when a White couple appeared just outside our window, no more than two yards away. They were aged perhaps thirteen or fourteen: the boy was nowhere near shaving age. And there they stood, continuing their mating prelims – deep kissing, the boy fondling the girl's breasts, she fumbling between his thighs and neither concealing symptoms of advanced sexual excitement.

In certain areas such behaviour is now very much part of the British cultural environment. What was unusual was not being able to avoid a momentary close-up view; normally one hurries past, feeling (in my case) a mixture of depression, disgust and compassion. When the Mirpuri and I involuntarily looked at one another no common language was necessary. His distress was painful to behold; and there was *fear*, too, in his eyes. Realising that my having been a co-witness was aggravating his embarrassment I moved to a back seat; and he moved to a seat from where no more daylight lechery could be inadvertently glimpsed. I felt absurdly upset on his account and even more absurdly mortified on behalf of my own race. To the average Mirpuri the fact that such incidents can happen in Britain – and do regularly and visibly happen – seems justification enough for restricting their women-folk even more than in Mirpur. Surveying Britain's urban scene through Brown eyes, one realises that what we think of as fanaticism could also be described as outraged decency.

Having devoted so much space to the oppression of Muslim women, two points need to be made clear. Firstly, I have never been a 'Women's Liberation' activist; to me the roles of wife and mother – though I personally never fancied the former – seem as honourable a profession as any other and more important than most. Secondly, I deeply respect Islam for its influence on the character and behaviour of sincere believers. (When all the theological and metaphysical arguments are over, taming human nature is, as far as I can see, the main function of the world's great religions.)

In Bradford, as elsewhere in Britain, most Muslim boys (and some little girls) go regularly to their mosque school to learn the Qur'an by rote. Whites often comment, "Poor kids! Never given time to play or watch telly – bullied off to sit on the ground learning mumbo-jumbo!" Such remarks make one question the efficacy of multi-faith R E programmes. How do you convey to those Whites who have completely lost touch with the Christian roots of their own civilization that for devout Muslims (or Hindus or Sikhs) life really does have a spiritual dimension? How do you explain to people who are indifferent to all forms of religion that Islam is the pivot of a believing Muslim's daily existence? It is not a separate mental area that you move into when you go to the mosque but a way of being, just as Catholicism still is for many in Ireland, especially among the older generation. The Mirpuris' religion provides a steadying sense of communal identity and pride, useful in times of adversity or stress and extremely important when individuals feel rejected, despised or threatened. There is a popular theory that Browns would make better citizens (i.e. more British-like and therefore better) if they gave up all that 'mumbo-jumbo'. People seem not to know that at mosque schools children are also taught the code of conduct by which, as good Muslims, they are expected to live. In Britain their *maulanas* lay special emphasis on the immorality of hooliganism, vandalism, mugging, theft, laziness at work. To suggest that the abandonment of this training would make them 'better citizens' is ignorant nonsense of a peculiarly irritating kind.

Within days of arriving in Manningham my antennae had told me that it was a safe district; no adrenalin flowed as I walked down dark streets late at night, I felt no anxiety about my bicycle (or even its pump) being stolen. One morning I went out early and the postman left a large parcel on my doorstep, in full view of the neighbours; it was still there when I returned at 6.15 p.m. People often spoke, shudderingly, of the Yorkshire Ripper, who murdered one of his victims just around the corner from Boston Street. But he was an Outsider . . . Manningham lacks its fair share of crime, by British standards, because as yet its Muslims are an uncommonly law-abiding lot. Their crimes are usually domestic, caused by that relentless feuding which for centuries has been endemic in Mirpur. In the privacy of their homes knives can come out very quickly and be used very savagely, perhaps to settle an old score with a man just arrived from Pakistan who may have rashly assumed that in the new homeland an ancient grievance would be overlooked.

However, even Bradford has a fringe of rebellious young men who proclaim that they've had Islam and want to "sort this place [i.e. Britain] out". If Mohammed Ajeeb's forecast is proved correct, and Brown youngsters are 'unable to withstand Western values and culture', then my forecast is Big Trouble Ahead. The prospect of thousands of jobless young Muslims, untamed by Islam, adrift in the inner-cities alarms me much more than that other problem – at present attracting so much attention – of thousands of jobless young Blacks on the loose. The virtues of the Muslim community – industry, forward-planning, group-loyalty, agile thinking, efficient team-work, purposefulness – could, if deprived of a legitimate arena, produce a law-and-order problem that would make the Blacks' sporadic outbursts of despairing violence seem trivial.

When an authoritarian religious mould breaks within a generation the youngsters who can cope flourish, leading freer and richer lives. But what happens to those with no tradition of thinking things out for themselves, because for centuries that was discouraged, or of self-restraint, because always restraints were imposed by an acceptable authority? Once that authority has become irrelevant all the brakes are off and there is no steering wheel and the downhill rush can be very swift.

Again there is an Irish comparison. In Britain now one meets many Irish adolescents from 'decent' homes who, soon after going on the dole and settling in some DHSS squat, have reached the bottom of the hill and are leading lives of reckless immorality – or maybe amorality, since they seem unable to distinguish between what is moral and immoral. They are into hard drugs, petty thieving, casual sex, drunkenness, fiddling the social security services – life becomes one hectic, squalid orgy of traditionally forbidden fruits. Their degradation would seem marginally less awful if at least they were enjoying it. But they never strike one as happy young people. Nor do their Mirpuri equivalents.

I met my first Mirpuri drop-outs in a large, dingy Sikh pub off the Leeds Road on the other side of the city from Manningham. There were few customers during that lunch-hour: only six Brown youths playing pool and two White teenage girls mesmerised by fruit machines. As I sat scribbling notes one of the Browns approached (something very unusual) and said, "You're the person who took Naseem away." It was a deadpan statement; I couldn't guess how he viewed my intervention. But it would be normal for him to disapprove so I looked apologetic. This was about a fortnight after the incident and it startled me to realise that our meeting had become common knowledge. We had seen nobody on our early morning walk to the bus-stop past curtained, unlit windows.

"You can't scratch your arse in Manningham", said the young man, "but everybody knows. Even if it's the middle of the night. That's why I want to get out and say fuck to them all. I want to live the way I want to live!" He emptied his glass and added, "You're fuckin' lucky you haven't had a brick through your window. We don't like outsiders interfering – makes the disgrace even worse." Clearly he was on Naseem's side, though I suspected she wouldn't find him a very congenial ally.

Ahmed sat opposite me and beckoned his friend Abdul and we all had another pint. They were aged twenty-one and unemployed; both their families' small shops had closed within the past six months, one very recently – I had shopped there on first arriving in Boston Street. "Our people are going more to Morrisons [the local supermarket]," said Abdul. "Everything is fifteen or twenty per cent cheaper and now our kids know English to do the shopping. With most dads on the dole you can't go on buying dear. The imams say we should, to support the community, but that's because *they* own so many businesses! They want to make us feel guilty if we buy outside."

"It's better this way," said Ahmed. "Not for *us*, but better on the whole. It's fuckin' stupid carrying on like we were still in Pakistan, keeping away from everyone who doesn't belong to us. Naseem was right to say shit to it all and get out. I'd do the same only I've no exams. No one at my school gave a fuck about Asians passing exams. And you won't bother, will you, if there's no one to tell you you can?"

I asked if either had ever had a job. "I worked for two years after school," said Abdul, "at the machine tools. Then they threw half of us out."

"I worked in our shop," said Ahmed, "from seven in the morning to bloody eleven at night! I wasn't sorry when it closed. My dad's still on the buses but no way will *we* ever get on them. Not now and being Asian – they just look at you and spit!"

"Maybe there's something in London or somewhere," said Abdul, "but not here – this is No-Hope-City!"

I reminded them of Bradford Council's 'positive approach' to Brown problems. They were only vaguely aware of the Council's Race Relations Policy and scoffed when I outlined its possible benefits. "It's all *talk!*" said Abdul. "I've lined up for nine jobs since I was sacked and always a White kid got it. I'm not trying any more. We have our pride."

Ahmed said, "Even if the Council spilled its guts to help us they couldn't. You people are like us, you stick together when there's fuckin' trouble. Why shouldn't you? Everybody does. And this recession, as they call it, is bad fuckin' trouble!"

Both had recently quarrelled with their families – apparently about drinking and girls – and had left home to share an empty semi- derelict house with two other drop-outs. "It's no good families going on like we were still in Pakistan," said Ahmed, "when half of us haven't even been there!"

"And don't want to go," added Abdul. "We're Bradfordians and that's the way we want to live. You can't live two ways at once."

I asked if they had any White friends – perhaps from school days? "Not school sorts," replied Ahmed, "but lots of White friends along Lumb Lane!" (Manningham's red-light district.) They both sniggered then, like callow White fifteen-year-olds. I found them a not very attractive pair yet felt rather touched when they invited me to meet their squat-mates next evening. Later I realised that entertaining a lone White woman (even 'of uncertain age') was just another gesture of defiance towards the Mirpuri Establishment.

Their terrace house was in a narrow, steep cobbled street of unrelieved squalor: broken glass strewn on cracked pavements, collapsed garden fences and hanging gutters, variegated garbage piled outside unpainted front doors, windows uncurtained or boarded up, roof slates missing. There are few such streets in Bradford, thanks to the Browns and the Council. It is more usual to turn a corner and find yourself looking at rows of carefully restored little dwellings, their brick or stone façades cleaned of smoke-deposits, their drain-pipes, gutters and outside woodwork painted in gay contrasting shades of red, green, white, blue, pink, yellow, orange, black. Some areas that once were desolate slums now have an almost W8 look. Had there been no immigrants to buy these houses they would have been demolished and replaced by yet more of the baleful 1960s tower-blocks – which fact alone puts Bradford forever in the debt of the Browns.

The front door was ajar and Ahmed shouted to me to enter; no one of course stood up when I appeared. What might once have been a front parlour smelt of mildew and stale cigarette smoke and unclean bed-rolls (on which we sat) and take-away fish'n'chips fried in over-used oil. The window was boarded up and light came from a small kerosene lamp that recalled many an evening on the sub-continent. A meagre store of fashionable garments on dry-cleaner hangers depended from the mantelpiece. Behind the door a large cardboard carton was three-quarters full of empty milk bottles and beer cans. On a wooden box stood a primus stove, kettle, packets of tea and sugar and four mugs. There was no other furniture. But numerous female near-nudes, provided by Messrs Murdoch and Maxwell, decorated two of the damp-stained crumbling walls.

Ahmed and Abdul said "Hi!" but in response to my "Salaam Alaikum" Ashfaq and Hashmi merely lowered their heads and glanced sideways at each other and laughed uneasily. A certain amount of beer had to flow before the conversation did; foreseeing this, I had brought ample supplies of a strong brew.

We talked for nearly four hours, mostly about the unfairness of life however you look at it . . . Among my companions' main grievances was the amount of money still being remitted to Mirpur. Ashfaq – at eighteen the youngest of the group – had visited his ancestral village for the first time as a twelve-year-old and never recovered from the shock. It was a twin shock: the material backwardness of Pakistani rural life and the unreal topsy-turviness of some families owning big British cars they couldn't drive (brought out by a relative since returned to Britain), and many families having new three-storey houses but only using two ground-floor rooms – and most families displaying as ornaments electric toasters, carving knives, food-mixers and microwave ovens while the cooking was still being done on mud-stoves. Ashfaq – the most intelligent of the quartet – argued that the rhythm of working and saving in Britain but spending in (or on) Mirpur would have to be broken. "*Our* generation needs all that cash that's pouring away. We need it *here*, to make something of our own future – what's the use to us of all these gadgets and cars and houses out in Mirpur? *We're* never going to live there. It was different when my grand-dad came first in the fifties on his own. It made sense then to send all he could back home. But when my dad came, and then called my mum, they should have saved for us kids the way you people do. Even now men on benefits are sending back money every month, so's the village won't know they're not doing well! It's all stupid face-saving and it drove me out of the house. *I'm* not handing over half my dole like I'm told I should!"

On marriage three out of the four were evasive. They seemed not at all anxious to choose their own brides, perhaps because they couldn't imagine themselves coping with married life as jobless husbands lacking *biraderi* support. But one day they would marry, Hashmi said, since it is the duty of *every* Muslim to marry; remaining single is not an option. Abdul and Ashfaq agreed, though many of their previous remarks had been calculated to show me how successfully they had emancipated themselves from Islam. Only

Ahmed stuck to his new irreligious guns. "Screwing around's O K for me," he swaggered, tossing one beer can into the corner and opening another. "There's no shortage in Bradford – going cheap, with all the competition!" Throughout the evening his language and sentiments had been exaggeratedly crude and this I sensed made his squat-mates uncomfortable, in conversation with a woman.

I cycled home depressed by the contrast between those young men, with their severely fractured personalities, and the 'average' Mirpuri youngster who remains part of the community. For all their emphatic approval of the breakaway Naseem, they retained their view of women as essentially inferior creatures: and that view seemed much worse when shorn of the protective attitude that traditionally goes with it. This and similar encounters made me appreciate even more Islam's 'taming' influence. Within such young men (and women) is an empty space that cannot possibly be filled by what is available to them of European culture. I hoped for their own sakes that all four would soon become reconciled with their families, as many Muslim drop-outs do.

2 · Poor Britain

Most newcomers to the North of England comment on the Bradfordians' *smallness* – of body, that is: their hearts are very large. Although of only average height, I seemed to find myself almost always looking down on the local men and women. They are living reminders that Britain's Age of Affluence ('never had it so good!') happened too recently to remedy the damage done by generations of deprivation and debilitating working conditions.

Whenever I felt my natural cheerfulness being undermined by life in one of Britain's most recession-battered cities, I reflected that a young council-housed couple on the dole now enjoy a far higher standard of living (though they rarely give the impression of enjoying it) than their working grand-parents. And they are incomparably better off than their forefathers (and mothers) in the 1880s, not to mention the 1830s. By the standards of Britain's past, or of the global present, there is no poverty in Mrs Thatcher's sceptred isle. Or so it can seem, when you are sitting in your pad reading about the endemic diseases that ravaged Manningham's exploited workers a century ago.

Then reality strikes, when you spend an evening sitting instead in a little Pakistani-owned café-cum-amusement arcade, watching groups of White schoolchildren wandering in from a cold winter's night, scantily clad in trendy garments, and for hours playing the machines – their faces pale and pinched, their eyes dark-ringed from years of late-night television, their hair dull, their teeth sugar-sabotaged. What they spend during the evening on those machines, and on chewing-gum and packets of junk-food and bottles of dire beverages, would buy the ingredients for a wholesome meal if they had anyone at home with the skill and the will to cook it. In Britain today there may be little poverty based on lack of cash. Yet the inner cities have been stricken by spiritual and emotional impoverishment – creating an aura of degeneracy, irresponsibility, hopelessness – that is no less harrowing. You cannot live close to it, even for a few months, without being anguished by the sense of human lives going to waste in a rich country through mismanagement of resources – state resources on the part of incompetent governments, personal resources on the part of ignorant individuals. Increasingly these bottom-of-the-pile Whites feel they have been written off as expendable; having served their purpose during the industrial booms of the past they are now without a use. Therefore, they argue, no government will do more than subsidise them just enough to keep them quiet, while the rest of society goes about its still-profitable business. And of course they do retain one use. Despite their limited cash, they are valuable *en masse* as consumers to those who assiduously exploit them: the fashion, entertainment and junk-food industries. One vignette symbolises for me the end of that exploiting road – you can surely go no further.

A young couple – undersized, unkempt, pallid – had just emerged from the Thornton Road supermarket. They were teenagers, but the parents of a very small baby with a rash-patchy face who was whimpering angrily in a shiny new pram. The husband carried several packets of disposable nappies, the wife a bag of cling-wrapped instant meals and tins of fizzy drinks. Having unloaded these goods into the pram she opened a tin of coke, filled the infant's bottle and thrust the teat into its toothless (and likely to remain so) mouth. Then she halved a bar of some revolting bright pink substance and gave one portion to her husband before they slouched off, chewing. I stood watching them go in a state of blank despair. No, they were not poor; you don't buy disposable nappies and instant meals and tinned fizz if you're *poor*. Yet they were visibly undernourished; very likely their mothers – probably still in their early forties – had not often, if ever, cooked an old-fashioned meal. The cycle of our modern-style poverty is by now well established. And what of their coke-soothed infant? But my imagination preferred to shy away from his/her future.

I find this consumer-society deprivation even harder to take than Third World poverty. It seems monstrous that in an advanced Western country a large section of the population should be fated to live in such a state of degradation, mollified by convenience foods and convenience nappies but with no more – perhaps less – chance of developing as human beings than their forefathers had in the mills and the mines. Nor am I prepared ever again to listen politely to top-of-the pilers deploring the fecklessness of bottom-of-the-pilers. Those who condemn working-class families for 'not managing their money properly' usually have shares in companies that devote millions annually to persuading people to spend unwisely. The advertising industry employs some of the cleverest people around and few seem able to withstand their campaigns. Therefore it is neither logical nor just to criticise bottom-of-the-pilers for failing to do so.

That evening I wrote in my diary:

What's happening to Britain? ? ? The Welfare State is a shambles, Thatcherism is a divisive and cruel disaster, inner-city schools offer a parody of education, the media are mostly in millionaires' pockets, the police become increasingly corrupt. Here, as in Ireland, the party-political system has in effect broken down, failing a large section of the population. But it's even worse here: no P R. So a government with a mere 46 per cent of the votes, for whom only one-third of the electorate voted, can win the sort of majority that lets it go on bulldozing for years. An odd sort of democracy! A few people talk of forming a National Government to cope with the crisis: but only a few . . . While the rich are getting richer, that is unlikely to happen. Yet extreme socialism (more hand-outs, nationalise the weather) is *not* the answer tho' one can sympathise with the many youngsters who feel it is. To sit here in Boston St and hear Mrs T. enthusing on the wireless about "everyone becoming a capitalist" is very bad for the blood-pressure: even by her standards, a singularly insensitive remark. Does she know what life is like at the bottom of the pile? Not in a thriving grocer's shop but *really* at the bottom – what chance does she suppose the average Bradfordian on the dole has of becoming a *capitalist*? She makes me want to pick up a red flag and rush out to lead a demo. Today I've been feeling even sorrier for the local Whites than the Browns, who seem much better at coping psychologically with unemployment – so far, that is. They have lower expectations and support each other in adversity as most Whites no longer do. But both these factors will change as time passes.

The culture shock involved in my first experience of a European 'deprived area' was severe. It is one thing to read or hear about Britain being 'a divided society', it is quite another to experience that phenomenon as it affects individuals. The buzz-phrase 'Britain is two nations' used to irritate me; like everywhere else, Britain has always had rich and poor – with the disparity formerly much more gross. But Bradford taught me exactly what the phrase means. Three and a half million unemployed leave some fourteen million directly affected by unemployment out of a population of fifty-six million. And the two nations are made up of those not on the dole – from bus-drivers to peers of the realm – and those who know that they and their children have no realistic hope of ever again being employed fulltime. That divide between Haves and Have-nots is stark and tragic and dangerous. It is a much more complicated issue than the traditional divide between those with wealth and those without it. The Have-nots are tragic and dangerous because, though few of them will ever die of starvation or exposure in a Welfare State, what they have not is *hope*. Neither of course was there much hope in the lives of previous generations of Have-nots; but the present generation has been differently conditioned. And their employed working-class neighbours *have* motor cars, deep freezes, holidays abroad, gadget-filled kitchens and all sorts of future *possibilities* for themselves and their children. The Have-nots are like prisoners in an encampment surrounded by wire-mesh; they can see how their more fortunate neighbours live but cannot escape to join in the competition with a fair chance of personal effort being rewarded.

In ten months I met few of those reprobates so beloved of right-wing commentators – men-who-don't-want-to-work. Most human beings do want to work regularly, though not necessarily very vigorously, unless they have been born on a South Sea Island, or into some other equally fruitful and enervating climate – or have been educated to fill their days agreeably with 'leisure pursuits'. I met many more of that other sort of reprobate, the furtively working dole-receiver. But they were rarely true bottom-of-the-pilers. This fiddle requires a jumping-off point: a little spare cash, some skill, useful contacts – assets the most deprived don't have. I also met quite a few apathetic men in their early twenties who have never been employed – or only briefly – and seemed near to qualifying for that doom-laden label 'unemployable'. If you leave school at sixteen and spend all or most of the next six or seven years on the dole, you are likely either to lose the will to work or to prove an unsatisfactory worker should a job eventually turn up. Therefore most parents urge their young to go on Youth Training Schemes or accept almost any sort of part-time work to avoid the mental and emotional consequences of permanent idleness. Numerous White parents told me of their worry because a son or daughter had returned from the Job Centre determined *not* to do part-time work that would reward them with only £6 or £7 a week more than the dole. I could see both points of view; if you are longing for a full-time job with reasonable prospects it seems futile to spend twenty-five hours on a boring temporary job to earn a measly £6 or £7. (Brown youths, reared with different attitudes to State hand-outs and not so inclined to defy parents, are much more likely to accept such jobs – but much *less* likely to be offered them.) The parental argument that work-experience, however ill-paid, will improve the chance of securing a full-time job is not weighty in areas of forty or fifty per cent unemployment. And the other parental argument, that it is healthier to work part-time than to lie in bed until two o'clock every afternoon, is not even listened to.

The class-hatred openly expressed by many of Bradford's White Have-nots – pub acquaintants, men making their half-pint of Yorkshire bitter last three hours – took me by surprise when I was new to the scene. As someone whose previous experience of England had been almost entirely confined to the other side of the divide – Hampstead and Cambridge, Dorset and Hereford-shire, Dorking and Rye – such deep hatred seemed to generate an atmosphere of un-English extremism. It took me some time to adjust to a world where everyone was on the miners' side (we were then hearing almost daily reports of miner-versus-police violence) and where I would not have been acceptable as a drinking companion had my accent been English middle class. Yet this was the world, not so long ago, of *Mary Barton* and *Shirley*, of Poor Law riots and Chartist riots. It was just as genuinely English as the other side of the divide. I recalled E.P. Thompson's observations in *The Making of the English Working Class*:

The British people were noted throughout Europe for their turbulence, and the people of London astonished foreign visitors by their lack of deference. The eighteenth and early nineteenth century are punctuated by riot, occasioned by bread prices, turnpikes and tolls, excise, 'rescue', strikes, new machinery, enclosures, press-gangs and a score of other grievances. Direct action on particular grievances merges into the great political risings of the 'mob' – the Wilkes agitation of the 1760s and 1770s, the Gordon riots (1780), the mobbing of the King in the London streets (1795 and 1820), the Bristol riots (1831) and the Birmingham Bull Ring riots (1839) . . . The most common example is the bread or food riot, repeated cases of which can be found in almost every town or county until the 1840s. This was rarely a mere uproar which culminated in the breaking open of barns or the looting of shops. It was legitimized by the assumptions of an older moral economy, which taught the immorality of any unfair method of forcing up the price of provisions by profiteering upon the necessities of the people.

In those inner-city pubs the 1830s and 1840s sometimes felt very near. On one occasion mobs of unemployed Bradfordians attacked Horsfall's Mill and were themselves attacked by Special Constables. Both sides used pistols and two youngsters, including a boy of thirteen, were killed. Chartist agitation continued for a decade in and around Bradford, causing much alarm to the Brontë family in nearby Haworth Parsonage. Royal Commissioners investigating factory conditions were assumed (no doubt rightly) to be on the side of the owners; they were habitually referred to as 'the enemy' and harassed whenever their coaches stopped to change horses. A Poor Law meeting held at the Court House by Mr Alfred Power, a Factory Commissioner, was disrupted by a mob who pelted him with stones and mud as he retreated to his rooms at the Sun Inn. For his next meeting the Court House was barricaded and forty Hussars were stationed in Bradford – not quite enough, because by noon six thousand angry Bradfordians were storming the building. They smashed almost every pane of glass before being dispersed by 'the edge of the sword' and pistol shots; those arrested were taken to York Castle for trial. In 1844 Bradford Moor Barracks was built in anticipation of further disturbances. In 1985 Bradford's city centre had to be cordoned off to ensure the safety of Sir Keith Joseph when he decided to visit the university. Some respectable Bradfordians considered this precaution unprecedented and shaming and 'all because of those Pakis'. Race relations problems and industrial decline problems – two ingredients in the post-imperial fall-out – are now ominously interacting.

Communication with my Have-not friends was not always easy. More than once I was told to stuff my liberal intellectual crap – "When you're working class, with no choices, you're not interested in *thinking* – you only *feel*." That is a verbatim quote, representative of many reactions to various of my comments. It came from Bill, an ex-intercontinental truck driver who when I first met him had been unemployed for ten months. His remark made me realise to what an extent the middle classes do take choice for granted: choice of school, career, house, doctor, hospital when necessary, entertainments, times for holidays. If you start from the bottom of the pile your choices are almost nil.

In April Bill found a job, driving from Leeds to Germany, Greece and Turkey. I met him one evening when he had just got back from Germany and he said reflectively, "You know, the Germans have everything organised much better than us but they don't seem any happier. In this country we had the balance about right in the '60s and early '70s. Now it's lost. And there's something very dangerous about us now – about the working classes. We don't just hate, we have spite and malice. People think we're so stupid we'll lie down quiet forever. But you don't need brains to go violent if you're pushed far enough – and that woman is pushing us to the edge!" (That too is a verbatim quote, except that Bill didn't use 'woman' but the canine equivalent.)

Bill's point about 'not thinking, only feeling' struck me as very English. It is hard to imagine an Irish Have-not disclaiming all interest in thinking; the less he had the more he would feel a need to think about *why* . . . The same anti-thinking attitude was apparent when I talked with the striking miners in their Alamo Hut at Corton Wood – which induced a flicker of sympathy for the Coal Board. If you must negotiate all the time with people who are determined to feel rather than to think, you surely have a problem. And how can this attitude be changed? Through education, in theory. But in practice the children of anti-thinking parents are not usually receptive to being taught how to think at school. Most of the White inner-city children I met regarded school as an ordeal to be endured before graduating to the 'freedom' of a job – or the dole queue. But then they came from some of Britain's most deprived housing estates and no doubt their parents also regarded 'education' as an unavoidable but meaningless prelude to adulthood. The teachers in such schools find their professional lives somewhat dispiriting, hence the vicious circle of mediocre (or worse) teachers in schools where inspired teaching is most needed. Or is it unrealistic to hope that 'deprived area' schools could ever supply – to any significant extent – those incentives lacking in pupils' homes? Many inner-city teachers who themselves think (they don't *all*, I was disillusioned to discover) argue that the chief needs of their White pupils are consistent affection, firm discipline and sympathetic listening – to make up for a domestic scarcity of those commodities. That was the conclusion long since arrived at by Barney, Headmaster of High Hill Comprehensive, which I visited regularly to discuss travelling and writing and race relations with groups of fourth- and fifth-formers.

More than sixty per cent of High Hill's 1300 pupils were Brown; some ten per cent were Black or mixed race. The school had been built twenty-five years ago and looked about ready for demolition. A crude oblong block, in the worst traditions of 1960s 'functionalism', both its exterior and its interior invited (and received) vandalism and graffiti on a grand scale. (There must be a link between the present level of vandalism and the surroundings in which vandals spend their formative years.) Yet amidst all this unhuman grimness, in the Art Department, one suddenly came upon a wondrous display of paintings and drawings – mainly the work of Brown pupils. Sadly, the school could not afford a Music Department; only Bradford's middle-class State schools now provide music lessons – paid for of course by parents, who also supply the instruments.

Barney gave me my introductory tour of High Hill one sleety February noon. Entering the main hall from the playground, we passed a group of sixth-form Browns watching two Pakistani boys scrapping – nothing serious, but they had overturned a litter-bin, scattering its contents. When Barney requested them to clear up the mess one could sense resistance flowing from the whole group; yet almost at once he was obeyed. Somehow he had left no scope for defiance though he gave the order almost casually. On our way down a long corridor, where hundreds were queuing for the second dinner sitting – supervised by a hard-pressed non-NUT staff – I noticed that Barney seemed to know most pupils by name. The available accommodation does not allow everyone to eat together, so supervision of this hungry, restive queue is a daily ordeal. When a tall, burly, truculent-looking Pakistani tried to jump the queue Barney checked him and for a moment quite a nasty confrontation seemed inevitable. But Barney ignored the youth's aggression, put one arm around his shoulders, dug him in the ribs and simultaneously reinforced his reprimand while defusing the situation with a show of affection – *genuine* affection. "Body contact is important," Barney observed later, as we ate at a table with two Pakistanis, one Sikh, two Hindus and an ex-Kenya Gujerati Muslim. The staff, including Barney, always queue and eat with the pupils, eighty per cent of whom have sixty-pence vouchers which procure an adequate meal from a moderately varied menu – including halal meat twice a week. (For most Whites this is their only cooked meal of the day.) Pupils must pay themselves for extras or second helpings. The majority of local White families have long-term-unemployed fathers; if either parent is working, it is likely to be mother. It surprises no one that High Hill's White pupils are far more troublesome and less studious than the Browns.

Minor crises crammed that lunch-hour; it was, I later realised, a typical day. In the playground a six-foot Black boy was plotting with his multi-racial fellow-trouble-makers; as Barney sauntered towards the group it dispersed. A fifteen-year-old Mirpuri girl had to have a chit to go home at once because her father's sister's husband had died suddenly. A weedy fourteen-year-old White boy, bleeding from the mouth and sobbing desperately, was brought to Barney to be comforted; he had been beaten up on the playground and a hunt for the culprits was started. Someone spilled a cup of lukewarm coffee over the arm of another weedy White boy, pale and spotty with troubled eyes; he claimed to have been scalded and became semi-hysterical. Barney was concerned but brisk – "We'll just put a little sugar on the burn and watch the skin change colour." Afterwards he said, "So many of them are aching for attention, as *individuals* – they need to feel they're important, even for a few minutes, to *someone*!"

It is satisfying to watch anybody doing anything superbly well. To keep order in a big multi-racial inner-city comprehensive is not easy at the best of times, but to achieve this when seventy per cent of your staff are on and off strike, and will never do 'dinner duty', is truly remarkable. No one could *impose* discipline under these conditions, yet somehow Barney unfailingly *maintained* discipline. And he did it through love – which sounds mawkish in cold print, but watching him operate I realised there could be no other explanation. Modern teachers have no sticks and very few carrots. Instead, they must display an attitude that makes their authority acceptable. Barney's attitude was caring and imaginative, yet he was always shrewdly on the alert and never sentimental or weakly hesitant. He had no illusions about his pupils' capacity for breaking every rule made by God or man. But he respected them deeply, as individual human beings – each and every one of them, however unappealing they might seem to outsiders. He also expected them to respect him: and they did. His standards were not always upheld, yet as inner-city schools go High Hill was extraordinarily civilised. Barney's realism must have had a lot to do with this. He pretended not to notice the breaking of rules that simply could not be enforced in such a school in the 1980s and during the lunch-hour many Whites sloped off to smoke, drink or canoodle, leaving the excellent sports facilities to be enjoyed by the more moral Browns. Yet on issues to do with personal relationships – consideration for others – Barney was unyielding and the general atmosphere reflected this. One of his staff said, "If there were enough Barneys around there wouldn't be any football hooligans!" But then that's rather like saying, "If there were enough Gandhis around there wouldn't be any wars." And an Urdu teacher (quite a few Browns do A Level Urdu) exclaimed one day in the common room – "This is a blessed school! Our Head is the embodiment of nobility!" By then I had come to the same conclusion, though I might not have expressed it so arabesquely.

Someone decided that I should choose a few action-packed passages from my own travel books and read them with multi-racial groups of a dozen or so. Then we would engage in illuminating and inspiring discussions designed to stimulate an interest in *books as fun* (not school-work) and *authors as people* (not teachers in disguise). A lovely idea, which, alas! remained in the realm of the desirable unattainable. It was a snag that several of the White fourteen- to sixteen-year-olds couldn't read, but the main problem seemed to be my mere existence. Roving in remote places has accustomed me to being seen as an odd or even frightening apparition, but to be so regarded in the heart of my own civilisation rather threw me. The effort to communicate with some groups recalled occasions when I had to overcome the suspicions of wary hill-people who, if not openly hostile, could quite easily have become so. Our speaking the same language (more or less) should have helped; but when people are far away on the other side of a vast chasm a common language is not much use. Little progress was made until we abandoned the printed page, by mutual consent, and settled down to a series of 'unstructured' chat-shows. Then it became clear that most of those youngsters were not, as I had at first supposed, abnormally stupid. They were simply *uneducated* – after ten or eleven years' schooling! – to an extent I would not have believed possible in any Western country towards the end of the twentieth century. Some High Hill pupils might be classified as ineducable, but my groups were the doomed victims of a system that had failed them. 'Deprived backgrounds' cannot be solely to blame for failure on such a spectacular scale. Many of the younger inner-city teachers I met were themselves so uneducated, and so sullenly uninterested in their jobs, that their appointments baffled me until I discovered what young teachers are paid. However, in both Bradford and Birmingham I also met permanently over-worked men and women who put heroic efforts – too rarely acknowledged – into overcoming the handicaps of their inner-city pupils.

Comprehensive school staffs must learn to live with many occupational hazards but monotony is not among them. One morning during the post-literary era, when everyone had got used to my existence, some of the Tuesday group decided to clear the floor and treat me to a dazzling display of break-dancing; I had admitted to not knowing what it was and by then they were all concerned about various gaps in my education. A week later two White fourteen-year-old girls beckoned me into a corner, showed me two boxes of contraceptive pills and asked me which type I would recommend; this gave me an opportunity to lecture the whole group on the long-term health-risks of oral contraceptives. Then there was the memorable occasion when a fifteen-year-old White boy, no bigger than your average Irish ten-year-old, burst into the room at 10.30 a.m. very drunk on vodka. No one else seemed to think his condition worthy of note; the Brown girls present looked disdainful but not even slightly surprised.

Whenever possible I steered our chat-shows towards race relations and one morning two sixteen-year-old White girls – disregarding the presence of two Sikhs, two Hindus and five Muslims – informed me that they felt they had "a right to be racist". One gave as her reason, "Me Dad and two brothers are out of work years past." The other explained, "I've been on drugs since I was six because of all them Blacks!" Patient questioning revealed her meaning. Blacks lived on one side of her family's council house, four young Sikh men lived on the other and both households enjoyed late-night music sessions: so she and her siblings were regularly supplied with sleeping-pills by their GP. (Such noise-nuisance is very uncommon in Bradford.) The Brown reaction to this racialist aggro was illuminating. All nine Browns looked at those two Whites with a sort of pitying tolerance – as well they might, being light-years ahead academically – and remained silent. I found myself involuntarily and absurdly thinking, 'The wisdom of the East!'

High Hill shared a dinner-hour problem with other schools in Brown areas. At irregular but quite frequent intervals, three or four Pakistani youths would cruise past the playground in a beat-up car and lure a few of the more daring Brown girls away to enjoy a pre-purdah flirtation. (The *most* daring brought taboo Western garments to school and changed for these assignations.) This lawlessness, though severely discouraged, was not easily controlled when a skeleton dinner-hour staff had to cope with 1300 pupils. However, *flirtation* is the operative word since only one Brown pregnancy marred High Hill's reputation.

In contrast, White pregnancies were commonplace and I saw a few proud sixteen-year-old mums visiting the school to show off stylishly dressed babies to ex-school-mates and staff. Not all those infants were 'little accidents'. Motherhood offers certain emotional and material advantages to a bored teenager with no 'status' or job prospects; and generous handouts to unmarried mums ensure that not all parents are averse to premature grandparenthood. But in most cases the advantages are soon seen as disadvantages. At fifteen or sixteen it may be very exciting to have a gurgling baby with which to play real-life dolls. At eighteen or nineteen, when your contemporaries are free every night to drift from pub to disco to amusement arcade, it's not much fun to be anchored in your rent-free pad by a fractious toddler. One of the most distressing of all inner-city sights is the loud-mouthed and short-tempered *very* young mum dragging an often scared-looking three- or four-year-old behind her.

April 25 was a bizarre day on Bradford's educational scene – as on many others all over Britain. At 10.00 a.m. I found High Hill's Militant pupils planning an anti-Youth Training Scheme strike – a march and rally at noon – while the seventy per cent of the staff members who were NUT planned a march and rally for 2.00 p.m. In normal circumstances most of the teachers would have been co-operating with Barney to restrain their pupils from downing pens and truanting. But on April 25 they were in no position to criticise strike action: what's sauce for the teacher is sauce for the pupil.

I followed the pupils as they bore a huge red banner towards the city centre to join other thirteen- to sixteen-year-olds outside the new Police Headquarters, a grim brick and glass building overlooking Town Hall Square, Bradford's traditional rallying point. Their placard slogans were uninhibited: 'SPIT ON THATCHER!' – 'FUCK SLAVE LABOUR!' – 'SHIT ON YTS!' No more than a thousand rallied, to the chagrin of the organisers, and most were from the very bottom of the White pile. Their bright yellow Militant stickers looked particularly good on foreheads surmounted by multi-coloured punk hair-styles. They formed a heart-breaking crowd: underfed, ineducable, unemployable, ostentatiously chain-smoking, already bored with life and vulnerable to manipulation by anyone who came along – National Front, Anti-Apartheid, CND, Militant Left, they wouldn't see much difference. Only a few Brown boys were present (of course no Brown girls) and scarcely a dozen Blacks. Yet a Pakistani was the MC and the fieriest pupil-speaker was a fifteen-year-old Black boy. Judging by crowd-response, the most popular speaker was a leader of the Labour Party Young Socialists, a crazed-looking girl who ranted on about Anti-Imperialism, Women's Lib, Anti-Racism, Troops Out, Animal Rights, Anti-Capitalism – a confused spate of negative bitterness. Then representatives of each school spoke; their powerful Bradford accents, distorted by the public address system, prevented me from understanding most of what they said but I didn't feel too deprived.

Before the meeting two frowning young men distributed a document on behalf of the Workers Internationalist League (no apostrophe). One side of the closely typed foolscap sheet dealt with the past fifteen years of Pakistan's tortuous domestic politics and ended with a demand for 'a freely elected assembly of workers and peasants to govern Pakistan'. The other side was headed: 'FIGHTING RACISM: Build a Labour Movement Campaign':

> As the Tory government steps up its attacks on working people so racism becomes an outlet for those, especially white youth, who having been fed racism by the bosses system see black people as scapegoats ... Kinnock has scabbed on the miners heroic strike by condemning miners 'violence' ... When British imperialism fights wars against Ireland the labour leaders support it fully ... So the struggles of the black community and the fight against racism and fascism are clearly linked to the fight against the bosses system that causes it ... Build solidarity for black self-defence. The Police are a key pillar of the racist state, they cannot be reformed or made 'accountable'.

The Workers Internationalist League should perhaps simplify their vocabulary. In the unlikely event of my young friends ever attempting to read such a solid block of prose, their bewilderment would be considerable. *Scapegoats? Solidarity? Accountable?* Yet the abundant literature of the Far Left is not so much paper wasted, as some like to imagine. In certain unhappy circles it is quite influential.

As the agitators (one can hardly call them leaders) successfully rabble-roused there was not even one pillar of the racist state in sight; tactfully, they were observing from within. Suddenly the M C announced that the rally was over and ordered everyone to disperse quietly. (Where to? Their schools were closed and their teachers visible in the near distance, demonstrating outside the Town Hall.) By then the children were thoroughly inflamed, excited and aggressive, yet with no target for their anger. Mercifully they didn't go on the rampage as had happened a few weeks earlier, when pupils protesting against the teachers' strike did considerable damage – including smashing the windows of Bradford's only bookshop, which seemed sadly symbolic. Instead they began to fight among themselves in a desultory way, ignoring all the M C's pleas – "Disperse at once! Don't make trouble! Someone will get hurt! We don't want any arrests!" A few yards from me a boy was thrown to the ground and kicked on the head and ribs by two girls. Other girls pulled them away as a very large policeman appeared – just one, slowly strolling towards the scene of action and looking benevolent. A group of police looking determined would certainly have started a mini-riot but his appearance marvellously caused the mob to melt away.

It is comforting to dismiss such events – "Pupils will do anything to break the monotony and look how few turned up." However, those now sowing seeds of hate among the (non)-working-class young are quite skilful. The Far Left's disunity leads many to regard it as an irritant rather than a threat – an extremely disruptive irritant, yet one that can always be kept under control in stable, sensible Britain. And I daresay it can, at an ever-rising price. As James Robertson wrote in *The Sane Alternative: A Choice of Futures*:

> Superior, censorious, insecure people like to see other people kept in their place. Among the professional, business, financial and bureaucratic middle classes in the countries of North America and Western and Eastern Europe today there are many who fear the prospect of disorder more than they fear the prospect of neo-fascism or neo-stalinism. In times of uncertainty there will always be many members of the police and military forces ready to impose law and order with a firm hand . . . Very few people admit that they would welcome this kind of future. But there are quite a lot who undoubtedly would.

'Racism' and 'British Oppression in Ireland' were equally popular themes in the several Communist weeklies on sale (30p. waged, 20p. unwaged) in Bradford's city centre. With so many Red splinter-groups around I could never sort out th'other from which, but most young paper-sellers looked alike: poorly dressed and ill-nourished, with bad teeth, broken finger-nails and angry hopeless eyes. Their journals' Irish articles had predictable head-lines: 'Hands off Ireland!' 'Unite to Fight the PTA!' 'Irish Freedom Movement Defies Censorship!'

One afternoon I bought the TNS (*The Next Step*: Review of the Revolutionary Communist Party) from a twenty-four-year-old who had never had a job. He asked challengingly, "D'you support Troops Out?"

"Not just at present," I replied. "Most Irish feel the consequences of their going could be even worse than the consequences of their staying."

"Imperialist chauvinist!" shouted the young man, clenching his free fist.

My remark that 'chauvinist' was peculiarly inappropriate provoked a tirade about the future of Ireland when "the puppets of Westminster" (Dr FitzGerald and Mr Haughey) had been overthrown, to make way for "true patriots" (INLA) who would establish a *genuinely* democratic thirty-two-county Socialist Republic.

I pointed out that few Irish will vote even for our conventional Labour Party, never mind a 'Socialist Republic'. But the young man was uninterested in reality and wittered on about 800 years of "Protestant imperialist persecu-tion of Catholics", overlooking the fact that 800 years ago there weren't any Protestants. He betrayed a remarkable ignorance about Ireland's past and present, yet his rage was as extreme as though he'd been born in West Belfast. It was also infectious. I don't easily become enraged and it's easy to sympathise with discarded youngsters who take refuge in the fantasy world of revolution-round-the-corner. But when he called me "a traitorous bitch" I suddenly and fiercely resented being told what to think about my own country by someone who didn't know Derry from Kerry. Losing my cool, I voiced this resentment, rather loudly – provoking further abuse which caused passers-by to swivel their eyes in our direction. It would of course be un-British actually to *turn the head* when noticing a strangers' quarrel.

I later described this encounter to a White anti-racist friend who said, "So now you know how angry *Blacks* feel when *you* talk nonsense about *their* problems. *They* know the score, *you* don't! *They're* the victims of White racism, you're just an observer sitting on the fence making silly remarks!"

In certain inner-city circles my nationality was, at least initially, advantageous; and it could have been even more so had I accepted the role in which I was often automatically cast – 'I R A sympathiser'. The Provos, being near the top of League One in the world propaganda championship, have secured much support among young bottom-of-the-pilers of all races. Some of their admirers know much more than my paper-selling adversary about Irish history and politics, though naturally their informants have given them green spectacles through which to view Northern Ireland's tragedy.

At the end of a meeting with one militant Black 'community leader', who had had much to say about the usefulness of bombing campaigns to 'prove a political point', his hitherto silent companion suddenly asked me – "Have the police called on you yet?"

To the amusement of both, I was somewhat taken aback. So the leader explained, "You come from Ireland, you've been living in a squat-area, you've been meeting all sorts of groups like us – don't you *expect* the police to call?"

I confessed that I did not, that my career had been so dull and uneventful no police force had ever had occasion to call on me – which admission did nothing for my status in that particular group. Some people fancy that if you are not a police suspect you must be a police informer; they ignore the intermediate area occupied by most citizens.

In Leeds 'poor Britain' seemed even more harrowing than in Bradford. I found it impossible to think positive about that city, which I occasionally had to visit for a variety of reasons. Its deprived areas are almost frightening in their ghastly desolation.

One cold, cloudy Sunday afternoon, between luncheon and supper appointments, I went walkabout for lack of an open pub or café. All was silent, apart from a gale-force wind tearing around tower-blocks, rattling empty beer and coke cans across the streets, flapping torn plastic sheets caught on rusty barbed-wire fences and sending litter swirling over wastelands strewn with disposable nappies, broken crockery and glass, discarded garments and furniture.

Then I found myself entangled in the university complex. We all think we've seen the ultimate in architectural aberrations but until you've wandered forlorn through the dead grey concrete canyons of Leeds University you've seen nothing . . . It recalls the sort of nightmare you might have (and I have had) after too much homemade tequila mixed with Mexican brandy. Around corner after corner sprawls yet another brutal, sterile vista of spiritless, heartless, mindless angularity, the blocks linked by glass and steel corridors like chutes in a flour-mill. The few curves are concrete outside staircases (I suppose fire-escapes) of a peculiar coiling obscenity. The few flecks of colour are doors painted repellent synthetic shades of pink, orange, blue and mauve. Ugliness on this scale is not just aesthetically displeasing: it's a form of depravity. Henryk Skolimowski was surely right when he diagnosed modern architecture as a symptom of the West's moral decay.

By 5.30 a rather large drink seemed an excellent idea; my Islamic luncheon party had been teetotal. Innocently I assumed the pubs would now be open, if I could find one. But nothing anywhere was open: no pub, no café, no hotel or restaurant, not even a Fish'n'Chipper. When an isolated Pakistani off-licence-cum-huxter-store appeared on the edge of a mini-precipice, overlooking a polluted beck and an assortment of abandoned factories, it was 6.30. I then discovered that on the Sabbath alcohol cannot legally be sold before 7.00 p.m.; but luckily the couple behind the counter were from Swat and the Wali of Swat is an old friend of mine. At once the law was broken and I scuttled gleefully away clutching a tin of Newcastle Brown. But where to drink it? A slashing rain-storm had just started (that was all Leeds needed) and only a United Reformed Church – looking like an enlarged public lavatory with a tower – offered any possibility of shelter. The door was being unlocked for the evening service so I lurked in a dark corner and hastily swigged before the congregation arrived.

Much later, after an excellent meal with Coorgi friends, my shoulder-bag was snatched near a Pakistani junior brothel which incidentally I'd been investigating; Leeds offers all sorts of exotica. As I had prudently transferred my wallet and notebook to buttoned-down pockets the snatcher got only two mini-cigars and a biro. He was a skinhead – White of course.

In that area numbers of small children were playing on waste land near a new housing estate at one o'clock in the morning. When I first saw them I thought I was hallucinating. (Coorgis are not teetotal.) But it was silly of me to be so astounded; a substantial number of the human beings who live in such an environment must mutate quite quickly into something almost sub-human. It only surprises me that Leeds United Football Club doesn't have many more psychopathic fans. By the time I had found the all-night taxi-rank my nerves were more than slightly on edge. The different atmospheres of inner-city Leeds and inner-city Bradford are remarked on by many, yet the two cities are only nine miles apart – and now almost merging.

Once I visited Sheffield, when escorting a runaway Mirpuri girl to a 'safe house' – the home of her sympathetic married cousin. All around that city vast industrial edifices are collapsing; others are so Victorian-solid they just look eloquently derelict; others have been recently demolished, leaving mounds of rubble and twisted steel girders strewn over many acres. Beside abandoned steel-works, weeds have obliterated enormous expanses that not long ago were workers' car-parks. Their affluent car-owning period didn't last long . . .

As a newcomer to England's North I was awed by the sheer size of mills, warehouses, furnaces, pit-heads – and by the soaring factory chimneys, some quite beautiful but few still smoking. The End-of-an-Age aura is overwhelming. Everyone knows that whatever the future may hold there cannot be a revival of traditional industries; if no one wants your steel or your woollen goods you can't go on producing them. However, this grimly simple fact is not always accepted by redundant workers who feel both personally devalued by unemployment and conscious of the whole framework of their community having been smashed.

On the return journey from Sheffield a fifty-eight-year-old man seated himself beside me; he was clutching a large parcel and anxious to talk. A redundant steel-worker, he had been to his first grandson's christening. Traditionally, in Sheffield, the paternal grandfather tears a corner off his own apprenticeship papers and, after the baptism, puts it into the baby boy's tiny fist. His son, also recently made redundant, wanted him to follow this tradition but he refused. "I told him – 'That was a custom that meant something, it wasn't like kissing under the mistletoe. Now it means nothing and we mustn't pretend. This baby has to fit into a new world, we can't help him the way we always did before.' " He unwrapped his parcel – it was the family bible – and showed me the entries, going back 208 years, of the generations of his family who had worked in the steel-mills of Sheffield. "We were craftsmen, all of us," he said. "You wouldn't last long working furnaces and tempering blades if you didn't know what you were doing." Together we gazed silently at those pages of carefully inscribed names and I realised that my companion was very close to tears. So was I.

Apprenticeship-paper traditions do of course have another aspect. The tearful grandfather acknowleged that trades unionism run amok has contributed to Britain's industrial decline – which in places like Bradford and Sheffield one tends to think of as 'collapse' rather than 'decline'. He was but one of many redundant or retired workers whom I heard condemning the restrictive practices of their unions. A retired Birmingham car-worker (a devout Methodist) told me that for the last ten years of his working life he endured a state of permanent moral crisis because union directives forbade him to do 'an honest day's work'. He therefore felt guilty every pay-day, knowing that he had earned only half his weekly wage. In Tower Hamlets I talked with an ex-docker who described how three men were habitually employed to do one man's job. And so on and on . . . No doubt the trade union argument is that if those three men had not been doing one man's job, *two* men would have been on the dole. But would they? Or would a more efficient labour force have meant the survival of British docks? My diary holds the following entry for April 9:

> Why can this government not see that the real threat to Britain's stability comes not from the Far Left but from the *causes of disorder*. 'People Before Profit' may sound like one more mindless slogan on a fringe-group banner. Yet those three words do provide the solution to what too many solid citizens conveniently think of as an *insoluble* problem. And the Far Left are not so stupid they can't see what's wrong, though their method of righting wrongs could never work.
>
> Inner-city life must be taking its toll: this morning the Polish swimming-baths attendant gave me a half-price ticket, assuming me to be an O A P. He speaks very little English, despite forty years in Bradford, so it took time to persuade him that I'm not (quite). The baths and sports centre now have restricted opening hours because of government cut-backs – in a city where the majority of under-twenty-ones have nothing to do and nowhere to go . . . In the sports centre cafeteria I talked with a Sikh youth who wondered why, with so many jobless, no one could organise a group of volunteer workers to keep the centre open for the benefit of the whole community. I explained that trade unionism precludes that sort of practical Brotherly Love. A young White man sitting nearby overheard me. He stood up, moved closer, leant over me and said, "You bitch! Why should the poor work for nothing when the fuckin' millionaires who run this fuckin' country get richer every day?" I could think of no reply, perhaps because there isn't any. Being exposed almost daily to the naked flame of British class-hatred makes the self-destructive trade union bloody-mindedness at least half-comprehensible. The fixed mental habit of regarding 'the bosses' as 'the enemy' is so deep-rooted (and was until recently so justified) that it's unreasonable to expect it to have changed in the course of one 'pampered' generation. It might have changed if the attitudes of 'the bosses' themselves had changed; but mostly they didn't. There is something admirable in the workers' refusal to be satisfied by a spectacular improvement in their *material* standard of living. The yearning now is not *really* for higher wages or shorter working hours. It's for something much more important and much more difficult to grant: respect.

Sharing my 'poor Britain' observations and reflections with the inhabitants of more fortunate regions did little for my personal popularity. Some old friends could be thought-read – "There she goes again! And turning even crankier since she went to those awful places!" The reaction is natural; you get it too, even more strongly, in the salubrious quarters of New Delhi, Lima or Mexico City, a few miles from some of the world's worst slums. And not only the callous ignore injustice. If there is nothing you can do about it – because 'that's how things are' – why get all steamed up? Does you no good, does 'them' no good. So write a few more cheques for your favourite charities and think about something else.

Happily, England is rich in individuals, groups, commissions and sub-committees who do get steamed up and regularly draw social injustice to the reluctant attention of the Great British Public. Their efforts may be derided – understandably – in the inner cities, where it seems nothing ever *happens* as a result of all those conferences and reports. But they do represent water dripping on the stone of general indifference. And they are responsible for an increasing awareness that what is tritely termed 'the recession' is something much more. It is not a temporary malfunctioning of the Western economic machine, soon to be put right by the expert repair work of Reagan, Thatcher *et al*. It is one more symptom of the end of an age. And, as it is always a waste of time tinkering with an obsolete machine, people's intuition is telling them that now mankind – together – must invent a new one.

To quote James Robertson again:

> It is the search for alternatives, for ways of avoiding disaster, that should occupy our minds – not the prophecies of doom. Mounting pressure on the carrying capacity of the earth, combined with increasing resistance to the present inequitable distribution of the earth's resources among its peoples, must soon begin to push us towards permanently sustainable patterns of economic activity.

3 · Domestic Dramas

Invitations into Mirpuri homes did not come readily; patience was needed. Informal social intercourse with Whites is not customary, apart from those Whites who have started with a professional reason for calling and become friends. (Happily there are numerous such relationships.) I could probably have attached myself to a 'pro.' as a first move, but it seemed best to make contacts independently, dissociated from all branches of the R R I. In the end this proved a sound policy, giving me access to a wide and uninhibited variety of views.

I swam daily in the Edwardian Betjeman's-Delight Manningham Baths on the corner of Drummond Road and always took the same route, often at the same time – which meant regularly meeting the same women, as they returned from escorting children to school. Gradually, in response to my greetings, timid little smiles turned to relaxed big smiles, and next to brief shy conversations if some English was spoken, and then to longer footpaths chats during which I would mention that I had visited Azad Kashmir. This information usually roused a new animated interest in me and my doings, followed by invitations to drink tea and eat Bombay mix and spicey Punjabi savouries. I also used this technique along other routes, in Manningham and elsewhere, and found that once a breakthrough had been made on a certain street others soon followed; for multiple reasons, there is much inter-house toing-and-froing of womenfolk.

Most of the homes I visited were well-kept, sparsely though adequately furnished and luxury-free – apart from the now obligatory television set, video machine and transistor-cum-tape-recorder. A few elderly women eventually let their hair down, with the aid of a grand-daughter interpreter, and spoke wistfully of the good old pre-television days when their husbands took them out, suitably veiled, to see Asian films at the Mirpuri-owned cinema. This was always a monthly treat and given an indulgent husband it could be weekly. Now many of that generation never go out.

The purdah-quarter is usually the back-room of a terrace house, which may also be the kitchen – or the living-room if a kitchen-extension has been built on. In back-to-backs the situation is more complicated and wives may have to retreat to the bedroom when non-kinsmen call. The front parlour is reserved for menfolk and their visitors, in winter frequently to be seen sitting wrapped in blankets before a puny one-bar electric fire while their women (who are not in every respect oppressed) enjoy sub-tropical heat from the main stove in the *zenana*. As in their villages, the wife serves her husband, and any guests he may have, and then waits to eat with the children when he has finished – not before. Even in a few households where the husband seemed outwardly Westernised, meals were never family affairs. When a husband rather than a wife had invited me to eat I was treated as an honorary male and fed in the front parlour. The families on my visiting list varied in the strictness of their purdah-observance. In some homes pre-puberty daughters, or sons of any age, brought the food from the kitchen to non-related male visitors; in others the wife did appear, her head always covered, and laid the dishes on a low table before silently and swiftly withdrawing, leaving the host to serve his guests. I was relieved to note that in Bradford, as in Pakistan, not a few husbands – when unprotected by the presence of sons or other males – were well and truly hen-pecked within the privacy of their homes.

Even when there is no language barrier, Mirpuris tend to be reticent with Whites. But slowly defences were lowered, probably because of my knowing their homeland and being slightly more *au fait* with their religion and customs than the average Bradfordian. A complex criss-cross of reactions to life in Britain was then revealed. Three wives (in their late twenties or thirties) confided that for all Bradford's drawbacks – an atrociously depressing and inconvenient climate, less freedom of movement than in the village, loneliness for parents left behind, suspense about unemployment, fear of children going off the rails, resentment of husbands Westernised enough to go out whoring, drinking and gambling, financial demands from Mirpur that couldn't be met – for all these disadvantages they were glad to be in Bradford, away from the tensions and constraints of a joint-family existence with unsympathetic in-laws. All three were devout Muslims ("Muslim from the heart", as one put it). Yet I noticed them inciting their daughters to defy paternal diktats to the extent of gaining as many educational qualifications as possible and looking for good jobs – which, in their mothers' view, would make them more attractive to the right sort of forward-looking though not irreligious ("Allah forbid!") young man. There's many a family row yet to come in Manning-ham.

Another sort of wife, in the same economic and social bracket, sees Britain as a wonderland. Water from taps; heat and light at the touch of a switch; free medical treatment; free good schooling (good by Pakistani standards); a new rented video film every evening – what more could anybody want? But some wives live in a classic state of dull resignation to *kismet*: this is how it has to be – why bother balancing advantages and disadvantages? For those women life in exile is cold, hard, rather frightening, very bewildering and certain to be forever alien. When asked directly, some admitted they still longed to go home (after perhaps twenty years in Bradford!), some looked confused and gave no answer, some said, "Here it's better for our children." But that last opinion often sounded like a husband-echo.

Many of the older and less successful Mirpuris endure the worst of both worlds. They are more conscious of racialism now than when they arrived: partly because it has objectively increased, partly because their own sensitivity has increased. Some are depressed by separation from ageing parents and flying home has become cruelly expensive. Vast numbers are jobless and of those an astonishing proportion remain unaware of the State benefits to which they and their families are entitled after a quarter-century or more of honest toil. Some who know what is available are so hampered by the language problem and daunted by the paperwork involved that they shirk the unequal struggle – being illiterate in all languages. There is no basis in fact for the notion that 'immigrants are bleeding this country white', a favourite though singularly inept phrase of the racialist press. According to a Bradford Council Report:

> [the Browns] have a vastly lower social services referral rate [than Whites] and significantly under-use most services. This reflects the national pattern. The Asian and Afro-Caribbean communities have a younger age-structure than the population as a whole. There is a predisposition towards self-reliance and containment in meeting social and family needs . . . This may be a good thing: it may demonstrate that black people can cope better with the pressures of modern society . . . but . . . we think that is unlikely. It is not possible to say what the ethnic minorities' needs 'ought' to be. All that can be said is that they have certain characteristics in common with other client groups who *do* make use of the services . . . More than twenty specialist posts, mainly in social work, were created in 1982 . . . More black people have used social services since those workers were employed and a variety of questions about social services provision has been raised.

That report worried me a little. Everything must be done to ensure that jobless citizens receive the benefits to which they are entitled, but the Brown 'under-use' of social services could be over-remedied. It would be crazy to encourage Browns to become State-dependent in such areas as the care of the old. Millions of Whites have been demoralised by over-dependence on hand-outs and I hate to see naturally self-reliant Browns being ensnared in the excesses of that system.

Sitting one day in an Asian Advice Centre, waiting for a friend to have his immigration papers conundrum decoded, I realised how quickly this can happen. Two tri-lingual Brown men and two tri-lingual White women were sorting out legal and bureaucratic problems for non-English-speakers, or for any Brown defeated by those form-filling marathons which are the price of State support. As someone whose mind glazes over at the first glimpse of a government form of any kind – and stays glazed – I felt for the glum-looking queues perched on narrow benches around the walls. Heading one queue was a wavy-haired Mirpuri Adonis: radiantly healthy, six foot three in his socks with broad shoulders – a newish arrival who spoke not a word of English. But it seemed he had canny advisers. When his turn came he handed a four-page foolscap form to one of the women who spent forty minutes, exactly, filling it in. It was a claim for £7.20 to pay for the replacement of an accidentally broken window pane. The money would take about four months, the translator estimated, to come through. Meanwhile how many desks would that form traverse? How many filing-cabinets would shelter it for a day, a week, a fortnight? Into how many computers would its multifarious details be fed? All to provide £7.20 to a strapping young man who allegedly had paid someone else to replace a window pane, though at home in Mirpur he could and would build a whole house with his bare hands and the assistance of a few brother-cousins. The British Welfare State was a lovely idea before it degenerated into a multi-billion pound muddle.

However, such lunacies do not cancel out the genuine need for more advice of the sort Bradford Council is trying to provide. It seems Mirpuris do generally 'cope better' because loyalty to their *biraderi* ethos excludes from their lives many modern stresses. Yet sustaining the *biraderi* in an unsympathetic environment creates other stresses, ranging from the imaginary fears of some Pakistani-born wives, who feel threatened without extended-family support, to the sexual problems of some Bradford-born young men who resented their imported brides but were afraid to say so. Moreover, any group abruptly transferred from a remote corner of Asia to a European city will inevitably have quite a high incidence of 'nervous disorders' and some older Mirpuris suffer from a chronic lack of physical well-being attributable to no specific disease. But until each Brown community has produced its own professional helpers only limited aid can be given. White social workers, doctors and psychiatrists, however kindly and well-equipped with background knowledge, cannot have the necessary 'feel' for a Brown culture.

Even where apparently straightforward needs are concerned, there can be major cultural complications. One day my Bradford-bought bicycle (Brontë) went flat half-way down a slummy little street in Lidget Green, another area of many Mirpuris. At once a shabbily dressed youngish man, sawing planks in a tiny front garden, offered to mend the puncture. The wind was icy and he invited me to shelter in the hallway of a house almost as decrepit as the drop-outs' squat. As the tyre was levered off, four skinny unwashed children crowded curiously into the hallway and to make space for them I sat at the foot of the bare stairs. The eldest, a handsome boy of eight, was Dad's darling and allowed to make quite a nuisance of himself – revolving Brontë's pedals, using the pump to beat the mudguard and switching the lamps on and off. It took me several minutes to realise that he was a deaf mute, though clearly not at all mentally impaired. When I asked which special school he attended his father said he could never go to any school – but that didn't matter because everyone loved him so much.

Impulsively I abandoned my 'non-interference-with-other-cultures' rule, though aware of the futility of doing so. In suitably circumlocutory style, I suggested that such a bright lad could benefit enormously from special schooling – all sorts of talents might be discovered and developed – his whole life would be different . . .

The father smiled and cuddled his son, gently removing from him my repair outfit and looking down on him with affectionate pride. My advice made no impression. Handicapped children are a disgrace, a punishment from Allah. They may be given special love – and usually are – but they must be kept hidden from mocking non-family eyes. There are believed to be a disproportionate number of such children in Muslim families, first-cousin marriages being so common. But they don't show up in the statistics.

Many Brown domestic crises are caused by the immense strength of family affections. It is a religious duty to respect and obey one's elders, but beyond and above duty is love. And in most Mirpuri families the love-level is very high. (In others it is very low; but those are a tragic minority who for reasons beyond the outsider's discernment have become almost brutalised.) When the duty to obey is underpinned by love, but new circumstances make disobedience seem inescapable, young people can find themselves in a state of potentially – and too often actually – suicidal inner conflict.

The strangest case in my Bradford experience involved a family to whom I had become exceptionally close. In 1965 the then newly (and happily) married parents had arrived in Britain, Farrukh's parents being already settled in Manningham. Their eldest child was a spirited and beautiful girl of nineteen whom I first met in the Central Library. Unlike many Mirpuri girls, Sai went there regularly not to meet a boyfriend but to borrow books. Biographies and travel books were her favourites and she bore me home in triumph to meet her parents, as though I were some sort of hunter's trophy. Her thirty-five-year-old mother, from whom she had inherited her beauty, spoke no English; she looked about twenty, despite having had eight children by the age of twenty-seven. Sai later told me that after the eighth baby her mother colluded with a discreet doctor and had a "little operation", about which she did not feel it necessary to consult her husband – who would certainly have withheld his consent. Some Muslim wives are now conspiring to spread the 'disinformation' that the English climate causes infertility around the age of thirty. As Mirpuris are disposed to believe anything of the English climate, the conspiracy works well; several gullible husbands told me this interesting scientific 'fact' about their community.

In 1978 Farrukh lost the factory job he had held since his arrival. He doggedly looked for another, found one, was again made redundant, found a third in Halifax but lost it within six months when that factory also closed. It would have been futile to look for a fourth so instead he trained as a plumber – not an 'approved' training, but enough to enable him to offer a cut-price twenty-four-hour service to the Brown communities of Bradford, Keighley and Leeds. His father lent him money to instal a telephone and buy an eleven-year-old motor car which was kept on the road through the ingenuity of his eldest son – who claimed with a charming grin that *he* had to provide a twenty-four-hour garage mechanic service. As Sai observed, "These days it takes three generations working together to keep one man off the dole!"

When I met the family in February Farrukh had been plumbing for a year and was doing well enough to survive – just. The four-roomed terrace house was spick and span but austere: no three-piece-suite in the front parlour, four beds for ten people, no trannies or video machines, only a black-and-white television set presented by Farrukh's father. A lean-to kitchen had been constructed at the back by Farrukh and his sons and the family ate well but cheaply; much time and little money was spent on the evening meal. All eight children – three girls and five boys – were a delight, the two youngest boys riotously mischievous but sufficiently under control not to be tiresome. At 7.00 p.m. the six still at school settled to their books in the front room. Farrukh sadly confided to me that only Sai was 'academic'. But he insisted on the discipline of regular study – "It's good for all children." His own seemed cheerfully resigned to their routine; in that household the love-level was very high.

Sai had achieved three Bs at A Level and planned to become a social worker among the Browns. She was happy with the prospect of an arranged marriage, in the distant future, to someone looking for an emancipated working wife. No problem there, I thought; one couldn't imagine parents such as hers choosing an unsuitable husband.

Late one evening at the end of March there came an urgent knocking on my door – Sai, swollen-eyed and frantic. Her home was only ten minutes' walk away, or five minutes' run. She had no time to explain anything before her eldest brother appeared on the doorstep, breathless and angry. She refused to return with him. They argued passionately in Punjabi and he tried to drag her away by the arm. It seemed time to intervene and when I promised to escort her home next morning Hassan reluctantly agreed – but stipulated not *too* early, to prevent gossip about her having spent the night away from home. Already, he reckoned, some gossip was unavoidable; obviously that, rather than the details of the quarrel, had aroused his anger.

Sai soon regained her composure under the influence of strong tea. The day before, Farrukh's brother had returned from a three-month visit to their village with a £10,000 offer for Sai's hand: to be paid in sterling, not rupees. The proposed bridegroom was a thirty-eight-year-old small-time entrepreneur, already locally notorious because his first wife had deserted him on grounds of cruelty and he had divorced his second wife on grounds of infertility. He was a kinsman of both Sai's parents.

My first – perhaps melodramatic – thought was that this character must be a cog in the heroin-trade machine. How else could a Mirpuri afford – or why would he be willing to pay – £10,000 as an entry-fee to Britain?

We talked all night. The alternatives formed a trap from which there could be no honourable escape. Sai could say "yes", sacrificing her whole life – her whole *self* – on the altar of 'many-ness'. Or she could say "no", devastating much-loved parents by her disloyalty, depriving much-loved siblings of a chance to make something of *their* lives, sacrificing her whole family on the altar of 'one-ness'. I could perfectly understand her torment of mind and heart. From a detached White point of view the plan was monstrous; from a detached Brown point of view it presented a dilemma; from Farrukh's point of view it offered his sons a narrow exit from the poverty trap. He was conscious of no dilemma, could see no possible excuse for Sai's reluctance to co-operate – though he had, she said, expressed regret about the burden she would have to carry. Her mother supported Farrukh; only Sai's sixteen-year-old sister could appreciate how she felt.

If Sai – a British citizen – went to stay with grandparents in Mirpur and became personally acquainted with her fiancé, to an extent that satisfied the British immigration authorities, he could return to settle with her in Britain. (He planned to live in London, which made it all that much worse: Sai wouldn't even have the comfort of her family nearby.) Initially the husband would be granted only a one-year residence permit; then, if no one suspected that the marriage's 'primary purpose' was settlement in Britain, he would be allowed to remain permanently. Thus Sai could not ditch him, on arrival in London, without dishonouring her family who had accepted his cash. Even if she did so after the first year, he might be deported. In consultation with her uncle, Sai had been chosen out of many British-born girls belonging to the same kin-network. For this plan's success, the wife would have to be of guaranteed integrity and emotional stability – not likely to have a nervous breakdown and flee to the nearest police station to confess all.

This marriage would be against the spirit of the law, but not the letter. Anyway I found myself unconcerned about the legality of the proposal. A law which is so comparatively easily evaded and discriminates so blatantly against women commands little respect. (Brown men permanently resident in Britain, even though *not* British citizens, are legally entitled to import spouses from the sub-continent; Brown women may do so *only* if they are British citizens.) Moreover, Farrukh's motives were touchingly pure. He was not greedily 'selling' his daughter, he only wanted to have five hard-working sons instead of five sons 'living like beggars' – his rather blinkered perception of all those on the dole.

Unable to think of anything constructive to say, I asked if there was a remote chance that this marriage might not be quite so awful as it sounded. Life in London, for someone with Sai's interests, could be more stimulating than life in Bradford. And perhaps this fellow (his name had not been revealed) would be pleased to have a studying or working wife? But no: he would not tolerate any whiff of emancipation. This was why his first wife, who came of a relatively emancipated Lahore family, had deserted him.

Feebly – and uncomfortably aware of the fact that though writers may be poor they are not Farrukh-poor – I suggested next that £10,000 is no big deal, when you think about it, and given time Dad might realise this.

"But you know what someone like him could do with it!" said Sai. "Starting with so much he'd set up *all* the boys. It makes him sick to think of them going from school to the dole – I've seen him *crying* about it!" (This I could believe; Farrukh was an odd mixture of practicality and emotionalism.) "And Mum's as bad, she stays awake worrying they'll get into trouble when they're hanging around all day. They could get mixed up with anything – last week Dad caught two of them reading the T N S!" Sai sounded as though her brothers had been detected poring over hard porn.

I wan't even tempted to advise Sai to opt for 'one-ness', though I desperately longed for her to be able to do so. From my perspective the alternative was shattering to contemplate. But only she could decide which of the two hells on offer might least painfully be endured. Nor indeed was she looking for advice. She had come to me partly because she couldn't take the supercharged home atmosphere for another moment and partly because she hoped discussion with an outsider – yet someone fond of the whole family – would help her to make up her own mind. But she seemed no nearer a decision at 5.30 a.m. when she slumped to the floor in a stupor of exhaustion and slept for three hours.

I did not sleep; 5.00 a.m. is my habitual getting-up time when my body-clock signals action. Besides, I was much too distressed by Sai's problem to do anything but sit drinking strong coffee and brooding ineffectually. Either choice must lead to lasting unhappiness. Only a Farrukh decision to scrap the plan could deliver Sai from misery – and that seemed beyond the bounds of psychological possibility. His whole career proved his tenacity, his single-minded resolve to be self-reliant, his pride in family independence. Had he personally been required to sacrifice his happiness to his sons' future he would have done so without hesitation; Sai was not, I felt sure, being victimised merely because she was female. In this case, less love might have helped. Then Sai could have chosen 'one-ness', weathered the resulting family storm and gone on – guilt-free – to live her own life. Despite the intensity of Mirpuri cultural conditioning, she was a natural loner; that had been my first impression of her when we met in the library. But she was also a person of powerful affections and being a loner doesn't mean you can be happily callous about those you love. Life had taught me that a very long time ago, which may be why I was so chewed up by Sai's dilemma. For me it had echoes.

As Sai breakfasted I ventured to question 'this fellow's' motives for spending so much money on getting into Britain. Sai too had thought of the 'heroin connection' and challenged uncle with the possibility. But he had seemed very shocked – the fellow, after all, was a kinsman! Apparently naked ambition was the motive: a conviction that a smart businessman – smart enough to be able to pay a £10,000 entry-free – could do very much better in Britain than in Pakistan. What, I wondered, was the nature of his business? Sai had asked, uncle had been evasive . . .

Now there were only five days to go; uncle had promised a definite answer within a week of his return to Bradford. If Sai said "yes" she could be in Mirpur, for the first time, by the end of another week – surrounded by relatives she didn't know and confronting a fiancé who in the cold light of dawn seemed to resemble the villain of some unsuccessful Victorian melodrama. As I left her, still undecided, at her garden gate – we had agreed it would be tactless for me to go in – my own conditioning almost took over and it was an effort not to plead with her to say "no".

That evening I went to bed even earlier than usual and was dragged from a deep sleep by another late caller, Farrukh's youngest brother – not the match-making uncle but Akram, who had migrated only in 1980 leaving his family in the village. I had met him twice and disliked him a lot. He was Farrukh's opposite: shifty, lazy, a heavy drinker and chain-smoker, forever sponging on his brothers (Sai told me) and indifferent to the welfare of his wife and children whom he hadn't seen for five years. Sai seemed a little afraid of him.

During the first half-hour Akram's limited English made me wonder if I were imagining things. When the overall pattern of his thinking at last emerged my defences went up; with Sai I had been in a familiar area of basic Muslim family pressures but Akram was trying to take me into dangerous territory for which I had no compass. His tortuously presented suggestion was that I should give the immigration authorities an anonymous tip-off about the Sai conspiracy. Only Akram would ever know who had informed them and they would certainly use the information because of their relish for keeping Browns out. Thus could Sai be rescued . . . If I really wanted to help her, this was the only way to do it. And it could not harm Farrukh because no one could *prove* his intention to conspire. The tip-off would leave the conspirators with no choice but to scrap their plan; disappointing for Farrukh, wonderful for Sai . . .

Akram's consistent avoidance of my gaze made me uneasy. As he waited for my reaction the silence became oddly tense and I felt threatened without quite knowing why – apart from the obvious family feud trip-wires all over the place. Sai's welfare was certainly the last of Akram's concerns and whatever he was up to I didn't want to be involved. There was no guarantee that playing his game really would benefit Sai; it was impossible to judge what the consequences might be for her, for Farrukh, for their relatives in Mirpur, for the go-between uncle. However, I too was a little afraid of Akram – of his evident instability and furtive ruthlessness. It seemed unnecessary to antagonise him at midnight in my pad so I said his plan sounded good and suggested we meet at opening-time next day, in the Brown Bull, to discuss details.

When Akram had gone I wondered how many insomniacal neighbours would deduce that I had been providing him with a foretaste of the Islamic Paradise; many Mirpuris suspect the worst of women (however moth-eaten) who live alone. Next I wondered if somehow his machinations could be put to good use. What if I told Farrukh that treachery was being plotted, without specifying by whom? How likely was it that he would guess by whom? Very likely – so did the attempted rescue of Sai justify my taking the risk of provoking bloodshed? Maybe just superficial knife-wounds, but maybe worse . . . What then if I told Sai herself, arguing that *now* her duty to the family required her to say "no" – because "yes", with treachery in the air, could endanger the whole clan? But to avert the risk of bloodshed (a very real risk, as Sai would understand) she couldn't explain her reason: that she was acting not out of selfishness but out of loyalty, to protect the family from entanglement with the law. She would however be delivered from 'that fellow' and at peace with her conscience, even if her parents felt betrayed and shamed by her insubordination. So the final question was, could she or should she be expected to take the responsibility for using my information to solve the worst of her problem while *not* implicating Akram? Foreseeing the pressures likely to be applied in reaction to her "no", I could not be sure that I was taking the right course. Given my complete ignorance of Akram's motives, I might be making a horrible mistake. But by 8.30 a.m. I was on my way to Farrukh's house.

Hassan opened the door, looking annoyed – as well he might, at breakfast time, though I didn't feel that was the reason. He said his father had left a few hours earlier to do an emergency job and his mother was ill. (Nervous exhaustion, according to Sai, which didn't surprise me; I was feeling a bit that way myself.) It wasn't easy to talk with Sai in such a tiny house; the Easter holidays had started and all the children were at home. So I asked Hassan if she might come to my pad and after some hesitation he gave his consent.

Sai was no nearer a decision and also showing symptoms of nervous exhaustion. But she listened attentively to my account of Akram's plot and, even before I put my argument in favour of her saying "no", she herself saw this development as a possible escape route. But her first question was: "Why did he need you to inform the authorities? Why couldn't he do it himself?" That point had also puzzled me, until I remembered that he was literate in no language and spoke the sort of English that requires patience and practice to understand. He wouldn't find it easy to report anything to the authorities – anonymously – in a manner sufficiently convincing for them to take the report seriously. (Most people, including educated Browns and Blacks, often forget how constricting it is to be illiterate in a literate world.) And knowing how fond of Sai I had become, it was natural enough for him to assume I would co-operate. What puzzled me much more was his apparent confidence in my not reporting his plot to Farrukh, should I disapprove of it. But Sai had an explanation for that. If I did tell Farrukh, Akram would accuse me of inventing the story as part of my 'Save Sai Campaign' and Farrukh would believe him, being already inclined to blame me for Sai's unfilial indecision. Why the word of a proven bounder should be preferred to that of a disinterested outsider was beyond my comprehension. But Sai seemed convinced that it would be, and that Akram could rely on this reaction. With every moment that passed I was feeling more out of my depth in the murky and tempestuous waters of this family crisis.

However, at least Sai felt that she could now say "no" with a clear conscience. But she was evasive about whether or not she would attempt to justify her decision – and if so, how. For the first time she seemed to be putting up barriers, where normally she tried to demolish them. My hunch was that she perfectly understood what lay behind Akram's plot but considered it so unsavoury, so discreditable to the family or the *biraderi*, that loyalty forbade her to discuss it – for which I admired her all the more. Previously she had not concealed her contempt for Akram but now there was a perceptible closing of the ranks.

As I escorted Sai home we co-ordinated our next moves. By then it was almost opening-time and while she was breaking the news to her parents I would be in the Brown Bull, telling Akram that I had just learned the marriage plan was off. "He won't be pleased," said Sai enigmatically. "Why not?" I asked. "He seemed keen enough to stop it!" Sai made no reply. But she was right. Although Akram put on an unconvincing show of relief he plainly felt thwarted and disappointed. That was the last but one of the case's many bafflements.

The final bafflement was pleasing. During the following days I longed for news of Sai but judged it diplomatic to keep off the scene, being unsure of my post-crisis status *chez* Farrukh. Then one evening a note from Sai was pushed under my door: her father would like me to visit next day.

That was a happy evening. The family atmosphere seemed mysteriously unimpaired by recent events and an unusually elaborate meal was served by Sai to Farrukh, Hassan, the go-between uncle and myself (as honorary male). Recent events were not mentioned but when Sai saw me to the gate she briefly and expressionlessly informed me that Akram had returned to Mirpur – for good.

Some time ago, in Belfast, I discovered that a bicycle has a use other than transportation. If you don't have a genuine puncture – as you frequently do, in areas where throwing stones at empty bottles is seen as a harmless form of free amusement – you can pretend to have one. Or you can derail your chain and look for help to put it right, thus getting to chat with people who (because you are Southern Irish on the Shankill, or White in Bradford or Handsworth) might not spontaneously communicate. To get chatting with Zia and Hussain, I derailed my chain.

My interest had been engaged not by either of those young men but by a pathetic girl – the wife, I deduced, of one of them – who early every morning was to be seen crouching on the pavement in front of their greengrocery, sweeping with a dustpan and brush. When I first noticed her I was walking past and stopped to look at the limited window display and ask a question – not expecting (though she did look timid) that she would scramble to her feet and flee in terror. A very new arrival, it seemed; and a very unhappy person.

Brontë's chain came off one Friday afternoon: bad timing on my part. Zia had just returned from the mosque – Hussain was not around – and so was clad in immaculate traditional garb. He might justifiably have claimed ignorance of bicycles but instead he hurried off to change into jeans and a sweater before messing with Brontë's oily chain. We had quite a long and coolly friendly chat. His parents had come from near Hazro town, so this was my first close encounter with a Campbellpuri family. (Most of them settled in Birmingham.) He and Hussain were then aged four and three; they had been back to their village once to visit grandparents. When I had loaded my saddle-bag with far more fruit than I needed I pedalled off, hoping that satisfactory foundations had been laid.

During the next fortnight progress was slow though I lived almost entirely on fruit and often pressed large bags of bananas, apples or oranges into the hands of astonished friends. If this family was typical, Campbellpuris are much more White-resistant than Mirpuris. By the end of two weeks I had thoroughly cleansed my bowels but gleaned only limited information: that Mina was Zia's sixteen-year-old bride, who had arrived from a small village in Chhachh just a few days before I first saw her; that Hussain was away visiting relatives in Birmingham; that their father had died suddenly three years after their arrival in Bradford. Not until Hussain's return was my fruitarianism rewarded.

Hussain had literary ambitions; he wrote poetry in both Urdu and English and longed to have it published. Zia had informed him that A Writer was now their best customer and within moments of our meeting Hussain had invited me to drink tea in the purdah-quarter over the shop.

Mina was not visible but could be heard pot-walloping in the background. Mamma – a stout lady in her early forties, with a pale, round, smooth face – did not greet the *Gore* (White). She sat cross-legged on a padded quilt in one corner, motionless apart from an occasional adjustment of her *dupatti*, and stared at me with unveiled hostility while I talked with her son.

Hussain told me he had learned Urdu – a language not normally spoken by migrants from a one-acre farm near Hazro – at a Birmingham mosque school, while he was living with an uncle in Sparkbrook after his father's death. In 1983 he graduated with a good history degree and applied unsuccessfully for teaching jobs. He acknowledged that many young White graduates are also jobless but thought it ironic that he had to remain unemployed while educational experts proclaim the need for more Brown teachers in multi-racial schools. He referred to the 1976 PEP report, *Facts of Racial Disadvantage*, which found that seventy-nine per cent of White graduates were in appropriate jobs, compared with thirty-one per cent of Browns or Blacks. A year later a national survey revealed that forty-one per cent of White male workers were in managerial or professional jobs, compared with twenty-six per cent of Brown men and eleven per cent of Blacks. The discrepancy here is less than might be expected, remembering the origins of most Brown migrants. More than one-third of Britain's hospital doctors being Brown no doubt partly explains this – but only partly. Mirpuris and Campbellpuris are often described as 'primitive peasants' by other Pakistanis, yet I met an extraordinary number who had availed themselves of British educational opportunities to leap from their inherited world of illiteracy to impressive academic heights. A recent government survey of school-leavers in six LEAs found that five per cent of Browns went on to full-time degree courses as compared to four per cent of Whites and one per cent of Blacks. Hussain told me that a survey of 500 retail businesses in Bradford, Southall and Leicester discovered that sixty per cent of Asian traders are graduates, as compared to nine per cent of White traders. "People think we're behind counters because we're fit for nothing else," said Hussain. "But many of us don't have a choice, even after we've put all we've got into studying."

Inevitably, Hussain urged me to stay for a meal; all Pakistanis, at home or abroad, are genuinely upset if you leave their hearth (or gas-fire) without not only eating but over-eating. By then, however, my nerve had almost broken under Mamma's baleful stare; so I made suitable excuses and departed, having arranged a meeting next day in the more relaxed atmosphere of a pub. (Hussain had already indicated that alcohol-wise he was liberated.)

That was the beginning of an eight-month saga which at irregular intervals I observed from the periphery – with increasing anxiety.

Campbellpuris, like Pathans, maintain a stricter form of purdah than Mirpuris, which explains Mina's reaction on that morning of our first encounter. She had mistaken me for a man, a not unusual error among Brown women; I have a deep voice and my garb – especially on an ice-bound Bradford morning – might be described as asexual. In her village, which she had just left, Mina was kept in the strictest seclusion, emerging from her home compound only rarely – to attend a wedding or visit a local saint's tomb – and then totally enveloped in a *burkah*. It was therefore brutal of Zia to order her to appear unveiled in the shop and on the public footpath: almost the equivalent of ordering a White woman to appear naked in public. But he, though no liberal, had decided that to get the most out of his wife, as a worker in Bradford, purdah rules must be relaxed; he even had hopes of putting her to work in one of the few still-functioning textile mills where a group of young Campbellpuri wives had been employed for some years. Mamma disapproved of Zia's decision and accused Mina of damaging the family honour by being a loose woman, though she well knew that her son had ordered this brazen behaviour. Zia, however, as the male head of the family, could not be directly defied; and Hussain said his brother was indifferent to the injustice being suffered by the new bride at her mother-in-law's hands – or tongue. What went on in the *zenana* was not his concern and he continued to go out with his friends every evening to their local club, as is the tradition, leaving Mina to be chewed up yet again.

Zia had wished for an imported bride (more docile) but Hussain was hoping his uncle in Birmingham would soon find him a suitably educated British-born girl. Their two sisters, aged twenty and twenty-two, were well married to Birmingham shop-keepers and the mothers, respectively, of three and four children – adored by Hussain, whose wallet was stuffed with photographs of them all at various stages of development. (That was another source of conflict with Mamma; she believed photography to be irreligious.)

Hussain and I met weekly in a pub. As time passed he admitted that he was unable to remain as aloof as his brother from *zenana* tensions. Being a kind and imaginative young man he felt the strain of sharing a small house with a terrified sixteen-year-old who was almost always in tears. One evening towards the end of April I found him drinking brandy instead of bitter and his hands were shaking. "I think I must go away," he said. "He's beating her now."

I made no comment; Mina was Zia's property and the Qur'an gave him the right to beat her. In Punjabi the traditional terms for a married man mean 'master' and 'owner'. I'm told most of Britain's Punjabi-speakers now use a Farsi-Urdu term meaning 'husband', but this semantic change does not always signify a changed attitude. Before we parted Hussain had decided to move back to Sparkbrook.

Soon after, the younger sister, Nazu, brought her three children to visit granny and stayed a month. She often served in the shop – replacing Hussain – which infuriated her mother; so the *zenana* atmosphere became even more fraught. But at least Mina now had a co-victim and a good ally. Nazu was an articulate and strong-minded young woman; we had many long conversations over the counter, not often interrupted by customers. (Sometimes Nazu would nod towards the pavement, drawing my attention to Brown children carrying home large Morrisons' supermarket bags of fruit and vegetables.) I soon learned why Hussain had been so upset that evening in the pub: Mina had just attempted suicide. Nazu believed that like many another young bride she would have become inured to mother-in-law bullying; what she found unendurable was the violence of her sex-life with a man she had grown to hate. "For her it's like being raped four times a night!" said Nazu, banging her clenched fists on the counter. "In the evenings I see her growing more and more afraid when bedtime is coming – she dreads him touching her and she has no relatives in Bradford. So when she got pregnant she tried to stop it –

she can only get away if he thinks she's barren. Then when she couldn't stop it she tried to hang herself. Now my mother won't let her be alone even for five minutes!"

This revelation left me too shattered to say anything coherent. Circumstances had not allowed me to get to know Mina – even to the extent one could, across the language barrier – but I had developed an odd affection for that frightened, rather beautiful young face with its large sad hopeless eyes.

That night I had a very strange experience. It wasn't (or didn't seem to be) a dream; it was more an acute heightening of awareness – a grim sort of enlightenment. I woke at dawn knowing with all my being the precise significance of what Mina was suffering. Not just intellectually knowing but feelingly knowing. And not just *Mina* but all women anywhere who are forced into a sexual relationship with a man they hate or fear. It then seemed to me almost incredible that any woman of reasonable intelligence should have reached the age of fifty-three before attaining that rudimentary understanding. I felt humiliated by the cocoon of complacency which for so long had protected me from a sufficient sympathy with the sufferings of millions. Yet of what use is *sympathy*? Mine could not help Mina.

The weeks passed, and Nazu reported, "She's very sick with this baby." We agreed her sickness was more likely to be of the mind and heart than the body.

At the end of May I left Bradford; Nazu was to leave a few days later. On my return during June for a brief visit I called at the shop to enquire after Mina. Zia smiled blandly and said, "She's OK."

Meanwhile, in Birmingham, I was occasionally meeting Hussain in a Small Heath pub run by a fiercesome six-foot Mayo woman who made a habit of checking her regular customers' cigarettes to ensure they were hash-free. Uncle had found him a suitably educated girl with two A Levels and he had talked to her and she was personable; yet he seemed oddly unenthusiastic.

"I could go to Sweden," he said unexpectedly one evening. "I have an engineer friend there earning £250 a week and he's built himself a house costing £80,000. He can give me a good secure job. There are many of us going there now, straight from Pakistan – and some going from here. They don't have so much prejudice there. It's a better country for young people. You can lead an independent life. Here it's like Pakistan, with family everywhere watching you."

"Would your fiancée like Sweden?" I asked. "Might she not miss her family?"

"She's not my fiancée," said Hussain. "She's only a *suggestion*."

Some weeks later, in the middle of August, we met again. I had just returned from another weekend in Bradford and Hussain enquired, "What's happening at the shop?"

"Do you not get news?" I asked.

"How?" said Hussain. "My mother and sister-in-law are illiterate, my brother hates me – how would I get news? Only about the business, we hear all about that, but not about people."

Alas! I had no news about people either; only that Zia had as usual said Mina was "OK".

"But she's not, is she?" said Hussain. "What will she do when the baby comes in December? Will she kill it?"

I stared at him, utterly unable to think of any response.

"She needs to get away," said Hussain, "before somebody turns violent."

I gathered my wits and suggested, "Might it not be better after the baby? It often is – things can become more humanised."

"No!" said Hussain. "She needs to get right away – far away!"

There was a short silence. Then, "You mean to Sweden?" I asked.

"Yes," said Hussain.

And so it was. They disappeared, overnight, in the first week of September. On subsequent visits to Bradford, I bought my fruit at a Mirpuri shop.

4 · Races Apart

The scene was a small, smugly affluent pub which caters for 'the White Highlands' of Bradford – steep ridges where the prosperous live in handsome residences far above all those little Brown-packed streets. (Remembering descriptions of Bradford, pre-smoke-control, one realises why the wealthy built higher and higher as industry developed.)

The time was 6.15 p.m.: high-tea time for Bradfordians, so there were only two women and a man at the bar, all aged thirty-ish. As the muzak had not yet been switched on, their conversation was audible; though not White Highland residents, they seemed to be regulars. Perhaps they worked nearby. I sat just behind them and took out my notebook to jot down the afternoon's impressions. But soon I had something else to jot down.

First woman: They're the dregs!
Man: There's some good ones though.
First woman: No, they all have filthy habits.
Man: But a few of them work hard.
First woman: No they don't! They're just filthy cheats – that's how they get rich! Honeyford's right – they're just a bunch of drug-pushers!
Second woman: They're moving in on me. A Paki doctor's buying the house opposite.
First woman: Hope he's not the one I know – that shit locks up his wife every morning when he goes out to work!
Man: What happens if the house goes on fire?
First woman: He wouldn't care! Burn one and buy another!
Man: But that costs money.
First woman: He'd have her insured like the furniture!
Second woman: Them Pakis don't eat decent food. They just make a fortune selling filth to us fools.
First woman: Jamaicans eat goats' meat and horse meat – like dogs!
Second woman: It's the hot food makes 'em so stupid.
Man: They're not all stupid. There's some right bright lads at George's school.
First woman: Not bright – just criminals they are – clever like criminals.
Second woman: The women are worse than animals – babies every year.

First woman: You know why? There's money in it here! Back where they come from they wouldn't have more'n one!
Man: But they don't have no way to stop children out there.
Second woman: Abortions!
First woman: The government castrates all the men – I read about it – cheaper'n giving them benefits!

On that last remark the three finished their drinks, said "Cheers!" to the tall blond barman and disappeared.

I put my notebook away and collapsed into despair; perhaps my resistance had been lowered by a hard afternoon with an Irish priest who regarded Muslims as pagans, which is theologically incorrect, and was drafting a letter to his bishop suggesting the exclusion from Catholic schools of Muslim pupils unwilling to attend daily Mass. Snatches of similar pub conversations are often to be heard in Bradford, but usually background noises prevent one from following the exchanges closely enough to write them down verbatim. So my despair-inducing experience was also a valuable coup.

Later I tried to understand why that conversation had been so exceptionally distressing; and I realised that it represented the concentrated essence of Britain's race relations problem, undiluted by even a spoonful of hypocrisy, diplomacy or self-restraint.

Personal contact with Browns probably explained the man's comparative tolerance; very likely he had Brown work-mates. The women's shared attitude seemed typical of working-class Whites who avoid all contact with 'them'. (It is also typical of many middle-class Whites, though they would express it differently.) I wondered then – how *territorial* is all this? Now many Bradfordians object to the cooking smells of curry; a century ago they objected to the cooking smells of bacon and cabbage, the traditional Irish dish. (Not that Bradford's Irish, a century ago, could afford to cook bacon as often as Browns cook curry.) The sense of being invaded, especially if your own status in society provides little sense of security, must stimulate very primitive feelings. Then, to justify the hatred you find within, it becomes necessary to build up an image of a cruel, dishonest, dirty, lazy, drug-pushing community – the sort of people it is proper to despise, if you are 'decent English'. So you eagerly snatch at fragments of half-understood information: about the institution of purdah, Sanjay Gandhi's sterilisation campaign, the smuggling of heroin from Pakistan – and thus you 'prove' that the invaders deserve all your scorn and hatred. This fanatical prejudice is way beyond reach of any government legislation, any R R I campaigning. If people *need* their misinformation and misunderstandings, to give a virtuous gloss to emotions they may well be subconsciously ashamed of, they are going to keep every mental door firmly locked against the admission of facts about the invaders. Most depressing of all, they are likely to infect their children, particularly in areas where there are few or no coloured pupils in the local schools. It appalled me to think that those two women are the mothers of

Bradford's twenty-first-century adults. Can it be that pessimists who predict a bright future for the National Front are in fact realists?

A week or so later, I was in a very different sort of hostelry, a dingy little pub near High Hill School. At 1.30 p.m. it was patronised only by three half-pint drinkers: two crew-cut, heavily tattooed, pool-playing young men and a gaunt, seedy, stiff-jointed pensioner who moved to sit beside me on recognising my brogue. He was a Bradford-born ex-soldier and his best army buddy had been from Co. Sligo. After the war they served together in East Africa. "Those were the best days of my life, in Africa! Lovely climate, lovely people – Masseys and Keecoos they were called. Real men, they were – we got on like we was brothers! I even liked 'em when they was fighting us. I remember the day . . ." And he reminisced for another fifteen minutes, recalling individuals, the landscape, birds, plants; his eyes would have been glowing if less rheumy. "*Paradise* it was!" he concluded. "That's where I'd live this minute if I was a rich man!"

He asked then why I was in Bradford and when I told him a spasm of hatred distorted his friendly old face. "They're horrible, those people! Horrible! You take my advice and keep well away – they have diseases. They're dirty and deceitful and they won't work. They're only here to live free off the rest of us and they breed like flies – ten and twelve children some of them have – and the best of them have eight. Horrible they are! A fifteen-year-old Paki kid had a baby – it was in the papers – she was found in an old factory off the Thornton Road with it – horrible they are! A kid she was, still at school. Contaminating the country, that's what they're doing – contaminating us all! We all think they're horrible – no one likes 'em. Live in filth they do – take my advice and keep well away – catch anything off them you could!"

This almost feverish antagonism was clearly based on the concept of 'Pakis as invaders', not on any form of racism or colour prejudice. And it contained a strong element of 'scapegoating'; the repugnance felt by people of his generation for schoolgirl pregnancies was being focused on one exceptional Brown case, while he sought to blame White 'immorality' on 'contamination' by the invaders. He would not have believed me had I told him that in Britain the proportion of unmarried mothers among Browns is one per cent as compared to nine per cent among Whites and thirteen per cent among Blacks. Nor would he have believed me had I tactlessly commented that as a widowed Brown father he would have been leading a more comfortable and less lonely life. Both his sons were working in Saudi Arabia and he explained sadly, "They never come to Bradford now. They have fine houses, I hear, near London – and smart wives in good jobs. I haven't seen them for three – maybe it's four – years. But they send cheques at Christmas." His case was a classic example of that filial neglect considered sinfully cruel by Browns.

Every day heightened my awareness of the extent and intensity of local animosity towards 'them'. If I were to extract from my Bradford diary all the anti-Brown remarks I chanced to hear, and all the impassioned accusations I listened to, those passages alone would add up to a stout volume. But is all this true racialism in the dictionary sense – 'belief in the superiority of a particular race'? Or might it be more accurate to describe it, in many cases, as xenophobia – 'a morbid dislike of foreigners'? It can often seem that working-class Whites are reacting against Browns and Blacks, as they once reacted against the Irish, because they are *different* – and now, increasingly, are seen as threatening competitors on the schooling, employment and housing scenes. A typical comment came from one angry young Keighley man – "Stuff your tolerance! Keep that for your middle-class friends – *their* kids aren't losing schoolbooks and jobs and space to live!" There is some jealousy too, interwoven with *inferiority* feelings because so many Browns have done so well in their little businesses (a few of which have by now become quite big businesses), though starting from the same base of economic disadvantage as their White neighbours. All these negative emotions are understandable, though it is hard on one's tender liberal sensibilities to have to listen to so much violently expressed hatred every day of the week for months on end.

Word-juggling with 'xenophobia', 'ethnocentricity' and 'racialism' may seem a mere game for on-lookers, irrelevant and indeed irritating to the victims of prejudice. But not so. The future of Britain's ethnic minorities depends on which of these reactions to outsiders is in fact predominant.

In a Shipley second-hand bookshop I talked one day with an octogenerian Jew who came to Bradford from Germany in the 1930s. He said, "We soon discovered that immigrants have to keep in the shadows, keep their heads down, accept hostility for a while and work hard – which is what the Asians around here have always tried to do, but now the anti-racists won't let them! They want them out of the shadows, marching on the streets with placards, and *that* won't do their community any good! For many years we've had no problems. My four grandchildren are all married in Yorkshire and no one ever thinks of them as *Jews* . . ."

Jews however are White. And *colour* – not religion – puts Browns and Blacks in a category apart from the many other immigrants who have settled in Bradford over the years.

The veins of Bradfordians must be awash with Irish blood (perhaps one reason for my feeling so at home among them) and the similarities between the early Irish settlements and the Pakistani settlements are fascinating. C. Richardson noted in *A Geography of Bradford*:

> Something like Irish ghettoes had developed by 1841 and they persisted throughout the 19th century. By 1861 a number of these areas had become wholly Irish . . . Linguistic, religious and occupational class differences distinguished them from the rest of Bradford's population . . . four-fifths of which was non-Catholic and generally anti-Catholic. The Irish included non-English speakers and had little to give but toil and sweat. They came mostly from peasant backgrounds and were not welcome in 19th-century Bradford; this as much as anything caused them to congregate in their established quarters . . . They made up 81% of the total

Bradford population of hawkers and pedlars; 62% of the 'other labourers'; 25% of the charwomen and washerwomen ... There were no Irish house proprietors, bankers and agents; they had only three-eighths of their share of the shop-keeping group ... As late as 1900 Irish quarters had a crude death-rate more than twice the Bradford rate.

The differences that emerge between Paddys and Pakis are also fascinating. Most Pakistani migrants were peasant *farmers* – small (albeit very small) landowners who migrated voluntarily to better their not hopeless inherited positions. But most of the nineteenth-century Irish came from one of the poorest sections of contemporary rural European society and, after generations of exploitation, had no alternative but to emigrate. Lacking the Pakistanis' industry, thrift and *biraderi* incentives to earn and save (though of course many did remit money home when they could), no Irish self-servicing network of businesses was at once set up. The original Irish immigrants were at even more of a disadvantage than the original Pakistani immigrants – obvious candidates for what the sociologists call 'transmitted deprivation'. But they were White and, as C. Richardson records, eventually they merged into the rest of the population:

> Irish migration continued throughout the 20th century and initially favoured the inner-city areas. As new waves of brown-skinned immigrants from the New Commonwealth began to enter these areas, the former occupants moved out ... those who have been in Bradford longest edging into better property . . . The Irish ethnic group is in process of being dispersed voluntarily as people move up the social scale.

Job discrimination, consistently practised by employers, trades unions and White workers, is making movement up the social scale impossible for most Browns. On arrival they took the worst-paid jobs, though at home many had been skilled workers. As time passed it would have been normal for a proportion to graduate to skilled jobs in Bradford, or to supervisory or administrative positions. Yet few did, whatever their aptitudes. And it is hard to see how they can avoid being condemned, by discrimination, to generations of 'transmitted deprivation'. One would like to think that xenophobia (essentially short-term) rather than racialism (essentially long-term) is 'the dominant gene' in British reactions to Browns and Blacks. Within some groups and individuals it probably is; but all the evidence suggests that Britain's coloured minorities are primarily the victims of *racial* prejudice, reinforced by both ethnocentricity and xenophobia.

When the Easter holidays started, and Bradford's midday temperature rose slightly above zero, the streets and laneways of Manningham came suddenly alive and bright and happily noisy with throngs of small Brown children. Looking into the future, I often felt heartsick. They are such beautiful children, and so carefree and high-spirited now – but ten years hence ... ? A country that cannot look after its own White 'sub-proletariat' offers little hope to Browns and Blacks. It is disconcerting to catch oneself thinking like Enoch Powell, but occasionally I was driven to wondering furtively if Mirpur – or wherever their parents came from – wouldn't ensure them a better future than Britain's demoralised and potentially anarchic inner cities. No State support, but more dignity, self-respect and stability – altogether a more *human* way of life. Many youngsters of both sexes are now being de-civilised by Britain's 'cultural environment'. In Birmingham I swam every morning in the local baths, regularly used by groups of schoolchildren. One day a score or so of Brown sixteen- to seventeen-year-old girls arrived without their PT instructor and while they changed I lingered in my cubicle, peering out unobserved. Their language and behaviour were vile. Had they been White I would scarcely have noticed, but remembering the graciousness of their equivalents in Pakistan and India it grieved me to witness how being British-born had debased them. However, they *are* British-born and for them 'repatriation' would not be repatriation but exile from the land of their birth. As a rescue plan for this new unwanted generation of Browns and Blacks it is not realistic, only fleetingly tempting to dreamers.

I often cycled out to Keighley, an Aire Valley town some nine miles from Bradford; to its fury it was amalgamated with the newly created Bradford Metropolitan District in 1974. Keighley has a strong personality of its own, many fine buildings, a population of about 60,000 and a dependent hinter-land: so naturally it resented being reduced to vassalage. Its prosperity was also based on the textiles industry and it now has a large and unwelcome Brown overflow from Bradford.

On my first visit I paused on the edge of the town to ask the way of a tall young Campbellpuri wearing a finely embroidered shirt and loose panta-loons, all spotlessly clean and meticulously ironed. (It was a Friday.) He apologetically conveyed that he spoke no English and we salaam'd politely and parted. That was at the junction of a main road and a short cobbled cul-de-sac of attractive terraced stone houses. Half-way down the little street a White woman stood in her doorway talking to a White man as he mended her window. Noticing my need for guidance she came hurrying towards me with characteristic Yorkshire kindness. I went to meet her, leaving Brontë unlocked at the corner, and the window mender yelled, "Don't leave yer bike there – them Pakis'll nick it!" She didn't know the address I was seeking but offered me the use of her telephone – and then insisted on making me tea because my destination was a few miles further on.

As I was leaving I remarked, "What a lovely street!" – which provoked a startling eruption of molten verbal lava.

"Lovely houses, yes, but we've no peace to live in them now with all them Pakis crowding us out – they're like plagues in the Bible – there isn't a street round here left decent and free of 'em! I can talk out straight to you because you're from some place else. In this town now we daren't speak the truth except to our friends – we'd be called racist if we did, like that poor teacher in Bradford! There's no one left to stand up for *us*, all they care about is them Pakis – making life easier for *them*! And a dirty thieving dangerous lot they are, forcing us out of our homes and streets with threats and persecutions – breaking the gutters and digging the pointing out of the walls to make us leave the houses we were born in! And if we dare complain to them new authorities in Bradford likely enough we'd end up in the courts for being racist or summat! Money they offer too, great wads of notes to bribe us out of our homes!" I interrupted then to ask in neutral tones where they got the money. "From cheating and thieving – and from a government that won't give us enough to keep our schools and hospitals and old folks' homes open. Nine and ten children they have and they won't take a decent job so's they qualify for everything free – free milk, free school-meals and their own dirty meat, free clothes, shoes, medicine, heat, fuel, light – even free telly licences! And special teachers, no less! And for why? For because their parents are too lazy to teach them English before they start school! So our kids must hang back waiting for them to catch up and then they're taught about all them people like whoever started that Paki religion. And no more Christian hymns because the Pakis don't like them – so why don't they go back where there's no Christians? Or let them run their own schools and pay for them too – then maybe our kids would have new books and classrooms fit to sit in, not the way they are now like they were bombed!"

At that point five small Brown children passed by the end of the cul-de-sac on their way to a nearby park: three neatly dressed little boys carrying hockey-sticks and two little girls in gay *salwar-kameez* with long glossy plaits. My companion literally bared her teeth; never before have I seen a human being look like a snarling dog. "Watch them – see them – there they go, the dirty little rats! Swarming everywhere! We used to go to the park regular with our Spotty, now we can't go near the place with them all over it! Spotty hates them too!"

Keighley's park is vast, with ample space for any number of White dog-walkers and Brown children to go their separate ways. But this insensate outburst was, I soon discovered, standard stuff in the Keighley area – where there is still much resentment of Bradford's take-over and one notices an extra emphasis on the fact that no one will stand up for the Whites.

On a later visit, a retired textile worker said to me, "You should have come here long ago and seen our town the way it was before them blacks were off-loaded on us, pushing Bradford's problems out to folks that never asked for them. Thirty years ago Bradford was encouraging them over – I said then we'd no business filling the country with blacks. And now they've thrown them out our way, to make a slum of Keighley!"

More ominously, his twenty-year-old (unemployed) grandson added, "No one listens to us any more – we're only the English! So they don't know what's coming. They've made us afraid to speak up – look what they're doing to Honeyford! So we're not warning them we won't stand for it much longer . . .'

"That's right!" said grandad. "And I won't be blaming our lads. And most people in this town won't blame them. If there's no one will listen or help we must look after ourselves."

I remembered Northern Ireland, where some travellers find it hard to believe that among their genial pub acquaintances are men who can and do attack their neighbours with a clear conscience – also reasoning that 'we must look after ourselves'. Within the next few weeks, several people (including a social worker and a police officer) told me that the National Front was gaining support throughout the Keighley area. Since that time there have been an increasing number of after-dark attacks on small groups of Brown youths by large gangs of White youths.

On Saturday 13 April the British National Party held a Bradford Council election meeting in Hutton Middle School, Eccleshill, an area notoriously supportive of the National Front. The main speakers were the BNP candidate, Mr Stanley Clayton-Garnett, a former Bradford headmaster, and the BNP national chairman, John Tyndall – he who did time during the '60s for running a paramilitary organisation which sported full Nazi regalia. Later Mr Tyndall was a leader of the Greater Britain Movement, which stated in its programme:

> For the protection of British blood, racial laws will be enacted forbidding marriage between Britons and non-Aryans. Medical measures will be taken to prevent procreation on the part of all those who have hereditary defects, whether racial, mental or physical. A pure, strong, healthy British race will be regarded as the principal guarantee of Britain's future.

During a subsequent Council debate on the admission of the BNP to Council property it was explained that under the 1983 Representation of the People Act permission could not be refused. The Tory and Liberal members defended the principle of free speech for all, but Mohammed Ajeeb (who a week later became Lord Mayor) wondered if the Council would have ignored Hitler's activities had he lived in Bradford . . .

Eccleshill is a bleak and sordid suburb of 'modern' but dwindling industries and newish council estates mainly occupied by Whites (including many Irish), with a few pockets of Blacks and even fewer of Browns. Before the meeting everybody expected trouble; it was too good a 'confrontation opportunity' to be missed by Bradford's jobless anti-racists and Far Left. But luckily 13 April was – even by Bradford '85 standards – meteorologically remarkable. An icy gale drove horizontal sheets of rain across the hill-top on which stands Hutton Middle School and none but the hardiest faction-fighters or most selfless idealists turned out. Had it been a gloriously sunny spring afternoon, loud with birdsong and caressed by zephyr breezes, the hundreds of police tucked away in vans around every corner might have had to exchange their thermos flasks for riot-gear. (But I doubt if that sort of afternoon ever happens in Bradford.)

A selfless idealist named Jerry accompanied me and we arrived at 1.00 p.m., an hour before the meeting was due to start. Already traffic had been diverted from the area and a long line of police (including one Brown) stood shoulder to shoulder across the wide Victoria Road outside the school. The BNP group were to park their bus beyond that line and be escorted into the school through a gate defended by the police. The two hundred or so anti-BNPs were keeping themselves warm by making vigorously impolite gestures towards the fuzz while chanting – "Scum! Scum! Scum!" Or – "Two – four – six – eight, *we* don't want a fascist state!" Or – "*Smash* the BNP! *Smash* the BNP *Smash! Smash! Smash!*"

As Jerry sadly observed, "Just another rent-a-mob, longing to prove their virility. If they had steady jobs all week they'd be at home on a Saturday afternoon washing the car or putting a new cupboard in the kitchen." I took his point, while inwardly questioning the virility of the White sub-proles; they looked almost under-nourished enough to feature on a Famine Appeal leaflet.

At such meetings the police try to balance the number of supporters from each faction and the crowd was enraged when an officer announced that only fifty demonstrators could be accommodated in the school. Mob-hatred, however mini the mob, is always scary. It is also depressing if one sympathises with the mob's grievances and so regrets its betrayal of a 'good cause'. Jerry said gloomily, "These are showing the other side of the NF coin – think how impressive if they'd organised a peaceful, dignified protest!"

The arrival of the small BNP group provoked a frenzy of shouted abuse, jerking arms and pointed fingers. Watching the police escort them across the playground I felt a chill that had nothing to do with the weather. There was no mistaking the comradeship between police and BNP in this situation where both were being jeered at by the Far Left. On the whole Bradford's police handle difficult confrontations tactfully and I am not suggesting that any of them is an active supporter of the BNP – though it is not inconceivable that some of them might be. That afternoon, however, it was disturbingly plain that when the chips are down the British police and the Far Right belong to the same tribe.

Jerry and I failed to get into the school and, with many other sodden and shivering rejects, adjourned to a nearby Pakistani café. Profiteers would have taken advantage of our misery but as anti-BNPs we were all heroes and heroines; the owner halved the price of tea and offered unrestricted supplies of free biscuits.

Before we had time to thaw a look-out yelled that the meeting was over. Everybody surged out, the mob eager for action – and they got it. The *Yorkshire Post* sensationalised what followed with 'RIOT' headlines but the event might more accurately be described as a nasty scuffle, during which I lost my escort and moments later found myself lying on the road under a few very large (it seemed to me) policemen. Thirteen anti- B N Ps – Brown and Whites – were arrested and at about 3.00 p.m. we all went home. Another selfless idealist, who had got into the meeting, told us that a vigorous five-minute punch-up forced the police to end the proceedings within quarter of an hour – at the request of Bradford Council's acting Chief Executive. Mr Tyndall, who was kicked on the leg, said afterwards, "We are going to complain to the police authority about the closing of this meeting. The public of Bradford will hear about what has happened today and will draw their own conclusions."

Most Bradfordians concluded that the 1983 Act compelling local authorities to allow political extremists the use of Council buildings should be changed. It seemed to be generally agreed that the maintenance of British democracy does not demand official co-operation· in the organising of provocative racialist rallies, masquerading as election meetings.

However, Bradford's Browns are less worried by occasional B N P/N F attempts to abuse the political system than by their behind-the-scenes activities. Not long after the Eccleshill affray a young Pakistani couple invited me to supper in Leeds. The doctor husband had recently joined the staff of a Bradford hospital and bought (as he thought) a small semi-detached in 'the White Highlands'. When he arrived at the estate agent's office to conclude the sale he was told it was *off*, not because of any better offer, or because the neigbours had complained, but because the estate agent had been personally threatened by the National Front. The fact that both he and my friend refused to inform the police astonished several people to whom I mentioned this case. It did not astonish me. The first lesson you learn, as a student of Northern Irish affairs, is that most of the time *intimidation works*.

Some young middle-class Browns, whose circumstances have so far insulated them from active discrimination, resolutely refuse to admit that it exists in Britain; they evidently feel happier regarding it as a mass-hallucination of their working-class compatriots. I met two such characters in my local one evening, both post-graduate students at Bradford University. The Leicester-born Sikh engineer – an accountant's son – was tall, fair-skinned, handsome, thoughtful and slow-speaking. The Bengali, in Britain on a two-year student visa, was small, dark-skinned, handsome, quick-witted and eloquent. For these two Indians, English was their only common language: an example of beneficial imperial fall-out. The Bengali, who planned to follow in father's footsteps and become a Calcutta politician, was deeply in love with England after a year's residence. He remarked enviously to his friend, "Your life here will be simple and straightforward – you're lucky. I'll have to become quickly corrupt and that's bad. I'm not a naturally dishonest fellow, but what can we do? Going along with Rajiv on cleaning up corruption won't work. When there's a system, you must go along with *that*." He had been elated to discover that 'present-giving' is not built into the British educational system. "If you study hard, then you can get a degree! I like this way! But maybe if I was stupid I wouldn't like it!"

Both men insisted that Britain is a fair and tolerant country. "No one has ever shown prejudice against me," said the Bengali. "*I* think it depends on your own attitude."

"That's it," agreed the Sikh, "you find what you're looking for." Yet half-a-pint later he was telling us that as he and his wife moved furniture into their new White Highland home three small boys stopped to watch and shouted loudly to each other – though standing side by side – " 'Why are Pakis moving into such a nice house?' 'Bet they'll have fifteen kids!' 'Bet we'll see them killing sheep in the garden!' "

"Don't you regard that as racial prejudice?" I asked.

The Sikh laughed. "No, we just thought it was funny – cheeky little brats!"

By that stage a friend of mine had joined us: Ann, a fervently anti-racist social worker. She now leant forward, shook the Sikh by the shoulder and said, "But it's *not* funny! Can't you see that *this* is the essence of racism, that any little brat, just because he's White, feels free to jeer at someone like *you* just because you're Black?"

"I'm *not* black!" snapped the Sikh. And then, catching the eye of the Bengali, who was not far off black, he blushed visibly – thereby proving his point. (And, incidentally, a few other points . . .)

The argument continued, Ann asserting that any insulted 'Black' should lodge an official complaint with the Commission for Racial Equality and follow it through, thus making Whites realise that, whatever their personal prejudices, it is neither socially nor legally acceptable openly to reveal them. "By taking it as a *joke* you strengthen racism, you encourage the idea that Blacks are so inferior they can't or won't stand up for themselves, you're saying, 'We accept we've no *right* to complain about ill-treatment, we're second-class citizens and we must put up with it.' Think if you were Whites moving into that street – you'd find those kids' parents and you *would* complain and they'd get a good thrashing!"

Ann's last remark seemed a bit over-optimistic but I could see her point. I could also see the Sikh's when he argued that for a non-White (Ann winced at the term) to criticise local children would establish a pattern of high-level hostility between the newcomers and their neighbours. He conceded that the boys' remarks – probably learned at their mothers' knees – proved the existence of low-level hostility. "But," he asked, "how would it help for us to take those kids seriously?"

"I'll tell you *exactly* how it would help," replied Ann, clutching her glass so tightly it seemed likely to shatter in her hand. "It would be one more push towards *genuine* equality – not just equality on paper – for every British citizen. O K, yours would be only a small push. But when everybody pushes together things happen. Little groups of activists can't do much – no one takes them seriously and they annoy a lot of people. Blacks must unite and *push together*. Legally and peacefully and quietly – no great demos or dramas or speches – but taking up every little racist incident and making sure the guilty parties never get away with it. Then gradually Whites would begin to look at Blacks in a new way. But I know I'm wasting breath ... Look at Bradford's Pakistanis, always fighting about funds for new mosques while their brightest kids go on the dole because even the dumbest White kid gets preference!"

On my next visit to High Hill school I sought the views of a group of three Whites and eight Browns on how best to deal with 'racist incidents' – ignore? retaliate personally? complain to the authorities?

During the previous weekend one of the White boys had been set upon, while walking home alone, by four Pakistani contemporaries yelling, "Cream-bun!" – the Browns' rather disarming equivalent of 'Nigger!'

"They kicked me arse and threw me in a ditch,' Charlie recalled cheerfully. He didn't particularly resent being 'bashed'; it was an occupational hazard in his area if you were reckless enough to walk around alone and vice versa for the Browns. None of the group seemed to regard his experience as 'a racist incident'; it came into the category of legitimate gang-warfare governed by unwritten laws. Four malevolent Browns could have given Charlie a hard time; kicking his arse and throwing him in a ditch was merely ritualistic – what you're in honour bound to do if you happen to encounter a lone cream-bun.

Fifteen-year-old Fred's weekend story was very different. A sixteen-year-old girl (not a High Hill pupil) had offered him fifty pence to join her gang of Paki-bashers. Already she had recruited five boys and two girls and their targets were not contemporaries but small Brown children who, having been beaten and terrorised, were to be told – 'If *you* went home to Nigland there'd be jobs for *our* Dads!'

"So what did you do?" I asked.

"Told 'er to fuck off with 'er shitty pence!" said Fred.

Rather naïvely, I persisted – "But did you tell anyone who could do something about it? Your parents? The police? The Headmaster?"

Fred shook his head, looking suddenly uneasy. "He can't say nowt," explained Charlie, "for he'd get beat up himself if he sang – they'd *know*!"

In the inner cities you learn young about intimidation.

Some of racialism's most hurtful manifestations are beyond range of legislation, protest or campaigning.

One dark and sleet-scourged May afternoon (no darling buds around) I had a 5.00 p.m. appointment in a city-centre hotel. When I arrived wet and cold at 4.35 the foyer was empty and a young waitress, hurrying past, called out, "Sorry luv! Teatime ends 4.30!" But then, without any appeal from me, she relented. "Is it just a pot of tea, luv?" I nodded. "Hold on then luv and I'll rush it to you!" Gratefully I thought: Typical Bradfordian – they *are* kind people!

At that moment two prosperous-looking Sikhs appeared, obviously just off the train. They called out an order for two teas but were curtly told, "Teas over for today." As they were registering at the desk my little tray arrived and the waitress muttered – "Think they own the place, that lot!" She would accept no payment, never mind a tip. "The cash is all locked away – this is just a pot on the side to warm you up!"

Was that a 'racist incident'? It is unlikely that the waitress would have served two Whites who arrived at that moment; she had, after all, just finished a tiring day's work. But had I been Brown she would almost certainly not have been moved to pity by my weather-beaten condition.

Later that evening I talked to the Sikhs as they drank orange-juices in the bar and to them it had *felt* like discrimination. "But we're used to it," said the elder of the two, an East Africa-born wholesale merchant in his fifties. "It happens all the time in this country – it doesn't upset us. But you do *notice* it . . ."

"It upsets *me*," said his nephew. "I've been through school here and I've had too much of it. I've even had my turban taken while I was swimming and kicked around the corridors. You remember things like that." (The Sikh turban is not a mere head-dress but of sacred significance as one of their religion's five symbols.)

Uncle's reply came as though triggered by the very thought then darting through my mind. He said, "But you must remember Africa, where *we* discriminated against Blacks."

Emboldened by this frankness, I asked, "Do you discriminate against them here? Do you employ any Blacks?"

Uncle thought for a moment before answering. "I wouldn't say we *discriminate* against them. There's a bit of fellow-feeling in England, where we all suffer from White prejudice. But we don't employ any Blacks – we've tried, but we find they don't work at the same pace as our own people."

"*I* don't think there's any fellow-feeling," said nephew, who was somewhat lacking in traditional respect for his elders. "The Blacks here are worse than in Africa, from what I can remember. At my first school in London they did nothing but make trouble and then squeal about being got at. If you were a teacher you'd get at them too – you'd have to, to give the other kids a chance to work. My parents put me in a fee-paying school to get away from them."

"Prejudice is against our religion," Uncle reprimanded him. "Guru Nanak taught that all men and women are equal before God."

Nephew frowned at the ceiling and said no more.

On the following evening I was again discussing racialism with Sikhs, this time a couple who had forgotten much of Guru Nanak's teaching.

Baljit, the wife, always wore Western dress, as do quite a few Sikh women long settled in Britain – foolishly, since the *sari* or *shalwar-kameez* is so much more attractive than most Western garments. She was a good-looking woman who would have been a lot better-looking if not clad in a purple sweater and brick-red skirt. In her view it is sexist for wives to remain sartorially tradition-bound while husbands can freely express their personalities by choosing from a wide range of garments. "Most Asian women", she informed me, "long to dress Western but daren't. Even if they don't worry about sex-equality they hate missing out on the *interest* of fashions. Of course we've our own fashions, but they're not the same – based more on the *quality* of materials, and on accessories, than on original design and style." Not being fashion-conscious myself – to put it mildly – I had never thought of that particular 'lack' in a Brown woman's life.

I first met Baljit at the Bolton Road Gurdwara. She worked for the DHSS and on discovering my 'mission' (her word) she immediately invited me to supper. At 7.00 p.m. I found her preparing an elaborate Punjabi meal in the cramped kitchen of a terrace house off Wakefield Road, in an area to the east of the city centre where the earliest Sikh migrants settled. Unusually, her building-contractor husband – not long home from work – was meekly slicing onion and cucumber. "When we left Uganda we moved in here quickly," she explained. "We were just married – no children – we thought we'd soon find something better. In Uganda my parents had a ten-room bungalow and eight servants. But life in England is hard and we're still in this shack . . ."

"But soon we'll move," said Manjit, who was small and dapper but sad-looking.

"You've been saying that for twelve years," retorted Baljit, handing him a dish of tomatoes for slicing. Theirs was not, I felt, one of the more successful arranged marriages.

Baljit summed up all Bradford's race relations problems in one word: *Muslims*. "Do the Sikhs make problems? No! Do the Hindus make problems? No! *We* can adjust, we don't expect the whole Metropolitan District to turn itself inside out to suit *us*. Whose country is it anyway? And these disgusting men – they let their wives die in childbirth rather than have a male doctor near them! Half of them should be in jail for manslaughter – and the other half for cruelty."

We ate in the living-room, neat and clean but characterless. It might have been in any White terrace house, with an unheeded television chat-show making conversation difficult from one corner. I had the impression that this family went to the Gurdwara in much the same spirit as many Anglo-Irish families attend church: to meet 'their own' and show the flag. Both sons – aged nine and eleven, rather spoiled – smirked as they listened to their mother telling me how exceptionally well they were doing at school.

"We're always spoken English with them," said Manjit, "so they got away to a good start. This craze for teaching British Asians Punjabi or Urdu or Gujarati or Bengali is *stupid*! What they need on the job-market is fluent English. D'you know that one in five of Bradford's schoolkids speaks an

Asian language at home? And for the next decade that percentage will be increasing. What a handicap to give your kids starting school!"

"And to make it worse," said Baljit, "Mirpuri kids are brainwashed every day at the mosques. So they grow up afraid to fit into the ordinary life around them – no wonder they can't get jobs! Fanatics, sticking together in their ghettoes like no one else was fit to mix with!" She scorned my suggestion that the Mirpuris' reluctance to compromise with British customs might be a sign of deep insecurity rather than fanaticism; and that their 'sticking together' might be inspired by the need of a community-on-the-defensive to maintain its own clear-out, self-reassuring identity.

This couple were among several Sikhs of my acquaintance who stated bluntly that Mrs Gandhi had 'asked for it' and who saw no need to conceal their satisfaction that she had 'got it'. They were however pleased that Bradford had had no major disturbances either after the invasion of the Golden Temple or after the assassination. (Never mind what happened in Delhi or the Punjab – where of course they had never been.)

"All our Asian religious leaders were clever," said Baljit. "They got together and kept the lid on – even the mullahs and imams in Bradford!" But with her next breath she loosed another diatribe against Pakistanis in general and Mirpuris in particular. "They're a bigoted, bullying, treacherous lot!" Whereupon I recalled that pub conversation overheard in the White Highlands . . .

Many such dishes of Brown and Black prejudice varied my daily diet of White prejudice. 'Stereotyping' – the vice most abhorred by anti-racists – is not peculiar to Whites. In Bradford, Mirpuris deplored the loose living of Gujarati Muslims who allowed their *wives* to drive delivery vans . . . Blacks deplored Pakistani heroin-dealing and Sikh arrogance. Hindus deplored Muslim faction-fighting and Black laziness. Sikhs deplored the sharp practices of Gujarati merchants, the drug-peddling of Blacks, the Mirpuri ill-treatment of women – and the dangerous politics of Sikhs attached to rival Gurdwaras. And so on and on, in apparently infinite permutations and combinations of misunderstanding, dislike, jealousy, contempt, fear, ignorance, resentment. I sometimes wondered: So what's special about White prejudice? To which my anti-racist friends replied: "Prejudice plus power equals racism." In their view other people's prejudices are relatively innocuous but ours is lethal because we have the power to *act* upon it – to discriminate. This equation seems to me unhelpful. In many homogeneous societies the powerful act to the detriment of their powerless compatriots; and the worst of British racialist aberrations looks benign compared with, for instance, the Indian and Bangladeshi governments' treatment of aboriginal tribes. True, two (or two thousand) wrongs don't make a right. But to focus on British prejudice-cum-discrimination as though it were an isolated, unique phenomenon makes it still more difficult to understand: and it must be understood before its effects can be ameliorated. It does indeed have certain unique features on which British anti-racists tend to concentrate. This makes sense; they can do little about the Bangladeshi government's treatment of the Chittagong Hill Tribes or the Japanese treatment of the Ainu. But the longer I spent on the 'race relations' scene the more important it seemed to me that we should not lose sight of the *universal* nature of the problem of discrimination against defenceless minorities.

On the eve of my departure for Bradford, while travelling to Hampstead by tube with my publisher Jock Murray, I had had occasion to think about one of the more primitive aspects of race relations. Opposite me, on Jock's left, sat a black African couple with negroid features so pronounced that they recalled the sort of cartoon nowadays banned as 'racist'. On Jock's other side sat two Indian adolescents, a boy and girl who were extraordinarily good-looking by our standards – though not all that unusual by Indian standards. To me there was a certain piquancy about this row of five people: my publisher reading his *Standard*, flanked by the raw material for our next book. From the Indians' fine-boned features, lustrous eyes and glossy hair my gaze returned to the Africans and because I had to be part of my own investigation of racial prejudice I acknowledged what might otherwise have been suppressed – that their appearance repelled me. At once I felt a twinge of guilt but it quickly subsided when I recalled that many Chinese find Caucasian features quite repulsive.

For some people the basis of racial prejudice is a physical distaste so strong that it deters them from establishing normal human relationships, yet antipathy based on skin-colour or features has become an awkward subject to discuss publicly. In my youth people talked of 'colour prejudice' or 'the colour bar' rather than of racialism, and those who were not white had no objection to being described as 'coloured'. There was even a League of Coloured Peoples, established to 'improve the welfare of coloured peoples in all parts of the world', which as a schoolgirl I enthusiastically supported. But by now it has become as indelicate to refer to people's colour as it was in the 1950s to mention penises or vaginas. And this is regrettable, since it deflects attention from one of the roots of racialism – while obscuring the fact that Blacks are more vulnerable to 'visual' prejudice than Browns. The sort of parents who would absolutely forbid their daughter to marry a Black Oxford graduate (if parents were still in the business of controlling daughters) might very reluctantly give their consent to her marrying a Brown layabout.

Occasionally I found myself being coldly unsympathetic to talented Browns or Blacks who seemed to be wasting their gifts on anti-racist careers within the RRI. I remember especially vividly an acrimonious evening in one of Bradford's many excellent Pakistani eating-houses, which are not at all like the phoney Oriental restaurants that afflict London. My companions were three Muslim professional anti-racists in their thirties – non-Bradford-based, all university graduates. Hashmi was East Africa-born and had visited Pakistan only once, as an adolescent. Mahomet was Lahore-born but came to Britain at the age of three and had never been back. Muzaffer Khan was born and schooled in Natal, visited his ancestral village Pathan for two years, then migrated to live with an uncle in London and eventually collected a First from Oxford. None of the three could complain that they personally had been thwarted in Britain, yet each was rabidly prejudiced against Whites – an altruistic prejudice, Hashmi pointed out, since they were concerned about the "ill-treatment" of their less privilged fellow-Browns.

I had known Muzaffer Khan ('Muesli' to his friends) for years, having twice stayed with his grandmother in Peshawar, met him at intervals in Britain and watched his 'conversion' to anti-racism as an ideology. His friends I had met a few times in London, while doing my race relations prep.

"This will annoy you," said Muesli, handing me a cartoon book, *How Racism Came to Britain*, produced by the Institute of Race Relations. He was right. In the Preface the Institute's Director, A. Sivanandan, asserted that 'Ethnic minorities do not suffer disabilities because of ethnic differences, but because such differences are given differential weightage in a system of racial hierarchy.' This is classic 'anti-racist-speak', denying the stark fact that a non-European cultural background is a handicap which has to be overcome before ethnic minorities can succeed in any European society. It is a handicap not because it is necessarily less valuable or 'civilised' but because it *is* different and those who have been conditioned by it must adjust to European culture before they can achieve what Europeans call 'success'. (Which may not always be worth achieving, but that's another matter.) This anti-racist doctrine is pernicious; it discourages Blacks and Browns from making essential adjustments by laying *all* the blame for anybody's lack of success on the 'White system of racial hierarchy'.

How Racism Came to Britain – the third in a series of 'Anti-racist Educational Books for Young People' – is cleverly aimed not only at schoolchildren but at those who have left school unable to cope with anything more demanding than cartoons. Its accounts of British empire-building, the post-war recruitment of immigrant workers and the unjust operations of British racial prejudice are factually accurate. The facts however are so selected and presented that read through Brown or Black eyes they add up to an incitement to hatred.

"What is this supposed to do for race relations?" I asked acidly.

"For one thing," said Hashmi, "it's to make White kids aware of the crimes of their imperial past – to take the shine off it – to show what a filthy racket it all was."

Mahomet added, "But it's even more important for Black kids to read it, to learn why they should feel *superior* to Whites, not *inferior*. Black kids brainwashed in White schools need all those facts in there."

Muesli took off then. "For centuries the British tried to kill our self-respect – all that has to be undone. Black kids must be made to feel self-confident, self-assertive, not afraid to go out and fight for their rights, not cringing and accepting crumbs falling from White tables!"

I suggested that it might do more for racial harmony to foster an acceptance of the reality of racial and cultural differences but to present them as less important than our common humanity.

"Cultural imperialism!" muttered Hashmi, bent over his curry.

"We don't want racial harmony at *your* price," said Mahomet. "*We're* naming the price nowadays." He was quietly angry: but very angry.

"She's always been wet," Muesli explained apologetically, "and I think she's getting worse."

"You call it wet?" snapped Mahomet. "*I* call it dishonest! She wants to look like she's all for racial equality, while she's trying to coerce Blacks into lying down under racism for ever!"

Hashmi looked at me with disdain. "You're really no better than Powell," he pronounced, "only a bit more diplomatic."

Muesli came to my defence. "It's two different forms of racism. He dislikes Blacks and wants us all to go home and leave his lovely England undefiled. Dervla *likes* Blacks!"

"Wow!" said Mahomet. "Big thrill! So who cares?"

Muesli looked discomfited; he was our host and his party wasn't going too well. For the rest of the evening my lightest remark seemed likely to be taken amiss. I said, "I suppose this is what you might call a private Race Awareness Training session – and I'm not joking. It's helpful to me."

Mahomet leant forward and said. "OK, let's raise your awareness. Don't you recognise your own assumptions of cultural superiority showing through in everything you say?"

"Yes," I admitted, "I do recognise them. But I call them 'acknowledgements of cultural differences', rather than 'assumptions of cultural superiority'."

"Now that *is* dishonest!" exclaimed Muesli. "Don't you see it's nonsense to talk of 'not thinking about superiority or inferiority'? Most Whites *don't* think about their superiority. It's just there like the beating heart of White society, keeping it going. You don't notice your heart beating but when it stops you die. Whites don't notice their superiority operating but when they lose it their society will collapse."

"And that", Hashmi intervened, "is what anti-racism is all about. White society the way it is now must be *made* to collapse – somehow. We'll only get justice for Blacks when *everyone* admits that *all* cultures are equal."

I longed to plead, "Don't be so intense about it all! Just relax! You'll never sort anything out if all the time you're thinking and speaking and acting in ways that *heighten* tension . . ." But then, as Hashmi had made clear, improving race relations through reconciliation is not the name of the anti-racist game.

Instead of retiring that evening at my usual early hour, I went for a cold moonlit walk around Lister's Mill. Life on Britain's race relations scene often reminded me of swimming off Cape Comorin, being tossed this way and that by powerful conflicting waves and never feeling quite in control of one's own actions or reactions. The connotations of that phrase 'racial superiority' are so repulsive that it is extremely difficult to admit to such feelings. Often too it is difficult to diagnose them with any certainty, to be sure they are not simple feelings of *personal* superiority – not a very laudable emotion either, but one which in certain situations many people seem able to entertain without self-reproach.

My own personal definition of a racialist is – 'Someone to whom human beings are less worthy of respect and consideration if they belong to another race'. If one accepts that definition it is impossible to agree with those anti-racists who insist that *all* Whites are racialist – or with the absurd argument that *only* Whites are racialist. Most Whites are indeed prejudiced in favour of their own race, in the sense of 'having an unreasoning predilection for it'. But this does not necessarily imply *antagonism* towards other races or a belief in the *superiority* of one's own. It is possible to be subjectively prejudiced in favour of the group to which one belongs, and which gives one a secure sense of identity, without objectively believing in its superiority. Even if I wanted to, it would be an intellectual and emotional impossibility for me to believe in the superiority of the White race. No one who has spent much of the past quarter-century travelling among other races, sharing their diverse ways of life, could fail to recognise that each race has certain outstanding qualities which, if set beside the flaws of the White race, might be described as its 'superior' points.

We all belong to a minority, to a particular group with which we have most in common. Clearly I would have more in common with a Black or Brown writer than with an English tycoon or an Irish farm-hand. And my negative feelings about the tycoon or the farm-hand, if expressed and transposed to an inter-racial context, might be diagnosed by some as 'racism'. When I put this point to an Indian writer friend in London he challenged it shrewdly. "But", he said, "is there not one level of your being on which you would feel more at ease with the tycoon or the farm-hand than you do with *me?*"

I had to admit that there is. But that level is very superficial; the ease would be based on certain unimportant cultural conditionings common to all Europeans – not on anything that really mattered to me or the tycoon or the farm-hand. So if I had to be shipwrecked on a desert island with one of the three, I would certainly choose the Indian writer.

Walking up a steep cobbled laneway, between silent little terrace houses packed with Mirpuris, I remembered two short items in that morning's *Guardian*. One reported riots in Gujarat, following an official decision to reserve fifty per cent of government jobs and university places for the lower castes. It seems upper-caste Gujaratis are no more partial to positive discrimination than White Bradfordians and 'several' people had been killed when police and paramilitary forces were ordered to fire on the rioters. Just below that item a Karachi riot was reported: 'Ten people died after police fired on crowds. One unarmed policeman died after he was dragged out of a rickshaw, sprinkled with petrol and set alight.' Such news items promote a happy glow of racial superiority among the Great British Public. Undeniably, countries where police and troops are *not* ordered to fire on rioters are in some sense 'superior'. Yet this has nothing to do with race. General Dyer was White. The South African government is White. The Brazilian *fazendeiros* are White. The Nazis were White.

In the shadow of Lister's Mill I accused myself of having been unduly critical of my anti-racist friends. Muesli, I knew, had been pushed into the anti-racist camp by two experiences of cruel job-discrimination when Whites less qualified, both academically and temperamentally, had been preferred to him. Hashmi, as a university student, had frequently been refused admission to local pubs and dance-halls. Mahomet had repeatedly been spat at and stoned in a Suffolk village where he worked for three months. Is it not too easy for me – White, professionally secure, self-assured – to condemn the aberrations of non-White anti-racists? I have never been discriminated against – or only once, when a Cork barman refused to serve me a *pint* of Guinness because in that pub pint-drinking women were thought to be unseemly. Enraged, I wrote a blistering letter to the Guinness Chairman in Dublin. So who am I to advise others, people who have experienced *real* discrimination, to be 'relaxed' about race relations?

On the way home I passed a solitary elderly Mirpuri wearing a turban and Kashmiri garb. If a White man on the sub-continent wears local dress he is regarded as an oddity, a drop-out, in some way a fake. If a Brown man in Britain wears his own traditional garb he is often scoffed at as a primitive peasant. He should be signalling his acceptance of White superiority by wearing Western clothes . . .

In *The Triumph of the West* J.M. Roberts observed: 'Wherever they went – to Isfahan, Delhi, Canton – Europeans were sure their own achievements, values and religion were best.' He was writing of the sixteenth and seventeenth centuries; but nothing has happened since to lessen White arrogance – and a lot has happened to increase it.

5 · How Anti-Racism Came to Britain

'Anti-racism' sounds good – naturally, since it means being *against* something *bad*. Yet Britain's anti-racism movement is disquieting. It can only make life more difficult for Browns and Blacks. It is irrational, provocative, destabilising; and White racialism created it. British anti-racism is a direct response to the flexing of National Front and Powellite muscles during the 1960s and early 1970s.

Before myself becoming a migrant labourer in inner-city Britain, I had not fully appreciated the importance – *and durability* – of these influences. On both the race relations and Irish scenes Enoch Powell had seemed to me a one-man 'lunatic fringe'. But that opinion was revised when I heard him quoted, time and time again, to justify savagely racialist attitudes.

One incident was typical of dozens. At an Oak Lane bus-stop late one evening I made a non-committal remark about the news from South Africa to the only other waiting passenger, an elderly White Bradfordian. In reply he by-passed South Africa, swung his arms around in a gesture encompassing all of Manningham and said, quite quietly, "I'd *shoot* them all, men, women and children. What thanks did I get, after five years fighting for my country? Only to come back to my own city over-run with dirty *vermin!* Here they're all around us, every street like a sewer full of *rats!* Powell was right. He said *The people of England will not endure it.* And he understood why we shouldn't endure it, why we should take England back for the English – a good man, Powell. If you gave me an armoured car and some ammo I'd clean this place up overnight. And if I don't have the chance my sons and grandsons will. *They* won't go on being the toad beneath the harrow, like Powell said we are – a menace he said they were, a growing menace. He was right. He knew the score. But no one listened to him when they should . . ."

Mr Powell has done for race relations in Britain what Ian Paisley has done for reconciliation in Northern Ireland. Despite his scholarship, his anti-immigrant campaign seemed on a level with Mr Paisley's speeches. Having identified the public's sorest points (and his inner-city findings paralleled my own twenty years later), he further inflamed them by repeatedly exaggerating some real problems and imagining others – such as the 'domination' of 'the rest of the population' by 'immigrants'. His carefully chosen phrases aroused anger, resentment and contempt. 'Immigrants' were presented as parasites who had come to Britain unbidden and contributed nothing to the nation's welfare. England, he lamented, "had saddled itself, without necessity and *without countervailing benefit*, with a wholly avoidable problem of immense dimensions". He did not refer to Sir Winston Churchill's post-war Caribbean tour, during which he appealed to Jamaicans to – "Come and help rebuild your Motherland!" He forgot that in 1962, as Minister for Health, he himself had refused to improve on a two and a half per cent pay increase for nurses because, as he explained, if they didn't like his award he could recruit lots more from the West Indies. He never mentioned the Caribbean recruiting campaigns of London Transport and the British Hotels and Restaurants Association, which in 1956 set up a recruiting office in Barbados. Nor did he recall that Englishmen and their local agents were then seeking labourers, in India and Pakistan, for the textile industries and foundries. In 1955 Smethwick Labour Exchange reported, 'Coloured labour from the Commonwealth is greatly easing the labour shortage.' In 1968 Enoch Powell insisted, "Supplying labour or skill has nothing to do with immigration." This is what he himself has described as 'the logic of Goebbels – a big, black, bold, brazen lie'.* It is shocking to find a man of his intellectual power so manipulating the bewildered, the fearful, the insecure and the ignorant.

The Powell–Tory split made many people happy. The British assured each other that this proved how distasteful racialism is to all political parties – and, by implication, to the Great British Public. They ignored all evidence to the contrary. Yet, as James Prior recalled in his autobiography:

> From Enoch's point of view, his sensational [Birmingham] speech had the desired effect. He became a national figure overnight. The Smithfield meat porters marched in support of him to the House of Commons. Mail began to arrive at Ted's office literally by the sackful; 99% of it backed Powell. But I wonder if he really knows or understands to this day the filth he collected to his side. A number of letters were so vile that it was offensive for the girls in Ted's office to read them: Others carried their message by including excrement.†

The Powellite gospel is acceptable to millions, who still see Powell as 'the brave realist' – the self-image so skilfully projected some twenty years ago. Powellism did not fade when the NF waned as a political force towards the end of the 1970s.

Coincidence hardly explains the simultaneous waning of the NF and waxing of the New Right, whose aura incorporates the Powellite colour.

---

* Enoch Powell, *Freedom and Reality*, Elliot Right Way Books (1969)
† Jim Prior, *A Balance of Power*, Hamish Hamilton (1986)

From the ethnic minorities' point of view the New Right is a much more serious threat than the NF and its offshoots. These have never seemed respectable enough to attract mass-support; they are too overtly intemperate and the British like to think of themselves as a moderate people. The New Right however seems very respectable indeed, to unwary citizens, and in its ambience people can uncork their racialism and call it patriotism.

Twenty years ago optimists were looking forward to the 1980s when a generation who had never known the Master-race feeling would at least be free of the most unpleasant feature of British racialism – disdain for 'natives' – even if they remained xenophobic. But alas! most of today's young Whites have inherited the Master-race virus and are susceptible to New Right racialist messages – which come in many forms, the most pernicious being often oblique.

In Mrs Thatcher's post-Falkland speech, on 3 July 1983, she tub-thumped triumphantly:

> When we started out, there were those who would not admit it . . . but in their heart of hearts they too had their secret fears that it was true: that Britain was no longer the nation that had built an Empire and ruled quarter of the world. Well they were wrong. The lesson of the Falklands is that Britain has not changed and that this nation still has those sterling qualities which shine through our history.

It is easy for the sophisticated to laugh at this pathetic disinterring of a long-dead lion. But the racially prejudiced masses who read the *Sun*, the *Daily Mail* and other Tory sheets remain susceptible to such fantasising. Britain's race relations have not been improved by the influence of a Prime Minister who sees building an empire and ruling a quarter of the world as a virtuous activity requiring 'sterling qualities'. This imperial revivalism can seem merely tiresome until you begin to notice its appeal for large sections of the population. It encourages the racially prejudiced to continue to display 'those sterling qualities' by keeping in their place 'people with a different culture' who are threatening to 'swamp the British character'. Those last quotes are from a *World in Action* Thatcher interview on 30 January 1978. And on 17 February 1986 she was at it again, her voice vibrant with enthusiasm about "Britain's pre-eminence . . . that is ours by right". At present poor Britain is being led backwards; and a hazard about moving backwards is that you can't see where you're going – you could be over a precipice before you knew it was there. In Brown and Black circles I often heard the fearful comment: "The way things are now, NF attitudes are being made to seem OK, though no one in government would ever *openly* approve of them."

During the 1960s and early 1970s, while Immigration Act debates were preoccupying the politicians and the toxic fumes of Powellism were spreading over the land, thousands of young Browns and Blacks were growing up in Britain. Some had migrated as small children, others were British-born, and of that generation many came to deplore their parents' passive acceptance of racial prejudice. As they observed the well-meaning but mainly ineffectual activities of the government-sponsored R R I, and listened to the supportive but meaningless statements of amiable non-racialist Whites, and experienced the failure of two-faced trades unions to give them a fair deal, they concluded that Justice could be won for minorities only through tough positive action: vigorous *anti*-racism would have to replace flaccid *non*-racialism.

These activists and their White sympathisers believe that the English must be made to do a big re-think. They must be brought to an understanding of the appalling cruelty of racial prejudice – the suffering it inflicts on individuals all over Britain every day – and must be shown how it also damages and impoverishes their own community. Anti-racists demand a questioning of all inherited assumptions about Britain's imperial past; what, for instance, is the historical basis for Mrs Thatcher's claim that ". . . the British character has done so much for democracy, for law and order . . . throughout the world"? They argue for the modification (and some for the abolition) of restrictions on immigration. They assert that Britain is now a multi-racial society, a fact which must be reflected in school curricula. They insist that the centuries-old stereotyping of Blacks and Browns must be "strongly redressed". They challenge British society – "It's not enough to say 'I'm not racist' – what are you *doing* about it?"

As anti-racism began to make itself heard and felt, large sections of the British public took umbrage. People often do, when their faults are pointed out; especially if the correction of those faults requires the abandonment of that on which their *amour propre* depends – and more especially if their critics are seen as a) inferiors and b) ingrates. Yet apart from their opposition to immigration control, and their insistence that all of Britain should be treated as a multi-racial society, there is nothing unreasonable in the anti-racists' demands. Unfortunately however, most anti-racist activists are handicapped by seething anger and impatient intolerance – both understandable but unhelpful to the cause – and by total incomprehension of the English temperament. Their strategies and tactics often suggest that they are, paradoxically, unaware of the strength and potential viciousness of British racialism. They behave like a zoo vet in charge of an injured tiger who says, " O K, I'll go into his cage and give him physiotherapy – it'll hurt him a lot but he'll feel better after. It's what he *needs* to cure him." The tiger wouldn't agree and what would happen to the vet?

Although anti-racists are themselves driven by emotion, they make no allowances for the fact that, in Charles Husband's words, "Ethnic relations cannot be studied as a clinical cerebral 'problem'. A comprehension of the nature of ethnicity resides as much in the heart and bowels as in the head."* Overlooking this complication, anti-racists attack British racialism as though it were a monolithic, clearly defined ideology like Nazism (with which they frequently compare it) and so could be fought with the weapons of quasi-political campaigns – *against* stereotyping and 'institutional racism', *for*

---

* Charles Husband (Ed.), *'Race' in Britain*, Hutchinson University Library (1982)

multi-cultural education and Black Studies. As White resistance to such campaigns hardens, the frustrated anti-racists become increasingly abrasive and truculent and on many issues quite paranoid. Their excesses are now notorious and would be comical if the pain behind them were not so real: anti-gollywog, anti-'Baa-Baa Black Sheep' and so on. In the 1980s it is odd to read Sheila Patterson's 1963 opinion that White children's 'aversion and apprehension' when Blacks came to their neighbourhood 'may have been counteracted by the homely and well-beloved gollywog, by children's rhymes like "Ten Little Nigger Boys" and "Eeny-meeny-miny-mo", by books such as *Little Black Sambo* or *Uncle Tom's Cabin* which present coloured people as inferior but agreeable, and by the popularity of "nigger minstrels".'*

The coming of anti-racism to Britain nonplussed many non-racialists who sympathise with the anti-racists' sense of desperation but deplore their methods, while hesitating to oppose them publicly lest that might give comfort to 'the enemy'. Non-racialists worry about 'the trivialisation of race relations' that follows on media coverage of ludicrous controversies about Robinson's gollywog or 'Baa-Baa Black Sheep' – controversies which deflect attention from real problems like job-discrimination and physical harassment. The prejudiced public pounce delightedly on such debates to 'prove' one of their favourite arguments – 'They're just loaded with chips!' Then, when genuine grievances are exposed, they feel justified in dismissing those, too, as 'imaginary'.

In any humane society the quest for racial justice should be a non-party issue, as Bradford Council tried to make it, and another non-racialist worry is the identification of anti-racism with the Far Left. Some see this coalition as a natural development because so many of the ethnic minorities' disadvantages are shared by their White inner-city neighbours. If it represented a genuine getting-together of the deprived of all colours it would obviously be healthy, but instead it represents an alliance of anti-capitalist extremists and therefore frightens off much support. Many English people, who may belong to any (or no) party, are genuinely concerned about 'good race relations' but refuse to be in any way associated with 'hectoring Lefties'.

Within their own communities Black and Brown anti-racists are viewed with unease by most of the older generation – the original immigrants – and by many of the British-born. They are seen as an increasingly disruptive lobby which is lowering the ethnic minorities in White esteem – 'All those Blacks are turning nasty and making absurd demands.' Some of their campaigns are criticised as goads to British racialism and their Far Left links are deprecated by conventional Muslims, Hindus and Sikhs. Also, they are blamed for deliberately cultivating the seeds of anti-White racial prejudice that have been sown in many young minds by personal experience of discrimination and harassment.

As yet anti-racists represent only a small fraction of their communities but

---

* Sheila Patterson, *Dark Strangers*, Pelican (1963)

they have recently become influential out of all proportion to their numbers. Their machinations vitiated the most strenuous efforts of the Rampton and Swann Committees on several issues of major importance and resulted in a report – *Education for All* – that had to make up in repetitive guff what it lacked in guts. More importantly, the often bizarre inhibitions induced by anti-racism have muzzled many people, of all colours, who care so deeply about race relations that the loss of their honest public comments is a tragedy. This sudden growth of influence puzzles many because anti-racism is far from being a compact, united movement; it is in fact an obsession rather than an *organisation*. As individuals, anti-racists display a bewildering – and sometimes conflicting – diversity of motives, compulsions, ideals, convictions, ambitions, impulses, guilts. Many Blacks and Browns are anti-racist simply because they have had agonising difficulties in their personal relationships with Whites. Many anti-racist Whites are profoundly ashamed of British racialism and naïvely see co-operation with anti-racist extremism as the only adequate expiation for their country's sin. It seems to me a mistake to over-emphasise the anti-racist–Far Left alliance. I found the movement alarming not because it is 'Lefty' but because it works so destructively on the emotions of thousands of discriminated-against youngsters who wouldn't know an ideology from the cat's breakfast. Moreover, unless the Tories keep their post-1987 election promise to alleviate inner-city miseries, anti-racism is bound to expand.

In Bradford alone, according to a 1984 Council estimate:

> By 1986 we expect the city's black population to have increased by a further 6,000, by 1991 by a further 13,000 and by 1996 by a further 10,000, giving a total of about 91,000. Some immediate implications of these figures are that by 1996
> a) a further 5,000 to 7,600 black families will be formed;
> b) there will be a further 10,000 to 12,000 Asian children aged 5–15 years;
> c) a further 11,000 to 18,000 black people will be looking for work.

The Council rightly stresses that these consumer-society-bred children will not settle for second-class citizenship. Unlike their parents, they don't compare life in Britain with life in the village and count their blessings; nor should they be expected to do so. The original Mirpuri immigrants – a stoical and practical breed – arrived with one aim only: to diminish the poverty and enhance the status of their families back home. Because of their industry, frugality and foresight, most succeeded in this. They also – incidentally – improved their own standard of living. Their spartan Bradford homes are spartan only to our eyes. Life in a back-to-back, with running water, electric light, a gas-heater, a television and video machine, hospitals and schools nearby, a shop on the corner and a little cash in the pocket – such a life is opulent compared to village life in Mirpur. This comparison, which can so easily be misappropriated to excuse social injustice and nurture passivity, understandably infuriates anti-racists. Yet it explains why so many tens of thousands of Mirpuris (and others) chose to remain in Britain despite its being an implacably racialist society. Also, the general benefits of living in an orderly democracy are appreciated by the older generation as much as specific racial insults and injuries are resented. Many Browns think it strange and wonderful to be able to register for welfare benefits, and collect them from a government office, without first having to scrape together the money for a bribe and then regularly slip a percentage to the paying-out clerk. They freely acknowledge this – though sometimes in a whisper, anti-racists having made it seem disloyal to admit such things out loud. However, these comparative advantages, enjoyed by all Britain's ethnic minorities, are obscured by anti-racist propaganda and the British-bred generation is scarcely aware of them. They are concerned only with the disadvantages inflicted on them by racialism, which they know – often from personal experience – has become more virulent even within their own short lifetimes.

Some Whites choose to see the anti-racists' aggressive campaigns as just one more unfortunate consequence of allowing 'all those people' into the country. Yet theirs is but one current in a river of anger flowing through the chasm that now divides British society. It is of course the most obvious current – at present – because anti-racist emotion has been so inflamed by the White pretence that racial prejudice is *not* widespread in Britain. The English can be supremely tolerant of those against whom they are prejudiced and this confusing ingredient in the inter-racial pudding explains why so many Whites are able to evade the reality of their own prejudice. They sit back admiring Britain's 'civilised tradition of tolerance' and subconsciously expect those who benefit from it to be suitably grateful and not belly-ache about *discrimination*. British tolerance has allowed them full citizenship (not like those wretched ethnic minorities in Germany, France and Switzerland!) and access to every State benefit. What more can they expect? Given the fact that they are not *really* (only legally) British, is it reasonable for them to expect equality of opportunity in jobs and housing? This distinctively English mix of tolerance-cum-prejudice fuels the anti-racist argument that anything less extreme than their approach would be futile in a society saturated with complacency about its 'fair treatment of ethnic minorities'.

I had chosen Manningham as one of my inner-city bases because of Bradford Council's reputation as a pioneer of 'vigorous positive action' against racialism. Bradford was also said to be 'the shallow end' of the race relations pool, a city that for generations has been successfully absorbing immigrants – Irish, German, Jewish, Polish, Ukrainian, Italian. (Yet even in Bradford repatriation is not a new idea; the city's Board of Governors decided in 1847 that 'all Irish and Scottish applicants for relief be forthwith passed home'.) Soon however I found that the water at the shallow end had become quite rough, partly because of the Council's vigorous positive action and partly because of the prolonged Honeyford controversy. (Those factors were not unrelated, as the next chapter will show.)

When the Council launched its new race relations policies in 1981 it explained:

> In Bradford, until relatively recently, the white and black communities lived apart and seldom came into contact; but factors have conspired against the continuation of this pattern . . . With the increase in expectations and competition comes the likelihood of conflict if needs cannot be met. The 'isolated pluralism' of the sixties and seventies had to give way to multi-culturalism with competition and interaction as the rule. In 1981, with the support of all parties, the Council embarked on its race relations initiative. Its aims were to bring about social justice by adopting policies and practices which would create:
>
> 1 Equality of esteem between different cultures
> 2 Equality of opportunity in employment
> 3 Equality of access to Council services
> 4 The development of services that were relevant to *all* sections of the community
> 5 The elimination of discrimination on racial grounds.

> The Council recognised the existence of racism and particularly 'institutionalised racism'; however its emphasis was on the effects of racism rather than its causes. It was decided that Committees and Directorates should be responsible for creating their own race relations policies (and) it was recognised that in the initial years some prompting, cajoling, encouragement and pressure was needed at the highest political and officer levels. To this end the Council established a Race Relations Advisory Council in 1981, composed of senior members of all parties. All policies which relate to race relations have to be submitted to this group for consideration and suggestions . . . More than one in ten people in employment in Bradford work for the Council which is by far the largest employer but its record of employment of ethnic minorities leaves much to be desired (only 2.9% of the workforce despite 13% of the population) and there is need to make special provision to enable members of ethnic minorities to enter certain professions and occupations. Word of mouth advertising of jobs will cease immediately. The Council will have to accept that there will be some loss of convenience from the casual filling of jobs. It is assumed that this will be regarded as a small penalty, set against the task of improving the racial balance of the Council's employment.

These policies seem at first glance humane and responsible, given the contemporary problems of a multi-racial city. But there was a fatal flaw in the Council's thinking – 'its emphasis was on the effects of racism rather than its causes'. *Why Bradford Needs Race Relations Policies* is a brave but foolish document. Its attempt to take the bull of British racialism by the horns merely set that bull loose in the china-shop of local race relations. Almost every day Whites told me what they thought of their Council's 'anti-racism' – and I didn't have to ask. By 1985 the subject had become such a local obsession that total strangers, at bus-stops or in cafés or pubs or supermarket queues, would without any prompting bare their racialist souls. (This was one reason why I loved Bradford – not because of the racialist souls but because so many Bradfordians were Irish-like in their readiness to communicate with anyone anywhere about almost anything.)

The comparatively modest sums deflected by the Council to the improvement of race relations were extravagantly exaggerated and there were bitter complaints that – "*We* need help more than *they* do! They get enough child benefits to live like lords!" The notion that "Pakis" should be encouraged to apply for Council jobs which traditionally have been "passed on" provoked incandescent anger. The fact that some schools were keeping dossiers of 'racist incidents', and punishing White children for verbally or physically abusing Browns, was interpreted as a persecution campaign against "our kids". The availability in some school canteens of halal meat, from animals slaughtered according to Islamic prescriptions, was denounced as "giving in to savages who torture animals to death!" Few stopped to consider – or wished to be told about – the reasoning behind their Council's new policy. Instead, there was a pervasive and unshakable belief that now Whites were being relentlessly discriminated against; and the stress put on the 'initiative' being a long-term policy, approved by all political parties, aroused feelings of despair and betrayal – "We've no one to speak up for us, they've all gone over to the Blacks!"

Some moderate R R I workers admitted to me in private that the Council had tried to move too far too fast, having apparently been unaware (inexplicably!) of the virulence of local racialism. They made the point that any Council, school, journalist, clergyman – any authority or individual in a position to influence public opinion – can help to deflate racialist myths and stereotypes: that indeed must be the way forward. But such a deflationary process can only happen like a slow puncture; it cannot be achieved like the bursting of a balloon.

Since the bureaucratic mechanisms for countering racialism have achieved so little, and the older generations seem in any case disinclined to have their racialism countered, what of the younger generation? Is it reasonable to hope for perceptible movement towards 'a solution' if new educational policies are carefully thought out and intelligently implemented? Many believe that only reformed curricula can cut the key that will release everyone from the trap of British racialism. But new educational policies are easier to enthuse about than to contrive. Here we are up against an omnipresent snag: reformed curricula must be designed by adults – the adults of today, the old gang of anti-racists and non-racialists, in confrontation with racialists.

The Great Debate on multi-cultural education, now more than a decade old, is and always has been amorphous for the sufficient reason that no one has yet produced a generally acceptable definition of 'multi-cultural education'. The debaters, both professional and amateur, are more often than not talking or writing at cross-purposes, thereby contributing lavishly to their own and the public's confusion. Recently £692,618 was spent on the 807-page Swann Report, *Education for All* (emasculated by bad race relations within the Committee of Inquiry), in which every possible mutation of multi-cultural education is dissected by swarms of experts. On 19 February

1985 it was presented to the then Education Secretary, Sir Keith Joseph. Among its scores of recommendations was: 'The Secretary of State should include a growing number of initiatives and pilot projects designed to develop a broader, pluralist approach to the curriculum within arrangements for education support grants.' Evidently this advice – part of the pith of the whole Report – left Sir Keith unimpressed. On 21 May 1986 he celebrated his retirement, and tried to push some stones off his successor's path, by stating bluntly that "mother-cultures" should be transmitted in the child's home, leaving the curriculum clear for unadulterated English schooling. He added, feelingly, that "multi-cultural education has become an almost meaningless phrase".

In 1980 Baroness Young, then Minister of State for Education, made a much wiser statement: "It is just as important in schools where there are no ethnic minority pupils for teaching to refer to the different cultures now present in Britain . . . It is a question of developing a curriculum which draws positive advantages from the different cultures."

Lady Young might have added that such a curriculum would now be essential even if there were *no* ethnic minorities in Britain. Any traditional 'mono-cultural' education – English, French, Islamic, Buddhist – is an inadequate preparation for life in the modern world. That is a truism, in civilised circles, yet the idea of a more cosmopolitan curriculum is resisted by many Little Englanders who seem to imagine that it must involve cultural contamination leading to leukaemia of the national spirit. But does some understanding of other cultures mean you have to love England less or become yourself less truly English? Is 'Englishness' so fragile that it cannot survive contact with other cultures? It doesn't seem so to me.

In racialist Britain the defenders of 'pure' English schooling are trying to preserve a dangerous situation which, if they succeed, can only become more dangerous. I was appalled to discover how many Whites, who for twenty or thirty years have lived in cities with large Brown populations, remain unaware of the differences between Sikhs, Muslims and Hindus. (The well-informed few of course know that Sikhs wear turbans, Muslims make a lot of fuss about meat and Hindus won't eat it.) One major obstacle to good race relations is sheer ignorance of those 'aliens in our midst'. If you know *nothing* about people you can believe *anything* about them; and the way is then clear for Powellism.

The contrast between Baroness Young's and Sir Keith's statements marks a hardening, within those six years, of the Tory attitude to ethnic minorities. And, in accordance with the grim logic of all such situations, anti-racism became more extreme during the same period.

Some of the confusion surrounding the Great Multi-cultural Debate has been caused by the intrusion of anti-racist obsessions. These do not help pioneer educationalists struggling to construct non-ethnocentric curricula. In Bradford multi-cultural and anti-racist education were introduced simultaneously, with the predictable result that traditionalist teachers who might have gingerly accepted the former were so antagonised by the latter that they gave their LEA's 'initiative' only minimal co-operation – in some cases just enough to avoid perilous confrontations with the Council.

'Anti-racist education' aims to cleanse schools of every taint of racialism, however inadvertent. This is a crazy ambition, given the subjective nature of so many definitions of racism/racialism, though obviously NF literature and graffiti must be eliminated from every British school: and *soon*.

Bradford LEA's anti-racist directive (LAM 6/83) stressed a particular problem: the fact that many teachers ignore 'minor incidents of racialist behaviour' – which may seem far from 'minor' to the victims. All schools were requested to keep records of all 'racialist incidents', giving details of 'the offence itself, the children concerned, the action taken and the sanction imposed . . . Heads are asked to inform the appropriate Assistant Director of all such incidents as and when they occur.' In theory this is fine; pupils should always be punished for ill-treating other pupils – period. But there is that definition problem . . . In tough schools where, regardless of colour, pupils regularly beat up one another (not to mention the staff), how can teachers be *sure* of the motive behind a particular incident? Did George Smith beat up Sher Ali because he hates 'Pakis' or because he had it in for Sher Ali personally? Moreover, once Sher Ali & Co. realise that 'racialist behaviour' has become an exciting issue may they not be tempted to provoke it on occasions, or to misinterpret a mere 'incident' as a 'racialist incident'? When one of my small Manningham neighbours was hit on the ear by a White-thrown snowball during a happy multi-racial playground romp his father promptly complained to the head teacher of a 'racist attack'.

Such – not unusual – cases partly explain why many Bradford head teachers derided LAM 6/83. As a breed, heads like to run their own show and feel quite capable of handling day-to-day problems, racialist or otherwise, without directives from anyone. Besides, they are no less ethnocentric/xenophobic/racialist than the majority of their compatriots and see little point in wasting time, thought and money on the 'special needs' of Browns and Blacks.

The anti-racists' views on children's books/stereotyping/prejudice fascinate me, as a non-English English-speaker. Most of my waking childhood hours were spent reading, so I was more exposed than the average English child to 'racist' literature. Yet as a non-member of the Master Race, and a citizen of a country plagued by England for 800 years, what those books reinforced was *my* stereotype (since slightly revised) of the arrogant, unimaginative, hypocritical and exploiting Englishman, rampaging around the world with a Bible in one hand, a gun in the other and an accounts ledger in his tin trunk. At no age did I receive an imprint of inferior peoples dependent on Whites for every sort of salvation; spiritual, material, legal, sartorial. The consistently unfavourable images projected of 'natives' were merely what I expected of English authors writing about their multitudinous victims – *my* ancestors' fellow-victims. This strongly suggests that the Swann Report was exaggerating when it stated: 'Images, both pictorial and verbal, are among the most powerful influences on how a child perceives the world and thus a major potential source of stereotypes of ethnic minority groups.'

Even very young children read critically or sceptically, if books fail to confirm the stereotypes *already* acquired from home, school and society. Thus the literary influence is secondary – important as a reinforcement of stereotypes, yet not capable of creating them against the current of a child's personal environment.

But how do Brown and Black children, born into a condescending White world, react to a juvenile literary diet that too often presents unflattering pictures of their countries, cultures and capacities? Depending on temperament, they may be made to feel either hopelessly inferior and ashamed of their parental background, or ferociously resentful – or a mixture of both. Does this justify banning from school libraries any book likely to lower Black and Brown self-esteem, while reinforcing White prejudices? The anti-racists say *yes* and there is a temptation to agree. Yet such censorship is not only impractical but repugnant to most Whites – too desperate a remedy. It would make more sense to counterbalance the traditional 'racist' volumes by *adding* to school libraries; which unfortunately is also impractical, in this era of cut-backs.

Books for classroom use are another matter; here vigilance is essential. Consider *Reading On Red Book 1* (7th edition 1968), which was still being used as an English reader in Leeds primary schools in 1982 (!):

> Perhaps Mary could finish her father's unfinished work. He had been interested in savages and backward races. Africa was the best place to find such people. Mary would go to Africa. She would go among the wildest savages she could find. She would spend her life studying cannibals.

One doesn't have to be a manic anti-racist to regard that twaddle as unsuitable for children of any colour in any country. And to Black eyes the *Little Black Sambo* genre is not much better, as Dorothy Kuya has explained:*

> We need to consider not whether the White children find Little Black Sambo lovable, or the White teachers think it a 'good repetitive tale', but whether the Black child and teacher feel the same way. As a Black Briton, born and educated in this country, I detested *Little Black Sambo* as much as I did the other textbooks which presented non-white people as living entirely in primitive conditions and having no culture. *I did not relate to them*, but the white children in my class identified me with them.

Advocates of anti-racist education see it as a corollary of multi-cultural education, but many advocates of the latter do not agree. And Little

---

* Bob Dixon (ed.), *Catching Them Young*, Vol. I, Pluto Press.

Englanders insist that multi-cultural education is a form of racial discrimination because without a pure English education the ethnic minorities, and Bradford's Browns in particular, will be condemned to a life-long and probably jobless ghetto existence – since only their schools can equip them with the necessary mental and social skills to make a success of life in England. Clearly too much emphasis on 'mother-cultures' in the classroom could have the effect of playing the racialist employers' game. Yet the multi-culturists' argument is much stronger. Unless Browns and Blacks are schooled in an atmosphere that acknowledges the value of *their* cultures they cannot develop self-respect and self-confidence.

In areas of many Muslims, there is a further argument for multi-cultural education. Without it, the tiny minority of fundamentalist Muslims who agitate at intervals for separate Islamic schools may gain support. At present few take them seriously. Yet they are not confined, as is often supposed, to the older generation; I met several young men who were even less flexible and much more belligerent than their fundamentalist seniors. For them being religiously hardline is also a way of asserting their personal/cultural identity in a 'rejecting society'. A booklet entitled *Muslim Children in British Schools,* produced by the 'Straight Path Monthly' with an address in Small Heath, Birmingham, gives the flavour of their thinking:

> Until Muslims can set up their own schools they should make sure their children are carrying out their duties as Muslims in state schools. Some parents allow their daughters to wear trousers to school and then change into skirts once they get there. Muslim parents should not sink so low as to make this compromise . . . Dance and music are both un-Islamic activities and Muslim parents should make sure even small children are excluded from them. All such activities are geared to create physical attraction between boys and girls which leads to permissiveness . . . Islam is totally opposed to sex-education. Parents should make sure their children are excluded from such degrading and dehumanising lessons . . . For boys it is not at all objectionable to take a shower after PE, provided that all the boys in the shower cover their private parts. It is not enough for Muslim boys to wear something and non-Muslims to be completely naked. LEAs do not insist that all boys wear something and this has caused quite a lot of problems as the Authorities will not alter their viewpoint on the necessity of taking a shower after PE . . . WE SHOULD NOT BE COWARDS AND BOW TO THE NON-MUSLIM EDUCATIONAL SYSTEM. Parents and local Muslim organisations must take up the fight . . . To Teenagers: YOU ARE MUSLIMS, LIVE AS MUSLIMS, BE PROUD OF YOUR RELIGION. SAVE YOURSELVES FROM THE FIRE OF HELL.

The victories of Islamic fundamentalism elsewhere, and the oil-money that could be made available to spread the contagion among Britain's Muslim communities, make 'pure English' schooling seem not only inadequate but hazardous. An upsurge of Islamic fundamentalism would do nothing for race relations in Britain. And some responsible moderate Muslims consider it not as remote a possibility as it may seem to outsiders.

*   *   *

In Bradford Sayed became one of my most helpful young friends. A thought-ful seventeen-year-old, he studied for his science A Levels even at weekends, while helping to run the family's large but no longer lucrative restaurant on the Leeds Road. "Folk here have no money now for eating out," he had explained sadly at our first meeting, on a Sunday evening when only one table was occupied.

Sayed's Old Delhi grandparents migrated to Pakistan in 1947 and in 1955 his parents moved on to Bradford. For twenty years his engineer father worked with one firm – the only Brown professional on their staff – and when redundancy came in 1977 his employers (noted for their 'good race relations policies') threw a farewell party. Then Sayed, aged nine, suddenly became aware of 'racism'. He remembers his father returning home in tears – "And he's not that sort. I was so shocked to see him *crying*, it really scared me." Despite the firm's policy, not one of father's colleagues, who had always been perfectly civil to him at work, attended that party; and most of them didn't even trouble to invent excuses.

Among Browns, racism of this sort ('discourtesy racism') is immeasurably hurtful – especially when it reveals, as so often it does, a strong strain of long-term hypocrisy. Most Browns (Muslims, Sikhs, Hindus; peasants, merchants, landowners) attach great importance to formal good manners, to the rituals of etiquette and ceremonial that govern certain occasions and events. They are frequently shocked by what they see as our brash informality or coarse insensitivity to the finer shades of inter-personal dealings, whether social or professional. When this prompts them to react in negative ways, Whites accuse them of 'having a chip and imagining slights'. But you don't need a chip to be wounded by the brutal ill-manners Sayed described.

'Discourtesy racism' is the most widespread form of the disease in Britain and its cumulative effect must be far more painful than gang-assaults, arson attacks, bricks through windows and excreta through letter-boxes. Only a tiny minority of Whites express their racialism violently. Yet it seems the majority are capable of, and if the situation arises are guilty of, discourtesy racism. It may (and certainly will) be argued that this insidious form of the disease is excusable – not malicious or deliberately unkind, merely the result of a blundering ignorance of other cultures, combined with a lack of imagination for which individuals can scarcely be blamed. To Whites such excuses seem adequate – but not to Browns or Blacks. And while discourtesy racism may cause the older generation to feel sorrow, hurt pride, betrayal and suppressed bitterness, their children and grandchildren feel anger.

We have now reached the very core of British racialism, almost as dangerous a place for writers as the core of a nuclear reactor. At that core lies something much nastier than unimaginative ignorance: an assumption, conscious or unconscious, that coloured peoples, whatever their personal attributes or attainments, are *lesser breeds*. Only this can explain why so many Whites are capable of treating Browns and Blacks in ways that they themselves would deplore in an all-White context.

The suffering caused by British racial prejudice, in its various forms, is ignored by most Whites and exaggerated by White anti-racists. About half-way through my inner-city year I discussed this point with a friend who is not Black, White or Brown, not Christian, Hindu, or Muslim. This Tibetan Buddhist speaks fluent English but has never resided in England. He commented, "It must be some sort of compliment to England that the Asians and West Indians are so disillusioned by their treatment here. It shows how people respect this country for being humane and upholding equal justice for all – I mean *within* Britain, not when they were colonisers. Is this why, as you say, 'some Whites ignore and others exaggerate'? Because of a conflict between Britain's domestic standards for Whites and her old colonial attitudes towards non-Whites? And is this why minorities can't accept being second-class citizens *in Britain* even if they'd take that status for granted at home, expecting nothing better from their own governments? When you think of the scale of cruelty and oppression and injustice and exploitation all over the world, is it maybe possible that the minorities here have only *small* problems?"

Thondup was right. Yet it doesn't really help someone who feels he has a very big problem to tell him it's *comparatively* small . . .

To counteract British racialism, anti-racists have imported from the USA a psychological device known as Race Awareness Training. Its failure-rate has made me think again about Race *Unawareness* Training as an alternative device. But that would require the dispersion of the entire population of Britain throughout the non-European world for at least a year, without enough money to live like tourists. This not very practical idea first occurred to me several years ago when I began to notice the influence on young Whites of travelling rough beyond Europe. Whatever their home backgrounds and early conditioning, the attitudes towards Browns and Blacks of many of those youngsters contrasts dramatically with those of the average non-traveller (or zombie tourist). To them Britain's ethnic minorities are – well, *just people*. Not necessarily the sort of people they particularly like, just other human beings about whom they have no self-conscious hang-ups; so they feel free to praise certain non-European characteristics without wondering if they are being patronising and to condemn others without wondering if they are being arrogant.

The current notion that racialists dislike coloured peoples and anti-racists like them has added to the confusions of the race relations debate. Liking or disliking is not the issue. I like my dog, my cats and even my goats much more than I like most human beings. However, my relations with them are quintessentially different from my relations with even the least likable representative of my own species. Yet in Britain now it often seems that Whites (anti-racists no less than racists) are so 'Race Aware' that they relate to ethnic minorities almost as though they belonged to a different species, who deserve better or worse treatment (depending on which camp you're in) because "they're not like us". This is the attitude which most travellers don't have. They recognise but are not uptight about the barriers that do exist between peoples of different colours, creeds and cultures. They know that these barriers must be negotiated, that the differences are important. But they also know that whether we are vegetarians or will only eat halal meat, whether we insist on arranged marriages or don't bother marrying, whether we believe in one god or eight thousand gods or no god – none of these differences is significant beside our common humanity. Some will say, "That's pie in the sky!" Yet it is not an ideal to be striven for; it is an objective biological and psychological fact. And, if clearly perceived, it should make us all much more laid-back about race relations: which could only do good. The cultivation of 'Race Awareness' tends to blur 'Humanity Awareness' – to obscure the simple, central and immutable reality that we are all human beings.

6 · The Honeyford Affair

... there is a very close connection between colour prejudice, anti-semitism, fascism, xenophobia and jingoism ... The common denominator in all these cases appears to be the fact that the prejudiced person sees the outgroup as in some way constituting a threat to his own personal security and status. Severe prejudice is a response to inner feelings of anxiety and insecurity ... often derived from childhood experiences of deprivation or frustration.*

ANTHONY H. RICHMOND

There are certainly Asian families who approve of Mr Honeyford's traditionalist approach to his job. They approve of progress by merit and 'a British education'. Strict discipline and the old values have a strong appeal to them.

COUNCILLOR MOHAMMED ADJEEB
(Lord Mayor of Bradford, 1985–86)

Some people say Honeyford is good, some people say Honeyford is bad.

Five-year-old Mirpuri schoolgirl,
March 1985

Soon after my arrival in Bradford I realised that I must, if possible, meet Ray Honeyford, then head teacher of Drummond Middle School in Manningham, and Jenny Woodward, who was leading the parents' campaign to have him dismissed. From the start of what came to be known throughout Britain as 'The Honeyford Affair', their personalities had been no less important – as determinants of events – than the abstract issues involved. Both kindly agreed to talk with me, despite their being importuned almost hourly, at that stage, by eager media beavers. I hoped that our conversations would clarify some of the more obscure aspects of the controversy, which indeed they did. But there was a snag. I liked them both so much that during our first meetings firm friendship foundations were laid. This was careless of me. Writers should remain aloof, clinically taking notes and not getting fond of people ... But it is always difficult to regard other human beings simply as raw material.

This complication was unexpected because of my preconceived images.

---

* Anthony H. Richmond, *The Colour Problem*, Penguin (1955)

Reading Ray's articles I had thought – What a ghastly man! Reading newspaper reports of Jenny's activities I had thought – What a ghastly woman! (Such is the power of the press.) Then, on meeting Ray, it seemed to me that those articles hid the amount of anxious thought he had given to the problem of educating children from an Islamic peasant background for life in modern Britain. Some believed that his extreme ethnocentricity made him an unsuitable head teacher for a mainly Muslim school, yet in my view it did not detract from the sincerity of his professional concern for his pupils. I felt it was unjust to accuse him of being 'racist'.

To the media Jenny was 'a virago' (the *Yorkshire Post's* favourite description); a raucous subversive feminist who addressed Militant groups of miners, teachers and other such rabble; a 'White woman who wears Pakistani clothes' and 'has West Indian friends'. Those last two eccentricities were noted in the *Sun* as symptoms of a severe personality disorder which meant that everything she said or did could be automatically condemned. Having allowed for media hysteria, I still didn't expect to find a keenly intelligent young woman, devoted to underdogs of every breed, widely read and with a delicious sense of humour – a scarce commodity in anti-racist circles. Her campaigning is inspired not by any personal grudge against society, or by political ambition (she is as apolitical as I am) or publicity-seeking. The media were maddened by her non-co-operation when they sought to 'spice up their Honeyford stories' with potted biographies of this beautiful young woman, whom they suspected of being closet upperclass despite her Manningham address. When all their probings were thwarted they began to use the adjective 'mysterious' in contexts which hinted at A Chequered Past. During the darkest hours of the Honeyford Affair, those references were the only light relief available to Jenny.

My 'cross-bench' situation baffled many White friends. When explanations were demanded I could only say that on first meeting Jenny and Ray I at once realised that in different spheres I had much in common with both. And it never occurred to me that because I couldn't whole-heartedly support either protagonist I should deprive myself of two valuable new friendships – which soon became four, as I got to know Jenny's daughter Jessica and Ray's wife Angela.

Jenny listened with polite restraint when I tried to convey why Ray seemed to me *not* a racist. Then she dryly pointed out that whether or not I accepted that particular label I couldn't deny that his writings had inflamed racial prejudice. Which is true. On race-related matters she was unable to comprehend my dogged professional pursuit of objectivity – which of course no one can ever hope to capture. She argued, "I don't think you *can* be objective about racism, at every level it has to be exposed for what it is. There isn't another side to the story that is worth listening to."

On this issue we disagreed profoundly though amicably. Of course 'there isn't another side to the story' in the sense that no form of racialist behaviour must ever be condoned. But racial prejudice is surely a mental/moral/ emotional defect to which most human beings are to some extent prone and for which there can be many causes, often elusive. Seeing it as one more human failing, I can't always condemn each of its manifestations without stopping to ask what prompted that individual in that situation to show racial prejudice. Thus I believe there *is* another side to the story which it is essential to listen to – because if we are ever to evolve beyond racial prejudice we must first understand its true nature.

*　　*　　*

On 3 May 1986, when I was home in Ireland writing this book, I heard a World Service programme on Britain's imminent local elections. The reporter explained why the 'ethnic' vote was so important in West Yorkshire and mentioned Drummond Middle School in Bradford with its 'sixty per cent Asian attendance'. (The true figure was by that date over ninety per cent.) He recalled that Drummond's headmaster had been at the centre of a 'prolonged and bitter controversy', following an assertion that White children in such schools are at an educational disadvantage. 'Deep wounds were opened, Mr Honeyford was forced into early retirement and Conservative candidates are now emphasising their support for the ex-headmaster.' The reporter spoke with quiet, detached BBC assurance. He was giving the Authorised Version of the Honeyford Affair and each of his statements was true. Yet linked thus their effect was to mislead.

By then the New Right had been nurturing this Authorised Version for almost two years. These powerful people are not to be confused with the puny Far Right – the British Movement, British National Party and National Front. Yet they travel close enough to that side of the road to find themselves occasionally driving along the Far Right shoulder: accidentally, of course, for they are ultra-respectable and would hate to be publicly associated with NF rabble or BNP demagogues.

The evolution of the Authorised Version was helped by an inherent media limitation. Many editors are interested in such controversies only when they provoke surges of anger or violence, or sensational accusations, or alleged injustices that tug at the heart-strings. Given the public's preference for dramatic simplicities, it is never worth studying a tangle of disputed facts and divergent perceptions. Yet during 1984–85 reporters frequently had to 'explain' in a few lines the background to Bradford's latest 'Race Conflict', a controversy obscure in origin and increasingly complex in development. Naturally they found this task impossible. Hence their contribution to the rapid growth of the Authorised Version: a brave headmaster had been cen-sored/suspended/punished/persecuted/hounded/denied freedom of speech/ bullied into early retirement because he had 'dared to stand up for the minority of White pupils in certain inner-city schools' and had 'criticised

Bradford's anti-racist lobby and multi-cultural education policy'.

The Honeyford Affair is of more than ephemeral interest, both as an example of right-wing myth-making and as a reminder that it is extremely dangerous to play party politics on the race relations stage, as both Right and Left did in Bradford during 1984–85. It is important to realise that ninety-nine-point-nine per cent of those who came to feel strongly about the Honeyford Affair – i.e., the entire White population of Bradford, plus millions of onlookers all over Britain – did not read, before taking up their positions, an unexpurgated version of that *Salisbury Review* article which is popularly believed to have 'started the row'. (In fact its publication marked the beginning not of the Honeyford versus Bradford Council conflict but of the parents' campaign to have Ray Honeyford dismissed.) Throughout the affair many people quoted selectively from 'Education and Race – An Alternative View'. Yet the public had no opportunity to judge its overall impact until Bradford's *Telegraph and Argus* reprinted it in full on 26 November 1985, at the end of the affair. It is difficult to estimate the merits or demerits of the anti-Honeyford case without reading that article but its author would not permit it to be included as an appendix to this book.

The timing of Ray Honeyford's appointment as headmaster of Drummond Middle School – April 1980 – was peculiarly inauspicious. Soon after, Bradford Council launched their anti-racist-cum-multi-cultural education programme and the new head saw both those novelties as massive obstacles to the academic advancement of children of all colours. Therefore, during the next few years, he publicly opposed his employers' education policies.

In November 1984 Bradford's Chief Executive described Ray Honeyford as 'a martyr without a cause'. This seems a little harsh. He does have a cause; he is passionately committed to 'good schools for all' and fervently supports the teaching of Christianity in all British schools, regardless of their ethnic content. In another *Salisbury Review* article (January 1985) he noted signs that the educational hegemony of the left was under serious attack and that the right were beginning to realise that support for independent schools is not enough. He insisted that the way most of the nation's children are educated should be of great concern to conservatives who believe in character training, the pursuit of individual excellence, and the unacceptability of moral and cultural relativism.

The last comment exposes Ray Honeyford's Achilles' heel as headmaster of Drummond Middle; if you consider moral and cultural relativism unacceptable, you are bound to have problems running a mainly Muslim school – with or without Council 'diktats'.

Here we must digress to consider certain idiosyncrasies of the *Salisbury Review* – subtitled 'A quarterly magazine of conservative thought' and available by subscription only. It first appeared in October 1982 and its editor is a co-founder of the New Right Conservative Philosophy Group. The other founder is John Casey, a Cambridge don who contributed an article, 'One Nation: The Politics of Race', to the first issue of the *Salisbury Review*. Mr Casey wrote:

> . . . there must be at least a potential problem should a community exist in large numbers, which defines itself because of its numbers, culture and other observable characteristics, in separation from the rest of the community . . . Do we not have the grave apprehension that the great English cities are now becoming alienated from national life . . . Large black and brown communities will turn Britain into a different sort of place . . . I believe that the only radical policy that would stand a chance of success is repatriation . . . The alternative would be retrospectively to alter the legal status of the coloured immigrant community, so that its members become guest-workers.

Mr Casey, remember, was writing in 1982, when nearly fifty per cent of 'the coloured immigrant community' had been born in Britain. The notion of legally transmogrifying them into 'guest-workers' would be comical if it were not more than slightly chilling.

In my pre-Bradford days I had never heard of the *Salisbury Review*; its circulation is about one thousand. However, I have by now read through ten issues and, since most people of my generation and bourgeois background carry a small-'c' conservative virus, I liked the views of some contributors on such topics as modern art and architecture and the calamitous fatuity of Britain's present educational system. But these were mere oases of agreement. Between them I found myself traversing a desert of superficial profundity. Contributors monotonously glorify 'the ideas of social continuity, national identity and tradition upon which durable political order depends'. And 'this serious journal lends its support to the idea that Britain ought to be British'.

'Common sense' is a favourite cop-out phrase of New Righters. 'Common sense' tells us that life was much more agreeable when everyone knew their place because the masses had not been exposed to disruptive notions about democracy and personal liberty, and when the nation was united in its loyalties – i.e. not diluted by alien coloured immigrants. 'Common sense' tells us that Britain was truly Great when women were industrious in the kitchen and submissive in bed, homosexuality was illegal, trades unions were meek, peace movements hadn't been invented, bishops didn't make rude socialist noises and murderers were hanged. The *Salisbury Review*, in brief, is a symptom of that authoritarian fever now infecting the Thatcherite segment of the Disunited Kingdom. As its editor has noted, 'Our opinions are not a million miles from those of a party which has twice in succession been voted into government.'

The passages in Ray Honeyford's articles most hurtful to Browns and Blacks were as tickles under a cat's chin to *Salisbury Review* readers. And apparently Ray doesn't realise the damage that could be done to his beloved England if the New Right had their way.

Roger Scruton, editor of *The Salisbury Review*, belongs to the 'Peterhouse School', a group which in 1978 published *Conservative Essays*. This book's message was summed up by its editor, Maurice Cowling – 'It is not freedom that Conservatives want, what they want is the sort of freedom that will maintain existing inequalities or restore lost ones.' We must pay tribute to this gentleman's frankness; there are many like-minded Tories around who don't advertise their wants. Mr Scruton defined his own political philosophy in *The Meaning of Conservatism*:

> In politics, the conservative attitude seeks above all for government, and regards no citizen as possessed of a natural right that transcends his obligation to be ruled. Even democracy – which corresponds neither to the natural nor to the supernatural yearnings of the normal citizen – can be discarded without detriment to the civil well-being as the conservative conceives it.

What would be the fate of Britain's Blacks and Browns post-'democracy'? In the April 1986 *Salisbury Review* Mr Scruton called for 'a new effort to integrate the Asian and West Indian communities into a social and political order that is recognisably British'. But if that effort fails? Then perhaps 'homelands' in remotest Scotland for all who refuse to become 'recognisably British'? Or would that upset the grouse, which are such an important symbol of 'social continuity'?

I am only half-joking. The 'Peterhouse School' is a political health-hazard because many of its journalist supporters are in a position to influence large sections of the British public. And the Honeyford Affair proved how quickly an ordinary, well-meaning Englishman can be turned into an innocent carrier of the New Right virus.

Ray Honeyford's background seems to have made him extra-vulnerable to that virus. He was born into the challenging world of a Manchester slum in 1934, when there were few State benefits. His hardline Protestant father – gassed during the First World War – could work only irregularly as a labourer. His devout Irish Catholic mother bore eleven children (seven died in infancy), while somehow earning enough to feed the family. At fifteen Ray took a job as a clerk in a small local firm and during the next decade continued to study by correspondence course for O and A Levels. In 1959 an acute teacher-shortage made it possible for him to do a two-year training course at Didsbury. Then, while teaching full-time at a secondary modern school, he took an M Ed in socio-linguistics at Manchester University's night school, followed by an M A in educational psychology at Lancaster. He is a man who enjoys learning and abhors the notion that 'pupil differences are simply a function of social circumstances'. His career followed a standard pattern and he would no doubt have relished greater recognition of his academic achievements. That would be natural, for anyone who had put so much effort into escaping from the bottom of the pile; it does not suggest undue ambition. It does however suggest that when his writing brought him into contact with the *Salisbury Review* group he was susceptible to its questionable profundity. In a *Telegraph and Argus* interview (29 March 1985) he said: 'I have met Roger Scruton on a number of occasions. He is the most brilliant man I have ever met. He sees my whole position as one of freedom of expression. I have had a large number of letters from academics over the last twelve months. They also see this issue as one of freedom of expression.'

Primarily the Honeyford Affair was a debate about a head teacher's suitability for his post, though secondary debates proliferated as time passed. But the pro-Honeyford faction viewed it as an 'un-English' attempt by an alliance of reactionary Muslims and rabid Lefties to muzzle a decent man who had had the courage to speak out against multi-cultural education and anti-racist pressure groups.

'Racist' is an unpleasant and ambiguous word and for months I experimented with 'ethnocentric', which simply means 'regarding one's own race as the most important'. Many (most?) Whites are ethnocentric, though not necessarily discriminatory in their dealings with other races. But ethnocentricity does foster 'District Officer' paternalism. And in present-day Britain it often leads to a conviction that Blacks and Browns have nothing to lose by becoming as British as possible as soon as possible.

When the 'Honeyford Out!' campaign began (March 1984) Bradford had just been through an inflaming series of race-related controversies – about the serving of halal meat in schools (approved by the Council), about the efforts of a fundamentalist splinter-group, the Muslim Parents' Association, to take over five schools including Drummond (thwarted by the Council), about the compulsory 'Race Awareness Training' of Council officers, including teachers, and about an allegedly racist assault at Wyke Manor School.

These conflicts had left a lot of diffuse hatred in the atmosphere. After the halal meat battle, the Education Committee chairman and his elderly mother were the victims of sustained persecution from an Animal Rights group rumoured to have N F support. Next a multi-racial group of anti-racists took over the Lord Mayor's City Hall room for an entire day in protest against criticisms of the Council's education policy voiced by the then Lord Mayor. When the occupation ended their spokesman told the press – "Today we had an objective, to bring out the racism within this Council and the racism of the civic leader and the racism of the politics that has existed in the Council chambers! Today can be seen as a great victory!"

It was unfortunate that Bradford's anti-racists were in such a militant mood when the most contentious Honeyford article was first publicised. Had the city's atmosphere been calmer, it might not have provoked so much strife.

By 1984 Ray Honeyford had been involved in several inter-racial controversies. In July 1982 a newspaper columnist reported a rumour that the Council had given a £100,000 grant to Checkpoint, a Black youth club, in response to threats of Black-inspired rioting. When Ray wrote to the *Telegraph and Argus*, on school writing-paper, urging an investigation of the grant by the district auditor, he was publicly reprimanded by the Education Committee for having written thus in his headmaster/Council employee role. More friction followed, when head teachers were directed to serve halal meat twice weekly to Muslim pupils, switch from a Christian to a multi-faith religious education syllabus and either attend RAT courses (a felicitous acronym) or forgo their right to help choose new staff members.

Ray Honeyford's first contentious article was published in the *Times Educational Supplement* in September 1982. During the next two years others followed, in the *TES, The Times, Yorkshire Post, Head Teachers' Review* and *Salisbury Review*. The Council, though enraged by these articles, dithered and waffled – even when the *Telegraph and Argus* printed a letter from their employee calling for public support for his anti-Council crusade. Towards the end of 1984 the Tory Chairman of the Education Committee suggested that the Council should try to 'buy off' Ray Honeyford because of his insensitive remarks, in a *TES* article, about Bradford's Browns in general and some of the Drummond parents in particular. But the Chief Education Officer declined to take such drastic action.

It was Mr Michael Whittaker, the Policies Development Officer for Educational Services, who drew the *Yorkshire's Post's* attention to an article by a Bradford headmaster hidden away in the *Salisbury Review* – and expressing sentiments likely to gratify many *Yorkshire Post* readers. Mr Whittaker did not consult his senior officers before making this move but doubtless expected them to be grateful for his initiative. It was likely to create so much trouble that they would have a good excuse for replacing a teacher whose articles had been described by the Council's Race Relations Advisory Group as 'the greatest threat to the new educational policy'. However, things worked out quite differently. When the *Yorkshire Post's* résumé of that article sent up the 'Honeyford Out!' rocket the Council lost what little nerve they had.

Instead of Ray Honeyford being required to move on, Michael Whittaker was seconded to the Home Office for two years.

Read consecutively, the Honeyford *oeuvre* reveals a man increasingly irritated by the activities of 'left-wing radical teachers', 'multi-racial zealots' and 'well-meaning liberals and clergymen suffering from rapidly dating post-imperial guilt'. His inconsistencies may be seen as one symptom of that irritation.

In 'Multi-ethnic Intolerance' (*Salisbury Review*, June 1983) Ray pointed out that the comparative failure of West Indian children in British schools had been recognised by many concerned West Indian parents who have set up their own Saturday Schools, in which youngsters are taught respect for authority – 'a concept correctly understood by the vast majority of West Indian parents as being central to the process of real education'. Yet six months later, in the fateful 'Education and Race – An Alternative View', he dismissed as 'almost certainly bogus', the argument that Black pupils fail because of teacher prejudice and an alien curriculum. Then he traced the roots of Black educational failure to the West Indians' family structure and values and to the political attitudes of misguided radical teachers.

What can have happened, in that brief period, to change so drastically Ray Honeyford's opinion of West Indian family values?

In *Trials of Honeyford*, a booklet published in October 1985 by the New Right Centre for Policy Studies, Andrew Brown quoted a memorandum written by Ray Honeyford for the Drummond School Policy: 'In a school as old as this there must be material somewhere which contains attitudes now considered out of date and inappropriate. If teachers come across this, I should expect them to have the common sense to throw it out, or, with older and more intelligent children, to use it to illustrate how times have changed.'

According to Andrew Brown, this memorandum was effective and Ray had assured him that 'to avoid giving unintentional offence the textbooks are checked over by every teacher as a matter of course'. Yet two months later Ray wrote in the *Daily Mail* (17 December 1985) that when urged by the Council's 'advisers' to vet the school's textbooks for anything that might upset any minority group he had refused to do so.

Clearly, Drummond Middle denied its headmaster 'job-satisfaction'. Almost every day, as one of his *TES* articles ('When East is West') is designed to show, 'unnecessary' problems tried his patience and forced him to go either against the grain or against his employers. "So why", many asked, "doesn't he bugger off and get another job?" But to Ray's numerous and vocal supporters, their hero's polemics proved his courage. While other teachers lay low, cravenly seeming to accept policies they despised, he stood up – again and again – to be counted, fearlessly exposing himself to the slings and arrows of outrageous anti-racist zealots.

In the article that fuelled the 'Honeyford Out!' rocket, Ray allowed his antipathy for those zealots to spill over onto all Bradford's Browns – and far beyond, to their countries of origin. His criticisms of Pakistan launched the parents' campaign to have him dismissed. He referred to the Mirpuris' motherland as a country which is corrupt at every level, which cannot cope with democracy and which since 1977 has been ruled by a military tyrant who, in the opinion of at least half his countrymen, had his predecessor judicially murdered. He dwelt on the Pakistani ill-treatment not only of criminals but of those who dare to question Islamic orthodoxy as interpreted by a despot. Also, he condemned Pakistan as 'the heroin capital of the world' and alleged that this 'fact' is now reflected in the drug problems of English cities with Asian populations.

Ray makes a point of never having left Britain; he prefers holidaying in places like Skye, which is consistent with his admirable non-trendiness – it is impossible to imagine him sun-bathing among the herd – and with his enthusiasm for all things British. However, this preference makes it difficult for him to draw an accurate pen-portrait of Pakistan. Frequently he complains, "One of the hang-ups we've got is that we must not criticise ethnic minorities." But a country's defects can be analysed without seeming to insinuate that all its inhabitants are A Bad Lot. In 'Pakistan Today' (*Asian Affairs*, June 1985), M.A. Rangoonwala, head of the multi-national Rangoonwala Group and a past-president of the International Chamber of Commerce, showed how this can be done:

> What are the contours of the political scene today in Pakistan? Essentially, it reflects a lack of political cohesion due to the bankruptcy of party leadership . . . It has faced frequent changes of government, a writing and re-writing of constitutions (and even their abrogation), three martial law regimes and so on . . . Despite such an unenviable record, Pakistan remains today one of the relatively stable countries in the Afro-Asian region . . . The common man in the street – the farmer in the fields, the worker in the factories and a host of other categories which contribute towards national production – have not let Pakistan down. Its economic and export performance is nothing short of a miracle when you consider the adverse circumstances and stiff competition a developing country has to face in the trading world of today. Its per capita income is $350, about twenty five per cent higher than that of the average developing country. The Pakistanis are a pragmatic people who are generally healthy, hard-working and talented. They have proved their mettle as workers, technicians, bankers, doctors, professors, entrepreneurs and in other professions all over the world. They make good citizens who would work diligently towards prosperity, given dedicated leadership.

The immediate grievance which inspired Ray Honeyford's criticism of Pakistan was the disruption of studies caused by parents allowing their off-spring to visit the Indian sub-continent during term time. Ray ended his article by asking, 'How could the denizens of such a country so wildly and implacably resent the simple British requirement on all parents to send children to school regularly?'

By 1984 Ray's inflexible opposition to those visits had aroused considerable bitterness among some Drummond parents. Soon after his arrival in Bradford he declared that he 'felt bound, both by professional commitment and the requirements of the law, to uphold the crucially important principle that compulsory and regular school attendance is essential to the educational progress of the child'. He sought the support of some other teachers, who shared his concern, and the DES was persuaded to put pressure on Brown parents to obey the law. But the consequent 'Discrimination!' outcry soon caused that hot potato to be dropped.

Ray then complained about being 'left with the ethically indefensible task of complying with a school attendance policy which is determined, not as the law requires on the basis of individual parental responsibility but by the parents' country of origin – a blatant and officially sanctioned policy of racial discrimination'. Oddly, he failed to recognise this DES retreat as an example of what he has described as 'the British genius for compromise, for muddling through, and for good-natured tolerance'. Journeys to India or Pakistan are rarely frivolous holidays; few Browns can afford such indulegences.

Children's visits may have religious motives, or be in response to a joint-family need that in parental eyes outweighs even the need for schooling. Many Browns are still going through a period of adaptation to their new homeland and feel a natural desire to maintain close links with relatives and villages.

According to Ray, these visits can 'vary in duration from two or three months to several years' and he estimated that they affect 'at least 1000 children in the area annually'. In fact few children miss more than one term, but teachers do find it exasperating when pupils suddenly disappear, often at a crucial stage in their education. However, much depends on the school's attitude. Academic progress need not be retarded if teachers give their pupils suitable holiday tasks and, on their return, treat their travels as an asset to be shared with their classmates – an approach that works well in some Bradford schools.

Unfortunately Ray was able to find 'no evidence that children's formal education benefits in any discernible sense'. Yet at High Hill school I found much evidence, in the essays of 'returned' pupils, of their having benefited enormously from their travels. This did not surprise me; I know from personal experience the educational value, to a young child, of seeing how life is lived on other continents. My daughter's education was disrupted for four or eight or twelve months whenever we felt like going abroad; Ray would have regarded me as the prototypical irresponsible parent. I provided no substitute teaching yet Rachel's academic development was certainly not slowed, and may even have been speeded up, by these extra-curricular peregrinations. It could be that regular schooling is not quite as important as educationalists imagine.

Another source of parent/headmaster friction was the serving of halal meat in Drummond. Ray commented in the T E S (September 1983) that the English regard the manner in which halal meat is obtained as cruel, since the animal is not stunned before it is killed. He felt uneasy about this, as the official in charge of school dinners, because how could ritual slaughter be reconciled with one of the school's values – a love of dumb creatures and respect for their well-being?

One might also ask, how do the English reconcile their love of dumb creatures with their consumption of factory-farm produce? Factory-farming causes incomparably more suffering than halal killing. I have closely watched the slaughtering of sheep in Muslim villages; when an expert butcher is in charge the beast becomes almost instantly unconscious as the flow of blood is cut off from the brain. Even if the butcher is less than expert the animal's suffering lasts only a few moments. But our factory-farmed pigs, hens and veal-calves endure unrelieved deprivation from birth to death. Muslims are rightly contemptuous of that English 'love of dumb creatures' which condones a lifetime of misery if death is preceded by stunning.

Also during 1983, Ray provoked much antagonism by informing the police that a few Drummond pupils had been severely beaten at their mosque school. Undeniably some imams are over-fond of corporal punishment – though the two accused in this case were acquitted for lack of evidence. What incensed Manningham was Ray's going to the police without consulting the boys' parents.

Thus an accumulation of anti-Honeyford feeling, among certain sections of the Drummond parents, already existed before the *Yorkshire Post* treated as 'news' the opinions expressed in a right-wing journal by a Bradford headmaster. And for those parents the linking of 'the drug problems of English cities with Asian populations' was the match to the fuse. No less than their White counterparts, Manningham's strait-laced Muslim parents fear and hate the hard-drug underworld. Ray Honeyford should have known that the present heroin trade was stimulated by White demand and is run by vicious people of all races. In the early 1960s I cycled through mile after mile of opium poppy crops in Afghanistan and Northern Pakistan; opium was then produced, as it had been from time immemorial, for *domestic* consumption.

Following the *Yorkshire Post*'s exposé, the extent of parental dissatisfaction with some aspects of Ray's headship became apparent. Several local race relations workers met to discuss the crisis, including Sher Azam of the Council for Mosques, Marsha Singh of the Education Department, Tim Whitfield of the CRC and Jenny Woodward. A week later all Drummond parents were invited to a public meeting and the Drummond Parents' Action Committee (DPAC) was formed to demand Ray's dismissal. After much discussion, Jenny was elected chairperson. In her own words, "This was a carefully thought-out position, based on the parents' experience that in the UK a White voice would carry more conviction." She soon became the campaign's acknowledged leader, not because she wished for that role but because no other committee member was capable of dealing with the many bureaucratic and legal complications involved. A few months later, when the Drummond parents elected her as their representative on the school Governing Body, she received more votes than the other twelve candidates combined.

The DPAC summed up its position in the *Telegraph and Argus* (9 April 1985):

A vote of no confidence in the abilities of the head teacher was passed (in March 1984) . . . It was suggested that parents be informed of the contents of the *Salisbury Review* article, with appropriate translations, and asked to vote privately on whether or not they felt the headmaster should remain in his post . . . Many people attended our weekly meetings and indeed they were closed to no one. However, the decisions taken as to whatever form of action should be followed by the DPAC were made by parents alone . . . The notion of multi-cultural education is to us an essential component of our children's education, in that it gives equal importance and respect to cultures other than 'British' . . . The main objective is obviously to eradicate racism from all our lives for the benefit of the whole. To the suggestion that the D PA C is out to curtail freedom of speech we would reply that no one is being criticised for expressing their feelings. [But] are those feelings in accordance with agreed upon policies of the employer? And are we, as consumers of the educational services, paid for by public funds, bound to accept the attitude of one head-teacher who finds himself in conflict with the policies he is under contract to follow?

This somewhat disingenuous statement unwittingly contributed to the evolution of the Authorised Version. No one could have organised an anti-Honeyford campaign based on disagreements with the Council about educational theories. Most Drummond parents, who come from a country with a seventy-six per cent illiteracy rate, are not remotely interested in debates about multi-cultural and/or anti-racist education. They value any form of education, ethnocentric or otherwise, and hope – touchingly – that given good schooling their children can prosper in Britain. Several jobless fathers who were my neighbours in Manningham gave education as their main reason for not returning to Pakistan. Had Ray confined himself to professional criticisms of multi-cultural education he could have gone on writing about it for the rest of his career without ruffling the average Drummond parent. However, the D PA C judged it expedient to use his non-co-operation with the Education Committee as their main weapon on the nationwide P R battleground. Meanwhile, within Manningham, their most effective weapon was the extent to which they alleged Ray had 'insulted' Islam, Pakistan and Bradford's Browns.

When the passages from 'Education and Race – An Alternative View' that appeared to have caused most offence had been translated, and shown or read to the Drummond parents, over 200 felt angry enough to sign a letter to the Education Committee demanding the author's dismissal – or, if they were illiterate, to authorise someone else to sign. This figure represented more than half the parents; Drummond's 520 pupils included many groups of two or three siblings. Had those parents foreseen how seriously the campaign would disrupt their children's education fewer might have signed. Once it had been launched they could not easily withdraw their support, though some became very uneasy about its conduct – for reasons both practical and ethical.

Ray's supporters condemned as mischievous the translating of isolated paragraphs to sharpen parental animosity. True, the D PA C's chosen quotations incited many Drummond parents to anger. Yet quoting out of context was not in this case tendentious; the offending remarks were capable of causing as much offence *in* context and the whole thrust of that article was, as the D PA C pointed out, likely 'to create or increase racial intolerance'. It was of course perverse to suggest, as some did, that Ray had intended that effect. But someone who accidentally smashes a delicate machine does no less damage than someone whose intentions are malign.

The formation of the DPAC turned the Honeyford Affair into a confused and confusing triangular conflict: – DPAC versus Honeyford, DPAC versus Council (because they refused to dismiss Honeyford), Council versus Honeyford (because he refused to implement their policy). Yet the media never drew a clear distinction between the Council's long-running educational feud with Drummond's headmaster and the parents' new campaign to have him dismissed because they alleged he was a 'racist' unfit to run a mainly Muslim school. They chose to concentrate on his educational pronouncements, rather than on his many controversial remarks, in a series of articles, about Britain's Blacks and Browns. Grotesquely misleading headlines appeared – for example, 'Head Speaks Out on Multi-cultural Education: Job at Risk' and 'Head "on Trial" over Criticisms of Multi-racial Schooling'. The professional angle was more palatable than the personal for White consumers. And so the Authorised Version began to take shape.

The popular press gleefully took up Ray's assertion that 'If a school contains a disproportionate number of children for whom English is a second language . . . then academic standards are bound to suffer.' Editors were not bothered by his failure to provide any proof of this assertion: he had said what their readers wanted to hear. (In fact he had used the *Salisbury Review's* favourite thought-stopper – 'It is no more than common sense that if . . .')

In contrast, minimal media coverage was given to a report published on 7 October 1985 by Mr Geoffrey Pollard, headmaster of St Andrew's Church of England First School in Keighley. Mr Pollard explained:

> As we started to take more Asian children into the school, I decided it might be wise to monitor our English pupils' progress with the Asian children's progress. I measured consistently for eight years to see whether the English children were suffering. It was my concern, just as it was the concern of Mr Honeyford. It seems to me that at the school in question [Drummond], there has been no objective measurement to see if what some people have said – rather emotionally – would happen, actually did happen. Over the years the English children in my school have on the whole scored something like six or seven points above the national average. That is in a school where at present we have 90% Asian pupils. And this school has ordinary White children – not middle-class. There is not much work done at home. Most of it is done at school.

As the Honeyford battleground expanded – from Bradford's City Hall to the House of Commons, the High Court, the Appeal Court and finally No. 10 Downing Street – more and more articles were written, speeches made, meetings held, resolutions passed and press statements issued about a Bradford head teacher's opposition to multi-cultural education. Yet no one ever paused to explain how, in practice, it was affecting Bradford's schools. What, precisely, was all the fuss about?

During Ray's headmastership, Bradford's contentious mountain of multi-cultural theory brought forth only a few mice. At Drummond these were: – the serving of halal meat; permission for Muslim girls to wear track-suits during PE lessons; separate-sex PE and swimming lessons; tolerance of occasional Brown breaches of the school attendance law; the adoption of a multi-faith syllabus for RE; the evasion of sex instruction.

These seem reasonable concessions to parental susceptibilities in a mainly Muslim school, yet Ray resented being made to grant them. Had he not defied his employers by repeatedly showing his resentment in public, he could have spent fifteen years quietly pursuing his own policy of conceding the minimum to the multi-cultural ideal. In a school where most children are well-behaved, content and achieving satisfactory academic results, it is virtually impossible for any LEA to reshape that school's ethos against the will of the head teacher. Multi-cultural education, in its present nebulous form, is unenforceable as a policy because its operations depend on the knowledge, attitudes, perceptions and gut-reactions of individual teachers. Working with the same syllabus and textbooks, one teacher could deliver multi-cultural and another mono-cultural education.

In June 1984, the Council's Educational Advisory Team inspected Drummond. By then Ray's relationship with 'the community' was so shambolic that the advisers' final severe recommendation was inevitable. Yet a close reading of their report reinforces a comment made at the very beginning of the affair by Mr Donald Thompson, Bradford's Principal Officer for Middle Schools – 'Mr Honeyford is very capable and runs a good school.'

Clearly Drummond under Ray was not the answer to a multi-culturalist's prayer. Yet the advisers, who were by no means 'pro-Honeyford', found much to praise. The school library was commended: 'basically good in comparison with other middle schools'. The pupils were said to be 'co-operative, well-behaved and industrious' and there was 'with very few exceptions, a comfortable teacher/pupil relationship which was the result of respect on the part of the pupils and the care and concern shown by the members of staff'. Relationships were consistently good between the Brown majority and their few White school-mates but 'the children learning English as a second language may lack the opportunities to hear and use idiomatic and colloquial English'. However, most pupils had 'developed a sound command of both written and spoken English'. Also, 'Considerable thought has been given to assessment, and in the head teacher's guidelines to staff he rightly stresses the importance of praise and of children feeling a sense of achievement.' On the negative side, there were criticisms of his dealings with parents – 'from a few of the letters sent to parents, the relationship between school and parents is not improved by the terseness of their tone.' The school was urged to 'openly acknowledge the value of different cultures and belief systems' and there was a reminder that 'In stressing the importance of a shared British identity, it is also important to remember that "British identity" is a developing concept, and one which allows for diversity of groups and of individuals within the one society.' On balance, however, it would be difficult to argue from this report that Ray Honeyford was anything other than a competent head teacher who worked doggedly to overcome the inadequacies of his Victorian school building and the sparseness of Bradford's educational resources. The advisers' few major criticisms were all to do with his reluctance to implement the Council's new multi-cultural policies. Yet they had to conclude: 'The situation, as it has emerged, must raise serious questions as to whether it will be possible for the school to continue to function effectively unless the head is able to regain the trust and confidence of a significant proportion of parents.'

On 22 October 1984 the Educational Committee responded to the Advisory Team's Report by giving Drummond's head six months 'to reconsider his relationships with parents and the community and the effects of his writings on those relationships and the life of the school'. A six-part head teacher's report was requested by the following Easter, dealing with school/parent/community relationships, the curriculum and the aims of the school. During this six months' probation period eight Council officials would monitor progress and all Ray's articles had to be shown to the Director of Education before publication. At once another shoal of 'Freedom of Speech' red herrings swam through the media. But the *TES* warned:

> It is most important to treat any attempt to make him a martyr to free speech with great caution. That would be naive in the extreme. There are many jobs which demand a certain professional reticence; being the head of a school is one of them. In certain jobs you cannot, when you write an article, separate your private opinion from the office you hold . . . However valuable Mr Honeyford's controversial views on multi-cultural education may be, by advancing them in the public prints he may have damaged his school as well as himself. It is up to him to mend his fences with his school community if he can, and if not it will be obvious that he has seriously undermined his own position as head.

On 9 November the Council offered an early retirement deal: £100,000 in salary and pension rights. But a head teacher with fifteen working years to go, at £15,000 a year, could not be compensated so cheaply.

There was then a three-month mid-winter lull. Many hoped that Ray could at last be forced out, at the end of the probation period, for having failed to 'reconsider his relationships with parents and the community'. This seemed a reasonable hope since his record indicated that he was not likely to compromise. When the catalytic *Salisbury Review* article was first publicised it was generally recognised that some passages were 'tactless'. The situation could then have been defused by an apology; most Drummond parents would have responded graciously to such a gesture. But Ray saw no need for an apology; in several interviews, with journalists and on television, he claimed the right to say what he felt and thought without reference to anyone's feelings. (An odd claim from a man who had approvingly quoted Burke in one of his articles – 'Liberty, too, must be limited in order to be possessed.') This insensitivity in relation to minority feelings was unfortunate. If a respectable, sensible-sounding, amiable-looking head teacher believed it was O K to say what he thought about all those Pakis and darkies, then surely it *must* be OK for Whites to speak out . . . Therefore no one should have been surprised to see (and hear) the DPAC supporters becoming ever more frustrated, angry and unscrupulous as the timid Council allowed the affair to drag on.

∗   ∗   ∗

When I arrived in Bradford, in January 1985, the public phase of the Honeyford Affair had already been damaging the city for ten months. Its origins were by then invisible beneath a rubble of investigations, allegations, exaggerations, contradictions, resolutions, threatened law suits, reports, assessments of reports, reports on assessments of reports, committee minutes, lies, rumours and leaks. I had to excavate energetically before I could even begin to understand what was going on.

It seemed that none of the protagonists (Ray, the Council, the DPAC) was in practice giving priority to good race relations though in theory all were dedicated to that cause. One evening, in an attempt to clear my mind, I wrote in my journal:

> Since most head teachers resent outside interference, and many distrust new ideas *per se*, is it wise for a LEA to insist on their abruptly adapting to the requirements of multi-cultural-cum-anti-racist education? NO
>
> Was Ray justified in criticising Bradford's new educational policies? YES.
>
> Had he used the correct channels to do so? NO
>
> Had his freedom of speech been unfairly threatened or curtailed? NO.
>
> Should an individual curtail his own freedom of speech, in the interests of common courtesy? YES.
>
> Was the DPAC's 'Honeyford Out!' campaign justified? YES
>
> Was it being run with due regard for good race relations in Bradford? NO

I soon felt mentally cross-eyed, through trying to see all viewpoints – which effort did not endear me to White Bradfordians. The majority were pro-Honeyford, a considerable minority were anti-Honeyford and both sides knew exactly what they thought – or, more often, felt. Honeyford was GOOD or BAD and no one was disposed to consider intermediate verdicts. Yet many Brown Bradfordians were, like myself, ambivalent about the whole affair – a fact which rarely seeped through into the national press.

Some of my Manningham neighbours, who had children at Drummond, denounced the DPAC for disrupting the school's routine. 'Honeyford Out!' seemed to them a dangerous rocking of two boats: the frail craft of Bradford's racial harmony and the even frailer craft (in permissive Britain) of respect for authority. They saw a headmaster as a respect-worthy figure whose authority should not be publicly undermined. Others had signed anti-Honeyford petitions or letters, when advised to do so, but admitted to having only a vague idea of what all the fuss was about.

Ray's virtues were more appreciated by the older generations. In several families the children would have beeen keen DPAC activists but for parental (sometimes grandparental) restraints. However, all schools no doubt have a percentage of pupils who would relish an anti-head campaign. There was much resentment of the fact that the Drummond interpreter – a Brown education welfare officer – was a Christian and so an unsuitable go-between in disputes centred on Islamic issues. (Although Browns are often criticised for not taking an interest in their children's schooling, they take far more interest than most White inner-city parents and are only prevented from showing it by the language barrier.) Many parents – not all DPAC supporters – complained about Ray's abrupt or dismissive manner, but the commonest reaction to it was sullen resignation.

All over Bradford many Browns agreed with Ray's anti-anti-racism. Drummond itself is not troubled by racialist behaviour but I met five Drummond parents, with older children at more mixed schools, who blamed the Council's anti-racist school policy for rising tension. They argued that White pupils from racialist homes are provoked by a policy which to them implies that the school authorities are anti-White; and such pupils know that they will have their family's sympathetic support if they relieve their feelings by attacking a Brown.

Opinions about Ray Honeyford varied not only from family to family but within families. One man resented an attempt to "intimidate" his son when the boy announced that he was going to Mirpur for three months; but his wife recalled Mr Honeyford's help when her husband was suddenly taken ill and she needed guidance through a tangle of DHSS forms. Also, attitudes were often determined or influenced by degrees of religious orthodoxy, or of actual or wished-for integration into British life.

Bradfordians of all colours indulged in fanciful speculations about who was *really* running the anti-Honeyford campaign. My own investigations satisfied me that there were no conspirators behind the DPAC scenes, that the organisers were what they seemed to be – a small group of parents who hated Ray because they believed him to be 'racist'. However, such conflicts invariably attract supporters from the Far Left and as the campaign continued these became so vocal that many onlookers (including myself, when a newcomer) mistook them for the instigators of 'Honeyford Out!' – forgetting the important distinction between *supporting* and *organising* a campaign.

During the second week of March 1985 the DPAC unnerved the Council by competently running an Alternative School at the Pakistani Community Centre for five days. It attracted over 200 of Drummond's 530 pupils, proving that the campaign had gained momentum during the winter recess. When the Council then looked at the wall it saw HONEYFORD MUST GO writ large.

On 22 March the Education Sub-committee met in the Council chamber, instead of in their usual room, to accommodate the crowd (local public and national media) who wished to attend this possibly decisive debate on the future of Ray Honeyford. The pro-Honeyfords tried to restrict the debate to Freedom of Speech. The anti-Honeyfords concentrated on the duty of a head teacher to implement Council policy. After six hours a motion of 'No Confidence in Mr Honeyford' was passed by eight votes to seven – i.e., The Rest versus the Tories. At last the Director of Education was in a legal position to dismiss his 'subversive' employee. Briefly – for about twelve hours – it seemed the affair was over.

Not so, however. Next morning the new Tory Chairman of the Education Committee, Mr Eric Pickles, condemned the vote as "Silly and juvenile . . . It will make the situation worse." He was right.

Ray's union – the National Association of Head Teachers (N A H T) – vowed to block any move to dismiss him. In the Commons, Mr Nicholas Winterton M P demanded that the government should defend him from 'further persecution'. White Bradfordians launched a 'Friends of Drummond' campaign, collected 10,000 signatures on a 'Defend Honeyford' petition and wrote sheaves of letters to Sir Keith Joseph, then Education Secretary. (Yet when Sir Keith visited Bradford University on 30 March he said he didn't know the details of the Honeyford dispute, which must be sorted out by the Council) *The Telegraph and Argus* letter-page became dangerously over-excited. One woman – with a sob in her pen – pointed out that a Bradford headmaster was being crucified for speaking the truth, as Jesus Christ had been crucified 2,000 years ago for the same reason. A *Times* leader ('Hunt the Heresy': 26 March) sounded no less demented but at least caused some mirth:

> Let us assume that the Head Teacher of the Drummond Middle School in Bradford is inefficient. There would have been ready signs long ago. Inspectors would be poking around; the annual pupil intake would be slipping as parents opted for other, better establishments; there would be staff-room dissension. The fact is, until last autumn, these revealing signs were absent: Drummond Middle School and its traditional disciplined approach was well-subscribed.

That ungrammatical leader-writer evidently imagined Manningham to be inhabited by *Times* readers who, if dissatisfied with their children's schools, could opt for 'better establishments'. And he had been misled by repeated references to Drummond's being 'heavily over-subscribed'. *All* Bradford's inner-city schools are heavily over-subscribed. As the Council noted in March 1985, 'A number of children in the inner-city areas have to attend a school other than that nearest to their home because of the pressure on school places . . . The authority hopes to open seven new schools in 1986.'

On 3 April Ray was suspended from duty on full pay to await the result of a Drummond Governors' inquiry into the whole affair. Because of his New Right-aided success in projecting the controversy as a Free Speech issue, the

Council was now trying to turn the spotlight away from his published writings and to prove enough 'professional incompetence' to justify dismissal. Their charge that he was not in tune with their educational policy has repeatedly been substantiated by Ray's own pen – for example, he believed that multi-cultural education, anti-racism and black studies had no place in an English school (*Daily Mail*, 18 December 1985).

Because of the national implications of the Honeyford Affair, Mr (now Sir) Marcus Fox, Tory M P for Shipley, was granted an adjournment debate in the Commons on 16 April. His pro-Honeyford account of the dispute was disgraceful; evidently he had not been fully briefed. Max Madden, the Bradford Labour M P, was not allowed time to make his anti-Honeyford speech but the *Telegraph and Argus* printed it in full. It was no less misleading than Sir Marcus's speech.

Meanwhile, on April Fools' Day, a Honeyford side-show had opened – put on by the Council's R A T officers.

Race Awareness Training, the craziest of all R R I ploys, was invented in the U S A. Judy Katz's handbook of 'Anti-Racism Training' – *White Awareness* – came out in 1978 and has been used by several British L E As, though the Swann Committee was warned that in America 'the trend in recent years has been away from specific Racism Awareness courses'. Using the 'power+prejudice+discrimination' definition of racism, R A T is based on the assumption that *all* Whites are racist but Browns and Blacks *cannot* be because in a White world they have no power. Whites who protest that they have never practised racial discrimination are told that they can't face the maggots of racism pullulating in their subconscious.

R A T 'workshop facilitators' run five-day courses devoted to 'unlearning and dismantling racism'. First the students – or patients – must be made to recognise and confess their own racism, then they must submit to having it cured. Many trainers are truculent Blacks or Browns and their displays of anti-White aggression form part of the therapy.

The lunacy of this enterprise must be apparent to anyone who stops for ten seconds to think about the psychology of the average British teacher – or councillor, or whatever. Their racial prejudice is a gut-reaction for which they are most unlikely to want any 'cure', least of all one that involves being personally abused by angry Blacks and Browns paid out of public funds. A committee to worsen race relations could contrive nothing more effective than a R A T course. Yet the Swann Report solemnly proclaimed: 'We believe there is an urgent need for research into the various Racism Awareness training programmes which have been devised so far and we would like to see the D E S funding an independent evaluation of the content and effectiveness of such courses.'

Thus are the wheels of the RRI kept turning. But it is monstrously irresponsible to urge the D E S to squander funds on such an 'evaluation' when in many inner-city schools three children have to share one textbook.

Bradford's RAT courses then had as 'workshop facilitators' members of the Black Checkpoint organisation and of Al-falah, the Islamic Youth Mission. These courses were compulsory for all Council staff – including head teachers – who interview and select employees. Anyone not 'race-trained' forfeited his or her right to have a say in staff appointments.

On 1 April (one would like to think the date was not a coincidence) a confidential memorandum from seven RAT officers to senior Council officials was leaked to the press by a person or persons unknown. It said:

> We believe that we cannot allow Ray Honeyford to attend a recruitment and selection course . . . To train him would give him credibility and power to recruit and show the Council to be colluding with a known racist . . . Given the racist views he has expressed a five-day course will not change him or make him anti-racist. Bradford's black community is losing confidence in the Council's policy. Those who implement it have to reflect community views and to train Honeyford would be a gross insult to a large percentage of Bradford's population.

The notion of Islamic Youth Missionaries and Black radicals 'training' Ray has a piquancy all its own. And, in view of the RAT doctrine that *all* Whites are racist, the illogic of the officers' position was no less diverting.

Ray sought a retraction of the 'known racist' accusation, plus an apology and libel damages. Two months later his union was seeking a High Court action because of the RAT officers' refusal to 'train' him but the case was not pursued. No wonder the 'anti-racist zealots' have gained a disproportionate influence in some areas. Their antics are taken far too seriously. That RAT memo was unworthy of Ray's attention – or anybody else's. It should have been dismissed as nonsense by the officials and local party leaders to whom it was sent and ignored by the media. Those who most loudly lament the power of the anti-racist lobby often strengthen it by over-reacting to trivial incidents – matters for laughter rather than for High Court actions.

As the Honeyford Affair became more embittered *facts* became more elusive and allegations went whirling across the scene like litter on a windy day.

On 12 April 1985 it emerged in the *TES* that that journal had rejected 'Education and Race – An Alternative View', though it had previously published a few Honeyford articles. This seemed to contradict Ray's statement exactly a year earlier (*Telegraph and Argus*, 13 April 1984) that he had chosen to submit it to the *Salisbury Review* because: 'I don't like intimidation any more than anybody else and the race relations zealots have created such an intolerant intellectual climate around these issues that I was trying to avoid publicity.'

On all sides, accuracy was a conspicuous casualty of the Honeyford Affair. On 30 March Sir Keith Joseph had explained – "My powers of intervention are extremely limited." Yet on 23 April his schools minister, Mr Bob Dunn, told the Commons that Sir Keith was making detailed inquiries into the Honeyford Affair under Section 68 of the 1944 Education Act, which empowers an Education Secretary to intervene in such controversies if he judges an LEA or Governing Body to have acted unreasonably.

The government was now openly on Ray's side, following his post-suspension defence in the Tory press as 'Decent Man Cruelly Hounded by Bigoted Muslims and Rabid Trots' – an interpretation of events that aroused perfervid nationwide support for Drummond's head, much of it inspired by raw racial prejudice. Now all good Tories had to be seen to be pro-Honeyford. Wide publicity was given to Sir Keith Joseph's keen interest in the fate of the 'Persecuted Head' and Bradford Council's all-party co-operation on race relations collapsed under the strain.

Because the pro-Honeyford lobby was rapidly gaining strength, Bradford's anti-racist groups united (for once) in an effort to organise a massive anti-Honeyford demonstration on 21 June – the eve of the Drummond Governors' hearing.

*   *   *

Back in Bradford on 20 June, after a three-week absence, I sensed increasing tension. People were longing for the Honeyford Affair to go away, literally at any price. One Brown friend commented, "The race relations boat has been so badly rocked, it's half full of water."

One doesn't love Bradford for its climate. Midsummer's Day, 1985, was marked by a strong swirling wind and cold drenching rain beneath the city's usual lid of Pennine cloud. But sunshine would probably not have augmented the anti-Honeyford turn-out. For complex political reasons, with which I won't detain us, the Honeyford Protest Committee, whose birth I witnessed on 12 May, had subsequently disintegrated and failed to attract any new support from outside (or inside) Bradford 8.

We assembled near the Pakistani Community Centre at 3.00 p.m., when Muslims return from their Friday prayers at the mosques; most of the marchers were young Brown men who might be described as 'professional' street politicians. The policing was excellent: enough, but not a provocative presence. I walked beside the escorting police van, pausing at intervals to watch everyone pass and note down slogans – 'We Want Education, We Get Racism!' – 'We Pay the Council, the Council Pays Hunniford!' – 'Don't Divide Bradford!' – 'The Governors Don't Represent US!' – 'Axe Hunniford!' That last banner was ominously decorated with a skilful drawing of an axe.

The crowd chanted so loudly and angrily that between high buildings they sounded like 4,000 rather than 400. "Honeyford *out!* OUT! OUT! Honeyford *out!* OUT! OUT!" Listening to this rhythmic hymn of hate, I felt a sick despair. What could be more inflaming to British racial prejudice than Brown marchers howling against a White? When two youths passed me I overheard one saying, "Gimme a razor an' I'd have their balls!" In the city centre an elderly White couple stood in a shop entrance, adjusting their umbrella. The scowling husband muttered something I couldn't hear, his wife smiled tolerantly and said, "But they're only savages!" Outside the City Hall I paused to talk to a young man who was clutching a briefcase and staring narrow-eyed at the marchers. He said, "We've got to remember something – it's taken us two thousand years to get civilised and fifty years ago that lot were still running round in loin-cloths! You gotta give 'em *time!*"

Like all Bradford's demos, this took place in the shadow of Police Head-quarters. (When the city centre was being rebuilt in the 1970s was it deliberately designed thus, with discreet policing in mind?) A few moist and grumpy-looking media people were sheltering on a raised pedestrian walk, overlooking the assembly place with its ornamental pond. As I stood near them, scribbling a few notes, a tight-lipped old lady – tiny, like so many Bradfordians of her generation – paused beside me and peered down at the chanting throng. She lowered her umbrella and said without preamble. "Sixty-seven years ago I left school – age of ten – into the mill. We knew all about 'ardship then! No grumbles over wages or we'd 'ave our fathers at us with a stick. I wouldn't vote for any party nowadays – not one of 'em! All soft! I'll not vote again till they bring back 'angin'! Whichever brings back 'angin', I'll vote for . . . The murders today – summat *'orrible!* With all them coloureds around, there's nothin' for it but 'angin'. Would they murder us in our beds if we'd 'angin'? I'd 'ang all savages – all them down there tormentin' that poor schoolmaster! Bradford was a decent place till they come. We'd lots of forners but they was decent quiet folk, not forever makin' trouble!"

I am not aware that any White Bradfordian has ever been murdered in his/her bed by a Brown; the reverse is much more likely. But before I had time to debate this point the old lady moved on.

As the speeches began I counted the marchers below me: 420 – hardly a mass-demo in a city with 62,000 Browns. There were eleven speakers: six Pakistanis, two Bangladeshis, one Hindu, one Sikh and one White. The Bangladeshi chairman, Mr C.M. Khan, was effective to the extent that he curbed the would-be rabble-rousers. Despite their efforts, and the high percentage of Angry Young (Brown) Men in the audience, everyone dispersed quietly at 5.45 – as they almost certainly would not have done, on a similar occasion, if White. Bradford's Browns are an inherently law-abiding com-munity.

I sought solace then in the Victoria Hotel bar, frequented by middle-class Whites, where a youngish businessman and his wife sympathised with my rain-soaked condition. (Bradfordians are like that.) When I had explained it, the wife sighed and wondered. "Why do we have to put up with them swarming all over our streets abusing that nice man? I think Mr Honeyford's *reely* nice!"

"It's a democracy," her husband pointed out, "so if you tried to stop them swarming they'd riot!"

Wife shrugged. "The *English* will riot if Mr Honeyford has to go! The Council won't be able to hold down their teachers – most of them are behind him."

"It annoys me", said husband, "when people say Bradford has an *Asian* problems. We don't – we have a *Muslim* problem. Mr Honeyford understands that. Those others – Hindus and Sikhs and so on – they're coloured too but they don't fuss all the time about their religion. With the Muslims it's all fuss. No school uniforms, must have halal meat, demanding separate schools, no swimming for girls, no music or dancing for anyone, just being awkward all the time. Why shouldn't Mr Honeyford try to knock some sense into them? Whose country is it anyway?"

"The worst trouble-makers", said wife, "are all those mosque fellas – the old boys who go round in pyjamas and lock up their wives. When they're out of the way everything will improve. They just don't want to merge in. It suits them to keep up the old ways. *All* men like to have their women under control!"

Husband then had a rush of tolerance to the brain. "Telly's done a lot of harm. When they see all those dirty American films they think that's the way we live too and they want to protect their girls. I went to a Council meeting when they were debating halal meat and things nearly got very rough but some of those old boys cooled it. Maybe the kids would be worse if they weren't treated tough by their elders."

'Well," said wife, "I just hope those Governors put that nice man back in his job!"

After a four-day hearing, a Drummond Governors' recommendation recognising Ray Honeyford's 'educational contribution', stating that 'the allegations against him have not been fully [sic] substantiated', and requesting his reinstatement *under the supervision of LEA officers*, was passed by only a narrow majority. Before the hearing all White Governors (except Jenny) received copies of Ray's *Salisbury Review* articles from the NAHT, with covering notes pointing out how innocuous these were. However, some of the pro-Honeyford Governors who had not previously read the articles disagreed with the NAHT judgement and became anti-Honeyford at voting time.

The Council's right to continue disciplinary action after the Governors' verdict was disputed by the NAHT, who sought a High Court injunction to prevent its doing so. They wanted Ray reinstated unconditionally, not merely for a further probationary period.

On 5 September Mr Justice Simon Brown pronounced in the High Court, "Once the school Governors decided against recommending dismissal, that precludes any further disciplinary process on the offences alleged. That situation means the teacher's suspension must fall.' The education officers then reinstated Ray, pending the hearing of their appeal against this judgement. On 16 September he returned to Drummond under police protection –

arriving at 7.30 a.m., three-quarters of an hour before a very angry D P A C picket of 200 chanting parents, pupils and supporters. Out of 530 pupils, fewer than 200 registered that day. There was a mini-scuffle as police kept the gateway clear for 'strike-breakers' to enter. Some children approached the school but, on seeing the picket, nervously retreated. Later, the Council warned that parents who failed to send their children to school could face prosecution.

The picketing continued all week and the D P A C said it would stop only when Ray Honeyford had been re-suspended. On 21 September I telephoned – from Handsworth – a Brown Bradfordian friend who reckoned the situation was dangerously out of control, with the Council taking no action against Brown law-breaking parents and tough elements within the White population daily becoming angrier. He said, "The only solution is for Honeyford to go voluntarily. But he won't until the settlement is right, which it can't be until the D P A C and Labour quit their 'no-reward-for-a-racist' policy. How much closer to the brink must we move before they give in?' Next day a D P A C press release suggested that they too were alarmed by the extent to which their campaign had run out of control:

> Various quarters have urged us to cool it . . . therefore, as a sign of good faith, the parents have agreed to suspend the boycott for two weeks . . . During this past week Bradford has been sitting on a time-bomb. This issue has divided the city. We have stepped back from the edge. There is a fourteen-day breathing space. The ball is now in the Council's court. If there is no light at the end of the tunnel after two weeks we will feel we have been forced by Council indifference onto the streets again. We urge that all parties take swift action to avert the lighting of the fuse of the time-bomb we are all sitting on.

This frenetic mixing of cliché metaphors – people sitting on time-bombs in tunnels throwing balls into courts – indicated that Jenny, whose literary ability exceeds that of many published writers, was no longer producing the D P A C press statements.

As 420 Drummond pupils passed through the school gates on the following Monday, they received anti-Honeyford stickers to be worn in their class-rooms saying 'Honeyford Out' and 'Ray-C I S T'. They were also given a contemptible leaflet:

DRUMMOND PARENTS ACTION COMMITTEE
Pupils Charter
Pupils you are engaged in a historic struggle to remove Ray Honeyford, your headmaster. Why? Because he has insulted your religion, and your culture. He has insulted your parents. That's why you have been on strike. On Monday you will be back at school, but the fight goes on. You have a part to play.

1 Do not be intimidated by the strike-breakers.

2 Do not be intimidated by Mr Honeyford. If he attempts to punish you report it to your parents or someone from the Action Committee. We will prosecute him.

3 We have no argument with your teachers, respect them. But if you see Mr Honeyford let your views be known. Honeyford Out!

4 There will be further half-day strikes.

5 Knock! Knock!
  Q Whose [sic] there?
  A Ray
  Q Ray Who?
  A Ray CIST
Do you have any more jokes about him? Let us know if you do.

Even ardent anti-Honeyfords (of the non-militant variety) condemned this leaflet. How many of these pupils will be mindlessly rioting on the streets of Bradford in five or ten years time? No doubt that is the ambition of whoever produced the 'Pupils Charter'. Jenny had had no part in its composition, but naturally enough most people blamed her for it. Between Far Left pressures on the DPAC and New Right pressures on the Council, the wretched Drummond pupils and their families were being squeezed to pulp.

On 27 September I returned to Bradford with a Mirpuri friend from Small Heath. Anslam was driving up to stay with a sister in Manningham whose husband had suddenly been called to Pakistan. Her daughter was at Drummond and because of the tension she feared being left 'without a man in the house'. (The daughter's verdict on her headmaster was shrewd: "Mr Honeyford tries to make us think like Christians even though he knows our parents want us to be good Muslims.")

Anslam collected me at 7.00 a.m. in the sort of car I like: fourteen years old and unable to achieve more than thirty m.p.h. unless going downhill. My fellow-passenger was an elderly White anti-racist named Milly, a fundamentalist Christian and fiercely anti-Honeyford. Strange bed-fellows are to be found in the anti-racist camp; manic Marxists and compulsive Bible-quoters.

The 'Pupils Charter' had angered Anslam; he thought it "sinful" to incite children to mock and abuse their head teacher. "It would be different if that man was a criminal – if he stole money, or drank so much he couldn't do his job, or played bad games with little boys. But fighting with the Council about education and being rude about other cultures isn't a *crime!*"

Anslam – like many others – wondered why the rest of Drummond's staff were seen as respect-worthy, despite their collaborating for four years with a 'racist' head. It was of course easier to isolate one man as the villain – Racism Incarnate! – and focus everyone's destructive energies on him.

Subsequently Jenny and I corresponded about the organisation of the anti-Honeyford campaign. She felt I was being 'grossly patronising towards the Mirpuri community', reminded me that I had never attended a DPAC meeting and asked:

Do you honestly believe that adult men and women would *allow* themselves to be organised along lines they found objectionable? By a foreigner? . . . From the inception of the D P A C and my election as chair, meetings were held weekly, sometimes twice weekly with parents. These were lengthy and verbose sessions, often lasting several hours, simply because each item had to be translated, discussed, agreed upon or not. In order to run a campaign effectively you have to have majority agreement otherwise your campaign fails at the starting-post. And this common agreement has to be sustained throughout . . . For you to suggest (as did the media) that 'all-these-peasants-were-told-what-to-do-and-say-by-White-socialists' is not only utter nonsense but incredibly insulting to the majority of parents who were involved in regular meetings and the taking of decisions at those meetings.

I stood corrected on the functioning of the D P A C. Yet many conversations in several cities have convinced me that most anti-racist campaigns worry most British Browns. The majority are well aware of the advantages of life in the U K; otherwise they wouldn't have settled in Britain and there would be no 'immigration control problem'. To emphasise this point is risky; such comments are often quoted out of context by racialists. Yet anti-racist attitudes and activities are at present doing so much damage that it seems essential to try to keep the matter in perspective.

Many stoical, pragmatic Browns and Blacks choose to seem to ignore racial prejudice because they have carefully considered how best to cope with their 'small-minority status' in Britain. Anti-racists scorn this 'cowardly' compromise. But as a direct result of the Honeyford Affair racialist attacks on Bradford's Browns increased dramatically, suggesting that a heads-below-the-parapet choice may for the moment be the right one.

On 27 September my first Manningham reunion was with an English-speaking family whose two older children were at Drummond. Both parents appreciated the school's Anglicising influence while deploring what they termed the head's 'insults'. Previously ambivalent about the D P A C campaign, they had been supporting it since Ray's reinstatement – generally seen as final proof that constitutional methods could never work. At the father's first D P A C meeting, a fortnight earlier, more than 200 enraged parents – many newcomers, like himself – voted almost unanimously for the picket and boycott.

At my next stop the youngest boy, a frail and timid ten-year-old, had been terrified when he tried to go to school on 17 September and was hunted home "by one of those Communists" – his father's description. (The 'Communist' in question is a committed socialist but also a devout Muslim; many Mirpuris, like many Irish, have trouble distinguishing between communism and socialism.) This family, though critical of some pickets' tactics, had recently been thinking things over and concluded – "There will only be trouble till Honeyford goes." They seemed unclear about the origins of the affair but were now resolved to go along with the D P A C "to end it all quickly because it's upsetting our children very much." By the end of September many families were in this mood. Yet they found it stressful when lively children were at home on wet boycott days and the loss of cheap school dinners was wrecking precariously balanced budgets. So an effective resumption of the boycott, post-truce, seemed unlikely; and it was feared that dwindling parental support might provoke more belligerent picketing. The police could not ignore attacks on strike-breakers' parents and the consequences of arrests outside Drummond were only too predictable. Throughout Bradford there was by then a feeling of desperation: among pro- and anti-Honeyfords, Council officials, local politicians, teachers, clergymen, policemen and the general public.

A new element in the affair alarmed me. It was being seen as 'a matter of honour' (Mirpuri style) by a small group of very angry young men and Ray was in more danger than the Council seemed to realise. His 'insults' had always been the mainspring of the psyops campaign to arouse anti-Honeyford feeling: for eighteen months he had been accused every day of 'insulting' Islam and Pakistan and the local Mirpuris. Thus 'Honeyford who insulted us' had come to loom large, as a challenge, in the consciousness of certain emotional young Mirpuris – and reinstatement was seen as yet another 'insult' to their community.

It is difficult to take this kind of thing seriously in modern England, where an insult is no longer a matter of life or death. We may feel resentful or vengeful or take a libel or slander action. But we don't think of washing away with blood stains on our honour. Some Mirpuris do. To them a man who has insulted their religion, parents, community and country is a *legitimate* target. And this is a deep-rooted tradition, not the sort that withers within a generation or two of settling in the more temperate climate of England. On more than one occasion, newly arrived immigrants have been knifed to death to avenge insults inflicted twenty or thirty years ago in Azad Kashmir.

On Monday 30 September the DPAC ran a one-day mid-truce school boycott, to prevent the campaign from losing impetus, and as Ray arrived the crowd released its ritual howl of hate. He was a brave man to withstand this sort of thing day after day and his apparent unflappability irritated the Brown pickets. Being used to getting strong emotional reactions from each other, they were narked by their inability to make any visible impression on British phlegm.

It disturbed me to think of the possible effects of this prolonged campaign on some children's development. In theory these pupils were merely being taught how to oppose racialism, but I was sickened by the extent to which they had been encouraged to feel and express hatred for one individual.

Later I said to Jenny, "How can such unthinking 'confrontation politics' solve anything? In a nuclear-threatened, propaganda-sodden world, isn't it essential to teach children to study *all* sides of a controversy?'

To which she replied, "Isn't that precisely the reasoning behind the DPAC campaign? That Honeyford refused to look at all sides and insisted on the British view alone? Those children whom you describe as being cruelly indoctrinated on the picket line know a great deal more about the campaign than you do! They after all know Honeyford the *headmaster*."

I saw her point. But unhappily such campaigns often build up their own sinister momentum, leading to developments never intended by the original organisers. Without intense emotional commitment no one would ever do anything to improve our world, yet justice and compassion evaporate when campaigners fail to strike a balance between feeling and thinking. And then their cause, however worthy, is discredited.

When I left Bradford that evening tension had been further heightened by news of Mrs Thatcher's invitation to Ray Honeyford to attend 'a private discussion of leading educationalists' on 2 October at No. 10 Downing Street. This bizarre *faux pas* would have seemed funny if Bradford were not already, in its Chief Executive's words, "sitting on a powder-keg". Many Bradfordians of all colours regard Mrs Thatcher as the greatest disaster to have hit Britain since the Black Death – and, as the *Daily Express* noted, 'The Prime Minister, with her invitation to Downing Street, has signalled that she sympathises with Mr Honeyford.'

All the teachers' unions, including the NAHT, condemned the invitation. Mr David Hart said, "the timing is not good. The situation is highly emotional in Bradford. Ray was as surprised as anyone by the invitation. I advised him to keep quiet about it but someone else must have told the press." The Labour Party spokesman on education, Giles Radice MP, summed up the general reaction – even among Honeyford supporters – when he wrote to Mrs Thatcher urging her to withdraw the invitation and describing it as 'frankly ridiculous'.

On 2 October, while Ray was contributing his mite to the No. 10 educational think-tank, three Brown anti-Honeyford parents were being elected to Drummond's new Governing Body. The previous Governing Body's reinstatment recommendation had determined the High Court's ruling; a contrary vote by the new Body could lead to Ray's dismissal. But that Body's full membership would not be known until 15 October, when it met to co-opt three community representatives who would bring the total to fourteen, including Ray. No one could guess who the ten Governors (three Brown parents, three Drummond teachers, two Tory and two Labour councillors) would co-opt.

The DPAC declared 15 October a Day of Action and the Council for Mosques directed all Bradford's Muslim pupils to boycott their schools on that date. A one-day sympathy strike of all Council employees was (unrealistically) hoped for; an afternoon march around Manningham was planned – and an evening mass-demo outside Drummond to mark the start of the Governor's meeting. The national media were put on red alert. The police put themselves on red alert. On 14 October I returned to Bradford.

After the election of three D P A C Governors – who had massive majorities for the second year running – it was no longer possible to claim that the D P A C represented only a cranky parental fringe plus Lefties. Yet many Manningham Browns remained critical of the whole campaign. On the afternoon of 14 October one young Mirpuri, standing behind the counter of the family shop near Drummond Road, complained: "All this will divide Manningham's Muslims for years to come and we need to be united. Half the parents who've been keeping kids away don't understand what it's all about. And most of those pickets don't know how or why it started – they're just layabouts looking for a bit of fun. I see them standing out there chatting and when the media come they tidy their clothes and comb their hair and go marching off to be televised. They don't belong here. I was born in Manningham and I've never seen most of them before. They're just making trouble for an area they don't live in. If we hadn't so many cameras around the whole thing would've died down long ago. I've had six cousins through Drummond since Honeyford came and they'd no complaints. He's done a lot to improve the facilities for Muslims, especially girls. But once a man makes a mistake everyone forgets the good things he did. A few fanatics who had it in for him stirred up all this trouble and the Council couldn't handle it. They should have sacked him when they suspended him, or else said they'd never sack him. When he was suspended this lot thought they'd won – then he came back and they went mad with anger. Now we could have riots here – this shop could be burnt down around me. It's the wrong time for crowds and marching. The kids all over Britain are just looking for trouble – they get all excited watching riots on telly. Tomorrow I'm closing this place even if I lose business – anything could happen . . .'

Ten minutes later, at a bus-stop on Manningham Lane, I watched two White Council workers erasing graffiti on a nearby wall. It said, below a large swastika, 'Pabio – N F Keep Britain Tidy – kill a wog or a jew a day – Oi'.

Beside me stood a unformed Mirpuri bus-driver, going to the Interchange to start his evening shift. We got into conversation and I remarked that in Bradford racialist graffiti is never allowed to survive long on city-centre walls. He looked at me sadly and said: "We don't need to see it written. We get it shouted at us every day – 'Paki go home!' More now – *much* more since all this Drummond trouble got so bad. Yesterday a man getting off the bus spat in my face. That happens a lot now. We feel it very much. It hurts when you know a lot of the people all around want to get rid of you, even though you're just quietly doing your job. I'm twenty years in Bradford and I'm lucky, I was never on security. I've always worked and paid my rates and taxes and bought my own house – my brother and me, we bought it together. My five children were born here and I'm bringing them up good Bradfordians. I tell them when they leave school they should take any job, even if they think it's not good enough, to keep off security. They'll never see Pakistan, I won't waste money sending them out. Why do they keep shouting 'Paki go home!' when Bradford is our home? How could I take my family back? They are British with British tastes and used to good schools and health care and so on. We're very well treated by the State – this country has a fair government. Even if the public turns more against us we *can't* leave! I couldn't do that to my children – it's too late now to force us out!"

I could think of nothing to say and was glad the bus came then. Had that Brown Bradfordian shown anger it would have been easier. Instead, he was close to tears.

On the other side of the city, in a tough Eccleshill pub with a BNP rally advertisement behind the bar, I found the air red-white-and-blue with sadistic racialism.

"I'd slash their dirty throats!" said one man.

"A few hundred petrol bombs would look after Manningham's rat-holes!" said another.

"Right – fry the rats!" said a third.

That exhortation brought the witticism – "If we'd a few more niggers here they'd fry each other, same as they did in Handsworth!"

British racialism can be literally nauseating. Listening for two hours to those men – aged eighteen to eighty – I remembered Jenny's hate-mail. It was then coming daily from all over Britain and those White reactions to her 'siding with the Pakis' smelt of Nazi concentration camps. A few months previously the police had warned her of a planned acid-attack; but it would take more than NF threats to deflect Jenny from her course. She and Ray have at least one thing in common – unflappability.

The then Lord Mayor, Mohammed Ajeeb, also received extra hate-mail after he broke his vow of silence about the Honeyford Affair by criticising the Council for reinstating Ray. Some letters were so pornographic that his Town Hall staff did not allow him to see them but handed them straight to the police. Many obscene telephone calls were made to his wife and sixteen-year-old daughter and the family home was repeatedly stoned.

Such psychopathic behaviour is never duplicated on the anti-racist side, which partly explains why most moderates, if forced to choose, would turn left. Some argue that these manifestations of racial hatred should be dismissed as mere symptoms of a way-out neurosis and two years ago I would have agreed. Now I see it all quite differently. Those who wrote to Jenny or Mohammed Ajeeb (and hate-mail comes from every social class) are of course unrepresentative in their lack of self-control – their display of fanaticism. But personal experience has taught me that they are expressing the feelings, suppressed but influential, of a large section of the British public. This is an ugly fact. Yet it is not safe to evade it.

The DPAC's encounters with the media were repeatedly distorted by the interventions of one Mr Amin Qureshi, who was devoted both to the liberation of Kashmir and to the downfall of Ray Honeyford. He was *not* a Drummond parent, though from the start the DPAC had unwisely and inexplicably tolerated him as a spokesman. This was a disastrous error. Because of the DPAC, emphasis on being controlled by *parents*, everyone (including myself) mistook Mr Qureshi for one of the campaign leaders. And because of his regular media appearances he soon came to represent, in the eyes of the Great British Public, 'Bradford's typical Paki parent'. Mr Qureshi's prominence throughout the campaign did an injustice to the 'typical' Drummond parent and inspired extra sympathy for Ray ("Poor man! Fancy having to cope every day with parents like *that!*")

The end of the Honeyford Affair also ended Mr Qureshi's career as a TV star. But in April 1986 he returned to Bradford's headlines in a new and startling role.

'Row over the Man who Met Gadaffi!' exclaimed the *Telegraph and Argus*. And there again was the familiar if not very well-loved face of Mr Qureshi, beside an account of how 'a leader of the campaign to oust head-master Ray Honeyford was among a 40-strong delegation from Britain that went to Libya for a four-day conference. All expenses on the trip for jobless Mr Qureshi (57) were paid for by the Libyan government. Mr Qureshi defen-ded Gadaffi: "If somebody helps the oppressed nations to get them freedom and equality, he will always be the target of capitalism and imperialism. Gadaffi was elected by the conference as the leader of all oppressed nations." '

This news item briefly convulsed Bradford and Mr Qureshi's compatriots frantically disowned him. Mohammed Ajeeb solemnly dissociated the City of Bradford from the visit. Councillor Abdul Hameed, Chairman of the CRC (of which Mr Qureshi is – or was then – a member), suggested that he should go and live in Tripoli – an excellent suggestion subsequently echoed in several letters to the *Telegraph and Argus*. Mr Qureshi then explained that he had been invited to Tripoli not as a representative of the anti-Honeyford cam-paign but as general secretary of the Azad Kashmir Muslim Association. This seemed reasonable, since Colonel Gadaffi is unlikely to have heard of the Honeyford Affair. But Ray's supporters were not impressed. They remembered that by the summer of 1985 most anti-Honeyford activists were not 'average' Drummond parents. Open Far Left support for the DPAC had increased in proportion to open New Right support for Ray.

By 15 October (the Day of Action to mark the co-option of three Gov-ernors) Mr Qureshi had become, as it were, a television anti-hero. Without his histrionics and laying on of angry hands, camera-crews covering the many demonstrations would have had little to make their journeys worth while. Each picket found him by the school gates, scowling and waving his arms and shouting – "These are all my childrens!!", a claim which drew predictable witticisms from the media-men. But his *pièce de résistance* came during a television interview: "*We're Mirpuris! We're* not interested in Freedom of Speech! *We* don't have any of that!"

At 7.45 a.m. on 15 October media people were swarming outside Drummond, pens and cameras at the ready. It was a mild, dry autumn morning: good 'protest' weather. The hundred-strong picket included the usual platoon of banner-bearing schoolboys, seven 'Socialist Workers' (their banner said) and twenty-six rowdy Rank-and-File Bradford teachers who were observing the Day of Action in defiance of the N U T. Theoretically all outside support was welcome but the stewards – responsible young Brown men, anxious to prevent violence – privately deplored the presence of these aggressive Whites.

As Ray's car approached, the ritual chanting, led by a thirteen-year-old, gained in volume and menace. Ray looked less insouciant than usual: in fact almost scared. So would I have been, in his position. The picket pointedly ignored the arrival of the rest of the staff. Only 183 pupils broke the strike and their appearance was the morning's flash-point. In preparation, the senior police officer at the school gate moved all pickets to the far side of the road, except for three Mirpuri members of the D P A C – and Amin Qureshi.

I was standing beside Mr Qureshi when he grabbed the arm of a White woman – Eileen Iqbal, an old adversary of his married to a Mirpuri – as she escorted a bewildered Brown schoolgirl towards the gate. Eager microphones were thrust towards his angry shouts and I dodged to one side as grateful cameramen zoomed in on this meagre excitement. Eileen Iqbal's confrontations with Amin Qureshi are part of the Manningham scene – mere neighbourly friction. Yet throughout the day news programmes repeatedly showed that "violent incident", thus giving a totally false impression of the Drummond Road atmosphere.

Soon after, a message came to the police about a sixteen-year-old girl in a nearby street. Her younger brother and sister were ready to go to school but two men waiting outside the house had threatened to smash their faces if they emerged. Both parents had gone to work; eldest sister wished to go to her own school but couldn't leave the children alone all day . . . Before long those siblings appeared, apparently unescorted, and were booed and hissed as they scuttled into the playground.

At noon about 500 marchers moved off into the Carlisle Road, led by a Brown youth bellowing "Honeyford Out!" through a megaphone. Most of the banners were hysterically vicious. One depicted Ray as a devil with horns, sitting writing at a desk below the legend: 'Honeyford writes with the blood of Blacks – D E V I L O U T!' Then there were 'Razism out!' and 'Bradford is not South Africa' – which last prompted a young *Yorkshire Post* reporter to mutter, "Indeed not! In South Africa that lot would have been locked up for good a year ago!"

Our route was confined to Manningham, to avoid possible N F attacks; we were accompanied by a few cops on motor-bikes while a police-van brought up the rear. The small boys carrying banners were followed by a line of unsmiling mosque elders with long beards, skull caps and baggy pantaloons.

Many of the over-excited schoolboys were naturally in an unruly mood, pushing and squabbling among themselves, attempting to dart into front gardens, casting predatory eyes on fruit displays outside greengroceries and occasionally converging on parked cars with intent to do damage. But the stewards maintained law and order forcefully; their methods, if used by White policemen or teachers, would be described in anti-racist circles as 'brutal assaults on innocent Asian children'.

At one street junction an OAP Council bus stopped to let us pass and a gang of youths pushed towards it yelling "Racist scum!" and "Tory bastards!" while giving the Harvey Smith sign. Three laughing old ladies with neatly permed white hair cheered me up no end by returning that sign, but several of their male companions were unamused and angrily banged on the windows. Later the same gang hammered on the side of a stationary double-decker while the White passengers stared out impassively and one elderly henna-bearded Mirpuri berated them from the bus door.

Some journalists were astonished to discover that Manningham was not flushed with 'Honeyford Out!' fervour. Many Browns smiled at the marchers, or waved or cheered. But most ignored this noisy demo with its entourage of uncomprehending media folk. In narrow cobbled alleyways between back-to-backs I glimpsed *dupatti*-draped wives peering nervously from behind garden walls or through half-curtained windows; some rushed out to collect toddlers, then slammed their doors. Brown youths knocked threateningly on shop windows, unsuccessfully urging fellow-Browns to join the demo. Manningham's few remaining White shopkeepers were tight-lipped and hard-eyed. At intervals the banner-bearing schoolboys – by now expert media collaborators – paused to arrange themselves suitably for the benefit of TV crews.

Back at Drummond one of the three new parent-governors, Nazim Naqui, addressed the crowd in English, emphasising that the Day of Action was not 'a left-wing plot' but had been organised because the Council refused to co-operate with the DPAC when they tried to remove Ray Honeyford 'through constitutional means, using the proper channels'. Then, in Punjabi, he begged the crowd to allow no violent incident to mar the day.

I spent the afternoon wandering along the march route gathering reactions – which involved buying a wide variety of objects for which I could think of no possible use.

"I don't like that Honeyford man," said one Lahore-born merchant, "but Amin Qureshi's no better! Our children and grandchildren will suffer for this. They shouldn't have noticed Honeyford. Let him write that he wanted – who reads his kind of thing? All this has killed good race relations in our city – and people like me, we started out from Pakistan but now we *do* feel Bradford is our city. That's why I felt angry and sad today, watching the crowd out there on the street. They haven't worked to get accepted like we did. They've always had it too easy. Not that it's all their fault. Look at that Woodward woman and Goldberg and all those Labour Councillors who should know better and even the MP. I was shocked seeing Max Madden with that mob. He'll lose votes that way – there's still more Whites than Asians in Bradford!"

That merchant was echoed by six others, men who have spent years quietly establishing themselves as respectable Manningham citizens and resent the behaviour of untypical Browns whose activities can be used to justify antagonism to all 'Pakis'.

The White reactions were standard.

"Who the fuck do they think they are, trying to tell us how to run our schools?"

"I'd sweep all darkies into the gutter where they belong!"

"Why don't they shut their mouths and be thankful *we're* paying for their bloody swarming kids to get free schooling? There's no schools where *they* come from!"

"Why shouldn't a man say what he thinks? This used to be a free country till all them buggers arrived – now people are afraid to speak their mind – afraid they'll be pushed out of their jobs by one of them mobs!"

"They're no better than wild animals running loose around the streets – like they were back in their jungles!"

By then I should have been used to such comments. But that afternoon's blind, mindless hatred left me feeling physically queasy.

Walking up Carlisle Road through the twilight I overtook groups of angry youths also on their way to the demo outside Drummond and already yelling – "Honeyford *out!*", "Ray-CIST!" During a long Day of Action, when minds are all the time focused on one object of hatred, vengefulness has too much time to reach boiling point. On the Drummond Road the atmosphere now felt very nasty indeed. At least 200 young men had arrived early and many more were quickly assembling. Teenagers and small boys were climbing onto the playground wall and violently shaking the railings while a few policemen strolled casually to and fro within.

Most pro-Honeyfords were already inside the school but Mrs Mubarik Iqbal had not yet arrived and schoolboys were watching for her car. Mrs Mubarik Iqbal lived in another district and her pro-Honeyford letters to newspapers were famous/notorious. A Punjabi, she has little time for Mirpuris and had told me a few months previously – "I wouldn't send *my* children to Drummond! That school has too many Asians!" The candidature of such an unsuitable representative for the Manningham community had done much to raise the temperature. When her car arrived a swarm of abusively screaming schoolboys surrounded it, banging on the bonnet and blocking her way into the playground. She was quickly rescued by the Brown stewards – the police standing alert but inactive close behind them. Bitter jeers followed her through the gateway.

About 150 parents expected to be admitted to the meeting, as was their legal right. When it was announced that there would be room for only sixty, because media people were taking up so much space, a tidal wave of rage seemed to lift the entire crowd towards the school building. Beside me a Pakistani sociologist from London exclaimed – "This is it!" But it wasn't. Some Brown leaders – I couldn't see or hear who – restored enough order to ensure that the school would not be invaded.

I tried to get into the meeting-hall (the school gym) through the back door – being used by Governors and candidates – but a polite policeman was adamant that no member of the general public could be admitted. Two yards from that door, and only six yards from where Ray was sitting throughout the evening, stood a police van with open door and driver at the wheel. Should the crowd turn rough, their quarry would instantly disappear.

At the main entrance, being used by media and parents, I 'did a Gdansk'. (By pretending to be a journalist, I had contrived to attend the 1981 Solidarity Conference every day.) Saying "Press!" briskly to an enormous P C, I swiftly slipped past him and forced my way down a corridor through a tumult of enraged parents and sulky cameramen – sulky because they had been ejected from the meeting after a five-minute 'photo-call'.

Close beside the two long press tables, Ray sat at the Governors' table beside Nazim Naqui, a remarkable man who had recently said, "I have nothing against Mr Honeyford as a human being and he is entitled to his opinions. I have never shouted at him. I have always tried to reason with him. I have tried to treat him as a friend." Ray seemed calm and was as expressionless as usual behind his useful beard – in contrast to the obviously tense and worried Nazim.

Moments after the eleven Governors had marked their voting papers the results were read out. Three pro-Honeyfords had been co-opted, including Mrs Iqbal. Therefore Ray's majority on the Governing Body was a secure nine-to-five.

Most of the evening's business remained to be done but because of the infuriated reaction to the vote a twenty-minute adjournment was announced. However, the disorder was comparatively mild; media reports greatly exaggerated it. The few men who seemed quite keen to get at Ray were quickly overpowered by the Brown stewards and forced outside. A *Yorkshire Post* reporter, rashly returning to the room, had his nose bloodied for no apparent reason as furious parents stampeded through the corridor to report to the waiting crowd. When the gym had emptied, apart from the pro-Honeyford Governors, Ray came over to me and we talked for five minutes. Then I decided that my duty as an observer lay outside.

Two policemen were blocking the door to the playground where yelling youths raced to and fro, flinging small stones at the school windows. "Do you *really* want to go out there?" asked one P C – solicitous for my grey hairs. He had to shout to be heard above the tumult. I assured him that I did and he reluctantly moved aside to let me pass.

Many more police were now in action, trying to clear the playground with the help of the stewards. As I dodged through to the road a fiery arc came over the railings and for a fraction of a moment I feared the worst – what everybody in authority had been fearing all evening. But it was only a fire-cracker. Beyond the gate the atmosphere was electric as groups argued furiously about whether or not the anti-Honeyford Governors should return to the meeting. I pushed through to the far side, looking for Jenny, and found myself beside a parked car at the edge of the crowd just as Nazim Naqui scrambled onto the bonnet to attempt to calm things. This seemed a futile gesture; by then the decibel level was so high you could hardly hear yourself think. In Punjabi and English he repeatedly appealed for *silence* – and within three minutes he got it. Total silence. You could have heard a feather floating. Only once before have I witnessed such an extraordinary feat of crowd-control through force of personality. That was on a memorable day in April 1967 when the Emperor Haile Selassie emerged from his palace, alone and unguarded, and defused a city-wide student riot in Addis Ababa.

Nazim said that he and his colleagues were about to return to the meeting; as the elected representatives of the parents it was their duty to do so. He promised that next day they would report exactly what had happened; then the community could discuss the next stage of the campaign. He advised the crowd to disperse at once; any violence could only damage the future of the Drummond pupils, the harmony of Bradford and the reputation of Pakistanis throughout Britain.

As friends helped Nazim to the ground – he was not then in good health – I thought: Allah be praised! Crisis over! But at once he was replaced on the car-bonnet by the Rank-and-File leader, a burly, bullying young White man who shouted – "Listen to me! I know I'm not a parent but all he said is nonsense! Those Tories have rigged the election! It doesn't matter what goes on in *there!*" He gestured contemptuously towards the school. "It's what happens out *here* that counts now! And what we need is action out here – action on the streets!"

I happened to be standing beside one of the Brown stewards, a young man who all day had been under tremendous strain as he exerted his authority to prevent any outbreak of violence. He caught my arm and said despairingly, "If they listen to *him* I can't stop them now! Christ! What we don't need today is youngsters who want to be fuckin' heroes!"

Mercifully the loud cheers raised by this Far Left plea were not widespread. The influence of a responsible Brown leader proved stronger than White rabble-rousing and the crowd began slowly to disperse. By 10.15 Drummond Road was deserted.

On the Day of Action scarcely 500 marched; fewer than 4,400 out of Bradford's 15,700 Muslim pupils boycotted their schools; fewer than 200 of the Council's 25,000 employees went on sympathy-strike. Only the Drummond boycott worked. Yet Bradfordians in general, and especially those directly concerned in the Honeyford Affair, were badly shaken by the realisation

that Manningham would have rioted had the police put a foot wrong outside
Drummond. (I said as much next morning to a senior police officer – an old
acquaintance – who was surveying the picket scene. He shrugged and smiled
and said, "It's easy for us here in Bradford – look at the co-operation we had
from the stewards!")

On 16 October only 104 of Drummond's 530 pupils registered. The
teaching staff's collective nerve was known to be at breaking point. It was
clear that the Council would have to bring out its cheque-book yet again and
this time think very big. The NAHT was now insisting on a settlement huge
enough to deter other LEAs from ever trying to sack a head teacher because
of anti-racist pressures.

I spent most of 16 October in Manchester with the Honeyfords; Ray's car
had had a breakdown and he couldn't get to school. By then the campaign
was tearing him asunder and for his wife Angela the strain was even worse, as
it always is for women when their men go off to battle. Also, she was being
worn down (as I would be, so I felt for her) by the relentless attentions of the
media. Ray was largely to blame for the controversy; he had provoked it, and
kept it going by refusing to apply the balm of an apology to the original
wound. Yet I longed that day for an end to his suffering. We all have character
defects – some very much worse than Ray's – but most of us manage to get
through life without being so heavily penalised for them.

The last phase of the affair, from mid-October to the end of November,
was prolonged by the Far Left's hijacking of the 'Honeyford Out!' band-
wagon.

On 17 October both Bradford's Chief Executive and the NAHT were eager
to reach a settlement. A few days later the DPAC (now chaired by Nazim
Naqui because Jenny's daughter had moved on to her senior school) withdrew its opposition to a generous settlement.

On 24 October an unprecedented meeting of the city's leaders – political,
religious, community, including the Anglican Bishop of Bradford and the
West Yorkshire Chief Constable – resolved to put pressure on all concerned
to make whatever compromises were necessary to avert disaster. The Labour
Councillors then withdrew their opposition to a settlement. But meanwhile
the picketing of Drummond, called off by the DPAC, had been taken over by
the so-called 'Drummond Parents' Support Group', a Far Left alliance
including militant trade unionists and the Sikh Federation. Their intervention
provoked the Tory Councillors to continue to oppose early retirement
because: 'Democracy is being tested about Mr Honeyford's right to stay at
the school and he has that right.'

On 13 November the Appeal Court reversed the High Court's pro-
Honeyford September decision. It ruled that 'The Council has statutory
duties to provide education for children in their area. If they did not have
ultimate power of dismissal they might find themselves thwarted in the

discharge of their statutory duties.' Ray was refused leave to appeal to the House of Lords and ordered to pay the Council's appeal costs.

Throughout November the Far Left continued to picket Drummond, whose headmaster was on extended sick-leave with 'a torn arm ligament'. At the end of the month came news that he would retire on 31 December; and his injury would prevent his returning to school before Christmas. The settlement provided for a total payment of £161,000, including an immediate lump sum £70,900. Mr Hart said, "This is the most substantial settlement that any teacher or headmaster within the state sector has ever achieved." The Lord Mayor commented, "The departure of Honeyford should not be regarded as a victory for any particular community." He was right; there were no winners in the Honeyford Affair – but many losers.

Two days after the settlement's signing, Lynda Lee-Potter's 'Authorised Version' Honeyford interview appeared in the *Daily Mail* (16 December 1985). Its headline lead-in referred to 'The man who fought his way from poverty, cared passionately for his pupils and had his career destroyed because he dared to speak out about problems in the class-room'. Lynda Lee-Potter had no difficulty in unravelling the Honeyford Affair. She wrote: '1985 will surely go down in history books as the year when a good man's career was destroyed because he said that in schools like his the English pupils are the real ethnic minority, and who can argue with the truth of that when in the first year at Drummond there are 123 children only one of whom is white?'

Next day came the first of a series of articles in the *Daily Mail* by 'The Hounded Head'. These revealed how deeply Ray had been affected by the long-drawn-out and merciless anti-Honeyford campaign. For almost a year I had been defending him against accusations of 'racism' and attracting a lot of flak as a result. However, these articles also indicated someone whose ethnocentricity operates unrecognised by himself (and many others) and influences many of his decisions and reactions.

In retrospect, the Honeyford Affair can be seen as a laboratory study of the dangerous chemicals now interacting on Britain's race relations scene – the New Right's hostility to 'ethnic minorities', the Far Left's hypocritical championing of those same minorities, the anti-racists' naïve belief that racial prejudice can be eradicated by relentless campaigning, the rise in unemployment which every year leaves more young Blacks and Browns with nothing to do but campaign, the swelling R R I bureaucracy with its vested interest in identifying (or inventing) race problems for the solution of which still more people need to be recruited. Bradford escaped an explosion. Britain may not, if those chemicals are allowed to continue to interact during the years ahead.

My neutrality throughout the affair was not a pose which, as a writer, I felt bound to maintain. It was entirely genuine, because I sympathised with so many of the convictions held by both sides. The insensitivity of Ray's articles shook me; his apparent reluctance to see any non-English point of view exasperated me; the ease with which his views could be remoulded frightened me. Yet I shared his impatient scorn for the woolly-minded wafflings of the R R I, the bullying tactics of the Far Left and the illogical fanaticism of 'anti-racist zealots'.

Some of the campaigning methods of the anti-Honeyford factions also shook me; their inability to see how much damage they were doing to race relations exasperated me; their refusal to recognise the complexity of that phenomenon known as 'racial prejudice' frightened me. Yet I shared their view that Ray was unsuited to run a mainly Muslim school in Bradford. Thus it was not difficult for me to remain sitting on the fence throughout the controversy; there was nowhere else for me to be.

PART TWO

HANDSWORTH
IN
BIRMINGHAM

The immediate impact of the demand for Negro slaves was felt among the West African peoples themselves. Previously orderly and politically fairly advanced communities were reduced to a condition of internal strife as more and more African chiefs and others succumbed to the temptation to get rich quick by deporting their subjects, in return for European merchandise . . . On the plantations of the New World the Negro slaves had to make a rapid adjustment to a completely different way of life from the one to which they were accustomed. A process of acculturation that would normally take several generations had to be achieved in a very much shorter period. It is not surprising that the scars are still to be seen on the face of West Indian society.

ANTHONY H. RICHMOND: *The Colour Problem*

7 · A Bed-sit in Handsworth

My first fortnight in Handsworth was well-spent lodging in a Black-run hostel for the homeless (*aet.* 18–24). Most of those young people had big problems. At best they were estranged from their families, at worst just out of prison; in between they had experienced every other sort of misfortune you could think of – and a few you couldn't. With three exceptions, they were disinclined to communicate with the White woman who had so inexplicably pitched up in their midst. Nor indeed did they communicate much with each other. That worried me, when I pretended to long for telly and joined them in their large, bleak sitting-room – minimally furnished with uncomfortable chairs, its pale green walls bare, its plastic-tiled floor chilly. The majority looked withdrawn, apathetic, mistrustful, hurt. Already life had defeated them; perhaps they were defeated the day they were born. They dreadfully contradicted the stereotype of ebullient, extrovert, noisy young Blacks.

The silence of that hostel was unnerving. People sloped in and out almost furtively, not belonging there (or anywhere), not audibly greeting one another, faces closed, eyes averted. A few of the young men had 'music-systems' in their rooms and it was a relief to hear blasts of reggae when Sylvia, who ran the show, was out. Then she would return, hurry upstairs, bang angrily on a door and demand less noise because the neighbours complained. Which I daresay they did. The hostel was in an up-market corner of Handsworth where some of the neighbours were White.

Matilda suddenly addressed me one evening, during the telly news. Aged nineteen – very tall, ebony-skinned, angry-looking – she was waiting for a DHSS flat after a final (she said) domestic row about her lack of religion. She made it clear that she was speaking to me only to let me know how much she hated Whites. Then she became reluctantly fascinated by my wanting to know why *she*, personally, hated Whites and we had several slightly more constructive conversations in my room. She was not yet a Black is Beautiful person, though by now she may have become one and for her own sake I hope she has. It then seemed to her worth spending £1.25 and 75p on *Black Beauty*

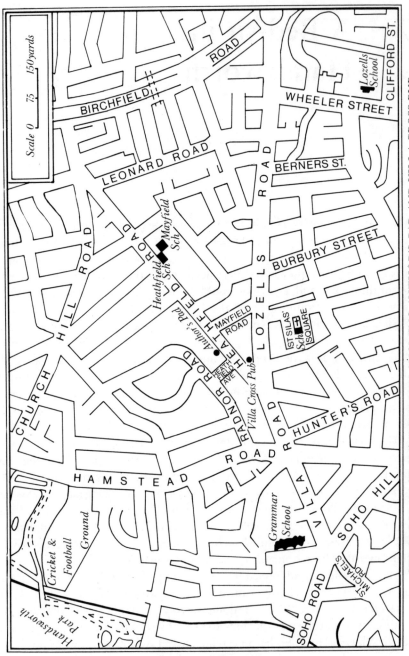

STREET PLAN OF HANDSWORTH SHOWING AUTHOR'S PAD AND VILLA CROSS PUB

and Hair (For the Beauty Conscious Black Woman) and *Root*, both glossy journals which kept her *au fait* with the latest skin-lightening lotions and hair-relaxing processes. Enabling Blacks to look less negroid is a multi-million dollar business, founded on a longing that fills me with an inexpressible sort of sadness. I can never get used to seeing 'relaxed' hair; its significance is shattering. And in America plastic surgery is common among wealthy Blacks. Father forgive us for we know not what we have done . . .

Matilda was the first Handsworth Black – the first of many – to tell me, "You're wasting your time! We're not going to tell you what we really feel and think – we're sick to our souls of Whitey *studying* us. You don't want to understand, you only want to have *theories* . . . Why don't you go home and write about your own problems? You've enough of them in Ireland, I've been seeing them on the news all my life!"

Matilda needed to despise me, to discredit my motives and jeer at my helplessness as a stranger in her world. (She was not alone in this, I discovered during the months ahead.) I was just one more patronising, blinkered, uncomprehending parasite feeding on 'The Black problem'. It is easy to sympathise with this point of view and I said as much. She wouldn't of course accept that. And she never did explain why she, personally, hated Whites; to do so would have been to let the side down.

Randolph was very different; he seemed almost eager to confide in Whitey. One of his problems was epilepsy, which had led to his being released from prison after serving two months of a six-months sentence. He was a gentle, shy, inarticulate person who at school had been relegated to an ESN unit. Within his family only patois was spoken and when he started school he understood very little of what anybody said. Yet he was far from stupid, though it took me some time to realise this.

For years Randolph had been day-dreaming about emigrating to Canada and working on a farm. Yet he rarely left Handsworth, where he had arrived from Jamaica at the age of two. The city centre frightened him; he seemed obsessively convinced that beyond his own territory he was likely to be attacked by NF gangs. Hour after hour, in his bare little room, he fondled his unattainable Canadian ambition. He had bought a large-scale map, and someone had given him a picture calendar (1979) of dramatic Canadian landscapes, and for six years he had been collecting postcards from Canada where quite a few Handsworth Blacks have relatives. "Blacks are *safe* in Canada," he said repeatedly.

Not until much later did I discover the source of Randolph's fear. By then I was in my own pad and he called occasionally for a chat. One evening he had had a few more beers than usual and told me that when he was nine his father, whom he adored, was attacked by two White work-mates on a building-site and suffered permanent brain-damage. He never again recognised Randolph and died three years later. His attackers escaped detection and Randolph's mother maintained that "the police didn't bust themselves – so what if there's one nig-nog less? Oi!' She herself suffered a series of strokes after her husband's death and died when Randolph was sixteen. His five younger siblings were then 'taken into care' and he moved to live with an aunt until his imprisonment. After that disgrace she – a pillar of her Pentecostal church – would have no more to do with him. Yet he was free of any bitterness against anyone. His acceptance of misfortune was almost disconcerting. He only wanted to be *safe*.

Lyndon was another young man with a day-dream, which had got him into Winson Green prison for eighteen months. He was a handsome fellow, not tall but well-built and graceful with fine features only marred by heavily bloodshot eyes. He knew nothing of his parentage; all his life he had been in care, moving every few years (five times) from one children's home to another. School had been meaningless: just more pushing around. Then at eighteen he qualified for a DHSS flat and suddenly was out on his own, expected to cope with society as an independent, responsible citizen – having all his life been a mechanically tended number on a list, never required to make a decision. He was of course still a number on a list and could have lived (I mean not *died*) on State hand-outs for the next fifty or sixty years. But he didn't fancy that idea. He planned instead to acquire enough money to buy a car and become a taxi-driver. So he stole the usual things – television and video sets, music-systems, tape-recorders – and had saved quite a bit when the law intervened.

Lyndon was a compulsive, excitable talker, yet he never seemed to be communicating with *me*. He couldn't, I sensed, relate to other people as individuals; he saw them as cogs in a machine – an educational, or law-and-order, or social services machine – and for him it was the machine, rather than the human being, which had an identity. I belonged (he decided, and wouldn't be persuaded otherwise) to the academic machine and he wanted me to tell him what young people *do* all day at university. His alone-ness was palpable and I feared impregnable. He always sat in the same position, on the edge of a chair, as though he were about to stand up and go; and while talking he stared upwards, his eyes travelling to and fro along the ceiling. During the summer he too came to see me at my pad – but only if I happened to meet him in the street and ask him in. Then I didn't see him any more and in the middle of October Randolph told me that he had committed suicide.

Handsworth has an appalling reputation. It is so maligned that until I had had time to form a personal opinion my nerves were all the time slightly on edge. People warned me never to leave Brontë outside the swimming-baths; however ingeniously swathed in locked coils of steel, most of her would be gone after quarter of an hour. Others warned me never to walk through Handsworth Park alone, day or night, and never to venture onto the streets after dark. I was also warned not to expect a regular mail delivery, because marauding packs of Rastas terrorised the local postmen. (Not many Rastas are awake at mail-delivery time and the Heathfield Road postman happened to be one of the few local Rastas lucky enough to have a job; but little details like that never deter myth-makers.) A dozen people warned me not to leave cash in my pad because it would be broken into at least once a week – and not to carry cash on me because I would be mugged at least twice a week. Had all those scare-stories come from White outsiders one might have attributed them to racial prejudice. But the majority came from residents – White, Brown, elderly Black – who seem to conspire most curiously to persuade themselves, each other and anyone rash enough to move into Handsworth that the district is a seething cauldron of violence and vice. Yet I constantly walked alone, day and night, all over the area (including the park) and was never once mugged. Nor was my pad broken into, though it represented a standing invitation to burglars having no catch on the window and easy access from the garden. Brontë might indeed have evaporated had she been left unguarded, but that situation didn't arise; Brum's traffic so demoralised me that I rarely used her. My mail-delivery too might have been unreliable had I not used Poste Restante – but merely because my doss-house had no letter-box. The truly astonishing thing about Handsworth is its *low* crime-rate.

Consider a few eloquent figures. In 1981 Handsworth's population was 56,300 – down from 65,037 in 1971 – and fifty-eight per cent were Black or Brown. The Whites are either 'respectable elderly' or at the very bottom of the pile – in fact hardly belonging to the pile, in too many cases. In that year seventy-two per cent of the district's births were non-White, as compared to forty-three per cent in 1966; so the White percentage will rapidly decrease in the near future.

In 1974 Handsworth's unemployment rate was four per cent. In January 1985 the male unemployment rate was forty-six per cent – almost double Brum's average and treble the national rate. And fifty-six per cent of the jobless had been idle for more than a year. An average of thirty-five people applied for every job advertised at the Handsworth Job Centre. In the Lozells area, where I had my pad, male unemployment was fifty-nine per cent when I arrived and ninety-one per cent of youths had *never* worked. Of 1984's school-leavers, only eight per cent of Whites, seven per cent of Browns and three per cent of Blacks could find employment by the end of the year. Community Programme figures showed how desperately young Blacks were trying to find work of any kind. Although Blacks form only about twenty-four per cent of Handsworth's population, they take up over eighty per cent of the CP jobs – mainly heavy building work. Yet only sixteen per cent of those who finished their CP scheme in December 1984 were able to get another job. (The national figure is about twenty-five per cent.) Those figures should be digested by the Tory MP, Mr Terry Dicks, who in August 1986 ranted dangerously – 'West Indians in general are bone idle . . . it's about time they were given a kick in the pants. Most of the West Indians here are lazy good-for-nothings, who came across to sponge and bring their way of life in the Caribbean to this country' (*Caribbean Times,* 5 September 1986).

According to the Department of the Environment, Handsworth is the most deprived district in Brum and among the most deprived ten per cent in England and Wales. The Department measures 'deprivation' by six indicators: unemployment, overcrowding, households lacking exclusive use of basic amenities, single-parent households, pensioners living alone, and families of 'ethnic origin'. Using those criteria, seventy per cent of Handsworth is in the '*extremely deprived*' category – i.e., within the worst two and a half per cent Enumerated Districts in England and Wales.

Having been battered by all those grisly statistics you might expect equally grisly crime figures. But not a bit of it. According to the West Midlands Police, 'The under-lying increase in crime over the period 1981–1984 is *less than one-third* of the City average.' [My italics.] Moreover, 'Offences against the person are rare, accounting for less than four per cent of all recorded crimes in the area.' So much for those packs of marauding Rastas and young Black muggers prowling the streets and parks . . . Burglary and car thefts account for thirty-nine per cent and twenty-eight per cent of Handsworth's crimes. And when you glance up the page at those unemployment statistics – ninety-one per cent of young men without hope of a job – is that surprising? What surprised me was to find Handsworth so comparatively law-abiding. (A riot, as we shall see in due course, is Something Else Again.)

The casual passer-by, or even short-term resident, would never suspect Handsworth of being *extremely* deprived. Apart from the forlorn little streets of Lozells and Soho Hill, it is, visually, a most pleasing 'residential area'. By a happy freak of topography, the unspeakable ghastliness of 'redeveloped' Birmingham is invisible from most vantage points within Handsworth, despite its being only two miles from the city centre. Until the 1930s, when it began to slide slowly down the social scale, the district had a history of modest prosperity going back to the Domesday Book. In the 1080s it was among the richest local manors with two holdings, many water-meadows, two mills, three adults per square mile and a value of £5. By 1300 it had an enclosed hunting park – a Leisure Centre for the Lord of the Manor. In the 1540s a hammer-mill was flourishing and by 1561 four blade-mills were operating and many specialist iron-workers had moved into the parish. Forty years later a new furnace for melting and casting iron was provoking the local environmentalists to complain about 'enormous mountains of cinders'. In 1761–2 Matthew Boulton ("I am very desirous of becoming a *great silversmith*") moved his massive complex of workshops and warehouses to a site on Hockley Brook, where the Boulton–James Watt partnership produced the world's first steam engines. This magnificent Soho Works, as depicted in 1839, had nothing in common with dark satanic mills or modern utilitarian factories; it quite closely resembled the Chelsea Hospital. Handsworth's first major employer was an enlightened man. He refused to accept pauper apprentices at the usual age of seven – no child under twelve was employed at the Soho Works – and he was much more concerned about the lighting, ventilation and cleanliness of his vast premises than are Handsworth's present-day sweat-shop owners. Most startling of all, in 1792 Mr Boulton set up a social insurance scheme for all his workers with wage-related payments and benefits.

The last of Handsworth's medieval open fields was enclosed in 1793 and in 1813 a National School 'for the gratuitous education of the children of the poor according to the system introduced by Dr Bell' was established. But in 1840 it was decided that Sunday Schools were more important, to remove 'labourers' children from noise and riot, and cursing and swearing in the streets on the Sabbath'. (Long before any 'darkies' arrived, Brummies were quite keen on rioting.) In 1854 the GWR provided Handsworth with a railway station (now no more) and in 1862, just a century after its establishment, the superb Soho Works was demolished, leaving Handsworth with only a few minor industries – a red lead factory, two corn mills and two breweries. Then the district was still a rural parish but housing developments soon began, mainly for factory owners, managers and senior clerical staff, and in 1874 Handsworth was described in Kelly's Directory as 'a fashionable suburb'. Most of present-day Handsworth appeared during the next thirty years: street after tree-lined street of substantial red-brick homes, some verging on villas with mock-Tudor embellishments and considerable gardens. Others, like my nine-room doss-house, have only six feet of garden in front but ample space behind. When the district became part of Birmingham in 1911 it had a population of 68,600. That included thousands of skilled factory workers, living in the Lozells and Soho Hill areas in four-roomed brick dwellings that open onto the street yet are quite substantial and attractive in their way. Now many such houses are occupied by Bangladeshis, the most recent and most impoverished of those new arrivals who would have so much astonished the compilers of the Domesday Book.

Handsworth's present façade of well-being owes much to the City Council's Urban Renewal Programme which, at the date of my arrival, had restored the exteriors of 6,300 properties (houses, shops, offices) – an activity curiously known as 'enveloping'. Local householders had also received 1,221 renovation grants and during my months in the district hundreds more houses were being 'enveloped'. But I heard much acute anxiety expressed about the effects of government cut-backs on Urban Renewal.

My own acute anxiety, as I observed so much busy beavering on every side of my pad, had to do with the composition of the work-force. In an area choked with unemployed young Blacks, aching for jobs, *almost all the construction workers were Irish.* Apart from enraging the Blacks, whose furious frustration everyone but the Council could appreciate, this meant that the millions allegedly being 'poured into Handsworth' were in fact pouring out of Handsworth every evening in the pockets of this Irish Mafia.

My search for a bed-sit soon revealed the extremity of Handsworth's deprivation. What lies behind some affluent-looking, recently enveloped exteriors is not Third World destitution but a Fourth World of squalor such as I have never before encountered. The half-adoption of a Western urban life-style, by very poor Blacks and Browns living in grossly over-crowded conditions, can lead to an out-of-control degradation unknown in the worst of Third World slums. (I mean degradation as distinct from hardship.) I once lived for a fortnight in the *barriados* around Lima without seeing anything comparable to what lurks inside many Handsworth 'envelopes'. But I'll spare my readers' sensibilities by skipping the worst of it and concentrating on the comparatively innocuous livestock.

In a Pakistani-owned house three cockroach corpses lay in the lodger's sink and several live cockroaches frolicked beneath it; mini-cockroaches by Ecuadorean or Malagasy standards – scarcely an inch long – yet I felt I could do without five months of their constant companionship. In a neat and polished Black-owned house all seemed tolerable (there was a perfectly adequate el-san in a garden-shed) until I noticed arcane and sinister smears on the wall above the bed. Fortunately these did not baffle me; I know a bed-bug slaughter-house when I see one. In a Sikh-owned house a spacious ground-floor room overlooking a leafy garden seemed paradisaical and the owner and I sat on the bed to talk business. A moment later my legs began to tickle and I vaguely scratched, as one does; then they tickled much more and I glanced down to see starved fleas swarming onto my bare ankles. The Sikh, looking amused, said the room had been unoccupied for six weeks and once someone moved in the fleas would depart. This seems to me a slur on their intelligence so negotiations ceased abruptly.

Bed-sit hunting is a good way to get the feel of an area and make contacts, but after a fortnight I had had enough. Rather cravenly, I ended up in an Irish-owned pad infested only by a half-grown kitten of infinite charm and exquisite beauty who had been callously abandoned by the last tenant. When she realised that I was on her wave-length she became quite ecstatic and stood on my lap and kissed my nose whereupon I at once signed a three-month contract.

Since January I had somehow acquired an unconscionable number of books so Des and Dan volunteered to help me move to Heathfield Road. These young Irishmen owned (or at least *used*) a beat-up untaxed motor-van and lived in a Fourth World squat – a genuine squat, where four or five people shared one room, as distinct from my genteel pad. Their house was in a dangerous state of disrepair and has since been demolished; no Urban Renewal beavers could do anything for it. It was an imposing eighteen-room detached residence in a large garden bounded by beeches and flowering chestnuts; trees are Handsworth's glory – wherever you look, they seem to fill at least half the skyline. However, within this shell of Victorian affluence all was reeking, sordid disorder, presided over by a chipped statue of the Infant of Prague, a plastic bust of President Kennedy, and technicoloured pictures of the Sacred Heart of Jesus, St Patrick ankle-deep in snakes, Our Lady of Lourdes, a simpering Little Flower, Pope John Paul XXIII (also simpering), a framed 1916 Proclamation and various other symbols of popular Irish Catholicism-cum-Nationalism. Perhaps it is not as absurd as it sounds to classify the Irish as an 'ethnic minority'. The description makes no sense physically, yet in certain surroundings it can seem psychologically or temperamentally accurate.

Des, Dan and their fellow-squatters were among the many thousands of Irish youngsters who have been settling in Brum during recent years – not to seek jobs, for they know none exists, but to escape from intolerable domestic situations. Contrary to popular belief, they get no more State support from the British than the Irish government, but British benefits come in a form that solves their particular problem. The DHSS was paying the owner of my friends' squat directly for their board (two meals a day) and lodging, while giving them £9.50 per week in cash. At home they would have been given £30 cash and had much more spending money, since most Irish parents take only £10 a week. However, in recessed Ireland whole families are now on the dole – perhaps a still youngish father and three or four grown-up children – which soon leads to friction in cramped council houses or high-rise flats. And Irish rents are too high for a jobless youngster to move into a bed-sitter, or even a squat – hence the attraction of the British system.

We set off for the hostel accompanied by Una, a nineteen-year-old Cavan girl pregnant by one of the boys; she seemed unsure which and they seemed happy to share the credit. All three were touchingly concerned about my feckless failure to sign on for the dole. "You're an EEC citizen," said Una, "so you're *entitled* to it. Why throw good money away? I mean, if you're just a writer you're not really *employed*, are you? I mean, you don't have real *work*, do you?" When I pointed out that writers sometimes have to work ten hours a day, seven days a week, fifty-two weeks a year they all thought this an excellent leg-pull and roared with laughter.

Arriving at my new front door – Flat No. 3 – we couldn't open it though I did have the correct key. It would have collapsed, being half-rotten, had any one of us leant on it. But I reckoned a half-rotten door is better than none so the boys went round to the side of the house and by shoulder-standing had gained entrance to my pad within moments. The inside catch had been put on the Yale lock by someone who had then departed – presumably – through the window. Later it transpired that the previous tenant, an Englishman of mysterious provenance, had returned to help himself to all the saucepans. As I didn't plan to cook during my tenancy this was of no consequence – to me. Brigid, my landlady, naturally felt otherwise, especially as the tenant in question still owed her five weeks' rent.

Brigid had gone to some trouble to reorganise my tiny pad. A rickety wardrobe and chest-of-drawers had been moved out to the landing and replaced by a biggish desk-substitute table, standing by the sash window. I felt very happy on that June evening, writing my journal by the open window. Directly opposite, some thirty yards away, was the kitchen wing of a semi-derelict three-storey house – painted an unfortunate dried-blood-red, which took a bit of getting used to. But just to the left of that stretched a glorious expanse of woodland, an unbroken line of beeches, limes, poplars, birches, chestnuts, ashes. Brum is to be commended for the zeal with which it cherishes – and when necessary replaces – its trees.

No. 45 had been worth waiting for; there I was at the very hub of Handsworth – or, in local terminology, 'on the front line'. (The significance of that phrase will emerge in due course.) The long Heathfield Road carries heavy commuter traffic morning and evening and is quite noisy even at night, many young Blacks being nocturnal in their habits. No. 45 is at the top end, about fifty yards from the junction with the Villa Road and the Lozells Road, and most of my immediate neighbours were young Blacks living in flats or squats. A little further down is a large Afro-Caribbean Centre, where special Saturday School classes are held, and just beyond that an enormous Nonconformist church has been converted into a Hindu temple. Within a few minutes' walk in other directions are a Vietnamese Centre, a Black Pentecostal church and the huge block of the Soho Road Sikh Gurdwara. Mirpuri families (many ex-Manningham) live on various streets leading off Heathfield Road and across the Lozells Road is a considerable – though self-effacing and not very noticeable – colony of Bangladeshis. My White neighbours were OAPs living in a newish but already dingy two-storey building opposite the Villa Cross pub. Handsworth is said to be the 'most multi-racial district' in all of Britain. I can believe it.

My local was the Villa Cross and the Villa Road catered for all other needs: Sikh supermarket, Gujarati newsagent, Mirpuri greengrocer, Black chemist, Sikh off-licence, Black take-away, multi-racial-staffed bank, all-White-staffed post office. It was then a grim street, always ankle-deep in litter and starkly reflecting both the poverty and the tension of this corner of Handsworth. No shop looked more than quarter-way to making a decent living and most shop windows – even tiny newsagents and pathetic cubby-holes selling cheap plastic toys – were protected by steel mesh. The mini-supermarket employed a bouncer; 'security officer' is too mild a term. He stood by the door – a squat, tough-looking elderly Black – and confiscated every customer's shopping-bag (or any other receptacle) as they entered. Although he could be quite charming, if dealing with Blacks or Browns, he positively vibrated with anti-White aggro. When I first tried to enter, he insisted that I must hand over my brief-case. It contained various vital documents (not to mention my journal, by then very fat and beyond price) so I turned away and heard him commenting loudly to no one in particular – "Bloody suspicious old cow!" On my empty-handed return half an hour later he pounced on me again and confiscated a newly purchased electric light bulb visible in my husky pocket. Two other Blacks – male and female – sauntered all the time up and down between the meagrely stocked shelves: the Villa Road substitute for electronic surveillance devices. Not surprisingly, White customers were uncommon in that shop.

It took me less than twenty-four hours to *feel* why my pad was said to be 'on the front line'. The Villa Cross pub, the Acapulco café opposite it (at my end of the Villa Road) and nearby areas were flamboyantly 'Rasta' territory. The fact that few of the so-called Rastas were true Rastafarians need not for the moment detain us. They were universally known as such, many wore dreadlocks and Rasta hats and all smoked ganja which the dealers among them sold openly, not only in the Villa Cross and Acapulco but on the wide forecourt of the pub and along the surrounding streets. This curious situation will be considered in detail in a later chapter. Here I am concerned only with the public perception of 'the front line', the effect on the neighbourhood of this group of a few score anti-White, anti-Authority young Blacks. They scared everyone, hence the area's perceptible tension – sometimes low, sometimes high. And they angered many, by their defiant holding of the ganja-dealing 'front line' against the police. Visually and emotionally they dominated the Villa Road, Lozells Road, Heathfield Road – their influence less noticeable the further one got from the Villa Road, yet extending in a diluted form throughout Handsworth.

To me as a newcomer they seemed an unattractive segment of the variegated local population. Their mien was deliberately hostile and threatening towards the world in general but particularly towards Whites (apart from their customers), and most particularly towards the police and all who might be considered police allies – for example, an elderly White female who clearly didn't 'belong' to Heathfield Road's squat-world yet had moved in. After 11.00 a.m., any excursion down the Villa Road involved running the gauntlet of those young men, some sitting on the low wall surrounding the Villa Cross forecourt, others hanging about on the pavement outside the Acapulco, or lounging in the doorways of the adjacent betting-office and taxi-office. By the end of my first day, during which I was to-ing and fro-ing a good deal in the course of 'home-making', I understood precisely what was meant by that term 'front line'; it is unnerving to be the object of such concentrated animosity. Later, when I came to understand a little more about the nuances of the situation, the 'front-line' catch-phrase irritated me. Yet I could still see why those powerful Villa Road vibes aroused anxiety and antagonism among most of my non-Rasta neighbours of every colour – and mixture of colours.

Birmingham's post-war reincarnation has obscured its interesting past. The newcomer, arriving at New Street station, can only feel shock/horror. That vast, ill-lit, grimy, low-ceilinged subterranean cavern seems to have been modelled on a Victorian coal-mine. Ascending to daylight via several escalators, one emerges into Britain's second city hoping for better things. But one doesn't find them. When Birmingham was re-designed in the 1960s it boasted of being 'The Car City' and so it is. If cars could speak they would no doubt tell us how much they enjoy scorching along the myriad wide motor-ways that make most of the city unlivable in for anyone who wants to stay even half-sane. Those roads go around and over and under the most repellant conglomeration of architectural aberrations I have ever seen concentrated in a city centre. To survey Birmingham from the top of a double-decker bus induces incredulity; it seems all this ghastliness can't be *true* . . . When you look up the sky is blanked out by brash metallic circular towers and immense angular blocks of post-war commercial buildings, interspersed with the decaying corpses of Victorian industrial triumphs. Weirdly coiling concrete car-parks also loom overhead; and when you look down hundreds more cars are parked in sinister shadowy areas between monstrous concrete struts upholding the motorways. The buses swing round and round in circles amidst a crazy confusion of other roads – above, below, beside – and the effect of so much traffic speeding on various levels in different directions is curiously menacing. One feels the heart and soul have been torn out of Birmingham (presuming it ever had either) and the few relics of its nineteenth-century splendour – like the Corinthian Town Hall – are so overwhelmed by the surrounding ugliness that they seem to accentuate rather than relieve it.

Many of the main pedestrian routes plunge into semi-underground shop-lined tunnels, all sullen and soiled and drab even on a bright midsummer day (not that there were many of those in 1985) and reeking of diesel. Alterna-tively, one can take an escalator up from street-level and go wandering for hours through endless abominations of neon-lit shopping arcades. There are also wind-swept pedestrian bridges high above the whine and roar of racing traffic. And sometimes one finds oneself lost for an indefinite period in long, low, dirty subways, or on footpaths by motorways from which there is no escape until you are miles beyond where you wanted to go. It is possible to walk in circles for hours, quite close to your destination, without ever getting to it. My sense of direction is, admittedly, poor. Yet even by Murphy standards it is remarkable to have lived in a city for five months without learning how to get around unaided. I was however consoled to meet Brum-mie after Brummie who confessed they couldn't direct me to X, Y or Z because "It's all a bit confusing". No wonder tourists are almost as rare as camels in Birmingham. And no wonder the unfortunate Brummies seem so much less congenial than Bradfordians. Living where they do must severely tax their humanity.

My city-centre excursions were kept to the minimum, but one Saturday afternoon in the middle of June I craved a bookshop and took a bus into New Street. Then I noticed that in Brum young Blacks, of the least attractive sort, impinge on the main shopping areas as they do not on London's West End. Many groups of four or five were roaming or loitering around, looking alienated and insolent and sometimes roughly shouldering their way through the crowds of White shoppers just by way of asserting themselves. Within two hours of wandering (and loitering) I saw three fights, all between Blacks.

As I was hesitating at a junction, wondering which way to turn, five young men pushed past me and accosted three well-dressed young Black women with straightened hair. When told to get lost they closed in on the girls, reaching for their breasts and jeering. (This aggro could have been because of their hair-style, regarded by some as a betrayal of the Black is Beautiful ideology.) All three girls were carrying umbrellas with which they vigorously attacked their molesters while screaming abuse. Their shoulder-bags were then grabbed and kicked into the middle of the motorway. Seconds later the fight spilled onto the road, almost causing a serious accident – whereupon the young men fled, pursued by drivers' curses and a police car.

In the second incident four leather-clad Black youths attacked two strolling Rastas – very unaggressive-looking types. They had their victims on the ground when four more Rastas rushed to the rescue from a posh coffee-bar and the leather-jackets legged it.

I saw only the end of the third fight: one bleeding Black sitting on the Cathedral steps, looking dazed, and three others disappearing at Olympic speed as a police siren sounded in the distance. In each case the White passers-by had pretended not to notice.

On the bus back to peaceful Handsworth I remarked to an elderly White man that in the city centre young Blacks seem very conspicuous. He shrugged and repeated an already familiar comment: "Here in Birmingham we're sitting on a Black time-bomb."

Later one of my neighbours, a young Jamaican woman, said, "All that's just normal in there, specially on a Saturday afternoon. Traders complain it puts shoppers off and puts up their insurance rates." She went on to point out that those unpleasant young men are a minute fraction of Brum's Black population; probably fewer, proportionately, than the fraction of far more destructive Whites who become football hooligans. Yet because of their conspicuous *colour* their truculent presence reinforces White fears of being 'threatened by outsiders' and confirms White prejudices against *all* Blacks.

Leaving aside occasional street brawls, or rude jostling through White crowds, that harmless Caribbean custom known as 'liming' also exasperates the English. On a BBC Radio 4 programme, in 1984, one of Britain's first Black police inspectors, Ron Hope, explained:

Something which has caused problems over here is the practice of liming, or standing on street corners just passing the time of day. In this country, traditionally, we discourage people from doing that, not only because of the obstruction but because also it may be intimidatory to people passing through an area. And this has caused problems in various parts of London, maybe more problems than anything else. Possibly we have to rethink the way we deal with Black people who stand on street corners. There is absolutely no reason to suppose they are up to no good. It's just a cultural trait, and no more than that.

In this respect, as in several others, the Blacks are indeed 'toasted Irishmen' (and women). It would never occur to me that liming is in any way odd or objectionable because I grew up with its equivalent – now, alas! being eroded by Ireland's new E E C prosperity. In small Irish towns not only 'corner-boys' but groups of eminently respectable citizens regularly stood or sat around on the streets for hours on end, discussing politics, sport, farming or whatever. Liming is often associated with sunny climes where it is natural to lead outdoor social lives: a category into which Ireland does not fit. Obviously it is temperamental rather than climatic, the mark of a take-it-easy and loquacious people who baffle the bustling and buttoned-up British. The tragedy is that White fear and resentment of liming, and the perverse police failure to distinguish it from 'loitering with intent', have goaded many young Blacks, like my Villa Road neighbours, into adopting intimidatory attitudes. 'Tragic' seems not too strong a word for this inexorable process, which it will not be easy to reverse. Essentially liming is an innocent and rather endearing custom and Blacks can scarcely be blamed for the hidebound Whites' suspicious and provocative reactions to it.

My next visit to the city centre was on 10 July, to meet a Trinidadian social worker at a Digbeth pub. Jasper was over an hour late and to pass the time I drew a pen-portrait of Brum's evening life:

A warm, petrol-scented evening. I'm sitting alone outside the Royal George at a wooden trestle-table set on a carpet of litter. Inside are only four customers; two undernourished White youths and a foul-mouthed Pakistani playing pool together, and a shrivelled old Irishman, half-drunk, with a deeply lined face and absurd-looking bright red hair. The barman – tall, powerfully built – grew up in a village near Peshawar. He still has a Frontier swagger that makes his Brummie accent sound tragical-comical. City-centre pubs can't make much at this hour – so few pedestrians around. Two young White men have just passed with lunch-satchels over their shoulders – lucky fellows going home from *work*! Almost opposite, across the dual-carriageway, is St Martin's-in-the-Bull Ring, Brum's 18th-century parish church. A handsome spire and stonework but the entire edifice – even the windows – *completely* blackened. Once no doubt the largest building here, now dwarfed by the sick functional fantasies of concrete cubism. Dominating all else is a loathsome circular contraption: alternate layers of glass and concrete with vile twitching crimson lettering round the roof exhorting the populace to E N J O Y C O C A   C O L A and electronically showing the time. Everything in sight is so *artificial* – shapes, textures, lettering, colouring – ersatz marble walls, 'clever' metal advertisement hoardings rusting and coming undone . . . But a few attractive stone or brick buildings remain, like the police station just down the road. Hard to believe this spot was the heart of a medieval market town. Traffic fast and frequent but not non-stop: people can illegally take short-cuts by leaping over the low wall in the middle of the road, and can even lift bikes over, to outwit Brum's barbarous planning and get to where they want to go in reasonable time.

A few minutes ago three teenage girls (one Black, two White) jumped the wall to buy cigarettes in the pub. Now a Black youth is sprinting across the road between the traffic; deplorable behaviour, yet I sympathise with his urge to defy the system. A Vietnamese youth – slightly stooping, sad-looking – is walking past my table alone. On the far side three young Hindus are hurrying up from the bus-station: a man with a neatly rolled umbrella, two graceful girls in shimmering saris carrying bulging brief-cases. An ancient grey-bearded Sikh with a stick is hobbling towards the bus-station, his wife following a few yards behind dragging two suit-cases. A moment ago the Black youth came out of the pub drinking from an open bottle of beer and scratching his head with a closed bottle. He paused beside me, glanced down at my notebook, said – "Fuckin' journalist!" and loped off, jumping high in the air for no apparent reason as he rounded the corner into Moor Street. Two boys (aet. 10?) paused to laugh at him. They are looking for a chance to dart across the road with their trick-bikes. One is Brown, the other a very unusual Black-White mix: light-brown negroid curls, blue eyes, thick lips, golden skin. By the bus-stop near the church stands a frail elderly White man in a Homburg hat clutching a carrier-bag of potted plants: his brave attempt to keep in touch with Nature . . . But at this time of day Whites are very much in the minority here. The few Council-planted trees and bushes look depressed and depressing. Now a flock of starlings is flying high above the spire, against grey shreds of cloud – and here comes Jasper, vaulting over the motorway wall!

8 · Singing on Sundays

Two of the main bases from which I operated were Black churches and multi-racial pubs. The former I found physically trying – knee-joints unused for many decades could, literally, be heard creaking – but to the latter I am accustomed.

On 16 June I attended my first Holy Marathon (10.30 a.m. – 1.10 p.m.) in a sort of United Reformed Church recently re-Reformed to suit Black tastes. The austere early eighteenth-century building seemed not quite in keeping with the sort of services it now sees – and hears. Its White pastor was fortyish, small, tubby, balding but with long ginger side-burns; he wore a plum-coloured lounge suit and tie and a primrose-yellow shirt. A brilliantly professional preacher, his every gesture, emotional voice-throb, homely aside and corny joke was perfectly judged to appeal to the ninety per cent Black congregation. And the other ten per cent – elderly White women and two Indian Christian families – seemed equally appreciative. His White assistant pastor was a very tall, born-again young man with horn-rimmed spectacles and a guitar. Under the influence of religious ecstasy (I suppose) he jumped up and down as though on a trampoline while playing the hymn-tunes. His spectacles would have fallen off if not attached to an elastic band and his sweat-shirt said – JESUS FOUND ME! The tubby little pastor jumped up and down beside him, looking perfectly ludicrous, and the congregation stood and sang and clapped and swayed and beat their breasts and moaned and in a few cases turned to their nearest neighbour to weep on the shoulder of a Brother- or Sister-in-Jesus. About three-quarters were elderly men and women, the latter wearing Ascotesque hats. At one side of the wide stage (impossible to think of it as an altar) sat a dozen youngish women clad in identical flowing purple robes and clerical-looking white cravats; the official choir, I assumed at first, but it seemed they were deaconesses of some kind. At intervals during the last hour, when people were really steamed up, several members of the congregation went to the foot of the stage, in response to Mr Plum-Suit's urgings, and entered into a 'healing relationship' with two (or in extreme cases three) Black assistant pastors who 'laid on hands' in a way that was deeply and unexpectedly impressive.

My reactions were split-level throughout. To me Mr Plum-Suit's spiel about witnessing for Christ and persuading family, neighbours and work-mates to seek Jesus was utterly nauseating. I also found the antics of the White pastors both embarrassing and slightly suspect, while being touched by the Blacks' vibrant faith (there is no other possible adjective) and the unmistakable authenticity of their fervour. I'm sure – well, *almost* sure – that Mr Plum-Suit was as devout as he seemed and fulfilled a need in the area. When he arrived from London in 1981 that congregation was down to thirty-four; within a few years he was attracting over 500 on Sundays (twice!) and 200 or so on weekdays. What bothered me was the patronising and manipulating element in the White pastors' leadership: I just wished they weren't there. Two Black assistant pastors also preached and were much less professional than Mr Plum-Suit but to my antennae much more genuine.

It didn't entirely surprise me when, at the end of the notices, Mammon reared its ugly head. We were informed that at a meeting of *all* Handsworth's Churches it had been decided to buy three nearby vacant shops because – "We want to capture this property for Christ! Lately in Handsworth all property and land is being bought up by these Muslims and other 'isms' – people who do not know the Lord! We can use these buildings for the Lord, to give witness to Christ in this area where his enemies are prospering. The price is £48,000 – if only forty-eight of you got together with one thousand pounds each, or four hundred and eighty of you with one hundred pounds each, these premises could be ours for the Lord! From a big bookshop we could spread the Word our neighbours here do not know – we could rescue them from darkness and vice! From a big food-store we could sell things Christians can eat! And perhaps we can set up some light industry to give jobs to the people of the Lord! Christ has directed us to capture this property – tell your friends that it is a great investment – there is no greater investment than spreading the Word."

It was not clear to me where '*all*' the Christian Churches of Handsworth came into the picture; Mr Plum-Suit seemed uncommonly eager to collect the full £48,000 from his own congregation. But I was pleased to observe that the premises in question went to Gujarati Muslims a few months later – yet another victory for Allah ... Mr Plum-Suit's hostility towards non-Christians – apparent both in his voice and on his face – was disturbing and brought an unwholesome response from the congregation. I have quoted his words verbatim; as he spoke I furtively scribbled them down in my personal shorthand.

Most of the congregation lingered in the church after the service and despite the disharmonious note on which it had ended the vibes were good. Little groups formed to exchange news and plan the week's activities; I was soon to discover that Black Pentecostalism is not just for Sundays but fills most spare moments of 'the saints'' lives. Several smiling men and women approached me to shake hands and welcome me to the congregation: heart-warming gestures, with no sense of people merely performing a polite or pious duty. But their acceptance also made me feel uncomfortable. I had no wish to attend their church under false pretences, yet it would have seemed rude to say bluntly, "I've just come to observe and meet people." Then to my relief Miranda appeared – a Heathfield Road neighbour who knew why I was in Handsworth and took charge of 'explaining' me. As the congregation slowly dispersed she introduced me to the Grahams (Evelyn and Clarissa, mother and daughter) and together the four of us walked down the Soho Road, past Handsworth's main Sikh Gurdwara.

Britain's Sikhs have 'adopted' Sunday as their chief day of worship and scores were entering or leaving the Gurdwara, or milling around the fore-court, while little boys with handkerchiefs on their top-knots dared each other to climb the high walls when their elders were out of sight. The marvellously bejewelled women were elegant in shalwar-kameez and the men's multi-coloured turbans added to the gaiety of the scene. Sleek, opulent motor-cars were parked up and down both sides of the wide street: a striking contrast to the few modest little vehicles to be seen parked outside Black churches. My companions, who had been loudly laughing as they recalled the fun of a recent Leicester Pentecostal convention, suddenly fell silent. Then, as we turned into the Villa Road, Evelyn said, "No pubs would be open here today if they'd kept those Pakis out!" I felt as though someone had kicked me in the stomach. This was the first – but not the last – time I heard a Black using the racialist blanket-term 'Paki' to describe any member of the Brown community.

I had of course already registered Brown/Black antipathy and had noticed a surprising (to me) ingredient in Handsworth's inter-racial pudding: some Whites and Blacks, of the older generations, seemed to see themselves as co-victims of the Browns. By now many of the Whites who most fiercely resented 'darkies' in the 1950s and '60s have either died off or moved away and a pleasing number of Handsworth natives regard the original Black immigrants – though not their more turbulent offspring – as respect-worthy folk with whom it is possible to live in a state of friendly neutrality.

When the first Blacks arrived in the 1950s there was full employment and they meekly accepted the worst jobs which no one else wanted. They were hard workers and spoke the same language (more or less) as their White neighbours. Many bought one-family houses, regularly paid their mortages, kept their homes neat-looking, tended their front gardens, went to church twice on Sundays and were no-nonsense parents who beat children if they misbehaved. Most such families have been living in the same houses for twenty or twenty-five years and are generally recognised as model citizens.

The Browns who followed the Blacks in the 1960s (mainly Sikhs and Pakistanis) were equally hard workers and also, in many cases, bought their own homes. The more enterprising among them then took over the Soho Road – Handsworth's 'High Street' – which now looks like a displaced bazaar. As time passed, those who prospered tended to move to more salubrious areas, driving in daily to their Handsworth businesses. They were replaced by more and more and still more immigrants from the sub-continent – culminating in the wretched Bangladeshis – until Browns far outnumbered Blacks. The Soho Road impression of a thriving local Asian community is thus somewhat misleading; most of Handsworth's resident Browns are poor and, because of unemployment, rapidly becoming poorer. Yet both Whites and Blacks cling to their stereotype of 'Smart-Alec Pakis – too clever by half!' Hence that anti-Brown alliance between certain sections of the Black and White communities, based mainly on envy of affluence and intolerance of 'heathens'. The poor Browns, unlike the 'respectable' Blacks, do not at all conform to White lower middle-class standards; in speech, dress, religions and customs they are, and apparently intend to remain, 'outlandish'.

The Grahams invited me to supper on the following Saturday evening. They lived near Handsworth Park, in a quiet, tidy, tree-line road of semi-detached stucco houses with rose-filled gardens. Like many Handsworth settlers, they had bought their home through a local authority mortgage, building societies being reluctant to lend to immigrants. It was an obviously cherished house, outside and in; numerous invitations to Pentecostal jamborees stood on the mantelpiece and elaborately embroidered religious texts (mostly of the warning variety) decorated the pink sitting-room walls between family photographs and pictures of Caribbean beauty spots framed by Theodore (Evelyn's husband) whose hobby was carpentry. On subsequent visits I was admitted to the kitchen, to watch elaborate Caribbean meals in preparation; there too Jesus-texts, printed on steam-proof plastic, were prominent.

Evelyn had come to England in 1955, aged twenty, and trained as a nurse. Three years later she married Theodore – they had known each other in Jamaica – though "he only had a dirty heavy job in a car factory". In 1981 he was made redundant and had since devoted himself to his own church, of which he was a Deacon. (He did not, I gathered, approve of Mr Plum-Suit.) Evelyn was still working, as she had been all her life, only taking time off to have three children – now all in their twenties. Clarissa was the eldest, a strikingly good-looking young woman who had recently qualified as a social worker and was engaged to Luke, a Black teacher. The boys however were a grievous disappointment and not mentioned during that first visit. Later Clarissa told me they had "gone Rasta" and were living in squats; not even D H S S pads but real squats in semi-derelict houses. One had fathered a child at the age of eighteen and been thrown out of the house by Theodore when the girlfriend (by then ex-girlfriend) arrived on the doorstep demanding marriage. Both sported dreadlocks and sold – as distinct from merely smoking –

ganja; so the family lived in tormenting suspense, expecting them to end up in Winson Green.

Theodore declined to discuss race relations. "We done awright," he said. "Don't do no good belly-achin'. If White we done better. But if Jesus wanted us White he'd a made us White – right?"

Evelyn was more expansive. "When I come first I thought: No! I can't live here, not even for a year! But then the shame! To run home and waste all that money! It wasn't *discrimination* – that hurt, yes, that hurt a lot . . . We didn't come expecting the English to be *cruel* – but the Lord gimme strength to keep cool, keep quiet, turn 'nother cheek when bad things happen. It was everything so gloomy I wanted to get away from – no sun or heat, all cold and rain and sharing one damp little room in Sparkbrook with three other girls and not enough to eat – I was hungry three months before I got into training. And remember I was one of the lucky ones, with good schooling. My father was only a poor cane-cutter, he couldn't read, he had nothing. But my mother she saw I was bright and she pushed and she pushed and she sent me into Kingston to live with my aunt and get good schooling . . ."

"But now", interrupted Clarissa, "good schooling isn't enough. Luke's fully qualified and all he can get is supply-teaching jobs, with months on social in between. That's because he's Black. He has no chip. I have no chip. But we have to face facts. It's no good nowadays *not* belly-aching. We've got to do *something*, if we don't want all our kids rotting away in ghetto dustbins. We need more Black Councillors and a few good Black M Ps – really *good* men, not into politics for themselves. That's the way to get things done in this country. Being angry and marching around with placards is all wrong. It puts people's backs up. If they see us becoming part of the British system, the way we're entitled to, they'll maybe take us seriously when we ask to be treated like equals – not demanding anything special, just to be accepted as Black Britons."

Theodore looked indulgently at his daughter, as though she were a five-year-old chattering about fairies in the garden. "You think Whites would vote for Blacks?"

"*Yes!*" said Clarissa. "They'd vote for the right sort of Blacks – the British aren't half so bad as people make out. But they're not going to vote for greedy men like push themselves forward now as 'community leaders'. Our churches should be thinking about all this. Young people should be told they're needed to work for the Lord *in politics*!"

The Grahams, like many of my friends much nearer home, managed to combine sincere religious fervour with implacable bigotry. It would be difficult to meet three more kindly, helpful and big-hearted human beings, yet the mere mention of Sikhs, Hindus or Muslims almost brought them out in a rash. Their comments on Birmingham's prolonged controversy about the Highgate mosque (the city's only handsome new building) were typical. The mullahs were then seeking permission for a two-minute loudspeaker muezzin call daily at noon – scarcely an unreasonable demand. (Two years previously their request for a three-minute call five times a day had been turned down.) Clarissa declared that the noise would upset old people in a nearby home. Theodore insisted that it would dangerously distract motorists on the dual-carriageway and workers in local factories. Evelyn almost shouted – "It's *sinful* to broadcast Muslim prayers in a Christian country! Those people don't really pray – they don't worship Jesus – their God is not forgiving! That's a fanatical, fearful religion with no love or mercy or joy! They believe evil comes from God who punishes them, *we* believe it comes from somewhere else and Jesus the Lord protects us from it."

"Right!" said Clarissa. "And you can't reason with them. They try to hide their retarded kids – they're 'a punishment from Allah'. So if the neighbours saw them they'd know the parents did something real wicked to bring such an awful punishment. What can you do with people like that? And the authorities pretend not to notice. I go to my boss and say, 'Look man, this child needs special schooling and he's locked up all day in a back-room' – and I'm told not to make trouble, we can't interfere too much! But I'm *paid* to see to those kids! Why is there one law for them and another for the rest of us? Luke calls this 'cultural law-breaking'. He says it's a menace to society – right? Those great fat businessmen running sweat-shops all round here, every day they're offering bribes to the police. O K some cops take them and some don't, but they'll never *prosecute* for attempted bribery. They say they know it's 'an Asian custom'! And when men are badly wounded and half-killed in fights at home the police turn another blind eye because 'that's their way of sorting things out'. You can't run a country like this! What's the use talking 'law-and-order' if it's only for some of us? Then the N F says, 'If the Pakis can carve each other up, why shouldn't *we* carve them up?' It's a bad scene, I see too much of it in my work. If I was an author like you I'd write a book about it!"

"What's worse", said Evelyn, "is the way those Anglicans encourage them with talk about 'we all worship the same god'! Shame on them! And now Muslims are looking again for separate schools, but why should my taxes go on children being turned against the Lord Jesus?"

"*And* against the State!" added Clarissa. "If they want separate schools they must pay for them – that's O K, they're entitled to that. And I can see why they want separate-sex schools, it's really a good idea, nowadays."

On which unexpectedly tolerant note I rose to depart, having accepted an invitation to accompany Theodore to a Pentecostal convention in Coventry on the following Sunday.

During the next few months, a variety of knee-testing and mind-broadening encounters with Black Pentecostalism justified my gut-antipathy to the unusual White leadership of Evelyn's church. Mr Plum-Suits are rare on the Black church scene; most congregations have untrained leaders – ordinary folk not 'above' their followers, either educationally or socially.

These men and women come to the leadership by popular acclaim. They are not 'career' parsons or pastors but earn their living how they can, sometimes in more menial jobs than the better-off members of their congregations. This spontaneity and informality has certain disadvantages: chiefly the risk of fragmentation, ever-present in all Black endeavours. Also, a dishonest pastor can easily exploit his or her congregation for personal gain and occasional scandals do rock the Pentecostal world. Yet the advantages seem to outweigh the disadvantages. In a society that consistently down-grades Blacks, Black Pentecostalism is in fact Black Power triumphantly in action, even if most church-goers don't think of it in those terms. This autonomous, distinctive Black world, organised by Blacks for Blacks and on which Whites rarely impinge, should be more valued than it is by anti-racists of all colours. True, the New Testament Church of God (Britain's largest Black denomination), the Calvary Church of God in Christ and the Church of God of Prophecy were all founded in the USA and are 'Black churches' only in Britain. But this by now is irrelevant. Some funding, to purchase buildings, comes occasionally from the States, yet within the past quarter-century 'Westindian Pentecostalism' has evolved as a way of worship peculiar to British Blacks and fulfilling their particular needs.

Nothing in Handsworth, where my experiences were quite varied, surprised me as much as my own reactions to Black Pentecostalism. At several three-hour services I didn't notice the time passing: partly because of the rousing musical content, partly because of the unpredictability of each service. There is no set liturgy and the congregation's belief that it is being led by the Spirit rather than the Pastor engenders an atmosphere of expectancy and creativity. Inevitably this 'group-thing' sometimes fails; then a feeling of anti-climax takes over and the Pastor has to retrieve the situation – usually by calling for more and louder hymn-singing. But such failures do not make the congregation's faith and fervour seem any less genuine. That word 'genuine' recurs again and again in my journal notes on Holy Marathons – perhaps because I started out so prejudiced against these displays of uninhibited mass-emotion.

The Black churches are authentic 'churches of the people'. Each member of the congregation can and obviously does feel that his or her contribution or need is as significant as anyone else's. There is a powerful sense of community, of people truly caring for and positively helping one another. 'Divine healing' is at the core of Black Pentecostalism and time after time I watched people in deep distress – men and women, young and old – answering the 'altar-call' and then returning comforted to their seats after the laying on of hands. Even in Mr Plum-Suit's church, where the leadership so switched me off, I was at once conscious of something extraordinary happening when this ritual began.

White theologians fight like cats about Black Pentecostalism: about the influence of West African tribal religions, the acceptability (or otherwise) of going into paroxysms or trances, the wisdom (or otherwise) of encouraging people to believe that they have received or may receive 'personal' messages from the Spirit. One theologian friend, who has never personally encountered Britain's Black Pentecostalism, wrote to me:

A real concern for many mainline clergy, and psychologists, is what happens to people when they come down off that emotional high? Cases of acute depression are being dealt with every day – people who have been swept up into the ninth heaven, and then fallen such a long, long way to ordinariness, which ricochets in their psyche as defeat, betrayal, disillusionment . . .

I wrote back:

It's easy to see how some (many?) White Born-agains might suffer thus, probably because of a basic instability that caused their 're-birth' in the first place. But my Handsworth friends and neighbours, far from coming off their emotional high and lapsing into depression, go home happily fortified against the difficulties, dis-appointments and tensions of daily life. For them the excitement of the service is not just an emotional fix – and more prosaic church-related activities are closely interwoven with week-day routines. Most religions have their occupational hazards, but I can't imagine Black Pentecostalism doing as much collateral damage as Irish Catholicism has done through its paranoid attitude to sexuality. Anyway religion is a mystery, not something to be controlled by theologians and given rules like a parlour-game. By its fruit ye shall know it. And most of the fruits of Black Pentecostalism seem wholesome. Doesn't every form of religious expression – rituals, penances, liturgies, pilgrimages, pujas, sacrifices, processions, trances or dances – have an equal potential for fulfilling the needs of individuals? Depending on their cultural background, emotional disposition, intellectual development, material circumstances . . . And isn't it therefore important to respect all religions, however zany by our standards, because they still mean so much to so many? It seems mankind is now evolving beyond the stage – many millenia long – when spiritual needs could be catered for by institutionalized illusions. We haven't yet found a replacement – but people are searching. Perhaps the present gruesome Fundamentalist Revival (Islamic and Christian) is part of our transition from one era to another?

Another common criticism is that Black Pentecostalism offers too easy an escape from reality – from the dreariness and frustration of inner-city life – and so politically emasculates its adherents. When they should be struggling to improve this world, they are ecstatically hymn-singing and concentrating on the next. I most often heard this complaint from young Blacks, who had reacted against devout parents and despised them for opting out. Yet my own observations did not confirm their stereotype. Although many church-goers do indeed keep their sights fixed on heaven – and some even regard it as sinful to think in terms of social reform – I met many others who were healthily angry not only about the issues that concern all Blacks and Browns in Britain but about the dangerous level of inner-city deprivation, which affects all races. Clarissa's view that the pastors should encourage young people to enter politics was quite common among her generation and it may be that the sort of Black parliamentary candidates best fitted to represent all communities will be found among 'the saints'.

One evening, in a rather up-market hotel bar near Handsworth Wood, I met two Jamaican social scientists who were already discussing Black churches when I edged my way into their conversation. (I don't always intrude on bar conversations, but this one was irresistible.) Neither of course was a Pentecostalist, to whom bars are anathema, but both fervently praised the Black churches. They were considering a survey to establish the correlation they believe exists between Black church-going, material prosperity and family stability.

"Black Pentecostalism is a major anchor," said Lionel (aged fifty-ish).

"And he doesn't mean it's our 'opium of the masses'," added Julian (aged thirty-ish).

"Look back to the '50s," said Lionel. "Think of the tens of thousands arriving here penniless, poorly educated, semi-skilled or with skills below the British standards for good jobs. Think how homesick they were – and spaced out by the sheer size of the cities and the pace of life. Think of the hurt and shock of not being *accepted* as British when they thought they were coming to their 'Motherland'. Think of the disappointment of not being able to earn big and send home good money. Think of the insults they had to swallow – often being treated literally like dogs. 'No coloureds or dogs' – and people refusing to work beside them because they didn't like their smell. Think of the cramped rooms they were packed into and the dismal cold demoralising English weather. Think of the boring drudgery of dead-end jobs and knowing promotion was unlikely however hard they worked to earn it . . . Add all that together and you wonder why the Caribbean community *didn't* soon become what so many Whites think it is – an inert mass of lazy scrounging lay-abouts. And why didn't it? Mainly, I say, because the Black churches helped people to keep their dignity through the worst of it all. *And* gave them a framework for living that made it possible for them to prosper. Not to get rich, like the Asians – but look around at the numbers who've done well enough, starting from nothing and shackled by prejudice every step of the way! *Why* have they done well? Because they never spent a penny on what they call 'worldly behaviour' – smoking, drinking, betting, entertainments. How many Whites on the same pay for the same time are still way down at the bottom of the heap, living in misery in Council high-rises, half of them up to their snouts in debt!"

Julian agreed with all this but foresaw the Black churches declining quite soon, or at least undergoing changes likely to drain them of their distinctive essence. "Already some congregations are showing signs of wanting to move into line with the traditional, disciplined, property-owning White churches, led by trained ministers. And that's dangerous – they could end up no better than America's Moral Majority!"

"Sure," said Lionel, "that's happening already. But it could be good in ways. At the same time you've more and more small congregations starting up through spontaneous combustion and worshipping hand-to-mouth in rented halls and people's front parlours. Maybe a bit of both is healthy. Westindian Pentecostalism *could* get very introverted and cranky and out of touch with reality. There's a strong argument to be made for a few more trained ministers. And some folk fancy a touch of formality, and the status of a church *building* of their own – they need that kind of reassurance. Others enjoy improvising every week, and don't want a trained smoothy for pastor, and think it's more Christian *not* to own property. So why not cater for all sorts?"

"And what about the younger generation?" I asked.

"Well," said Lionel, "the younger generation is made up of individuals, just like any other generation! Sure lots of them are revolting against church twice on Sundays, *plus* Sunday School in the afternoon *and* compulsory churchy activities all week. But lots more stick with it, voluntarily, right through teens and early twenties when you'd expect them to be running wild. It's hard to judge how much this has to do with their own needs and how much with sensible parents – not putting too much pressure on, so the kids don't feel they have to defy them. Then you get lots more who've kicked the whole thing for a few years and they hear of some new congregation – nothing to do with the parents' – and maybe it's one that likes a lot of drums so they go right back into the middle of it all. *And* give up smoking and drinking, which is pretty remarkable." (On the previous Sunday I had been to one such service, where the noise almost deafened me, and I reckoned some seventy-five per cent of the 400-strong congregation were under thirty.)

"But there *is* a problem here," said Julian. "And it's a big problem. It's the great 'minus' in Pentecostalism, after all the 'pluses' we've been giving it. Those kids hanging out on the Villa Road all day and half the night – people think they're the dregs of the Afro community and sure, OK, some are. But many have been driven away to that fringe by hyper-religious families. I know two of those kids got thrashed by their fathers when they were *eighteen* for coming home one evening at 11.00 instead of 10.00. In Britain in the '80s you don't get away with treating kids like that. They're in a squat now, when they're not sitting on the wall outside the Villa Cross. Lots of school-leavers get desperate with their home situations. They reckon it's all or nothing. Stick with the family life-style or swing right away into the good-timing blues world of reggae, booze, ganja and making babies ad lib. Growing up they've never had any experience of *moderation* – the atmosphere around them has always been *intense*. So if they can't handle the total rejection of worldliness they go right over the edge. And what to do? How to help them?"

"There's not much anyone can do," commented Lionel, "because anti-worldliness is the cornerstone of Pentecostalism. No reform is on. To relax the rules would mean the end of the Black churches. So the most you can hope for is parents coming round to the notion of enforcing the rules more gently."

He turned to me and added, "Don't look so depressed! Julian's exaggerating – plenty kids get out from under the heavy religious bit but don't go good-timing round the Villa Cross!"

In Handsworth I met few Blacks like Julian and Lionel; perhaps I didn't frequent enough up-market pubs – not that there are many of those. Both men would have been contemptuously dismissed as 'coconuts' (White inside) by my Rasta friends. They were also fair-skinned – the hallmark of professional-class Jamaicans – but had shown more concern for their less fortunate fellow-islanders than many successful Jamaicans do.

Walking back to Heathfield Road at midnight, past several locally notorious squats where blues parties had started (and would continue all night) I pondered yet again the problem of *colour*. Why do so many non-Whites (especially Afro-Caribbeans and most especially Jamaicans) want to look as Caucasian as possible, not only in skin-shade but in features, hair, figure? Anti-racists like to put all the blame on the omnipotent White imperialists who gave everyone else chronic inferiority complexes. Clearly this is part of the answer: an important part, in the Caribbean. But it doesn't explain the antiquity and extent of the 'white-is-good' syndrome. Both the Incas and Aztecs had ancient legends about a god emerging from the sea: and he was a *white*-skinned god, though they had never seen a white-skinned human being. When the semi-nomadic pastoralist Aryans invaded India *circa* 1500 BC they were divided into three social *classes* but had no restrictions on inter-class marriage or 'social mobility'. Eventually they came up against an urbanised and far more technologically advanced culture – the Harappan – whose people were dark-skinned and flat-featured. At that point:

> The first step in the direction of caste was taken when the Aryans treated the Dasas as beyond the social pale, probably owing to a fear . . . that assimilation with them would lead to a loss of Aryan identity. Ostensibly the distinction was largely that of colour . . . The Sanskrit word for caste, *varna*, actually means colour. The colour element of caste was emphasized, throughout this period, and was eventually to become deep-rooted in north-Indian Aryan culture.*

The Japanese, long centuries before they saw or heard of their first European or American, valued a *white* skin and looked down on their own sun-tanned peasantry. As Dick Wilson has recently pointed out:

> The Japanese think of themselves as yellow only when they have jaundice. The association of white with beauty, and black with ugliness, goes far back into Japanese history. White skin is essential to feminine beauty and as long ago as the eighth century women at court were putting white powder and rouge on their faces – to be imitated in the twelfth century by aristocratic men . . . In the summer of 1965 the mass-circulation paper *Mainichi Shimbun* could say in its women's column: 'Blessed are those white in colour . . . How can you become a white beauty? You should be careful not to expose your skin directly to the ultra-violet rays in sunshine

---

* Romila Thapar, *A History of India*, Vol. I, Pelican (1966)

. . .' A Japanese mother in the USA explains that her daughter is considered very 'white' by their compatriots. "Looking at her face, I often say to myself how white she is. As a mother I feel happy. But when I see her among Caucasian children in a nursery school, alas, my daughter is yellow indeed."*

Laurens van der Post has recalled having a long discussion with the late Chogyal of Sikkim about the origins of colour prejudice. He told the Buddhist ruler of his belief that the White South Africans' antagonism against Blacks is owing to "the Calvinistic heresy of taking symbolism literally and not seeing therefore that the 'black' they feared was a darkness in their own soul". The Chogyal replied, "You know, what you have told me explains to me for the first time why the Tibetans have always spoken of the Chinese as 'the black people', symbolically, of course."

This exchange is a reminder that 'black' has negative connotations beyond Europe. Much has been written, in Britain and America, about the role of the word in the English language. The black sheep of the family. A black day for me. Blacklisting, blackballing, blackmail, black-market, black thoughts, black looks, black marks, black souls, black ingratitude, a black future – the list is endless, the association of badness/misfortune/ugliness/inferiority with *blackness* is powerful. When my attention was first drawn to this semantic fact I tended, like most Whites, to dismiss it as an irrelevancy and laugh at the notion of emending the English language – for example, by renaming 'blackboards' 'chalkboards'. But when I got deeper into the complexities of race relations the association began to seem more significant. Numerous teachers assured me that five-year-old Black and Brown children are already conscious of being at a disadvantage, because they are not White – and are quite often found applying to their bodies every sort of substance, from scouring powder to Bleach, in heart-rending efforts to become less black. Yet the average Brown is far better-looking than the average White. And frequently Black is *very* Beautiful. Africans wearing splendid garments which suit their colouring and physique, as European clothes usually do not, make me wonder when the Black Power movement will set up an African fashion industry in opposition to the degrading skin- and hair-modifying industries. But such a trend might not have many Afro-Caribbean followers.

Africans and Afro-Caribbeans react differently to White colour prejudice. The former may resent it no less but they also despise it. The latter have a tradition of condoning and perpetuating it, while simultaneously resisting and condemning it. More than thirty years ago F.M. Henriques, writing about the society from which most of Britain's Blacks migrated, noted that Jamaicans, in particular, have for long been pathologically colour-obsessed and suffer from acute inner anxieties and conflicts caused by their society's 'White bias'. And in 1935 Marcus Garvey, the Jamaican 'African Redemption' crusader and Rastafarian hero observed:

---

* Dick Wilson, *The Sun At Noon*, Hamish Hamilton (1986)

> The Jamaicans hate themselves because they constitute a mixed population and their colour is the standard for everything. The people in Jamaica worship colour, that is the colour of the skin. They think it is the greatest and best thing in life, hence people who are even related by blood, if they are not of the same complexion, hate and despise each other. A British Governor . . . finds when he goes to Jamaica . . . a country divided on the shades of colour. The few real White people who are in the country being more sensible than the rest, allow the native population the freedom of their own thoughts, and so the coloured and black peoples carry on among themselves a peculiar prejudice that affects the natural life of the country. Not even hurricanes and earthquakes do much in getting them to realise their oneness.*

Jamaica's small upper class (higher civil servants and professionals) was always White or fair-skinned. The middle class (clerical staff, teachers, traders) was 'coloured' with a scattering of upwardly mobile Blacks. The other eighty per cent of the population was and still is made up of Black labourers and peasants. Fairness of skin and social status have for so long been linked in everyone's mind that an ambitious Black, who was doing well economically, would try to 'marry light' to give his children the priceless advantage of skin fairer than his own. According to Dr Henriques, 'A Fair man who marries a Dark or Black woman commits social suicide. A Black man, wishing to be socially successful, who does the same throws away the only opportunity he will have of "raising his colour".'† Most disturbing of all, mothers with children of varying shades (a common situation) usually favour the fairer-skinned offspring, with predictable results for the emotional well-being of their darker siblings. (This consequence of 'White bias' has unfortunately survived the passage to Britain, in some cases.)

Black anti-racists impatiently denounce such 'looking backwards'. To them Caribbean attitudes and customs – White bias, marriage patterns and so on – seem entirely irrelevant to the present problems of Britain's Blacks, half of whom have never set foot in the Caribbean and probably never will. They deny that their forefathers' (and mothers') colour hang-ups impinge on their own life and attribute *all* their colour-related difficulties to native British prejudice. Yet many of my personal encounters suggested that the situation may be more complicated. Some of my most awkward relationships were with fair-skinned Afro-Caribbeans whose top-of-the-pile position would have been assured in Jamaica but who in Britain are agonisingly conscious of being Black – or at best 'half-caste' – in White eyes.

For some 'dark' British Blacks, from the eighty per cent layer, White bias creates other problems. As Sheila Patterson has noted, the Jamaican preoccupation with skin-shades produces 'a tendency to interpret everyday situations, and particularly setbacks, in terms of colour'.‡ Very often, in Britain,

---

* John Henrik Clarke (Ed.), *Marcus Garvey and the Vision of Africa*, Vintage Books (1974)
† F.M. Henriques, 'Colour Values in Jamaican Society', *British Journal of Sociology*, Vol.2, No.II (1951)
‡ Sheila Patterson, *Dark Strangers*, Pelican (1963)

this is the correct interpretation of setbacks. Yet a Black who sees himself as inferior because Black, and is tensely expecting to fail, will be more likely to provoke discrimination than a relaxed Black with equal (or even lesser) qualifications.

Another side-effect of White bias was revealed by a thirty-five-year-old woman, a Black Power activist who came to Handsworth at the age of fifteen. "Here we're just dirt," she said, "not even noticed by Whitey, just shovelled away into corners and forgotten. At least back home we're in the majority and there's always some chance a majority can get organised and take over. Here we feel doomed, hopeless, trapped – dumped in what will become *real* ghettoes, like they have in the States, if no one pays attention to the way things are going."

Tentatively, I asked if she would ever consider going back to Jamaica, to help organise the revolution. For a moment it seemed she was going to attack me physically. "What d'you want?" she yelled. "Repatriation? Why should I give in to the fascists and run away just to please all you fuckin' Whiteys? This bloody country needs a revolution too!"

End of conversation . . .

Colour-based inferiority feelings run so deep in some Afro-Caribbeans that one fears it may be psychologically impossible for them ever to adjust to life in a White country, even if it is their birth-place. One Trinidadian social worker assured me that his British-born generation contains a higher percentage of 'White bias victims' than the immigrant generation. Thousands of those youngsters have nothing to do all day but brood over the disadvantages of being Black in an unjust racialist society. Genuine Rastamen, pseudo-Rastas, Black Power militants and Marcus Garvey disciples of assorted kinds are all striving to counteract their inherited White bias by cultivating pride in being 'out of Africa'; but the strong element of fantasy in this endeavour can lead to its having a destabilising effect.

It is an over-simplification to describe White bias as 'the most enduring legacy of slavery'. Its tap-root lies deep in the slave centuries but it has endured because *White domination* endured, after abolition *and* after 'independence'. Today the allegedly 'independent' Caribbean countries are dominated by multi-nationals like Tate & Lyle and Trust House Forte, whose profits are not shared with the Black eighty per cent. Had my Black Power activist friend (or ex-friend) chosen to argue with me, she might have pointed out that there are good reasons for Blacks – however bleak their prospects in Britain – *not* returning to the Caribbean. There is nothing to go back to and they are sensible to remain where they can at least obtain some indirect benefits, through the D H S S, from the continuing White exploitation of the Caribbean.

9 · Black, White and Browned-off

The Blacks, the Whites, the Browns . . . Any writer using those terms has to assume sympathetic readers who will make allowances for the limitations of language. I use them with Bhikhu Parekh's warning, quoted on the title-page, always in mind. It is indeed an 'impertinence' to write about a community of men 'as if they were objects under a microscope'. Yet it does help to know what holds a community together and makes it 'distinct and unique'. If it *is* held together and distinct . . . One evening in late June Black disunity – political and cultural – was vividly illustrated at a Black Women's Poetry Reading in the large bleak theatre of a local Community Centre.

I arrived early and studied the bookstall, run by three White feminists and offering Anti-racist, Far Left, Feminist, Anti-nuclear and Black Studies literature. It startled me to see copies of my own autobiography in the Feminist section. Subsequently a Nigerian woman, noticing my Irish brogue, asked me if I knew Dervla Murphy. I replied, "Slightly" – which is probably true.

The audience of fifty-four looked disappointingly meagre in that vast theatre. It was mainly Black – fair-skinned, middle-class Blacks – plus the Nigerian, about a dozen Asian and White women and five men. Two of the males were earnest, New Statesman-ish Whites; one was a tall, elegant, tweed-clad Kashmiri whom I mistook for an Englishman until he spoke; two were angry-looking youngish Blacks beside whom I sat. Even before the first reading began, an odd criss-crossing of subtle tensions was apparent in the atmosphere and the honey-skinned Jamaican chairwoman wore an 'I'm-expecting-trouble' expression.

The three poets seemed unaffected either by the smallness of their audience or by the electricity in the air; possibly they were used to both. Their poetry was superb: exhilarating, musical – at once sharpening the wits and wringing the heart. Poets often seem too smug or too shy when reading their own work but these women were stunningly effective. The sheer beauty of their language filled me with a delicious dizzy excitement. By far the most important message coming through to me was 'Wave-length is all! Forget skin-colour!' I was responding to those three people as *writers*: their Blackness and Feminism seemed secondary. Yet this was not how they saw themselves. Each was emphatic about being a *Black* woman before all else and much of their work dealt with the exact significance of being Black *and* a woman in the 1980s. This I found disconcerting. While I (and no doubt the other Whites present) were revering those three poets as creators of beauty, they were proclaiming that their separating Blackness was more significant than their unifying creativity, that their race mattered more than our common humanity. *They* were keeping a 'colour-bar' firmly in place. Yet as the evening developed I sensed that for them writing was in fact the most important thing in their lives. Recognising kindred spirits, I was rejoicing in this feeling of closeness when during the discussion session a haughty Jamaican woman stood up – tall and commanding in flowing African robes – to ask if the poets felt "the encounter" would have been more valuable and enjoyable without a White presence. All three were embarrassed – even distressed – by this question. Yet being honest they could only say "Yes", which hurt me absurdly while being very good for my arrogant White soul. (At intervals I need to be forced to acknowledge that other people's realities are just as real as my own.) Each of the three then explained, in fascinatingly different ways, that they *also* enjoy mixed encounters and regard them as important on another level; and they seemed sincere – not merely soothing the feelings of the few discomfited Whites. When the tweedy Kashmiri gentleman asked if the presence of Asian women also alters the nature of such encounters it was the poets' turn to look discomfited. The political need to affirm solidarity with all non-White women prevented their admitting that on such occasions they find the presence of any non-Blacks restricting: which clearly was how they felt.

Many of the poems, and most of the questions from the audience, had to do with growing up Black in Britain. It puzzled me that Lucia, at twenty-four the youngest of the three, was accepted as 'Black'. If she had any African blood it didn't show; she might have been Greek, Pathan, Italian, Turkish, Spanish. In fact she was a Trinidadian/Amerindian/English mix and one of the most beautiful women I have ever seen. Afterwards I was told that as a fifteen-year-old she had witnessed her best friend, a Barbadian girl, being slashed about the face by razor-wielding N F gangsters. The girl almost bled to death and needed plastic surgery. Lucia then threw in her lot with Britain's Blacks.

Charlie (Charlotte) had handsome 'Afro' features and hair and the sort of complexion some White women spend a fortune trying to acquire – a rich golden-brown. She had grown up in 'an exclusive suburb' in Edinburgh having been adopted, with her half-brother, by a White couple. Her father was Jamaican, her brother's father Nigerian; their White mother had them both before she was twenty. One of Charlie's poems described the shock of first coming into contact with Blacks when she went to London University at the age of seventeen; she had been the only non-White pupil at her girls' grammar school. At once she felt a longing to be *Black*: not White in everything but appearance. When a young Asian woman in the back row asked how her parents had reacted to this she admitted they felt personally rejected – "They were embittered but they have always tried not to show it." From within their White secluded suburb – "all well-bred and low-key" – they couldn't begin to understand that for people of mixed race life can be rough in the big wide world. "They couldn't imagine what I meant when I tried to explain that for my own security, emotional *and* physical, I needed to be a Black among Blacks." Also – "I'd have despised myself forever, as a coward and traitor to my Black half, if I'd chosen the soft option, which my brother did, and put everything into being accepted by Whites, being successful in their world by their standards."

Another young Asian woman asked, "Did you not feel *guilty* about hurting your parents so much?" (Having talked to her before the reading I knew she was a Mirpuri.)

"No," said Charlie, "I didn't feel guilty because I'd done nothing to make that situation. But I did feel very sad – I still feel sad, and they still feel hurt – they never came around to the idea of my living in a different mental world. I suppose you could say mine was a political decision in the widest sense. Yet really we have no honourable alternative. The decision is made for us, by Whites. At university I was called a Black bastard, a mulatto bitch, a dirty nigger, a half-caste cunt. So of course I wanted to be Black – you understand? You see how most of us have no choice, though we get a lot of stick for being poseurs, especially if we're very fair." She glanced at the almost-White chairwoman and half-smiled. "It seems to some our calling ourselves Black is an affectation. But White society has pushed us into a maybe exaggerated pride in our incomplete Blackness by sneering at our incomplete Whiteness. We three poets and anyone like us *could* choose to be White. We'd be *apparently* accepted as fully-paid-up 'equals' of the Whites because of our talents and reputation and what the media call our 'charm'. But then we'd be ditching the majority, the ordinary Blacks and mixed-race folk who have no special gifts and are treated like garbage. Or at best like handicapped people – handicapped by not being *White!* If we don't stick with them, who will? If we don't identify with them, insist on being considered Black and part of *their* culture and community, what hope do they have of building up confidence and self-respect?"

Lucia and Charlie both defined themselves as lesbians but Florence – in her early forties, very dark-skinned and the finest of those three fine poets – was happily married with an eleven-year-old daughter. Both her parents (White father, Jamaican mother) were academics who spent much time abroad and she was brought up in London by her Black granny – "the most influential person in my life". Like Charlie, she was the only non-White in her rather posh girls' grammar school and grew up acutely conscious of everyone "trying to be polite and pretending not to notice, as one might with a hare-lip or club-foot". It was during Florence's question-and-answer session that the chairwoman temporarily lost control of our 'encounter'.

Sparks had been flying sporadically throughout the evening – with increasing frequency – but thus far each shower had been firmly stamped out by the chairwoman before it could start a general conflagration. At one point, early on, the only *black* Black woman in the hall (the Nigerian) had described herself as "a *real* African", which provoked enraged protests from Afro-Caribbean Black Power adherents who like to think of themselves as just that. But most of the sparks had been coming from the two Black men beside me – Lloyd and Kelvin – who had attended the reading with sabotage in mind. Both belonged to a Black Militant group intermittently prominent in Handsworth for the past twenty years, though it has recently been becoming less militant and more socially constructive. They had repeatedly interrupted the poetry readings and been truculently argumentative during the half-hour wine-and-somoza break. Their comments became louder and more taunting as Charlie answered the Asian girls' questions. When she referred to "mixed race folk who have no special gifts" Lloyd – sitting beside me – rolled up a sleeve, tapped his light brown arm and yelled, "Why d'you think I'm this colour? Who were the bed-warmers on the slave-ships?" For over an hour I had been seething with angry contempt for his vile manners: but suddenly my anger was switched off. I looked down at his outstretched arm and was aware only of his anguish, his tormenting, forever-hopeless identity-search. And then that collective racial guilt, of which I so disapprove in theory, engulfed me with the force of a big wave that takes you by surprise from behind. But perhaps it is no bad thing to feel guilty about *what we are still doing* to the slaves' descendants.

As Florence began to answer a question about the 'under-achievement' of Black children in British schools, Lloyd and Kelvin became intolerably disruptive and insulting. Springing to their feet, they accused all three poets of trying to ape Shakespeare, faking concern for inner-city Blacks, trying to impress their audience with long words, being as patronising as Whites, boot-licking the academic establishment, knowing nothing about the realities of life for most British Blacks, contributing nothing to the 'Revolution' and imitating BBC accents. (Florence had the misfortune to speak with what used to be quaintly known as 'an Oxford accent'.) For a few moments the chairwoman tried to continue keeping her patience – being quietly firm, calmly reasonable. Then she too stood up, stamped her foot and requested all men present (all five of them!) to leave the room. This drew another fusillade of jeers from the Militants. Lloyd shouted that no bunch of bent women could dictate to *them*. Kelvin challenged everyone – "Who'll dare to throw us out?" In instant and rather remarkable response, we women – saying nothing – spontaneously drew our chairs in a tight semi-circle around the poets as the three innocent men meekly and sadly left the hall. The Militants made no attempt to force their way into our circle; I suspect they felt slightly intimidated by the vibes we were producing. But they remained in the background, sniggering and muttering about the three poems with which our 'encounter' was rounded off.

Walking home at midnight, between silent moonlit terraces of 1880s brick houses, I remembered Lloyd's outstretched arm and reflected on Charlie's use of the word 'incomplete' – "our incomplete Blackness, our incomplete Whiteness". That usage distilled the tragedy of countless lives, Lloyd's among them. Yet those three women – as human beings – and those three poets – as artists – were proof enough that 'mixed blood' can have gloriously 'complete' results. The problems is not miscegenation, but people's attitude towards it. All sorts of people: Black, White, Brown, mixed.

A young African acquaintance brought up this subject a few evenings later, in the Grey Dove. Asto was a twenty-three-year-old bio-chemistry student from Botswana, in his second year at Birmingham Polytechnic, and he had many tenaciously held theories. One concerned alcohol; he believed that nobody should drink more than a pint of beer in twenty-four hours. Another concerned miscegenation; he believed in a physiological antipathy between Caucasians and Negroes which will never be overcome by more than a tiny minority on either side and will always defeat the most strenuous efforts of 'do-gooders' to persuade people that race doesn't or shouldn't matter. "It's really a chemical repulsion," he assured me. "You'll say you don't feel it, because you've been mentally conditioned not to admit to yourself that you do feel it. But most people aren't so inhibited. And that's why you get so much opposition to mixed blood. It's unnatural."

"You sound like a spokesman for the South African government," I said. "Or even the Ku-Klux-Klan."

"That doesn't bother me," replied Asto, taking another small mouthful of his daily pint. "I'm not interested in politics. I'm only interested in race relations as a scientific issue. I feel bad in a room with a White person and a dog because I know he feels closer to the dog than to me – he doesn't really *relax* with me."

I pointed out that it is a common English idiosyncrasy to be more at ease with dogs than with human beings of any colour. But Asto wasn't listening. He said, "It *is* a scientific issue. People are afraid to admit to themselves that deep down they're physically repelled by Blacks. *That's* why they can't relax – not because they're repelled but because they can't admit it. Me and my White friends, we'd have better times together if they'd *admit* they'd hate their sisters to marry me. I don't mind admitting I'd hate to marry their sisters – White girls are only half-alive. Blacks marry them just to image-build, like moving from Lozells to Handsworth Wood. And Whites marrying Blacks is more of it, like being vegetarian and joining CND. And it's cruel, making babies who can never be happy adults. We need to be scientific and honest. People don't have to be guilty about scientific facts. If you're allergic to flour or cats or feathers you don't feel *guilty* about it! We could all be more relaxed together if everyone accepted this deep-down physical antipathy, built into us. It doesn't give one race the right to dominate another. It's nothing to do with superiority or inferiority. It's just being scientific and detached about *differences*. Most African people are soft and kind. Most European people are hard and cruel. That sounds like prejudice – I can see from your face you want to argue. But you only see Africans on TV, killing and burning and cutting each other's guts out. Suppose you were African and only saw war-films of Europeans bombing each other and newsreels of what they found in Hitler's camps in 1945 and documentaries about money fiddles in Wall Street and the CIA and Mafia woking together – *then* how would you see White people? Africans are soft and kind because we've stayed more human. We're still aware of all sorts of things you don't know exist. Europeans had to throw out important things to make room in their minds for all their new scientific knowledge. I can see how it works. I'm here eighteen months, studying hard and never taking holidays, and I'm beginning to do the same – maybe you have to . . . It's worrying me. I want to be a *good* scientist – really top-class – but I don't want to be hard and cruel! And I don't want to stay in Europe. I've been watching race relations in this country and all colours have big problems. You're a brave lady to be writing about them – put what I've said in your book and I'll buy a copy!" Asto finished his pint, picked up his initialled leather brief-case, looked at his solid gold watch and said, "Now I must go home, eat one tin of sardines and two bananas and study for four and a half hours." He seemed a very organised young man.

I was waiting that evening for Dinah, a Black child welfare officer who had befriended me at the poetry reading and suggested meeting for a drink. The Grey Dove was one of my favourite pubs, an interesting multi-racial hostelry on the borderline between Handworth and Handsworth Wood. Its lunch-time customers were mainly Irish enveloping workmen; its evening customers were prosperous-looking young people of all colours, many of them students. As a newcomer to Brum, it astounded me to see Brown girls (Hindu, Sikh and *Muslim*!) drinking and flirting in the Grey Dove with Brown (and occasionally White) boyfriends; an unimaginable sight in Bradford, unless they were prostitutes. There too I first noticed the fashion, among 'liberated' Brown youths, for imitating Rasta mannerisms and trying to speak Jamaican patois. Most of the Black women were trendily dressed, with relaxed hair and, quite often, White boyfriends. (Asto's 'chemical repulsion' theory would have provoked derisive laughter among the Grey Dove clientele.) White girls with Black boyfriends were less common but not remarkable, and mixed groups of friends regularly met – women and men, Blacks, Brown and White in every combination. There were always more single-race than mixed groups, but quite often as the evening aged small groups merged into big multi-racial parties. Judging only by the Grey Dove's atmosphere, one would assume Handsworth to be free of racial tension.

The young White customers I talked to were unanimous that they are far less prejudiced than their parents' and grandparents' generations. As one engineering student put it, "We've grown up with Afros and Asians so we just take them for granted – if they take us for granted. I hate those thugs on the Villa Road and I'd be scared to go into the Villa Cross – but then there's tough White pubs in Kingstanding I wouldn't fancy either. It's not people's *colour* we think about, it's their *type*. In here you get your own type, of all colours. No drugs, no tarts, no boozy fights and flick-knives. We just enjoy beer and talk and the machines perhaps and pool sometimes. But my father and his pals never come here now. It used to be their local, when all round was White, and you hear them cursing a bit about being pushed off their own patch. They've got nothing *against* coloureds, really – I mean, they wouldn't *harm* them. It's just they like being with their own crowd. So now this is what they call a 'young pub' – we don't often get people your age in here, meaning no offence!"

When Dinah arrived I told her about that conversation and we looked around the crowded and happily mixed pub and I asked, "Was that young man hitting an important nail on the head when he said it's type not colour that matters, to his age-group? D'you think from now on miscegenation might be part of the answer?"

"You should have asked Charlie", said Dinah. "We talked the other evening, after those crazy men went. I told her I worked with kids and she *begged* me – 'Use your influence to discourage more mixed babies! They can't be at ease with either community and both look down on them.' I agree. I do try to talk sense to the youngsters, but it's hard to make them look ahead. I've been watching it all happening for ten years. If mixed kids grow up and get hooked on Black Power they're like Lloyd, feeling White blood is polluting and going half-hysterical about being *fair*. If they turn the other way they're secretly proud of being not real black but discontented about being not real White. Like Charlie said in the discussion, they're incomplete both ways."

"But they're not, in fact," I objected. "That's only how people imagine them to be. There's nothing incomplete about Charlie herself, or Lucia or Florence – or any of the thousands of mixed-race people all over the world. Objectively there's no argument against miscegenation. And given more of it attitudes would change. The 'incomplete' hang-up would get to look silly and vanish."

Dinah stared at me for a moment with open contempt. Then she laughed, rather sourly. "You're all the same, you Whiteys! Fanciful theory! OK for filling books but it does *us* no good spreading your fancies around. I'm working every day with mixed kids and I want to see *less* of them – not more. Maybe you're right. Maybe in a hundred years things would be better. But that's making guinea-pigs of the next few generations. And we're talking about *human beings*, not lab. experiments. They say all Afro-Caribbeans have some White blood and my mum says one of her grand-dads was English. But I'm glad I don't show no sign of it. I'm no Black Power freak, it just feels good to be all Black. It feels *right*. I'd never marry a White man – I wouldn't want a batch of neurotic kids!"

Dinah was a formidable woman: tall, burly, stern-looking, sloppily dressed, slow-moving – but quick-thinking. Her main professional gripe was the separation of siblings when whole families were taken into care. "And it's not just Blacks, they mess everyone up. Last week I'd three White kids – eight, nine and eleven – pushed off in different directions. But the worst was in 1981, five kids under ten orphaned – parents from St Kitts killed on the M6. A beautifully happy united family . . . But those kids were torn apart and put in five different Homes when all they'd left was each other. The eldest's fourteen now – last month they had to put her in a psychiatric ward. Have those bureaucrats no hearts? Do they think kids are files of documents and you shove 'em in where there's space on the shelf? Then one day we'll see a commission set up to find out why there's so many disturbed kids around! And transferring is another craze they have. I've one sixteen-year-old, in care since he was a baby, in his twenty-second Home."

On the inter-racial adoption controversy Dinah was middle-of-the-road. "It's only those meddling anti-racist freaks say Black kids should *never* go to White homes. If couples adopt they want to give love and there's not too much love around for kids in care – and White love's better than no love! But it's true there's always problems for Black kids in White homes. And sometimes they're real big problems – I could tell you stories enough on that to fill your book. Softie parents make a lot of the troubles. The sort who adopt are softie anyway and sometimes they don't understand Black kids need real tough discipline. So do White kids, *I* think. But there's a lot of Black kids if they don't get it feel insecure and go all to bits. They don't want all this liberal shit about reasonable discussions and talking things over – they can't handle it and they get scared and *lonely*. They want to be told 'Do this and that, then and there – or else!' You wouldn't believe how lonely some Black kids get in White middle-class homes. All the love doesn't seem to get through to them. They've got everything – transistors, bikes, tape-recorders, trendy clothes – and still you get them running away at fifteen or sixteen, wanting back in their own world. The parents can't understand – how could they? – and then *they* go all to bits . . . More Blacks adopting is the answer. They don't like the idea, they're nervous about inspectors poking around checking out on them – asking if they've quarrels and how much they earn and so on. We should cut down on that crap. Anyone will tell you Black kids do better with poor Black families than with rich Whiteys."

Half-way through her third rum-and-coke Dinah suddenly became auto-biographical. She recalled coming to Britain from rural Jamaica in 1960, aged nine, not having seen her mother for six years. She didn't know who her father was and seemed to think paternity relatively unimportant, provided the parental colours matched. Her mother had married in Handsworth and she was greeted on arrival by three half-siblings. "I hated everyone," she said, "including my mother. I cried and cried to go home to my grandmother. She felt like my *real* mother. It took me a year to settle and I didn't feel happy until my step-dad disappeared one day. He just went. My mother was that upset they took her off to hospital. When she came out she thought I was fantastic, the way I'd looked after the kids – there was four of them by then. She got dependent on me after that and we got real close until she married again – well, not really, but he moved in. He hated me so I moved out. I went to an uncle who lived with his eldest boy in a flat. He'd left his wife when she got religious. He couldn't take it. She'd follow him to the pub and pray over him and tell him he was a sinner in front of all his mates! So he and Jimmy moved up here from London. Then Jimmy went Rasta and he found another women and I had to push off. I went to a hostel till I got my qualifications. All the years at school I hated it but I wouldn't be bullied. I knew what I wanted to do, I always wanted to work with kids. So I beat the educational bastards and got this good job. I'm lucky. There's lots of my age around in Handsworth would've been better off left at home with their grannies. All they can get is shit-work, if that – most of them are just rotting. Too many kids came over. Our parents meant well, thought we'd all get good schooling and good jobs. They couldn't know the schools wouldn't educate us and most of the jobs would go. But if I had to rot I'd rather rot in the sun!"

It was still daylight when we left the pub but Dinah refused to take a short-cut through Handsworth Park. "At this time of evening", she said, "it's full of drunken Irishmen attacking people with broken bottles."

The Irishmen in question happened to be friends of mine, amiable homeless OAPs who had chosen homelessness so that they could scrounge three separate dole payments. These they spent on large plastic bottles of cider which kept them in a state of mild, jovial intoxication twenty-four hours a day. It was impossible to imagine them attacking a mouse. But I said nothing. We're all entitled to our stereotypes.

The best coffee in Handsworth was to be found in the Holy Hole – not the café's official title, but its nickname among my irreligious friends. White American Fundamentalists ran this large, bright, hygienic coffee-shop-cum-bookstore on the Soho Road. An emotional Bible Belt male voice, reading from the Old Testament, provided the wall-paper noise. Long shelves were laden with religious cassettes, records, glossy illustrated Bibles and improving tracts. This was Big Biz Born-Againism; also on offer were tea-towels, trays, cushion-covers, T-shirts, table-cloths, egg-cups, calendars, diaries, pens and pencils – all inscribed with sickly-sweet pietist sentiments. The subdued-looking black waitresses never smiled, perhaps because they were supervised by a White American female with a mad glint in her eyes who at intervals stood in the doorway and sang a solo hymn for the benefit of the Soho Road's unheeding heathens. The customers were a stimulating cross-section of Handsworth residents, their only common denominator a willingness to endure this surfeit of piety for the sake of a decent cup of coffee.

The Holy Hole was my main venue for meetings with church-made friends, though many found its hard-sell atmosphere uncongenial; such rampant consumerism is alien to the Black Pentecostal ethos. However, a Born-Again café was preferable – most seemed to feel – to any of the local idol-worshipping tea-shop/restaurants, with their devilish aromas of joss-sticks and gaudy pictures of 'false gods'.

On a Saturday morning, not long after my conversation with Dinah, I had reason to remember and feel suitably re-chastened by her reproof, "We're talking about *human beings* . . ." Arriving at the Holy Hole to meet Marigold I found her already there and ominously swollen-eyed. She was of Dinah's generation and had also been sent from Jamaica to join a mother she couldn't remember; but her respectable church-centred youth was uneventful and secure. She became a nurse-attendant, married an English bus-driver and had two handsome sons, now aged nine and seven – both dark-skinned, but with their father's features. I had met Marigold while pad-hunting and she became – perhaps because of her mixed marriage – one of the few Black friends with whom I felt it unnecessary to be on guard, while discussing race relations. She in turn found it helpful, she said, to discuss her domestic tensions with a complete outsider.

Those tensions were caused, I had been given to understand, by her sons' reactions to their mixed parentage. But that morning Marigold said, "Can you see I've been crying all night? It's not only the boys – I should never have married White – it's too much of a strain for Phil." She paused as a waitress approached and blew her nose loudly as our order was being taken. Then she continued, "Being married to me is something an English husband has to live down, like he was a duke married to a shop-girl – know what I mean? It's easier for university types, and doctors and so on. They can get away with it – wouldn't you say? But some of Phil's mates are downright nasty. And don't say it's just joking and teasing because *I* know it's not!" The waitress returned with our tray and, her curiosity evidently aroused, dawdled around unnecessarily polishing nearby tables. When she had moved one, thwarted, Marigold leant forward, lowered her voice, and said, "I'll tell you quickly before Phil and the boys come to pick me up. I never knew how bad it was for him till yesterday. It was my birthday, see, and I drove in to collect him from the depot, for us to eat out, see, and Mum was looking after the boys. He'd bought me flowers – gorgeous big red roses – and they shouted filthy things at him across the depot. 'Will yer Fuzzy-wuzzy put 'em in her hair?' – and so on. And they didn't mean the hair on my head. Phil says they didn't know I was there, but they saw me, they were pointing at me – I was *meant* to hear. It showed me what he's had to put up with for years. He got so mad, he just went wild and tried hitting his mates till he was pulled off them. Now you've met Phil, you know he's not like that, he's not a fighter – you'd nearly say he was timid, right? So what was bottled up inside him over the years to make him turn so violent? I was scared, see, like he wasn't *my* Phil . . . And it showed me he'd be a happier man now if I'd never married him – a lot happier. My mum was right, she always said mixed marriages brought nothing but trouble. But who listens to their mum at twenty-two? And now there's two more kids caught up in it all as well – at school last week they told Norman he was a bastard because White dads can't have black kids and he came back crying and saying 'What's a bastard?' and 'Isn't Dad real for me?' "

"Never mind the boys for now," I said. "You're talking nonsense about Phil and *that* won't help the boys. You've told me you're both more in love than when you married, which not every couple can say after ten years. Phil's lucky and he knows it. You can't say he'd be happier without you. It isn't true. And the boys will be able to cope if they see *you* coping."

Marigold suddenly stood up, fumbling for her handkerchief, and hurried away towards a door marked 'Rest Room'. I was glad of the respite; this was the sort of tête-à-tête I found difficult even with her.

The impulsive White reaction to such 'racialist incidents' is (too) simple. "Forget it! Why let those yobbos worry you? What do they matter? Why should someone like *you* be upset by people like *them*?" But the victims of racialism are not White; they cannot be expected to react as we think they should. And Marigold's innate sensitivity and puritanical Pentecostalist background combined to make her extra vulnerable to the sort of scene she had described. British working-class soft-porn 'humour' can be excruciatingly non-funny and it does become 'downright nasty' when blended with racialism. Yet for her sons' sakes it seemed to me she needed to conceal her vulnerability, to show them that verbal racialism can be ignored – that to allow it to cause distress is to allow racialists a victory.

Phil arrived with the boys before Marigold's return. "Is she O K?" he asked anxiously. He was small, slight, nervy, unhealthily pale – and he worshipped his wife. When Norman and Gordon has rushed to the bookstore end, to marvel at children's bibles with pop-up pictures, he stood by the window and waved the waitress away. "I won't spend money in here," he muttered. "This gang of heaven-dealers should be sent back where they came from!" He looked down at me and asked, "Have you been getting the story? She didn't have a very happy birthday – I shouldn't've lost my cool – that's what really upset her. And did you get all that crap about she shouldn't have married me? I want out of this bloody fascist country. I want to get us to Canada, where our kids can grow up free and *accepted*. I'm looking for a trucking job – out there we could all feel *equal*."

"But don't you feel equal here, as a *family*?" I asked.

Phil shrugged and looked towards his sons, now watching a video of some Black American Super-Preacher. "How can we feel equal in this bloody country? People won't let us! When Gordon was seven he saw a thing on the telly about plastic surgery after Vietnam – skin-grafts and all that. And he comes to me and he says, 'Dad, could a doctor give *me* another skin, a White skin?' How can he ever feel 'equal' here, when that's what Britain did to him in his first seven years?"

Marigold reappeared then, looking almost cheerful. "I've been thinking," she said to Phil. "I've got to toughen up, see? For the kids' sake I've got to get real tough!"

"But you won't," said Phil bleakly. "You can't! And why in hell should you have to? *I* don't want you any different – it's other people need to change . . ." He moved towards the door, calling the boys. "C'mon lads, you don't want to waste money on any of that junk!"

Marigold's theory that 'university people and suchlike' find it easier to 'get away with' Black partners seems valid only to the extent that middle-class racialism is usually oblique; few academics would shout remarks across the campus about their colleagues' wives' pubic hair. But mixed-race problems are common to all classes and can be even more acute in homes dominated by the middle-class tendency to dodge emotional suffering.

My next encounter with a Black/White couple was bizarre. Joan (English) and Niko (a Ghanaian doctor) called to my pad one day, having been told I was a Villa Cross 'regular'. They were on the trail of a missing nineteen-year-old son and certain clues had led them to Handsworth from their prosperous home-town far away on the other side of Britain's Great Divide.

"We've never had problems," said Joan. "You know, *colour* problems . . . For twenty years we've been in the same house, always getting on *marvellously* with our neighbours – with *everyone* in the town. And our son and daughter did splendidly at the local school. Never any complaints about unpleasantness – they're both *gifted* children and so popular! But then a few years ago James became – well, *odd*. Didn't he darling?"

"Very odd," agreed Niko.

"But we thought it was just teenage moods and tenses – this dreadful loud music, shaking the whole house! And he began to read strange magazines – he sent away for them – they came by post from something called Ethiopian Federation Inc. – really *most* peculiar! Wasn't it darling?"

"Very peculiar!" agreed Niko.

"And all this time he wouldn't talk to us, he wouldn't *explain* anything. And then – well, then he began to let his hair grow under a funny hat like those boys wear around here. And really we thought that was quite serious – didn't we darling?"

"Extremely serious," agreed Niko.

"So I pointed out how *unhealthy* it is, always keeping the hair covered . . . He still said *nothing*! But one evening he came in and left his sweater in the bathroom and I picked it up and noticed a really *very* unpleasant odour! I've always had an *acute* sense of smell so I marched straight into his room and challenged him. I knew it was my duty. I asked him, 'Are you smoking heroin?' I thought that was the best approach – to take him by surprise and frighten him. But he wasn't a bit upset, he just said – 'Get lost, Mum!' in quite a kind way . . . Then a week later he was gone. One morning he told his sister he was a Rastafarian and wouldn't be coming home again. He said he could live on the dole. And now *she's* grown her hair and joined some lunatic Black women's group in London! But at least we know where she is, she's at the LSE and we have her flat address – though she doesn't seem to be there ever. And she won't come home and she won't communicate – will she darling?"

"She won't," said Niko.

"Then we heard from a friend of James – well, actually from his friend's mother – that a letter had come from Handsworth. So it seemed worth looking here because actually nineteen is quite *young* – isn't it darling?"

"*Very* young," agreed Niko.

"I mean, he could find himself in prison, if he's mixing here with all these shocking drug-smugglers and people of that sort . . . And what about his *career*? He's got a place at university for October – he can't give that up after doing so well at school! It's all so terribly *silly* – isn't it darling?"

"No," said Niko, "it's not a bit silly. I've told you a hundred times he had a problem and this is his way of working it out. He's not White."

I had long since decided that if Joan were my mother I would have left the nest even before I could fly. I looked at her now and saw that she was very angry indeed. She smiled – a Thatcherite smile, as though someone had pressed a button to switch it on. "Now you're being absurd, darling! *Of course* he doesn't have a problem! You're not White – do *you* have a problem?"

"No," said Niko, "because I'm Black."

My tiny room began to seem too small a stage for this drama. It would have been interesting to talk to Niko on his own, if only to find out how this most unlikely pairing had come about. But since that was impossible I looked at my watch, invented a city-centre appointment and hoped they would soon find their son – though for James's sake I half-hoped they wouldn't.

That afternoon I went to look for Shalli, who might or might not be at home, to discuss my morning visitors; there were some similarities between her story and James's. She however "didn't like the feel" of living on the dole and we had first met in the Job Centre, where she was drifting disconsolately from notice-board to notice-board, her hopes being dashed repeatedly by that fatal word 'experienced' . . . She was an unusually dark-skinned Pakistani – in complexion and features more like a South Indian – and being jobless in a Handsworth DHSS flat was her own choice. White adoptive parents had brought her up from babyhood in affluent Selly Oak, but on her eighteenth birthday she had run away from home. She was still working to perfect a Brummie accent, which she judged would make her more socially acceptable in her new milieu.

Walking down the Soho Road, I glanced into each little Pakistani café or restaurant: Shalli found her flat depressing and spent hours sitting in one or other of these *chai-khanas*, with a library book and a slowly sipped cup of tea. And sure enough there she was in a café near the Job Cente on the last chapter of Angela Davis's *Women, Race and Class*. "Have you read it?" she asked eagerly, all set for a heavy political discussion.

"No," I admitted, "I'm not sure it's my scene."

Shalli frowned and shook her head. "You should be more broad-minded – d'you only read books you think you'll agree with?"

"Well," I said, "when you begin to notice the sand running out, and when about fifty thousand new books are published every year, you're inclined to become more and more selective."

As I described my morning visitors, Shalli exclaimed, "I do know how that boy felt! Poor fellow! For years he must have wanted to escape – I was only twelve when I first thought of getting away from it all."

"But what, exactly, *is* 'it all'?" I asked.

"Devaluing," replied Shalli crisply. "My mother's great thing was – 'I'm colour-blind! I just don't *notice* people's skins!' So I was only a symbol of how 'liberal' *they* were. *I* didn't matter, the person I know to be *me*. They didn't even know *I* existed. Only their dark adopted daughter mattered. 'Aren't the Mullers splended – they don't seem to notice any difference!' I've heard their friends talking like that, when I was small and eavesdropping after they thought I was in bed! So because they didn't notice any difference, I couldn't belong. I'm not a status symbol for liberals – I'm me and I am different and they couldn't be bothered to think about the differences. Or maybe they were afraid to – maybe they didn't trust themselves to handle the differences. They sent me to a 'good school' – 'She's very bright, she'll do well!' I *am* very bright but I didn't do well. I didn't want to do well just to fit into the pattern. I didn't want to be anyone's successful experiment – can't you hear the chit-chat over drinks? 'Shalli's got such a good degree! You see they're just as bright as we are if you give them a chance!' And then string-pulling to slide me into some secure good job in an all-White world where everyone would be terribly nice to me because 'Shalli is just like us, really – she's quite exceptional.' I'm *not* just like them. I'm me, my parents came from Pakistan, they were Muslims, my father was a professor at Lahore, my mother came from Hyderabad India – I'm not someone from Selly Oak who happened to fall into a tar-barrel when she was small. I never thought about colour until I went to school and had to think about it. I don't suppose I imagined I was White, but I felt part of my environment and *British*. Then in class one day I said something about 'Our Queen' and the little boy beside me turned round and said, 'She's not *your* Queen! You're only a Paki!' I cried so much the teacher rang my mother to take me home early. That's the first time I remember her saying, 'I'm colour-blind!' It was a few years more before I began to realise what a monstrous insult that is. It really means, 'I'm so tolerant I can pretend everyone is White and therefore as good as me.' It's as stupid as saying you don't notice somebody's sex or age. You're not accepting them as a whole person, you're editing them to get the version you want. That poor James with that awful mother you've described – are you surprised he was driven over to the Rastas? Think of the humiliation, growing up seeing his father turned into something unreal! Why should he let her do the same to him? Why shouldn't he be half-African? He *is* half-African – that's *him*! If she wanted an English son she should have found herself an English husband. So there!"

It was always worth seeking Shalli out and asking her to explain things.

Whatever anyone's views on miscegenation, the numbers of mixed-race British-born children (especially Black/White mixes) is increasing and will continue to do so. And one of the cruellest consequences of British racialism is its inexorable pushing of every individual with a discernible quota of African blood into the Black 'camp'. An East African woman historian, based in Birmingham for the past twelve years, described this process to me as "an infringement of human rights".

While studying in Nairobi, Bamba had married an English academic and two of their four children are, she said, "by temperament and natural inclination" more White than Black. Yet all four, growing up in Britain, will be compelled to think of themselves as 'Black'. "Asians don't have to cope with this turn of the racialist screw," Bamba pointed out. "Most Asian-European mixes can pass for Southern European to escape discrimination. If they ally themselves with religious, cultural or political movements, and emphasise their non-European half, that's their choice."

Bamba likened the RRI to Corbusier's tower-blocks – "On paper the answer to every problem, in practice disastrous." She went on, "But I don't believe it was set up to deprive non-Whites of their political leaders. That's supposed to be a neat imperialist ploy – place them in their own little niches along the walls of the Establishment to keep them quiet. But if people can be so easily seduced into those niches, are they really good leadership material? If they cared about their communities' welfare, would they go along with so much dishonest thinking and hypocrisy? The RRI often makes bad worse – again like Corbusier. Why show people distorted reflections of how things are? Why all this 'black unity' propaganda, when everyone knows Asians are hated by many Africans and West Indians – and vice versa? If so many East African Asians hadn't come here relations in that area might be healthier now. The direct-from-Asia Asians and the Afro-Caribbeans might have moved closer, they share so many handicaps. But the ex-Africa Asians' anti-Black bias has been seeping through the whole Asian community – despite the ex-Africas being unpopular among other Asians. I've been watching all these inter-relationships for fifteen years. You can't measure an influence like the anti-Black bias – you just feel its effects in the air, like a weather-change. But you must allow for my own prejudice against Asians. I grew up in an atmosphere of bitter animosity between *them* and *us*. We saw them as an integral part of colonialism, co-operating with Whites to exploit Blacks. In their personal dealings with us they were as racialist as any White – often more openly, more contemptuously so. And they were such slick law-breakers you couldn't corner them. A sister of mine worked in a bank when we had currency export restrictions. Each member of a huge family would come in at different times on the same day and send off £10 – and go to all the other banks and do the same. So £600 might be exported in one day when the legal limit was £10! And we'd no controls efficient enough to stop this. Of course they foresaw being expelled and having property confiscated. And for generations they'd been contributing to East Africa's development in trade and commerce and the professions. But *why*? Why weren't Africans allowed to make that contribution? Because they might have 'got out of hand'! So bring in the Asians, encourage *them* to advance, then they've an interest in helping to suppress Blacks . . . And now they're showing the classic racism-based-on-guilt syndrome. Having got rich collaborating with Whites, they have to look down on Blacks – if you can feel your victims are inferior, somehow your conscience settles down. The other Asian immigrants, however they felt about Blacks, at least had no reason to *despise* them . . . Incidentally, d'you realise Gandhi didn't give a damn about South Africa's Blacks? That's glossed over now, it doesn't fit in with the myth. But all his campaigning for citizenship rights was on behalf of *Indians*. Seems it never occurred to him that Africans, who owned the country, might be entitled to the same rights! How ethnocentric can you get!"

I remarked that while the 'ex-Africas' were consolidating their middle-class position in salubrious suburbs, there did seem to be increasing solidarity between young inner-city residents of all colours.

"Yes," said Bamba, "but it's not a helpful solidarity. Who wants gangs of Asian and White youths hanging around with fake dreadlocks? How can that improve things?" She certainly felt no solidarity with Rastafarians. "To me they're puzzling and alarming. Yet we need to try to understand them – their influence is growing, though your Handsworth neighbours may contradict that. A few years ago they were more obvious – now you don't see so many dreadlocks and hats. But those were only a fashion, like punks' spikey hair. Their crazy mixed-up philosophy is still spreading and the anti-White bit bothers me."

I admitted that I found the phenomenon confusing. "Isn't pure Rastafarianism all about universal love and peace and justice, and helping the Brothers and Sisters in Africa?"

"Perhaps it is," replied Bamba, "But the pro-Black mystique can be easily bent to justify hating Whites – when 'I n I' *don't* live on a cloud of brotherly love. And that's what's happening in Britain. Jamaican Rastas mightn't approve, but over here their views don't count. I find it sad – so many Blacks driven into this sick fantasy world – Haile Selassie being Almighty God, the

Jews having been a Black race before they became Semites and so on. Naturally they're desperate for a culture of their own, but why do some Whites who should know better pretend to take all this seriously as a *religion*?"

I asked, "Is it any dottier than believing Jesus Christ was *literally* the Son of God? Billions took the Virgin Birth seriously for nearly two thousand years – and millions still do. It must have been invented because the early Christians *needed* to believe it, just as Rastas need to believe in Jah Rastafari . . ."

Bamba took this half-facetious argument too seriously. 'You're insulting all the sane, intelligent Afro-Caribbeans – ask *them* what they think of Rastas! You pity the poor uprooted, hybrid, decultured ex-slaves, so you want them happy and fulfilled with their own special make-believe religion – *rubbish*! Why encourage a neurotic cult just 'to make the Blacks happy'? It's like reading fairy-stories to toddlers! Why is it OK to feed Blacks all this garbage about Ethiopia as 'the foundation of their spiritual existence' and 'the home of their cultural heritage'? How many slaves were taken from *Ethiopia* to the Caribbean? How would you like your daughter to be exposed to such distortions of *her* history? Are you by any chance a closet racist?"

That evening I wrote in my diary:

> Trying to disentangle race relations in Britain makes me feel like someone trying to untie a multiple knot in the dark. What delusion of grandeur or reckless upsurge of false self-confidence ever gave me the notion that *I* could write a book on this hydra of multi-racial prejudice? So many convolutions of colour, class, creed. But mainly *colour*. I wonder how much we, the privileged-by-nature-white-skins, have been affected over the generations by the powerful pro-White bias of other races? How much did their envy of/deference to Whites, *per se*, promote the development of our arrogance and racial superiority complex?

Joan and Niko had given me their address, in case I should chance upon the dreadlocked James or hear news of him. Quite soon a rumour did reach me, on the Irish semi-underworld grapevine, about a fairish-skinned Rasta with a posh accent. He had been seen hanging around a notorious hard-drugs pub way beyond the Handsworth Rastas' territory. This was worrying; ganja is one thing, hard drugs are quite another. So at noon next day I took a bus up Trinity Road and through the penultimate ghastliness of that horrorscape between Aston Park and Salford Park. My destination was within sight of the ultimate ghastliness: Spaghetti Junction.

Any excursion out of Handsworth provoked a nauseated incredulity. I never got used to Birmingham's insensate ugliness. It seemed beyond belief that people – human beings, belonging to the same species as myself – could have sat down and planned an 'Urban Renewal' scheme like Birmingham's. During this bus-ride my feelings apparently showed on my face. An elderly, very fat Black woman leant forward, patted my knee and said wheezily, "Cheer up duckie! Whatever yo problem is, someone else has a wuss one!"

The pub's gable-wall was half-covered with pro-IRA graffiti. Inside, it matched its environmental setting. The lounge bar was enormous, L-Shaped, unfurnished apart from bile-coloured plastic benches screwed to the smoke-stained cream walls. Most of the benches had been ripped and their foam-rubber stuffing hung out like run-over rabbits' entrails. A machine was emitting punk-rock and a snarling Alsation paced up and down behind the bar to deter young Blacks from vaulting over and making away with bottles – so said the barmaid, a sharp-featured, shifty-eyed, peroxide-blonde Irish-woman. There is no pub even remotely resembling this in supposedly sleazy Handsworth.

In a corner near the door seven Irishmen – youngish and middle-aged; already half-drunk – were playing poker with dog-eared cards, closely watched by two anxious-looking women in plastic raincoats and nylon headscarves from Killarney. When the stakes went too high the women protested and the men cursed them. Around the bend of the L, four elderly Blacks in Homburg hats played backgammon, loudly slamming the dice onto the cigarette-burnt table. They were sharing two small bottles of Lucozade. No other customers appeared until near closing time, when a chubby, jolly, grey-haired Black man bounced in, greeted and was greeted by the Irish group and stood expectantly at the bar – behind which the Alsatian was still prowling and growling. The Black gave no order and I watched, mesmerised, while the sour-puss barmid laid in front of him one glass of port, one of sweet sherry and one of brandy, with an empty half-pint beer mug and a jug of water.

"Thank you my joyless angel!" said he, handing over the exact price. Very carefully he mixed the drinks in the mug, topped it up with water, took a thermos and funnel from a canvas shoulder-bag and poured his concoction into the flask. Then he filled the mug with water and beamingly clinked it on my cider glass before taking a long draught. "To flush my kidneys," he explained. "You a social worker?"

"Yes," I replied on the spur of the moment. "I'm looking for a young man with a problem." And I described James as best I could. The barmaid, who had already denied seeing anyone of this description, at once rang the bell for the third time and switched off the lights. The cocktail-mixer winked at me and said, "Talk outside, eh?"

On the pavement he extended his hand and introduced himself. "I'm a gentleman by name Archie Morgan – you're a probation officer?"

"No," I said. "I'm just looking for this missing youngster."

"He won't be back here," Archie declared. "Beat up to hell in the gents two nights ago – they kicked the shit out of him."

"Who did?" I asked. "And why?"

"Three Pakis – three to one's not cricket, eh?"

"But why?" I repeated.

Archie looked shrewdly up at me. "You're not a social worker! Or you wouldn't ask that . . . Ever hear of a sort of an animal called an 'informer'? I don't know nothin' about your young man, 'cept he didn't seem to fit the local scene – right?" He tapped his shoulder-bag. "You thought I was another crazy spaced-out Black man? But I'm just cowardly – evenings I drink *at home* – right? Never drink in the day, every evening drink the same hooch – 'Archie's sedative', my missus calls it!"

At the bus-stop we said good-bye. "Hope you find your fair Rasta," said Archie. "But for sure you won't find him round here – unless he has a death-wish!"

On the way home I dithered. Was the beaten-up young man James? If so, should his parents be told about his misadventure? Archie, who had got the story at second hand, might have been exaggerating. Was there any point in worrying parents? James was a legal adult; if he wanted to live dangerously there was nothing they could do about it. And yet, if my son were missing wouldn't I want news – even bad news – of him? Yes, I would.

Making a telephone call from Handsworth was always a memorable experience. First find your working telephone . . . There were kiosks, which doubled as public lavatories, on every other street. But as often as not the machine was either out of order or functioning so erratically that after a quarter of an hour you felt an almost uncontrollable urge to vandalise it. Few in fact had been vandalised; that is an uncommon crime in areas where most inhabitants depend on public telephones. Handsworth's machines were simply neglected by British Telecom. However, someone quite regularly drenched the kiosks with Jeyes' fluid and removed their complement of empty bottles, fast-food containers, discarded garments, newspaper parcels of disposable nappies, and used condoms and tampons. I could never decide which was the more asphyxiating, the stench of stale urine or the stench of stale urine plus Jeyes' Fluid.

In the fourth kiosk I got through to James's mother. She sounded strangely subdued. James had returned home the day before with five broken ribs and without three teeth. Before she could say any more the telephone made a noise like a distant road-drill and we were cut off.

10 · Black Talk

I remembered Bamba's anti-Rasta outburst when Walter addressed me at the Heathfield Road bus-stop opposite the Villa Cross. It was 2.30 p.m. and he had watched me leaving the pub. When I stood beside him he demanded, "Why you making a fool of yourself, always in and out of that place? Why you sit in there with prostitutes and no-goods? I seen you in my church, too. What you playing at? You're a book-writer – *I* know! But why you pay such notice to them bad boys? You think they got a religion? Jah Rastafari – worshipping false idols – blasphemy! There's trouble coming in Handsworth and who's making it? Your friends in there . . . Why do people say Blacks are lazy drug-pushing criminals? Because they drive down the Villa Road and this lot's all over the place and then they go away and tell their friends and write in their papers and books – 'That's what Blacks are like!' I'd shove your friends in a barbed-wire camp, with all their dirty women, and let the rest of us live law-abiding lives the way we've always done!"

Walter seemed unmollified when I pointed out that he had seen me in his church because I wasn't paying attention only to Rastas. Yet ten days later, when we chanced to meet on the Lozells Road, he apologised for having "attacked" me and invited me into a café for a cup of tea. He was a deeply unhappy man who had lost his job at the age of fifty and been unable to find any other work, even part-time or temporary. And he had chosen to make the Rastas his scapegoat. "If we didn't have them bad boys we'd be respected. Now I look for work and people think, 'Black man – bad man!' It wasn't like this before. Twenty-three years I worked, no trouble – then *bang*! and the whole place closed."

Walter sought comfort – it seemed not very successfully – in his church. Other middle-aged jobless Blacks sought it in the Crown and Rose, a small, spartan Black-run pub frequented mainly by the older generation, including several Irish regulars in the same no-hope situation. There I met Irving: very tall, very thin, ebony-skinned, usually sitting alone in a corner stretching a half-pint of bitter. We had several long, impersonal talks, chiefly about

Northern Ireland and nuclear weapons – subjects in which Irving took an uncommon interest. He knew my reason for being in Handsworth but seemed disinclined to discuss race relations. Then one lunch-time I was startled to see him ordering a double-whisky. There were only a few other customers, all standing at the bar, and when he went to his usual corner I joined him.

"I want to talk to you today," said Irving. "I mean talk about us Blacks. This is my second whisky and I've a lot to say. My sons would laugh if they could hear me now. They don't believe Whitey wants to understand – or *can* understand. Maybe they're right. But I get the feeling you're working at it. And if we give up even trying to talk to one another, what hope is there?"

There had been a police raid on the Rastas' Acapulco café the day before. The Handsworth air was thick with allegations of police misbehaviour. Not only the Rastas believed that hard drugs had been planted in the café. Irving unfolded his *Birmingham Post* and looked at the headlines and photograph. "How come", he said, "there happened to be a press photographer standing right by the Acapulco when the drug-squad arrived for their *surprise* raid? What does that tell you about the *motive* for the raid?" He ran his finger down the page and frowned and looked for one alarming instant as though he were about to cry. "How many reading that page will ever think how sad it makes *us* feel? Us who came from the Islands full of hope . . . The waste of all those kids' lives! My two sons are into their twenties – they've never had steady work – maybe never will. A few weeks here, a few months there and each time longer to wait for the next break. Today one's gone off to Winson Green – car theft. That's in the paper too."

"So that's why you're drinking whisky!" I said. "Have another?"

"Not until my talking is finished. Some whisky makes you talk better. More than that makes you talk nonsense. I'm taking a bottle home for Gerry, my wife. Today she needs it too. You come along with me and we'll talk nonsense all evening! Ever since Andy was charged Gerry won't go out, won't face the neighbours. I say to her, '*Why*? It's not us drove him to crime, it's nothing in his blood or his training, it's the world he grew up in!' You read in the papers, judges and M Ps and Chief Constables all saying, 'If these young Blacks can't keep the laws of this land they shouldn't be here.' But *they* didn't come here – *we* came, to 'help rebuild our Motherland', like Churchill said. What a chance Britain's missed! If this country wasn't so racist it could have paid off some of its old debts in the twentieth century . . . D'you understand what I'm saying? It could've let us escape from our past. You're a reading lady, you know our history. We were dirt, for centuries, no more or less important than work-animals. Then we were needed here, and that was a good feeling. To be needed, as *people*. To make our own decisions, to cross the sea independently, paying our own fares, travelling to earn a fair wage for honest work. That felt real good. A lot of us dreamed about saving to go home to start something of our own. In the early days most of us didn't come to *settle* – people forget that. We didn't come to invade cities and take them over. We had stupid ideas about how much we could earn and save in a few years – we were just ignorant about Britain. We thought here we'd be equal. Nothing special, just equal . . . But it was never like that and we had to adjust to the way it was and make the best of it. If it was the other way, if ourselves and our kids got equal treatment, we could have been so *happy*! We wanted to work hard for fair pay and have our kids grow up to do the same. Sure we wanted more opportunities for them than we ever had, if they were bright kids – if they could use good schooling. Isn't that reasonable? Isn't it only what every parent wants? Some kids are no good with books, even if they'd a prince's schooling – like some princes are no good with books! No one's complaining when dull kids don't get O's and A's. If they could've had steady jobs like us, we trained them up to work hard – harder than a lot of White kids, you can believe that! But we've thousands and thousands of bright kids, first-rate bright – only they don't show up in the statistics. At school they just get one message in teacher's eyes: 'Black is thick . . .' And now for most there's *no* job, good or bad. Everything's gone sour, for the kids and for us watching them – not able to help, not able to keep them up to our standards. The world offers them *nothing*. No goals, no security, no dignity, no hope . . . What use telling them 'Keep the law'? Having a nice orderly country with everything calm and everyone law-abiding is a two-way deal. You keep your part of the bargain, the country gives you a fair chance. If the country thinks you're too stupid to learn, shouldn't be here, can't be trusted, don't deserve a fair chance – why should *you* keep the bargain? You're given no opportunity, so you go make your own. And when you're young and Black and half-schooled, that's likely enough to mean breaking the law. I talk this way to Gerry and she gets angry and says I'm no better than the boys. She's wrong. I wouldn't break any law, ever. I couldn't, there's just something inside would stop me even if it seemed I'd every sort of excuse. But I'm an old man, nearly sixty, I've had my life. It was tough and always a struggle with low pay and Gerry having to work too. I never liked that, even though it's our custom. But I remembered where I started from and that was a lot tougher! So I was O K till two years ago with a steady job and a lovely wife and two fine boys – *bright* lads. But how can we ask kids born into this rich world and wanting *more* than their parents had to settle for *less*? That's not how real life works. You've got to think these things out. You've got to let your mind see the way the kids feel, even if it's against your own ideas and it shocks you and keeps you from sleeping at night. There's Black parents now feeling so let down and bitter they won't talk to their kids, don't even want to see them. That's no good. Look all around you in Handsworth, up and down every road – there's the third generation being pushed and wheeled and carried. They're going to need grandparents in their lives – desperately need them. That's one of our traditions, grandparents being important – especially grandmothers, half of us were brought up by grannies. It's dangerous to let that custom go. There's splits enough among Caribbeans here without *families* splitting . . . But you see what I'm saying about Britain losing a chance? Treated fair, we'd something to give this country. And if we were let give it, we'd have gained by giving. Are you understanding? We'd have gained what our people lost when they were made into work-animals. We came here to give and to gain – and now I'm not talking about money, wages, benefits . . . Then when we settled we wanted the same for our children. With fair schooling and fair chances, so many could have given so much! Andy could, for one, instead of lying now in Winson Green. Our kids had more to give than people in this country wanted to know about. British people never wanted to see us as *givers*. Why do they want so badly to have only their own picture of us? If only they'd stood back and waited and let us *prove* what sort we were . . . But they'd decided how they wanted to see us before we'd even started to get adjusted and fix our lives here. You think about that. Think about the way it felt to be in a little community of immigrants surrounded by millions of Whites all the time sending out strong hating messages. 'You're no good – you're not welcome – you're stupid, untrained, illiterate, dirty, lazy, noisy, smelly – you shouldn't be here – go home!' And think about how it feels to be born into and grow up in that . . . that *smog* of prejudice! And then next time you hear about problem Black kids, disrupting classrooms, just ask yourself – 'How many does it take to make a problem?' Told you I had a lot to say! And now we'll go home with our bottle . . .''

Irving understood when I explained that duty required me to hurry home and write all he had said in my journal, before the details were blurred by further conversation – never mind 'talking nonsense' over a bottle of whisky. We arranged that I should call to see Gerry on the following afternoon. "I'll be out," said Irving, "but that's good. You'll get Gerry's views spoken plain – women together!"

The Hamiltons lived on a road of three-storey semi-detached houses, built just a century ago and not yet enveloped. The solid appearance of these buildings was deceptive; most interiors were damp and disintegrating. This was Black flat-land with neglected, litter-strewn gardens and 'JAH' spray-painted on doors and façades. Many tenants were single youngsters, or couples living sporadically together and making babies almost – it seemed – absent-mindedly. Gerry told me that in their set of eight flats three mothers were under seventeen. "But they're *good* mums. I ask myself, are these babies better off than ours? Maybe that's the silver lining to unemployment! Mostly we were working mums, hardly seeing our kids. When mine were small I did late night shifts, eight to four. Home at five, sleep till nine, with the boys all day. Irv used to keep them up real late, so's they wouldn't wake me before nine. But many of my friends hadn't such good husbands – or none at all. Maybe never married, or husbands left them, or went back to the Islands. There was plenty construction work in Jamaica in the early seventies – over fourteen thousand Blacks *left* Britain then. Some reckoned they'd be thrown out anyway, after all Powell's talk. That was a scarey time. We thought of going back in '71, after thirteen years here. Irv could see his job was dead-end – steady, he thought *then*, but dead-end . . . I said no, let's stay cos the boys are doing O K at school – they were eight and ten. So we stayed and that was a big mistake . . ."

Gerry went to the tiny kitchen to refill the teapot. She was short and rather overweight and moved stiffly; she looked years older than her age – forty-eight. The three-roomed flat needed redecorating and was sparsely furnished; it must have seemed very cramped before the boys moved out. When Gerry returned I was glancing along home-made bookshelves of unvarnished wood holding a few hundred second-hand paperbacks, mainly history and sociology with a leavening of thrillers. Gerry nodded towards the shelves. "I thank the Lord Irv's a reader! That saved him, after the works closed. There's men around here on tranquillisers ever since the day they got their last pay-packet. Irv's still looking for work, any kind and any hours. He doesn't say but I know he is, like today when he's gone for a few hours. I never ask. It's hard enough hearing 'No!' every time without having to tell your wife you're not wanted. He hopes about everything but won't admit it. He tells himself one day Blacks will be O K in this country. I can't see it that way. I know I'm depressed in myself right now, with Andy where he is . . . But I've had these thoughts for years. In England we're doomed – doomed to wear shackles from generation unto generation, like it says in the Bible. Could be Irv has to believe it'll be O K or he'd see himself to blame for coming here, though *I'm* to blame for us staying. But how could we know it was a mistake? Which it was, ever leaving Jamaica . . . Irv had his skill, he could have got work – not as regular as here, not as good pay, not much future for children. But maybe they could have got to the States, which they can't from here – who knows? No good day-dreaming now! What's sure is we wouldn't have been degraded and spat on like here. Our neighbours always respected us, both families, Irv's and mine. O K we were poor, but so were they. Maybe we were all too greedy, thousands of us rushing to England planning to get rich quick . . . This country's taught us there's more important things than fat wage-packets – not that Irv or myself ever earned what we should – most of us didn't. Can you see English people changing? I can't, only in those small ways you make laws about. The *feeling* won't change. And even if it did it's too late for thousands of our kids. Their minds are fixed now, mistrusting and fearing Whitey – though they'd never admit the fear is part of it! Our boys are that way. If they walked into this room now they'd be rude to you, and that's not the way they were trained up! It's like they were still slaves, though they were born free British citizens, with the same rights as the Prime Minister. Isn't that a funny thought? How you can be born with all those rights on paper and it just never works out you're equal day-to-day . . . 'Emancipation' – it hasn't happened yet! Can it happen here for Blacks? No! How can you get emancipated from your past when things happening day-to-day keep you in touch with it? White men still controlling everything, still looking down on the niggers, still being cruel – no more whips but still keeping us in our place. And Blacks *letting that happen*! Irv talks like it's all Whitey's fault but I see two things making each other worse. There's English racism and there's our own *colour* hang-ups and general inferiority complex. The slave legacy, as they call it. OK, that's not our fault, that's what was done to us. But some Blacks go forward, ignoring prejudice, getting on in spite of it. How do they do it? People think they must be the bright ones – 'the *few* bright ones'! I say they're the toughies. They don't care what Whitey thinks, they'll just go right on doing their own thing, paying no attention to insults and discrimination. Some of that sort haven't half Irv's brains but they're not sensitive, the way he is. Don't mistake me – he has no chip. But he feels how things are in the atmosphere, prejudice gets through to him. Not so much to *himself*, but when he sees it destroying Black kids. Most Blacks aren't toughies, have you noticed? The Whites and the Asians can compete – both tough. We're softies – those Rastas swaggering around the Villa Road giving two fingers to the fuzz and scaring the whole place, *they're* softies! Softies covering up . . . Maybe you *haven't* noticed? OK, I'll try explaining – first, we all know Blacks can be very violent. We lose our cool, then it's really lost! But that's not being tough the way I mean tough. Men sitting up in London – politicians, businessmen, civil servants – they work out, 'OK, give 'em this much and that much, enough to keep 'em quiet, enough so they won't starve, and then forget 'em.' Forget the poor are human, forget they need hope – *that's* being tough! But that sort don't hit and knife people, so they think they're *gentlemen*! Have you noticed most Afro-Caribbeans getting on in UK are fair-skinned? People think, 'More White blood, more brains!' *I* say, 'More White blood, tougher!' *And* they arrived with more money and education, being 'middle-class'. 'Free People of Colour', they were called back in slave-times – sambos and mulattos and quadroons and mustiphinis and quintroons and octoroons – there was no end to the mixtures. But whatever sort of mix, they all worked for Whites keeping down real Blacks – even though Whites despised them. So there's another hang-up for some of our kids. Blacks going along with the English system, pretending not to notice insults, they get called 'traitors', still grovelling to Whites. Over and over I've told our boys, 'So what you want? How *you* change the system here? You just go along with it, make it work for you, forget slave-times! Maybe that way slowly you *can* change things. Seeing real Blacks getting on, getting over all the obstacles, might make Whitey think again about what sort all these Blacks are!' Irv says I'm too hard, expecting too much from youngsters asking them to swallow their pride – not thinking enough about what the bad *feeling* in this country does to them. But I say all these young 'Black Britons' have no choice. OK, they were born here, but Whitey's still in control and this is Whitey's country. So you got to adjust, the way we did when we came. It's not fair and it's not easy, but where's the other path leading? Scares me looking round at all these groups stirring things up – Rastas, Marcus Garvey warriors, Black

Sisterhood – all one way or another wanting *revenge* . . . The slave-legacy again – 'kick Whitey's system'. That's what's been getting our kids into sin-bins and E S N units for years and years. Mostly they're not bad kids or sub-normal kids – you couldn't have that percentage sub-normal in one community! But they've picked up all this Black Power aggro in the air and then the teachers can't think what else to do but get rid of them. I don't blame those teachers, when some kids are wrecking every class. But I do blame teachers who think every Black pupil is dumb. Irv says most teachers don't even know they're racist, it's so built in. O K, there's plenty like that around. But there's plenty more just bad teachers, too lazy to bother. They won't even try to understand the special *emotional* problems young Black Britons have. I watched our boys doing fine till about twelve, thirteen. Then when they started being teenage and moody their teachers just gave up and things went from bad to terrible. Like they do for thousands and thousands of other *bright* Black kids. I want all-Black schools, even if people say 'You can't have apartheid in *this* country!' Kids would come out of all-Black schools with better qualifications, more able to compete with Whitey – that's not apartheid! The *result* of what goes on now is more like it, leaving kids trapped in ghettoes for lack of O Levels they're well able to get with different teaching. Employers are always complaining some kids with no qualifications won't take shit-jobs – 'Slave-type' jobs – the way *we* did. That's true, but *why* won't they? Because they know if things were O K at school they *would* have qualifications! So Whitey can say 'They've unrealistic expectations' – we're always hearing that. But as I said to Andy's teacher, years ago, you can't expect bright kids, blocked at school, to sweep gutters – or polish hospital floors like me – for the rest of their lives. Why should they? Don't mistake me, there's plenty Black kids only able for shit-jobs – the good Lord gave 'em no brains and colour shouldn't get anyone into an office with a computer in front of 'em! There's thousands lying in bed at noon pretending they should be in good jobs only 'teacher was a racist bastard' – and turning down Y T S cos it's *work* . . . Layabouts come in all colours! Now you're looking hungry, after listening to all that, so I'm making us a good dinner."

Irving had returned a few moments earlier, touchingly equipped with a can of cider for my refreshment. As Gerry went to the kitchen he said, "It's how I told you yesterday – Whites focus all the time on *negatives*. Layabouts come in all colours, but do the English think of themselves as 'a lazy race' because there's English layabouts? Why no *positives*? Why no publicity in the media for what percentage of Whites under thirty and Blacks under thirty go to church every Sunday? You'd get a positive image of young Blacks being more teetotal, God-fearing and clean-living than young Whites. But the English only want images of Black muggers, rapists, knifers. They'd reject any information that tried to change the picture, like if The *Sun* had headlines – 'MOST YOUNG BRITISH CHURCH-GOERS BLACK'!"

Walking home after a formidably 'good dinner' (Afro-Caribbean food is more notable for substance than savour) I thought about Gerry's prediction – 'doomed from generation to generation'. My morning had been spent with an idealistic White friend who was adamant that Britain *must* – and soon – become a society in which no one is 'doomed' because of skin-colour. But Gerry's prophecy agreed more with my own uneasy intuition that, for reasons to do with Black as well as White attitudes, this transformation of British society is unlikely. One of her comments, I felt, had gone to the very heart of the matter. "How can you get emancipated from your past when things happening day-to-day keep you in touch with it?" 'The slave legacy' seems to most Whites a tiresome phrase: perhaps relevant for social psychologists but, as used by Blacks themselves, merely a glib excuse for present-day failures. Yet numerous long conversations with Blacks of every age-group convinced me that it still influences race relations in Britain. Irving had remarked that it takes two to make a problem; Gerry was aware that it also takes two to solve one.

The Rastafarian and Black Power movements, which Gerry so deprecated, are the most obvious attempts to achieve emancipation from the past. Unfortunately each builds inter-racial barriers and several Black social workers told me they worried about there being too little communication between British-born Blacks and Whites. Many of my own encounters with young Blacks involved no exchange of views; the Blacks simply delivered diatribes calculated to put me in my place. The similarity between those Blacks and the Orange and Green extremists of Northern Ireland disturbed me. A reluctance to communicate with outsiders is one of the most ominous symptoms of fanaticism, of a retreat into a mental ghetto, barricaded against reality, where genuine grievances can grow into diseased fantasies.

One prodigiously wet Saturday evening I attended a hymn-singing concert (the Pentecostalists' idea of frivolous entertainment) to raise funds for a church school in Jamaica. The venue was a ramshackle hall behind a huge smog-darkened brick church at the other end of the Lozells Road from the Villa Cross pub – where I would much prefer to have been at that hour. As the three well-known singers from Jamaica arrived fifty minutes late, and the hall's electrical equipment was then found to be defective, there was ample time for gossip about the audience's home-towns. Some congregations are much closer than others to their Caribbean roots and this was a mainly elderly rural-origins group, still interested in whose goat had been stolen, which stretch of mountain road had at last been repaired, who alleged what about which pastor in the home-town churches, who had got a visa for the States (and *how*), who had moved to Kingston (and *why*) . . .

Three grannies (whom I had already met at church services) told me they were planning a campaign to have their grandchildren's generation sent home to Jamaica for schooling – an ironic reversal of the colonial practice.

Evangeline said, "Our schools are supposed to be no good – old-fashioned, unimaginative, repressive. But my family and friends all came out of them able to read and write and do sums. Here in Britain we've thousands of illiterate school-leavers – so which system is best?"

Carol said, "Anyway best for *our* kids. They need discipline, from day one. They need to be *taught*, to be told what to do and when and how – not left to *express themselves* with paints and modelling clay and inventing dances. That sort of stuff is for playtime in the evenings, when they've finished their homework, which mostly they don't even get any more in this country!"

Dulcie said, "Teachers here just don't understand our kids, even if they're not racist and want to. They don't know how Black minds work, they don't know how Black feelings work, they imagine kids are being cheeky when they're just being a bit boisterous. Then the kids think they're being got at because they're Black. And the day that happens their education ends, even if they're another four years at school."

"Then there's a new problem for the little ones now," said Evangeline. "My own daughter's an example and there's plenty like her. She had such a bad time at school she turned Billy against White teachers before he started last year. I tried to make her see how silly that was – we had rows every day – but really you can't blame her. She's a bright girl – not *university* bright, but everyone said she could get four or five O Levels and she was mad keen on history. But they said she wasn't up to it and couldn't get O Levels and pushed her into C S Es. I went and made a fuss and what was I told? That she'd be wasting staff time and making a fool of herself and if she was that keen she could go to the library and read history books! So now Billy's being difficult, though before he went to school he was a good little boy. I've written to my sister, near Kingston, and asked her to have him. He can come back when he's eighteen, with a better chance of a job than if he spent years here in an E S N unit!"

I asked if they would support all-Black schools. "Yes," said Carol, "but they'd never be allowed in this country – not State schools, for every Black kid. And more fee-paying church schools wouldn't help the kids that most need help."

"I'm against them," said Evangeline. "It's giving in to racism. And you'd have attacks on the buildings and the pupils – and probably the staff too. Then where would you find teachers? There aren't enough educated Blacks and mostly those with education want better jobs – better than teaching inner-city kids in falling-down schools. And another thing you mightn't realise, some Black parents – my daughter for one – wouldn't want their kids taught by the sort of middle-class élitist Black folk you get with degrees and diplomas. This generation of young Blacks is very *awkward . . .*"

"So am I against," said Dulcie. "It could look like we were ghettoising ourselves and didn't want them to have White friends – which isn't true. It's mostly the teachers make problems in this area, not their own age-group of Whites.'

During the post-concert bun-fight I talked with Hubert, a widower aged sixty-five who had just returned from a visit to his eighty-seven-year-old mother. "I spend one month with her every five years, and this time I took my eldest grandson – he's fifteen. In the middle of the twenty-first century he can tell *his* grandson he met his great-grandmother, whose grandfather came from Ghana on one of the last slave-ships. He was twelve then, in 1809. My mother remembers her father talking about the owner's brand on his father's left breast. And he said being branded wasn't really painful though it sounds so cruel to us. Everything changed quickly when the new Africans stopped coming. Then we lost touch and became more and more – what? Whatever we are now! Which is something *special*."

Hubert left Jamaica in 1941, served in the RAF for eight years, then got a £14-a-week job in Birmingham. "By living sensibly I saved eight pounds every week. In those days a single man with no bad habits could live well on six pounds." When he married his Barbadian wife (SRN) he already owned his first taxi; by keeping his original job and taxi-driving at night he saved enough for a second. Then he gave up his job and when he retired in 1984 he owned a fleet of taxis in Birmingham and Wolverhampton.

"Anyone willing to work hard, not looking for too much money, can get on in this country. There's nothing wrong with Britain, the trouble is inside those youngsters. Black and White they're all the same, looking for hand-outs. My two sons and my daughter did well at school – I sent them to fee-paying schools, it was worth it – all three are in the forces since they were eighteen. No problems, no complaints, but when they're home on leave the agitators round here tell them they should have been promoted, they'll get nowhere working for Whitey – only so far and no further. Well, that may be so. But what should they do? Complain and be sacked? Resign and go on the dole? This is England and the best jobs and promotions will always go to English-men and women. That's human nature and you get it all round the world. If we'd stayed on the islands where would we – and our children – be now? I'd say I'd be still where I started from – a three-room shack without a lavatory or a tap! You've got to take the rough with the smooth. And if you keep your eyes fixed on the smooth you needn't notice the rough. 'Dirty coon!' 'Black bastard!' 'Lazy nigger!' – yes, you get it all. And what harm does it do? You *pity* people who talk and think like that, you don't let them *worry* you. The English are not polite, they have very primitive ways of treating people – not just Blacks, but each other. Of course the upper classes could be different, I'm talking about the ones we know. But they can't help it, the Lord made them that way so we should be able to forgive them."

As Hubert spoke I thought of Gerry's (unheeded) advice to her sons: "Ignore insults and prejudice and do your own thing." Her argument, which Hubert repeated, was persuasive; if enough Blacks successfully do their own thing, Whitey's attitude may slowly change. But change to what? – to regard-ing Blacks as Browns are now regarded, 'hard-working quiet people', not equals but 'coloureds' who can be tolerated because they don't make trouble?

I asked Hubert what developments he has noticed over the years, on his regular returns to Jamaica. He laughed. "So many I could write a book about them – forty-four years is a long time! But most came since we got Independence in 1962. My mother thinks it's all got worse and a lot of it has – now there's no control over inflation and taxes. There's an even bigger gap between rich and poor – and it was big enough before. The big business families have been too greedy to invest at home, when there's bigger and quicker profits abroad. Too many talented Jamaicans have migrated to the States, which is even worse for our future than money being sent out – and of course it follows from it. No investment at home means no opportunities for the talented. But saddest is the violent crime. I left Jamaica a peaceful, happy-go-lucky little place, now Kingston is bad as Chicago. It's gangland, and not just slum gangsters. Some of the nation's leaders are getting their slice from the cocaine trade – South America, Caribbean and on to the States – so you expect violent crime among the poor . . . But each visit I see improvements too. The old colonial churches are fading out – too tied up with the rich and the corrupt – nobody trusts them. So all over the island there's a true revival of faith – never before so many listening to the Spirit. And connected with this – or to me it seems connected – our 'White bias' is weakening. I feel now it's stronger among Blacks in Britain. Education is improving – but still not *good* – and people judge each other more on achievement than colour. There's big pride in our music and carvings and all our traditions. What used to be looked down on as 'folk-culture', people see it now as *national* culture. My grandson was really excited by that. He's grown up hearing the immigrant generation saying we've no culture, we lost everything when we were torn away from Africa – which is nonsense. There is an Afro-Caribbean culture. It's all the old West African cultures mixed in with the old Creole planters' culture – and *that* wasn't all European but influenced for centuries by the slaves. Not only our genes were mixed, but our spirits – and out of all that we've got something *special*. Isn't every culture mongrel, if you go back far enough? You just have to give it time to set, like jam! And now it *is* setting, in Jamaica. I wish more young Black Britons could go to see how it is, see they do have real cultural roots without chasing off to Ethiopia looking for imaginary ones . . . Sometimes I think, if the islands were properly run, it might be better for a lot to go back where their parents came from. Too many here are using what slavery did to us as an excuse. Back home they'd find their own generation growing out of the old 'Negro inferiority complex'. In my boyhood it was as strong as in slave days – the colonial regime needed it. So that's the greatest and the best change I can see in forty-four years. And I thank and praise the Lord for it . . ."

Gerry would have described Hubert as a 'toughie', able to ignore racialism and compete successfully in Whitey's world. (Although he was black Black – no discernible White blood there to make him tougher!) He represented a distinct 'school of thought'; only a few days later I met a woman in her mid-thirties who used almost identical phrases.

Denise had emigrated to Canada fifteen years previously and was home to help her parents move from a large house near Heathfield Road, where they had brought up their six children, to a compact new O A P residence – part of an attractive brick two-storey Council development off the Villa Road. Her father had worked for twenty-eight years as store-clerk in a factory, her mother for almost as long doing evening shifts in a hotel kitchen. "When Dad came home Mum went out – as kids we always had one parent around. And aunts and an uncle and cousins living near. We were secure. And Church helped in those days, though it's not part of my life now. It still helps my parents, as you can see."

When I asked Denise if Canada has race relations problems she replied sharply, "I never notice anything like prejudice or discrimination. I was brought up to ignore it – my parents always said this is a good country where you get a fair deal if you do an honest day's work. A lot of Blacks use racism as an excuse for their own laziness or stupidity. My youngest brother is into this anti-racism thing and he's turned down four jobs. He was offered them because my Dad spoke for him but he says they're all shit-jobs. If he couldn't draw good money from the State for doing nothing he'd take them fast and thank the Lord!"

Such conversations always bothered and confused me. It is comforting for Whitey to concentrate on the fact that some Blacks can ignore racialism and that dynamic characters like Hubert can prosper despite it. The temptation then is to deduce that it can't really be a major problem, that all Blacks could ignore it – a temptation to which Oscar Wilde's advice does not apply. One rejoices for those who have been able to build defences against racialism and live contentedly within them, but is this retreat from reality tainted by cowardice? Perhaps it has to do with that stereotype of 'the benevolent Motherland' which was deeply imprinted at school on the minds of the immigrant generation. A certain sort of personality finds it easier to practise life-long self-deception than to abandon a vision of 'goodness' and cope with profound disillusionment.

In many of her dealings with Blacks, the Motherland is a bitch. It is simply not true that in Britain Blacks 'get a fair deal'. And the compulsion felt by some Blacks to condemn those others who are unable or unwilling to build defences – a compulsion which invariably accompanies the 'I don't notice prejudice' syndrome – is very off-putting indeed. Since no Black can be unaware of British racialism, however successfully they may ignore it, the implication is that it *should* be ignored, that it is in some way justifiable (perhaps divinely ordained?), or at least so inevitable that it makes no sense to fight it. One White argument insists that Blacks who *can* ignore it are proving their emancipation from the slave legacy of White superiority. They believe in their own worth as individuals, and 'make the best of things here and now'. The counter-argument is that Blacks who accept second-class citizenship – for example, by accepting that being Black means being denied promotion, however well deserved – are proving themselves still firmly shackled to the principle of White superiority. And then there is that third argument, implicit in Hubert's questions – "But what should they do? Resign and go on the dole?" Very often opposing discrimination means saying, 'If I can't have a whole loaf I'll take no bread.' And people without bread go hungry.

Hubert may have sent his three children to fee-paying schools in the early 1960s for reasons no different from a White parent's. However, he is now helping to pay for his four grandchildren's private education because he has been so shocked by Black 'under-achievement' at State schools. For this he tended, characteristically, to blame Black parents more than White teachers. But he admitted – "By now Black kids have such a bad name *all* Black pupils are handicapped at State schools, whatever sort of home they come from."

Only 3 per cent of Blacks obtain in five or more higher grades at O Level, compared with 18 per cent of Browns and 16 per cent of other leavers. Only 2 per cent of Blacks obtain one or more A Level pass, compared with 13 per cent of Browns and 12 per cent of other leavers. Only 1 per cent of Blacks go on to university compared with 3 per cent of Browns and 3 per cent of other leavers. Concern about Black 'under-achievement' prompted the Swann Committee to bring out an Interim Report (*West Indian Children in our Schools*: The Rampton Report) in 1981. It considered every aspect of the problem except the most important – why have a few Blacks been able to overcome the obstacles common to all Blacks and succeed academically? Hope was expressed that the Swann Report would try to solve this puzzle. But some anti-racist Committee member objected to any such investigation, which might have exposed the unfavourable domestic circumstances of many Black children to racialist criticism and scorn.

Every morning I swam in Handsworth's vast Leisure Centre (opened in December 1984), often leaving my pad before 6.30 a.m. to walk to the Park by round-about routes. At that hour one of the long-recognised causes of Black 'under-achievement' was visible – and audible – all over Handsworth, as Black working mothers delivered their pre-school children (and babies) to child-minders' homes. Despite this being a daily routine, many children did not want to part from their mothers and I regularly witnessed harrowing scenes at garden gates or on doorsteps.

The Rampton Report commented:

> Many West Indian parents may not appreciate the importance to a child of an unstrained, patient and quiet individual dialogue with an adult . . . In order to help parents to recognise the many ways in which they can help their child's linguistic and conceptual development in the pre-school years, we feel that LEAs might usefully distribute information leaflets to all parents giving ideas and advice on constructive play and preparation for school.

This is an excellent idea, but working Handsworth parents urgently need something more substantial than leaflets – like several new day-care centres and nursery schools. In my own Heathfield Road–Westminster Road zone there were then (1985) 273 three-year-olds and only ninety-one 'official' nursery school places. (A new twenty-six-place nursery unit has since been opened at the Heathfield Junior School.) In the whole Handsworth area 83 per cent of the children registered at nurseries were Black or Brown (mainly Black) and over 43 per cent were from single-parent families. I was unable to find out the percentage of Black working mothers but everyone agreed it was very high; Black women can find jobs – often in sweat-shops – more easily than Black men. Hundreds of unhappy Black children know their mother only when she is exhausted at the end of a long, hard day's work and in no mood for 'individual dialogue' or 'constructive play'. She wants to get her young quickly out of the way so that she can briefly relax before going to bed early to be up early to deliver her child (or children) back to the minder before catching the bus to work . . . And very often her pay is so low that she must work seven days a week.

The local D H S S day-nurseries, which each cope with fifty or sixty children aged six weeks to three years, have waiting lists of 100 or 150; therefore child-minders, both registered and unregistered (illegal) are numerous. According to D H S S regulations, no single-handed paid minder should take on more than three children under five, including her own. But this rule is often broken and unregistered minders, themselves desperate for a little extra money, sometimes take on half-a-dozen children. Many Blacks spend most of their first five years in 'day-care'.

There are some minders of exceptional quality, both registered and un-registered, and their reputation ('better than a nursery school!') means that they have waiting-lists as long as the D H S S's. Gerry's niece (unregistered) was among those and having been sworn to secrecy I was taken to visit her one afternoon. She was not expecting us – the Blacks 'drop in' on each other, as the Irish do – and it was yet another very wet day. Yet we walked onto an astonishingly well-organised and cheerful scene. In the front parlour a clean, plump nine-months-old baby lay asleep on the settee, barricaded by cushions, while two toddlers happily messed about on the floor with sensibly impro-vised 'toys'. Gerry's niece was sitting on the stairs, from where she could see into the parlour, reading nursery rhymes from a library book to three four-year-olds. She was, in my eyes, of heroic stature: one of those people who actively *enjoy* being with small children (not my favourite form of wild life) and so can remain calm throughout a long day in their company. But it was not difficult to imagine the scene in a similar cramped terrace house on a wet day with a more 'normal' minder in charge. Some women take their protégés to play-groups; these are numerous in Handsworth yet can cater for scarcely half the numbers who seek to join. And lack of transport prevents many minders from using them.

I was reliably informed, by Gerry and others, that the average child-minder provides very restricted play-space, few toys, no books, poor food and little if any individual attention. The minder's nerves are usually frayed by noon – as mine would be by 8.00 a.m. – and the children's restlessness and noisiness is often curbed by methods that can do permanent psychological damage. Small wonder then that so many of these children are labelled 'difficult' or 'disruptive' when they start school and are soon relegated to E S N units, though their intelligence may be average or above. A complete lack of 'individual dialogue' and 'constructive play' during pre-school years, combined with the emotional insecurity inherent in the child-minder system, imposes a handicap not easily overcome.

I discussed this most distressing problem with a Black child psychologist who grew up in Handsworth but now lectures at a university elsewhere in England. She criticised Lord Swann for giving in to anti-racist pressure – "He should have insisted on a detailed analysis of the link between Black under-achievement and inadequate parenting." Her main argument was that Black pupils *en masse* are indirectly affected by those who can't cope with school – Hubert's point, to explain his grandchildren being privately educated. She said, "Child-minder victims have to seem stupid when they start school! Often they're backward in speech. Never having played creatively, they can't concentrate. Their insecurity leads to all sorts of classroom difficulties, from incontinence to aggression to hyper-activity to almost autistic withdrawal – then later to truancy. And many teachers, with low expectations of Blacks, are only delighted to have their prejudices confirmed. But it's a mistake to blame teachers for circumstances beyond their control – another reason why Swann should have gone into all this. The more teachers feel they're being made the scapegoats for Black under-achievement, the more they'll take it out on Black pupils – that's happening now, increasingly, all over the country. You can't expect ordinary teachers, working in demoralised inner-city schools, to sort out Black kids' special problems. But they are to blame in the whole area of diagnosis. If a child is naughty and Black, most teachers don't bother finding out whether he's normally naughty, in need of no more than firm discipline, or disturbed naughty. So thousands of perfectly normal pupils, from good secure homes, end up in special units for the abnormal – where they soon *become* abnormal. And fiercely resentful and frustrated. Naturally they feel society is unjust and against them. So there you have the rioters of the future. By now a whole anti-school cult is flourishing, with small children being egged on by older siblings and friends to defy the system – and sometimes by young parents, too. I don't see this vicious circle being broken without all-Black schools – at least for a while, maybe twenty-five years." (This is also the view of Carleton Duncan, one of Britain's few Black head teachers and an anti-racist member of the Rampton and Swann Committees.)

At an informal Small Heath gathering of teachers and social workers, who had got together to discuss the Swann Report, I infuriated one anti-racist White teacher by asking, "Why do Blacks have to emulate White academic achievements to be regarded as our equals? Why must they be seen as failures – 'under-achievers' – if they can't compete within an educational system designed for another sort of people?"

The young woman glared at me. "So what d'you want?" she snapped. "To see them all drummers and boxers and singers and sprinters?" Then she turned and walked away.

Later, I listened to twelve teachers (including two Blacks) heatedly – sometimes over-heatedly – discussing this difficult problem. In my notebook I jotted down the main points to emerge:

1 A considerable minority of Black pupils who 'under-achieve' do have the ability to get good exam results.
2 Too many White teachers assume that Black talent is *always* musical and/or athletic.
3 Among Black pupils there is *much* more musical and athletic talent than academic.
4 Anti-racists refuse to admit (3). Thus a school atmosphere is created in which blacks feel they are being down-graded if encouraged to develop non-academic gifts.
5 Many black parents do have unrealistic academic expectations for their children. These are fostered by extreme anti-racists, who lay *all* the blame for 'under-achievement' on racist teachers.
6 Many teachers are now afraid to encourage black non-academic talents, lest they be accused of 'racist stereotyping'. Therefore much first-rate talent is never used.

Half-way through this dicussion the two Black teachers walked out in protest against a suggestion that it might be time to forget stereotyping hang-ups, see each pupil as an individual and encourage him/her to develop to the full whichever gifts he/she might have.

Another discussion group (six teachers and two women social workers, all White) met to debate multi-cultural curricula but were soon onto the more immediate dilemmas posed by classroom discipline – or the lack of it. What came through most strongly was the teachers' physical fear of aggressive Black adolescents, both boys and girls. One man in his forties, who had always taught in multi-racial schools, remarked, "Even on quiet days, with all the Afros sitting at the back of the class playing cards, there seems to be a *threat* of violence in the room."

An older man wondered, "How much of that do we imagine? And if we're tense and waiting for trouble, does that provoke it? I'll never understand their signals – gestures, looks, the way they come into a room and sit or lounge about – what's called 'body-language' nowadays. Theirs is still foreign to me, after fifteen years. And mine must be foreign to them. A lot of trouble could start there."

"But what that means," one of the social workers pointed out, "is that neither side *wants* to learn! I'm not being personal, but all you've said shows a really powerful mutual antipathy."

"I don't know about *mutual*," said the elderly man rather huffily, "but there's massive hostility on *their* side. And every year it gets worse."

Afterwards, during tea-break, I heard an angry criticism of geography text-books. The speaker was a Black teacher who had walked out of the first session. She complained that African countries were depicted as 'primitive' – "It's all jungles, deserts, grass-huts, half-naked women, herds of cattle and wild animals! What does that do for the Black kids' self-esteem? And for the White kids' concept of where we all came from! Why not show how African cities are now, with skyscrapers and big cars and T V aerials?"

To me that was the day's most poignant remark. It is heart-breaking to hear – as one too often does – anti-racist Blacks demanding pictures of what *W*hites super-imposed on Africa to raise the self-esteem of Black children.

The elderly teacher with body-language problems gave me a lift home and remarked on the savagery of South Africa's militant Blacks, who had recently been much in the news. "I always remind myself we have to make allow-ances," he said virtuously. "They've different *codes*, if you follow me, and that goes too for our lot here. I mean, all this about necklacing, hacking people to death, cutting out livers and hearts for rituals, corpses being dug up and burned, slicing off genitals – it's primitive stuff, no doubt about that!"

"You think we're more civilised?" I asked.

He looked at me in astonishment. "*Think*? I know it! We all know it, it's only those looney lefties won't admit it!"

"And yet," I said, "most Whites don't oppose nuclear weapons – which would cause far more suffering to innocent millions than anyone endures while being hacked to death. Isn't it possible we're actually *over*-civilised? In fact thoroughly decadent?"

"That's an altogether different matter!" said my outraged companion.

Some fifty per cent of Handsworth's young Black mothers are unmarried; many others are already separated from their husbands and living alone or with a new partner. The older generation, of all colours, tend to regard these young women as promiscuous, improvident and irresponsible – as an unmar-ried White working mother I often found myself defending them, out of a sense of sisterly loyalty, and thus shocking prim friends. What White O A Ps and monogamous Browns and Pentecostalists deem 'promiscuous' is now normal behaviour for many young, of all colours and circumstances. (Or was: A I D S may alter that – though I doubt if it will.) However, the Blacks' reckless reproduction is undeniably creating a 'problem' generation. Their apparent allergy to contraceptives puzzled me and I asked two young mums about this – the only girls I became sufficiently intimate with to put such a question. Their replies were identical: "In bed you don't think of things like *that*!"

When one's economic situation is dire, and without hope of improvement, this attitude could perhaps be described as improvident. Yet it seemed to me that mothers who work seven days a week to feed and clothe their children cannot fairly be described as 'irresponsible'. This view is however derided by church-going Blacks. As Evelyn put it, "Those kids go to work for *fun*! They get bored stuck all day with a baby or toddler – they want to be active, with their own age-group. If being mums suited them, they'd get enough benefits to stay home. It's different for older women with three or four kids and a husband gone off, or out of work – they've no choice. They're *really* pushed – you want to know what poverty feels like, you ask them!"

The high incidence of single-parent Black families is not, as some Whites imagine, a result of British permissiveness corrupting the sons and daughters of pious, puritanical Blacks. Marriage was not a usual preliminary to child-bearing among the Caribbean working classes – though 'respectable' Blacks, long settled in Britain, are often reluctant to acknowledge this fact. In 1942 70 per cent of Jamaica's population were born out of wedlock. In 1961 only 22 per cent were legally married and 44 per cent of women were single parents. Being married was a sign of economic prosperity, not of social respectability or religious orthodoxy. Couples frequently lived happily together for twenty years, then married when already grandparents – because only then were they able to afford a good wedding-party. Many of the unmarried original immigrants – men and women – left one or more children behind them and regularly remitted money for their support if they weren't brought to Britain as soon as their fares could be saved. This essentially matriarchal system seems to have worked well enough in the Caribbean, but in urban Britain it is proving catastrophic.

Most grannies can no longer play their traditional part by grandchild-minding while mum goes out to work; often they themselves have a job, or are living in cramped quarters that make grandmothering impractical. More-over, in the British environment there are new psychological complications. Those among the immigrant generation who grew up seeing marriage as a mark of economic success, and who quickly realised that in the Motherland shifting sexual alliances and illegitimate children were non-U, acquired the marrying habit as part of their effort to 'better themselves'. Nowadays parents in this category often reject their children for behaving as they themselves behaved, at the same age, in the Caribbean. Yet this rapid adaptation to British 'respectability' did not obliterate the old tradition, itself based on a slave-era distortion of West African polygamous and matrilineal social structures.

"Have you noticed how many Black debates lead back to shackles and whips?" asked Clarissa (she whose brothers had 'gone Rasta'). We were considering the formidable ramifications of 'under-achievement' while en-joying a Caribbean meal in my pad – supplied by an excellent new black Take-Away on the Villa Road.

During the three months since I first met Clarissa she had left home, left Mr Plum-Suit's church and decided *not* to marry her teacher fiancé but simply move into his pad. Also, she had deliberately become pregnant. These dramatic developments she explained thus – "I suddenly thought, a few weeks before our wedding-date: This is silly! Why am I pretending to be another sort of person? To keep my parents happy! But whose life is it? Mine! Luke never really wanted marriage and neither did I, it was all to please Mum and Dad. And that was the wrong reason to get tangled up in legal complications. We want to enjoy each other, have a few kids, maybe spend the rest of our lives together – but then maybe not. I felt being imprisoned by marriage would be bad for Luke – I mean bad for our relationship – a threat to it. We know why our parents' generation took up British ways. They were desperate to be respected and accepted and they had this Jamaican dream about marrying and leaving working-class ways behind – even though Dad was always in his dirty heavy job! Now all that's changed. Soon after they arrived the change began but they didn't notice it! No one cares now in Whitey's world whether people are married or not, or have babies in or out of wedlock. So why let our parents force us into old conventions if they don't suit us? Some of my generation do want marriage and that sort of stability – O K, that's their choice. But it's bad if the reason is to make Whites think *we're* the same as *them*, under this Black skin. We're not, we're settled in our own sort of mould and you could say it's not monogamous. It's more natural and spontaneous and happy. Monogamy isn't natural for anyone, but Whites are so conditioned they can manage to regulate their families within it. I suddenly saw one day – I hadn't really been *thinking* about it, it just hit me – I saw there's no reason why we shouldn't love the way *we* love!"

By then I knew Clarissa well enough to speak out. "That's fine," I said, "but it does take us back to all these 'under-achieving' pupils. No need to worry about your children – you've the money and education to cope, even if it's not easy. But thousands of young Blacks happily doing their own sexual thing in inner-city Britain *doesn't work*. Too many kids suffer too many disadvantages as a direct result. As well as inheriting poverty and racial prejudice, they're expected to survive without emotional security. So what's the answer?"

"Lots *more* and much *better* day-care facilities and nursery schools," replied Clarissa promptly. But would Handsworth's White and Brown tax-payers agree?

However, many more Afro-Caribbean Self-Help centres, like the Marcus Garvey Day-Nursery on Linwood Road, and the Saturday School on Heath-field Road, would ease the pressure on children, parents and teachers. Such community-run 'support-systems' are immensely valuable. Linwood Road in June 1985 had a waiting-list of eighty; thirty-eight under-two-year-olds were being cared for daily and advice was given to young parents on every aspect of child-care, including health, nutrition and pre-school education. At the

Heathfield road Saturday School, forty five-to-fifteen-year-olds were coached weekly by Black voluntary workers. Here, as in numerous similar schools all over Britain, many under-achievers become achievers and despite their teachers' pessimistic predictions gain good O Level results. Unfortunately, 'official' attitudes to such Self-Help supplementary schools – which have been increasing in number since the late 1960s – are ambivalent. The Healthfield Road school, started in 1967 (in another building), received its first ever grant for equipment in 1983. Some L E As and individual teachers provide moral support, if nothing else. Others resent the competition ('interference') of non-professionals, especially when these prove the professionals' assessment of a child to have been quite wrong. Also, there are frequent objections that the Black Power approach to teaching Afro-Caribbean history and culture is 'subversive' and exacerbates classroom tensions by raising the pupils' level of 'anti-Whiteness'. In some cases this last objection is justified; certainly I was made to feel unwelcome at both the Linwood Road Nursery and the Heathfield Road Saturday School. In both places hostility might have been less had I used some of my 'Letters of Introduction'. But this I preferred not to do. I didn't wish to be politely tolerated, and shielded from the realities in this area of Black–White relationships, because So-and-So had said I was a person of consequence.

I visited the Linwood Road Nursery only once, feeling it would be wrong to distract the workers, and create bad vibes for the toddlers, by reappearing. But I often visited my anti-White neighbours on Heathfield Road, where the hostility gradually dwindled until I came to feel quarter-welcome – though no one ever actually rejoiced to see me, least of all the two snarling Dobermanns who guarded the entrance and were the most racialist dogs I have ever met. As one stood at the door waiting for admission they hurled themselves against their restraining wire mesh, only three feet away, slaverring to tear Whitey to shreds.

When new to Handsworth, it hurt me to be hated, despised, feared and suspected by many of my neighbours. At first I tended to react with confused, almost small-child indignation – This isn't *fair*! I'm *me*, an *individual*, someone who wants to listen to their point of view! Why must they treat me like an enemy just because of the colour of my skin? Just because I'm White! But I soon turned that around. Why do so many Whites admit that if a Black man overtakes or approaches them on a quiet street they tense up, half-expecting to be mugged? Because most Whites don't think of Blacks as *individuals* . . .

To a Heathfield Road resident, 'The Blacks' very quickly comes to seem meaningless. *Which* Blacks? The devoutly busy Pentecostalists, mapping a route to Heaven? The employed younger generation, drinking moderately with White and Brown friends in the Grey Dove? The friendly older generation, drinking immoderately in seedier pubs because they have lost their jobs and cannot resign themselves to the boredom and indignity of life on the dole while their wives are still working? The tiny minority of successful big businessmen who are never seen in Handsworth and if they were would probably be pelted with half-bricks? The defiant, despairing younger generation who have never had a job and use gradations of Rastafarianism to disguise their shame and express their anger? The genuine Marcus Garvey militants, who scorn ganja-smoking Rasta drop-outs and both practise and preach constructive 'Self-Help' and not-so-constructive anti-Whiteness? The middle-class intellectual feminists who half-want to be on the militants' side but are rejected by them? The many hopeless young who have allied themselves with no group or cult but live quietly and sadly in pads or squats, tacitly admitting defeat at the age of twenty?

Blacks, like Whites, come in all shapes and sizes; it would be odd if they did not. But as a minority they seem even more tragically disunited than the Brown communities.

11 · In and Around the Villa Cross

Within days of my arrival in Handsworth, the extraordinary contrast between the 'race relations atmospheres' of Bradford and Birmingham had become apparent. Bradford is a small, compact city and its 62,000 non-Whites seem much more obvious than Brum's 150,000 – which form by far the largest concentration of Blacks/Browns in Britain. Within Brum's inner-city 'Core Area' (total population 272,000) forty-three per cent of the residents are non-White. Yet in general the Brum atmosphere felt more relaxed; among White Brummies I heard few of the rabidly racialist remarks so common in Bradford. This may be partly because White Brummies are less communicative about everything than White Bradfordians, but it often seemed to me that the sheer diversity of Birmingham's non-White population reduced its potential for irritating Whites. Brum's racial mix includes the biggest settlement of Sikhs in Britain, and many thousands of Gujaratis, Pakistanis, Bangladeshis, ex-Africa Asians, Vietnamese – you name them, Brum has them. Perhaps racialism flourishes more obviously where issues are simple: Mirpuri Islamic orthodoxy versus White working-class paganism. Bradford Council's anti-racist/multi-cultural policy involves concessions to one conspicuously non-English set of demands and so provokes eloquent resentment of what is perceived as 'too much grovelling to the Pakis'. Birmingham's efforts to counteract racialism are an integral, taken-for-granted part of its 'Inner-City Partnership Programme', a scheme to help *all* deprived Core Area residents. It is revealing to compare the local newspapers. Almost every day Bradford's *Telegraph and Argus* gives prominence to race-related items, usually controversial. Reading the Birmingham newspapers, one would never suspect the existence of over 150,000 non-White Brummies. (Anti-racists of course see this as a bad thing: 'Sweeping the problems of prejudice and discrimination under the carpet.') Also, Brum's last Special Language School, for teaching English to children who only learn their mother-tongue at home, was closed in 1981. Bradford has three such schools and more are planned. Apparently the children of the large Mirpuri community in cosmopolitan Brum do not have the same language problem as their cousins (very often literally cousins) in Bradford's 'Little Mirpur'.

However, despite the overall sense of Britain's second biggest city being better able to cope with its Brown/Black population, I find the following entry in my journal for 25 June 1985: 'My conversations with White Brummies suggest a resigned indifference to, or muted distaste for, these "alien communities". Yet there is too a general awareness, found in Bradford only at the end of the Honeyford Affair, that things could "get out of hand" – i.e., that race riots are always a possibility. No doubt this is because of the huge Black population – approximately 75,000 – with its (real or imaginary?) potential for spontaneous combustion.'

In both Bradford and Handsworth (but especially in Handsworth) my material-gathering task proved even trickier than it had been in the tense sectarian ghettoes of Northern Ireland. There most people eventually accepted me as an outsider with no axe to grind. On the race relations scene, my being without an axe aroused many suspicions which were strengthened by my working methods, or lack of them. Blacks and Browns are used to their territories being closely studied by battalions of sociologists, anthropologists, political scientists, urban economists, educational psychologists – even theologians. They therefore expected me to talk jargon, employ an interpreter, present them with questionnaires, use a tape-recorder, interview Important People and go statistics-hunting in offices. My failure to do any of those things inevitably started rumours. Was I perhaps working for the Home Office, sniffing out illegal immigrants? Or was I in cahoots with the police, being paid to inform on drugs-dealers? Writers of books about race relations are not supposed to wander casually around back-streets, equipped only with their antennae and a scruffy little jotter, talking to 'unimportant' people.

Suspicion of my real purpose was, naturally, at its most intense in the Villa Cross pub – undisputed Rasta territory and at that time Handsworth's (perhaps Birmingham's) main ganja-dealing centre. Within days of my arrival in Handsworth, several people of all colours warned me never to attempt to drink there. The regulars, they said, do not welcome irregulars and any stranger unescorted by a regular was likely to be 'harassed'. This was particularly so at the beginning of June 1985 because the drug-squad had recently 'done' the Villa Cross. Nineteen regulars were ungently arrested and (allegedly) some £2,000 worth of ganja was collected from the floor where it had been dropped when the fuzz appeared. (And yet, by one of those strange coincidences that so baffle innocents on the ganja-scene, none of the main dealers was in the pub that evening.)

I cannot say how I might have reacted to my neighbours' warnings had the Villa Cross not been my geographical 'local', two minutes' walk across the road from my pad and therefore the pub I would in any case have used most regularly, irrespective of its Rasta ethos. That greatly interested me, but I was not going there merely to 'study the scene'. As a resident of No. 45 Heathfield Road the Rastas were my neighbours, their local was my local and I felt *entitled* to drink at the Villa Cross. To have avoided it would have seemed cowardly; in such situations one instinctively resists intimidation. (I vividly remember my sense of outrage on being told that as someone with a Southern Irish brogue I 'dare not' drink in Belfast's Sandy Row pubs.) Later came the realisation that my gate-crashing had been insensitive because the Villa Cross was much more than just another ganja pub. But without becoming a regular I could never had reached that awareness of the place's significance.

No one had specified what form Rasta harassment might take and I felt mildly apprehensive on first approaching my local at 8.00 p.m. one damp, chilly June evening. On the Heathfield Road side the pub's wide forecourt stands some ten feet about street level and a narrow flight of litter-strewn steps formed a short-cut for me. On those steps – half-concealed from the road – much ganja-dealing was done, either because the (White) buyer preferred not to enter the pub or because the (Black) dealer wished to conduct his business out of sight of rival dealers. I hesitated that first evening, seeing two young men blocking the steps. A dozen Rastas were sitting on or lounging against the wall above, staring fixedly at me while drinking beer or Lucozade from bottles. (Drinking from a glass is non-U in Rastaland.) My avoiding the steps would have involved walking the length of the wall, still being fixedly stared at, and going a long way round across the forecourt to the pub door. I chose the steps and squeezed past the trading pair with eyes ostentatiously averted. The forecourt drinkers – some wearing dreadlocks, some Rasta hats, some short-haired – all turned to continue to stare at me as I crossed the short distance from the top of the steps to the door. A few cars were parked nearby, including one that habitually flew the Ethiopian flag and belonged to a self-styled Rasta 'leader'. The sentinels (known as 'soldiers') were obvious; three men posted where they could observe the Villa, Lozells and Heathfield Roads and warn of approaching police vehicles or foot-patrols. Another three were blocking the doorway and at first made no move when I said "Excuse me". They looked me up and down with calculated insolence, smiled at one another above my head, made unintelligible remarks in patois, then moved aside just enough to allow me past.

It was a Wednesday evening and the enormous, high-ceilinged bar was only half-full but still redolent of ganja and vibrating with reggae. In its Edwardian youth the Villa Cross must have been quite magnificent. Standing at the semi-circular mahogany counter, I could feel everyone's attention concentrated on the unescorted stranger. It was a relief to hear the manager's Dublin accent; later I discovered that he had been in charge for eleven years, since the days when most of the regulars were Irish construction workers, then living in doss-houses all over Lozells. The barmaids were both friendly youngish Irishwomen, one from a village near my own home town. While waiting for my pint of cider I told her what I was doing in Handsworth – loudly, so that the scowling Rasta who had quickly moved to my side could hear me above the reggae. He was wearing a black leather jacket with a built-in bandolier; it looked like part of a little boy's Christmas 'Bandit Outfit'. His dreadlocks were superb and his general appearance and manner quite ferocious – or so I thought that first evening. As time passed he proved to be a most endearing character, one of the few who befriended (as distinct from tolerating) me.

I took my pint to a corner seat between two high, wide windows, one facing Lozells Road, the other overlooking the forecourt and Villa Road. All the windows were curtained from half-way down. The door was on my left, three yards away beyond a five-foot wooden partition which made this corner a semi-snug. On the bench against the partition sat a small slim nervous-looking Rasta, his locks tucked into a leather hat, and a tall sultry Black woman wearing very high-heeled scarlet shoes and a skin-tight lime-green dress. They had been arguing angrily when I took my seat; after a moment they moved out of sight, to the pool-table end of the bar. Then two young Blacks who were sharing a joint on my right also moved, leaving me alone in the corner. A large Black and White group in the opposite corner studied me briefly but intently, before forming themselves into a tight circle for trading purposes. I got out my jotter and settled to my usual evening task of note-taking. All the tables were badly knife-scarred: a result of the cutting of countless bars of cannabis resin. Business was slow that evening; in Handsworth there is very little money around by Wednesday and most of the action was centred on the pool-table. I left after about an hour, feeling elated. My reception could scarcely be described as cordial, but neither had there been any harassment. I assumed that no one had offered me ganja because of my advanced years.

The atmosphere was different on my next visit, two days later. I felt quite relaxed as I climbed the steps, politely greeted the row of unresponsive Rastas on the forecourt wall, and edged my way through an ebullient throng around the door. One man grabbed my shoulder and asked, "How much you give me if I fuck you?" But I took that to be his little joke. I had to queue at the crowded bar and there was much excitement in the air. Single men and pairs of men were closely watching the door (and each other), awaiting their weekly customers. Already, at 7.30, the air reeked of hash. Two pallid but bouncy little White boys, aged nine or ten, were doing a roaring trade fetching supper from nearby Take-Aways for hungry drinkers/smokers. Several Rastas were dancing solo around the floor, shaking their locks and shouting as they leaped in the air. Three teenage prostitutes were being wanton with Black youths in 'my' corner, but there was a vacant seat between them and a short-haired dealer. He was having trouble with his tiny silver ganja-scales and paid no attention to me when I sat beside him.

Placing my pint amidst a clutter of bottles, I took a tin of ten mini-cigars from my shoulder-bag and left it on the table while rummaging for my jotter and pen. Then I became aware that half-a-dozen Rastas had gathered around the table and were staring down at me, saying nothing. Their united, silent, unsmiling concentration was absurdly unnerving. I reached out for the cigars, intending to offer them round by way of breaking what felt uncommonly like a spell. But one of the men quickly seized them and shared them among his friends before throwing the empty tin to the ground near my feet with an extraordinarily eloquent gesture of contempt. Then, still not having addressed a syllable to me, they all moved away. It seemed my first visit had been in effect a surprise attack and no one then present had known what to do about it. But now the heat was on.

My note-taking abilities felt rather blunted so I took out a book instead of my jotter. John Lambert's *Crime, Police and Race Relations* was not perhaps the most appropriate volume to study in the Villa Cross but I had been reading it on the bus from Small Heath. As time passed more and more hostile vibes were sent in my direction, like invisible arrows. However, a few people did talk to me. The prostitutes (two Black, one Brown) were intensely curious about my presence in the Villa Cross. And a sad, seedy young White man told me all about his girlfriend who had just been jailed for smuggling cannabis from Morocco – "It was so *little*! Just for herself and me . . ." I stayed for two hours, to give my cigar-smoking friends the (false) impression that they had *not* intimidated me.

Next day I cancelled a supper appointment with a new Sikh friend, explaining that the psyops duel (Murphy versus The Rest) required my presence in the Villa Cross that evening. I somehow felt that in fact it wasn't versus 'The Rest'. On reflection, it seemed that if I could get things sorted out many of the Villa Cross regulars would allow me (wittingly or unwittingly) to glimpse an important area of Black life not otherwise accessible.

On that Saturday evening the same group repeated their silent harassment, but not until I was half-way through my pint and busily scribbling notes. They then tore two pages out of my jotter, shredded them with a flick-knife and threw the pieces over me like confetti. On the following evening, as I stood at the bar waiting to be served, the back of my husky jacket was skilfully ripped down its whole length from the collar. In the crush I didn't notice what was happening. But the ripper (he who had shredded the pages) at last broke his silence to draw my attention to what he had done, while stroking his knife-blade. "Around here you need to take care, see? Or your gear gets damaged – right? You wanna write down details, you do it somewhere else – see?"

Moments later, as I was gingerly carrying my pint through the throng, one of his mates chanced to knock the glass out of my hand: the sort of accident that can happen in any overcrowded pub, especially if most of the customers are boisterous young Blacks. I was picking up the pieces when Malcolm appeared beside me; he was wearing a Rasta-colours track-suit, instead of his bandit outfit, and for an instant I failed to recognise him. He said nothing but handed me a replacement pint and pointed to my usual corner seat. Then he ordered one of the little White errand-boys to finish collecting the broken glass and rejoined his friends around the pool-table.

By that Sunday evening my antennae had begun to register that the Villa Cross was a place of many under-currents, factions, moods and viewpoints. The campaign to scare me off was becoming, I sensed, rather an embarrassment to its organisers. They had probably not expected me to return after the notebook incident and were now losing both their cool and the support of the local regulars – as distinct from the weekend regulars, many of whom came from outside Handsworth. I felt certain they would be relieved to call off their harassment campaign if they could do so without seeming to have been defeated by Whitey. Next morning I had an inspiration, took a bus to the city centre and was fortunate enough to find one paperback copy of my own book on Ethiopia.

Even among pseudo-Rastas, there is a powerful mystique about the word 'Ethiopia' – a mystique which long pre-dates the founding of Rastafarianism in 1930. In 1911, when Caseley Hayward's *Ethiopia Unbound – Studies in Race Emancipation* was published, Ethiopia and Ethiopians were synonymous with Africa and Africans in the minds of many Caribbean Blacks. The novel's hero was in fact a young Fanti, educated in England, who returned to the Gold Coast to lead an early Black Power movement.

Marcus Garvey was much influenced by Casely Hayford's belief that: 'Afro-Americans must bring themselves into touch with some of the general traditions and institutions of their ancestors, and, though sojourning in a strange land, endeavour to conserve the characteristics of the race.' Few now remember that Garvey verbally flayed Haile Selassie for deserting his country after the Italian invasion. Garvey's criticisms were almost identical to those of the Ethiopian Communists who eventually overthrew the Lion of Judah.

To this day many Rastas are ignorant of Ethiopia's geographical location, but this does not diminish the 'power of the word'. Therefore when my book was observed beside my pint on the bar table many guards were lowered and many questions asked. Soon the news was spreading that I, personally, had lived and travelled in Ethiopia during the Emperor's reign. Then it emerged that I had also been the guest and protégée of one of Haile Selassie's grand-daughters – after which my Villa Cross tribulations were over. The Rastafarians, after all, believe Haile Selassie to have been not a mere prophet like Mohammed but God Himself. And you can hardly name-drop more effectively than by recalling your friendship with God's grand-daughter and producing photographs to prove it.

After that I was accepted as a regular. Not as a friend (apart from four young men), but as a tolerable acquaintance who was certainly not a police informer and could even be to some extent trusted. I never asked questions about anything, yet people talked more and more openly as the weeks passed, telling me when Red Leb was scarce, Pakistani Black plentiful or a new consignment of Moroccan Kief expected. Prices too were discussed in my hearing, and worried suspicions about spiked resin – but never, of course, sources.

However, there remained a small group – not associated with the original harassing brigade – who continued to resent and distrust me and whose regular taunting made quite heavy demands on my stoicism. "You're too old to be a whore but maybe you like watching? You come with me, I'll let you watch something bigger'n you ever saw before!" And: "What you hanging about here for? Still hoping for a man? Can't you find a White one?" And: "How many years you waiting for a Black man? You wanna take me home? I wouldn't go with you for a million!" And so on into more explicit details from which my gentle readers must be sheltered. Ironically, I would never have guessed *how* accepted I was by most regulars were it not for that permanently hostile group; their insults caused the rest to rally round me protectively and apologetically.

Before moving to Handsworth I hadn't understood the extent to which young Blacks' (especially Rastas') street behaviour is regarded as a 'public nuisance'. Much is made of their noisy exuberance, flamboyant gestures and general assertive effervescence – all of which is seen as verging on 'threatening behaviour' by the staid British Public. This censorious aversion to Black uninhibitedness should not have surprised me, given the English terror of revealing personal emotion of any kind. (Crowd support for a soccer team and mass-adulation of the Royal Family come into another category.) Yet to condemn Blacks for not behaving in public like English people does seem to take insularity beyond the bounds of reason. And the longer I perched in Handsworth the clearer it became that this basic temperamental discrepancy is among the main sources of Black/White antagonism. I could sympathise with – and share – disapproval of all-night blues parties which keep a whole neighbourhood awake until dawn. Those are indeed a public nuisance, a residue of rural traditions – when the entire community participated – which it is reprehensible to reproduce in any city, African, Caribbean or European. But it irritated me increasingly to hear Whites criticising Blacks for conducting their diurnal social life in the way that comes naturally to them and does no harm to anyone else.

Granted, as a newcomer to Heathfield Road I had been unnerved by the Rastas' holding of the Villa Road 'front-line'; but behind that particular scene there is a long history of 'Rasta versus Babylon' animosity. Having spent many evenings in 'my' corner of the Villa Cross, watching the action, it seemed to me that the Rastas' swaggering or sullen defiance of society was more defensive than offensive. Seeing them on their own territory, one realised that their exuberance really was capable of making what anti-racists describe as 'an enriching contribution' to British life. If they looked as happy on the streets as so many did in the Villa Cross, even the local Whites might eventually have developed a more favourable image of young Blacks. And it needs to be emphasised that their happiness was not usually alcohol-inspired. On one bottle of Babycham a young man might suddenly leap up and dance round the floor through sheer *joie de vivre*. Many of those youths were happy and relaxed in the Villa Cross simply because they felt secure; they were on their own patch. And there was an engaging innocence about much of the habitual bravado and frolicking: it was for instance 'cool' to light joints not with matches or cigarette-lighters but with long gas-stove lighters which dramatically spurted flames in all directions. I found it hard to remember that when first I heard of that pub it was presented as a vile sink of iniquity, a bit of Chicago gangland transposed to Handsworth.

However, petty ganja-dealing is a precarious way to make a living, quite apart from the risk of police raids, and the less innocent side of the Villa Cross sub-culture became apparent when anger flared between rival dealers. If big money was around – wads of £20 and sometimes £50 notes – one could sense the tension within seconds of entering the bar. And the presence of such wealth was usually accompanied by momentary displays of the rich men's flick-knives – weapons I irrationally find more frightening than guns. (Perhaps the police do too.) On such evenings – with connoisseur buyers sniffing at various bags of 'the herb' before making their choice, and carefully scrutinising the minute scales as purchases were weighted – extra sentinels stood on duty around the forecourt. Every evening Panda cars passed repeatedly, coming up the Villa, Heathfield or Lozells Roads but never stopping – just cruising past very slowly. Whenever one appeared in the distance there was a hurried superficial concealment of grass and resin, though everyone knew they could only throw their ganja to the floor if the fuzz did raid. As the police knew this dealing went on daily and nightly, and the general public knew the fuzz knew, there was a strong element of make-believe about the whole scene and it sometimes felt as though we were all thoroughly enjoying the 'Let's Pretend' excitement.

Except on very quiet evenings, the dealers were always alert, watching the door to spot their regular customers' arrival and get to them before someone else murmured an undercut offer. Ugly confrontations – rather scary to an outsider – were not uncommon. Then Kevin would pad quietly out from behind the bar, looking like an amiable teddy-bear, approach the angry rivals with no air of urgency, gently tap them on the shoulders and – now looking like a reproachful teddy-bear – whisper something in their ears. And that would be it: end of aggro. One could feel the tension slackening as Kevin calmly moved on to collect empty bottles – or glasses from those of us who used them – before shuffling back behind the bar.

Repeatedly I witnessed this defusing process and though Kevin achieved it apparently casually – all part of the routine – such situations obviously imposed an enormous strain on him; if his magic ever failed he would be likely to get a knife between the ribs. One didn't talk to him during opening hours because he could never relax for an instant; he also kept the forecourt scene under close observation, frequently going out to check on the open-air drinkers (and dealers). Although he is a man of few words, I once persuaded him to talk about his extraordinary role. "Well," he said, "you just have to think of yourself as a social worker, rather than a pub manager. All those poor devils need help, of one sort or another. Don't we all, in our own ways?" Under pressure he conceded that his job was stressful. "Yes, course you know things could get out of hand – it's always on the cards. When they're in a rage there's just one thing to remember – *never turn your back* . . ."

Kevin was as remarkable for his compassion as for his courage, a model of how to establish good race relations: no theory, all practice. He declared that he had no interest in 'race relations' and was plainly puzzled that anyone should want to write a book on such a theme. "I'm only interested in people living peaceably, respecting each other. I don't care what colour or religion anyone is, we're all just human with our own human weaknesses and strengths." He seemed genuinely unaware of the extraordinary nature of his achievement in 'keeping the peace' among his regulars, while retaining their affection and respect. Even the most implacable anti-Whites spoke well of Kevin, no doubt because they sensed that his simple respect for them was sincere: not something he believed he should feel, but something he *did* feel without ever thinking about it. A police force composed of Kevin-types could transform the inner-city scene. But then Kevin is not a 'type'; I have never met anyone else quite like him.

By 1985 the Villa Cross – partly because of Kevin's influence – had become immeasurably more than 'a pub'. For many homeless and hopeless young Rastas it was their special place; in that tiny area they, as Blacks, were psychologically in control and Whitey could intrude only 'with permission'. This feeling was of course largely based on the Villa Cross's reputation as a pub where ganja-dealing freely took place in defiance of Babylon. Many of the young Blacks rarely or never smoked, because they couldn't afford the herb. But the triumph of their group getting away with doing its own Black thing was at least as important as the pleasure of smoking, or the meagre financial gains from dealing.

It was easy to understand why Handsworth's elderly Whites so resented this enclave of defiant Black drug-dealers, an 'idle rabble' who had reduced their once respectable and attractive district to 'the depths of degradation'. Returning home one damp grey evening, through the midsummer twilight, it struck me that the environs of the Villa Cross were like some sinister film-set, with groups of ganja-dealers lurking in corners, broken glass crunching underfoot and the stern-faced look-outs posted at their three strategic points. On the steps down to Heathfield Road business was being done and as I descended through swirling dreadlocks one dealer shook both his fists at me and shouted, "Shit off, you blood-clot!" This would have been alarming in my novice days, but by then I could recognise Rasta joviality. And the Rasta in question had recently bought from me (at trade rates) a copy of my book on Ethiopia, so his apparent abuse was, when decoded, an almost affectionate affirmation of acceptance. But it didn't seem so to the two little old ladies (White) standing close together at the bus-stop near the steps. They assumed I had been taking a short-cut from the Lozells Road and one of them beckoned me and whispered, "Never walk across that way! They're a cruel dangerous lot. Like dirty black slugs, crawling out every evening when it gets dark – you keep away from there!"

It was also easy to understand why Handsworth's quiet-living, conventional, law-abiding Blacks were – if possible – even more anti-Rasta than the Whites and Browns. Again and again they lamented that these "so-called Rastas" – such a small minority of the Black community! – have over the years "given us all a bad name". In multi-racial areas like Handsworth this is something of an exaggeration; there the Whites can and do distinguish between Rastas and 'respectable' Blacks. But in Britain as a whole it is unhappily true that people tend to see the truculent anti-Babylon minority as 'typical Blacks', a distortion for which the media are largely to blame. The tragedy is that that 'lawless' minority is increasing annually, as more and more British-born Blacks leave school and find themselves at once on the dump-heap with no prospects of ever getting off it.

The equation 'young Black male equals criminal' is now deeply engraved on many Brown and White minds. It depressed me to find that most of those who live in 'the other Britain' were deeply sceptical when I pointed out that the average jobless Black, like the average jobless White or Brown, is not criminally inclined. This scepticism was clearly based on two complicating factors: a) to possess, smoke or deal in ganja is technically criminal: b) their skin colour, daring methods and reputation for intimidation make Black criminals seem both extra-conspicuous and extra-threatening and so create a false impression of the *extent* of Black criminality. I shall deal first with (b) and return later to (a).

My journal is stuffed with first-hand accounts of 'bad experiences' inflicted on Handsworth Browns by Blacks. Other crimes were reported to me at second hand but these I did not record lest they might have been damaged in transit. The Browns are peculiarly vulnerable, a community caught between fear of Rasta violence and distrust of a racialist police force. The following incidents are but a few examples from my collection; there are some twenty others, all very similar.

Outside a new supermarket on the corner of Grove Lane and Church Lane, a Sikh friend was packing groceries (for three families) into the boot of his car when two Rastas nicked the keys from the dashboard and disappeared. He idiotically raced into the shop to ring the police and emerged to find his car (naturally) gone. Next day it was found, undamaged, in a city-centre car-park. Apart from the groceries, the thieves had been rewarded with an expensive camera and a brand-new home-computer, not yet unpacked. Their victim told me he felt quite certain he could identify one, an Afro-Indian-looking man in his thirties whom he believed he had often seen hanging about a Rasta restaurant on Lozells Road. He had been disillusioned by the police lack of interest in his information and also by the witnesses' refusal to help. There were several witnesses, Brown and White, who saw the car being driven off; but when appealed to they all claimed to have 'seen nothing' and melted away.

At the junction of the Villa and Soho Roads a Mirpuri friend parked outside a newsagent's shop for little more than a minute, to pick up his weekly Urdu newspaper, and as he left the shop saw his car being driven off by three young Blacks. At that moment a Panda chanced to turn into the Soho road and he yelled to the PCs to give chase, his own car (a battered mini) being then no more than 100 yards away and easy prey for a Panda. But the police paused, to write down his name, address and car registration number, before taking off in what by then was mock-pursuit. One can only conclude, as my friend did, that the fuzz were unkeen to arrest three Blacks on the Soho Road at 2.30 p.m.

One afternoon in April, a Gujarati friend (Hindu, ex-East Africa) was standing at her sitting-room window lovingly watching her eight-year-old son riding his new BMX bike on their tree-lined cul-de-sac road. Suddenly a very tall Rasta came striding around the corner, lifted the little fellow off his birthday present, picked it up and ran away. Subsequently Lally saw that Rasta on several occasions accompanied by a little boy (presumably his own son) riding what was unmistakably the stolen bike. Yet she never even considered reporting this daylight robbery to the police. "We don't want more trouble – bricks through windows, or worse. My husband says we should be more brave, if more people stood up to those Blacks they wouldn't be such gangsters. But he didn't push me. He really feels it's a waste of time going to Thornhill Road. The police never seem interested in what happens to Asians."

One night in mid-August a Sikh house was burgled on a quiet road – mainly 'Brown bourgeois' – near Handsworth Park. The middle-aged wife (Ranzi, a good friend of mine) had seen two short-haired Black youths loitering about during the previous afternoon, staring through an uncurtained window at one of those collections of Hi-Tech equipment to which prosperous Browns are much addicted – the latest in everything, from video camera to music-system. As Ranzi was drawing the curtains, one youth approached with an implausible tale about their football having been lost in her back-garden, which allegedly adjoined their own. When she declined to admit him, his friend shouted abusively from the road. Ranzi then rang the police to report "suspicious behaviour" and ask for "an extra eye" to be kept on the house. She was told, "We're not a private security firm – your house gets as much protection as anyone else's."

At 3.15 next morning Ranzi and Dev were awakened by noises downstairs.

Fearing an attack on her husband, Ranzi tried to dissuade him from confronting the burglars and when he reached the sitting-room they were gone – as was everything of value in the room, plus a wallet containing £280 in notes which had been carelessly left in a shopping-bag hanging on the back of the kitchen door. Also, the curtains and long sofa – recently re-covered in gold-brown velvet – had been vindictively slashed with a knife and the burglars had urinated all over the new bottle-green carpet. To me this vandalism was much the most disquieting part of the story. By that stage of my inner-city career I was fully able to understand – without condoning – the jobless Blacks' impulse to steal from their comparatively wealthy neighbours; but I almost wept to see the vindictive devastation in that room, of which Ranzi had been so proud. Dev bitterly criticised the police for 'not being more alert', which was perhaps a trifle unreasonable. Their telephonic rudeness to Ranzi had been unforgivable (though not unusual), but it is hard to see how they could 'keep an extra eye' on every house in Handsworth considered by its owner to be at risk.

It shocked me that Dev had reluctantly agreed not to report this burglary, because Ranzi so dreaded being required to identify the culprits should the police succeed in catching them. Her fear of Rastas – and indeed of all but the most patently respectable Blacks – was extreme. She firmly believed that the police shared that fear, for which she didn't in the least blame them. But – "It means we've no protection, the Blacks can get away with anything. It's a reign of terror." She and Dev had only recently moved to this house from another part of Handsworth where they also had a Rasta problem – a very nasty one. In 1983 their next-door-neighbour, a Hindu doctor and close friend, had identified two Rasta car-thieves in court. As a result they were sentenced and their 'brethren' launched a retaliation campaign against the doctor. Within three months he had been forced out of Handsworth and within six months out of Birmingham. Then late one winter evening Ranzi's nineteen-year-old son was waylaid by three Rastas seeking the Hindu family's new address. He, foolish boy, simply refused to give it – instead of inventing an address. His face was then beaten to pulp and an iron bar was dropped on his feet, breaking several bones. That experience so scared him that he refused to report it to the police; and it also left its mark on Ranzi.

There was nothing intrinsically notable about any of my neighbours' experiences; by modern urban standards these were run-of-the-mill crimes. Yet a distinctive pattern emerged clearly from all the *reactions* to those crimes: a deep fear of Black violence (attacks on person or property), combined with a conviction that the police were reluctant to tangle with Rastas, either because of racialist indifference to the fate of *Brown* citizens or because the police had themselves been intimidated by implicit threats of 'big trouble' – for example, had the Panda pursued my Mirpuri friend's car-thieves, and arrested them on the Soho Road, they might have started a riot. One shrewd Black friend, first met in the Villa Cross, suggested that police ill-treatment of innocent Blacks might be partly explained by 'professional frustration'. If those Panda car P Cs really were inhibited from hunting their legitimate quarry, by fear of provoking big trouble at 2.30 p.m. on Wednesday, they would be that much more likely to beat up some inoffensive Black found wandering alone along the Gibson Road at 2.30 a.m. on Saturday.

No doubt professional frustration does in many cases exacerbate police racialism. However that may be, fear of Black violence is all-pervasive – whether admitted, denied or side-stepped – and it influences the whole area of Black/White relations, from education to policing to job- and housing-discrimination. It also means that Handsworth's Black criminals (who in general, according to police statistics, are *not* violent) have such an intimidatory effect on the population that they can pursue their careers of burglary, car-theft and other non-violent crimes with the minimum of interference.

One day Kevin was off duty (a family complication) and, coincidentally, that evening became slightly dramatic at the Villa Cross. Four Rastas who had just done a job arrived to celebrate, leaving their loot – or so the fuzz seemed to think – in a mini-van parked below the steps. Soon two 'plain-clothes' cars zoomed up, unrecognised by the sentinels, and the van was seized as the Rastas tried (unsuccessfully) to escape through a side-door. But meanwhile the loot had been transferred to another vehicle and driven off by Persons Unknown. Much hilarity broke out when everyone realised that the fuzz had been wrong-footed; it was remarkable how getting the better of the police (loot safe, never mind the four arrested) charged the Villa Cross atmosphere. Not long after the departure of the police, free-for-all fighting suddenly erupted (I'm not sure why) and I acquired a bantam-egg-sized bump on my head. I don't know what hit me: with so many missiles flying around identification was difficult. Probably nobody meant to injure *me*, but you can't be selective on such occasions. However, I did become a target when one of my foul-mouthed Rasta enemies followed me to the 'Ladies' – a mildly hazardous place at the best of time, far down in the cellar. He tried to grab a diamond ring I habitually wear – for sentimental rather than ornamental reasons – but luckily he was under-sized and easily dealt with. By then, however, a ready-for-anything mood had taken over in the bar so I nervously scuttled home, much earlier than usual. And that evening I wrote in my journal:

I can understand Whites and Browns being afraid of Blacks, at gut-level, in a way they're not afraid of each other. Yet why do I say that? Why can I understand it? When you think of the violence of White soccer gangs and N F thugs, not to mention the mob-violence so common on the sub-continent . . . Is this a deep-rooted racial prejudice on my part? Or is it to do with the Black/White temperamental/ cultural gulf being so wide one never knows quite what to expect of alienated Blacks? From our point of view they *are* unpredictable. And when physical violence is in question, *uncertainty* about its motives and manifestations and limits (or lack of them) triggers a *special* sort of fear – of the unknown.

My Villa Cross contacts led to many illuminating conversations, in Handsworth Park or someone's squat, with young Blacks who had already 'done time' and were prepared to discuss their attitudes to Whitey's conventional morality. They were not hardened criminals, or ever likely to become such, yet they felt no guilt or shame about past crimes and had no intention of avoiding similar crimes in the future. Their 'alternative morality' forbade hurting people; they drew as clear a distinction between violent and non-violent crime as between ganja-dealing and hard-drugs-dealing. Many financiers and industrialists cheat their competitors or the general public on a massive scale, yet would never hit an old lady over the head and run away with her purse. And many young Blacks consider it permissible to steal goods which are almost certainly insured – thus their main victims are gigantic corporations, over whose misfortunes few could shed any but crocodile tears.

British justice, seen through youthful inner-city eyes, looks unimpressive. Perhaps it is better than most other systems, but your average 'deprived' youngster – Black, White or Brown – is not concerned with its comparative virtues but with its rapidly worsening defects of which he is the most frequent casualty. In all Black circles, from Pentecostalist to Rasta, it is noted that British courts seem obsessionally protective of *property*. The *Runnymede Trust Bulletin* (No. 198) reported that in November 1986 Paul Parker – 'a vulnerable youth with a low IQ and no previous convictions for violence' – was sentenced to *seven years* imprisonment when convicted of affray and burglary during the 1985 Tottenham riots. Nicholas Jacobs was found guilty of affray and sentenced to *eight years*; he had been photographed by the police while thowing a petrol bomb. A week or so later Sebastian Guinness was sentenced to *four months* for possessing heroin and Rosie Johnson to *nine months* for supplying heroin to a friend who subsequently died after a heroin-plus-alcohol party. The heroin dealer who had sold the drug to those young people was sentenced to *four* years. Such unwholesome disparities between the sentencing of Black and White, rich and poor are commonplace; the examples I have quoted just happened to come to my attention while writing this chapter. Hundreds of equally shocking comparisons could be made – and are made, regularly, by outraged Blacks. These disparities breed dangerous cynicism and disastrously undermine *repect* for the law, without which no amount of 'tighter legislation' can ensure a law-abiding society. They also do even more damage to race relations in Britain than physical attacks on Blacks and Browns by the NF and their sympathisers. They are seen as 'institutionalised racism' triumphant – Babylon Rules OK. Throughout 1985–86 the British government ran a major (though ill-thought-out) anti-hard-drugs campaign, while the courts continued to treat the sale and use of those drugs by rich Whites as comparatively minor offences. Burglary and arson are attacks on property; heroin-dealing is an attack on human life. So why give heroin-dealers much lighter sentences than burglars and arsonists?

Most young Blacks, and many of their seniors, see the refusal to legalise ganja as another form of institutionalised racism; because it is a harmless recreational drug, official White prejudice against it looks to a Black like more anti-Blackness. Each year in Britain the pharmaceutical industry spends some £180 million on the promotion of drugs, including numerous addictive and damaging 'uppers and downers'. For over a century British doctors prescribed cannabis as a medicine without creating a single addict. Each year in Britain an estimated 100,000 people die of nicotine-related diseases and some 8000 of alcohol-abuse. No one ever has (or ever *could*) die of a cannabis-related disease or of cannabis-abuse. Given these facts, it is scarcely surprising that Blacks see the outlawing of *their* form of escapism and/or relaxation as discriminatory.

Being myself loyally addicted to nicotine and alcohol, and incurious about other people's drugs, I have never smoked pot/hash/marihuana/hemp-bhang/charas/ganja – the Rastafarians' 'holy herb' has more than 350 nicknames. Therefore I cannot say what it does to or for anyone, but apparently individuals react to it differently – for some it does a lot, for others nothing. The Great British Public displays an extraordinary ignorance about cannabis, which is often confused with hard drugs. In recent years some police spokesmen have deliberately fostered this confusion and the tendentious association of Blacks with 'Drug Barons' has become a feature of post-riot police pronouncements – an association which is gleefully headlined in such racialist newspapers as the *Daily Mail* and the *Sun*.

Cannabis-myths abound; to counteract the worst of them I shall now list a few facts:

1 Cannabis does not normally lead on to hard-drugs use; 'pot-heads' and hard-drugs addicts are very dissimilar types.
2 As it is not addictive there are no 'withdrawal' symptoms and cannabis users, unlike heroin addicts, do not develop a tolerance which requires them to increase their intake to get the same effect.
3 It produces no delusions or hallucinations.
4 It cannot cause either hang-overs or 'black-outs', such as people sometimes experience after too much alcohol.
5 It inhibits the aggressive instinct and regular smokers tend to suffer from a lessening of initiative and ambition – generally considered its most harmful effect.
6 It does not stimulate sexual desire and may even have the reverse effect. In 1846 Theophile Gautier observed – 'Romeo as a hashisheen would have forgotten his Juliet'.'

In January 1969 the Wootton Report recommended:

The association in legislation of cannabis with heroin and the other opiates is inappropriate and new legislation to deal specially and separately with cannabis and its synthetic derivatives should be introduced as soon as possible . . . Possession of a small amount of cannabis should not normally be regarded as a serious crime to be punished by imprisonment . . . the offence of unlawful possession, sale or supply of cannabis should be punishable on summary conviction with a fine not exceeding £100 or imprisonment for a term not exceeding four months, or both such fine and imprisonment.

Baroness Wootton and her learned colleagues had worked hard but were ill-rewarded. Their report inspired headlines like – 'NOW THE DRUGS FLOOD IN' (*News of the World*), 'CLASH OVER SOFT LINE ON DRUG TAKING' (*Daily Mail*), 'THE DEADLY PATH TO ADDIC-TION' (*Daily Express*). The popular press was, and has remained, deter-mined *not* to be instructed about the differences between cannabis and hard drugs. Nor did the politicians show any more intelligence. Mr Quintin Hogg, then Tory Shadow Home Secretary, insisted on the need to 'pursue the addicts of hashish and marihuana with the utmost severity that the law allows'. And soon the *Sun* was rejoicing – 'Labour and Tory MPs cheered Mr Callaghan when he announced that the cannabis penalties would not be altered.' Time, however, has vindicated the Wootton Report. The anti-cannabis law is unenforceable, as many policemen now privately admit. But meanwhile efforts to enforce it have 'criminalised' thousands of otherwise law-abiding citizens and led to a serious deterioration in relations between the police and large sections of the general public. When Lady Diana Cooper's flat was raided in 1968 no one accused the drug squad of misbehaviour during the raid, yet it provoked a special debate in the House of Commons and the Deputy Commissioner of the Metropolitan Police called personally on Lady Diana to apologise. No debates or apologies are inspired by the equally arbitrary (and often less disciplined) raids inflicted on the innocent inner-city victims of over-enthusiastic drug-squads. They take no less umbrage than Lady Diana did – but who cares?

On one level ganja's illegality has become a joke. When the Wootton Report was published in 1969 pot smokers were seen as an integral part of the distasteful hippy world; by definition they were anti-Establishment. But today's Establishment has many pillars – propping up Whitehall offices, Inns of Court, Anglican Deaneries, City boardrooms, officers' messes and the two Houses of Parliament – who have learned through personal experience that cannabis is not a dangerous drug. However, on other levels its remaining illegal is far from funny. All unworkable laws have bad side-effects and this one has thoroughly poisoned relations between Blacks and the police, who nowadays tend 'not to notice' White cannabis users while viewing young Blacks, *en masse*, as potential criminals. The sort of policemen who enjoy 'having a go at a coon' can stop and search (and rough up) their wretched victim while glowing with virtue because they are 'doing their duty, trying to stamp out crime'. After a few such encounters, otherwise law-abiding youths – automatically 'criminalised' by their ganja-smoking – may decide to break other laws and have the game as well as the name.

Meanwhile, in places like Handsworth, decision-making police officers live uncomfortably on the horns of a Black/White dilemma. If they try to enforce the anti-ganja law they may provoke uncontrollable Black violence. If they permit it to be publicly broken they are accused of allowing certain areas to become 'no-go, dominated by Black criminals'. While ganja remains illegal, the White majority feel entitled to ask, 'Why should the Black minority not keep the laws of this land? Whose country is it anyway?' They forget that most people assume the right to break laws which *they* deem unreasonable, unjust or discriminatory. In certain Arab countries the 'absurd' anti-alcohol law is consistently broken by resident Europeans and Americans. The fact that that law reflects the ethos of the Muslim majority leaves the minority's conscience untroubled as hooch is brewed in garages and regular drinks parties are arranged. "So why", ask many Blacks, "should we not break Britain's 'absurd' anti-ganja law?" In reply I sometimes pointed out the crucial difference between 'ex-pats' drinking in the Middle East and Rastas ganja-dealing on the Villa Road; the former try to break the law furtively, the latter glory in breaking it openly. (Or at least they did, in Handsworth, during the summer of 1985.)

There are three main arguments against legalising cannabis. Firstly, some dealers, no longer able to earn an honest though illegal living, might turn to hard-drugs dealing. Secondly, ganja's illegality is one of its attractions for Babylon-haters; deprived of that, they might seek more dangerous authority-defying outlets. Thirdly, in the future it may be found that ganjas does, after all, damage the health. When I smoked my first cigarette in 1952 – offered me by my father on my twenty-first birthday – no one suspected nicotine of hastening the deaths of millions. However, scientists have so thoroughly investigated cannabis during the past few decades that any threat to health would almost certainly have been detected by now.

The other arguments are slightly more weighty. Most ganja-dealers would grieve to see their merchandise legalised. Theirs is a 'small business', of a size much admired by Mrs Thatcher in other contexts, yet the majority make enough to run a motor car and dress well. To maintain this life-style, a few would inevitably venture onto the hard-drugs scene. But to assume that *all* redundant ganja-dealers would automatically become hard-drugs merchants is like assuming that all corner-shop tobacconists would automatically become heroin-pushers were cigarettes outlawed.

I asked three Black social workers (not themselves smokers but with no anti-ganja bias) to predict the reaction of young Blacks whose smoking represents 'two fingers to the fuzz'. Each thought it likely that if (a gigantic IF) the legalising of ganja fundamentally changed police attitudes and behaviour, most young Blacks would feel so relieved that new authority-defying gestures would not be sought. One of those workers had lived in New York during the mid-1970s when pseudo-Rasta gang-warfare, between rival groups of ganja-dealers, was prevalent. He foresaw a danger of similar developments in Britain unless ganja is legalised – "What else would you expect, with more and more intelligent, enterprising, penniless young men looking around for ways to make a living?"

Significantly, three senior police officers argued against any change in the law – "It would look like giving in to the Rastas." One added, "Then they'd have their tails up, thinking they could run the country!"

That same officer emphasised that in Handsworth, as elsewhere throughout Britain, Rastas are declining in number and influence. I never knew quite what to make of this belief, largely because (like ninety-nine per cent of Whites) I never knew quite what to make of Rastafarianism. Dreadlocks and other outward marks of the cult are certainly becoming unfashionable; even in the Villa Cross half the regulars were short-haired. But this may be, literally, a question of fashion; few of the Rastas I met knew much about the origins, beliefs and rituals of the cult. During adolescence they had fancied themselves as African warrior types, rebelling against Babylon, their parents, their teachers and – very often – the church of their childhood. Then, having outgrown that stage, some found their locks more trouble than they were worth and had them off. As one recently shorn friend explained with a grin – "It's our version of Thatcherism and Reaganism, we're moving to the right when we cut our locks!" He was of course being facetious; he then stressed that the waning of the dreadlocks fashion does not mean a waning of Rastafarian influence on the emotions of young deprived Blacks.

The fate of the poor in Kingston's slums fifty years ago and in inner-city Britain today cannot be compared. But British-born Blacks know little or nothing about the former and their awareness of deprivation, at the bottom of the British pile, is no less acute than their grandfathers' was at the bottom of the Jamaican pile. Hence their continuing openness to the revolutionary message within Rastafarianism, however confused their understanding of its religious (or quasi-religious) doctrines.

12 · Liming Rastas and the Law

The seed of Rastafarianism was perhaps sown by George Liele, an American slave preacher who in 1784 founded Jamaica's first Baptist church – and called it the Ethiopian Baptist Church. Soon it merged with African religious beliefs and flourished outside the 'orthodox' territory controlled by Christian missionaries. Most of those adapted Christianity to reinforce slavery or, after Emancipation, to encourage Blacks to remain 'meek and mild' and resigned to their lot. But the Ethiopian Baptist Church and its off-shoots encouraged them to be politically assertive and created an atmosphere in which, eventually, Marcus Garvey's Back-to-Africa Movement aroused wild enthusiasm. Next to Haile Selassie (their God), Garvey is the Rastas' most revered hero.

On 17 August 1887 Marcus Garvey was born at St Ann's Bay, Jamaica. He was the eleventh child of Moses, a bookish stonemason (of Maroon stock: no slave hang-ups there) and his devout wife Sarah. The Garveys could not afford Kingston school fees, so Marcus's mother engaged the local headmaster to tutor him privately until he was apprenticed to his godfather, a printer, at the age of fifteen. Three years later he moved to Kingston, got a job at a print-works and immediately became involved in political campaigning on behalf of the least articulate section of Jamaican society. During his early twenties he travelled widely in Central and South America, studying the appalling abuses inflicted everywhere on West Indian workers – who even at that date had been forced to emigrate by the thousand. In 1912 his only surviving sister, Indiana, helped to pay his passage to England where she was employed as a nanny. He worked in the Liverpool, Cardiff and London docklands, again gathering information about the deprivations and injustices endured by his fellow-Blacks, and studied for an unknown period at Birkbeck College – then an independent institution 'for the improvement of working-class minds' which admitted students without formal academic qualifications. Later in life he decorated his signature with 'DCL', though there is no evidence that he ever gained (or sought) a Doctorate in Civil Law. By far the most important outcome of that first visit to England was his contact with Duse Mohammed Ali, a Sudanese-Egyptian who was then the dominant 'Pan-African' thinker and had been living in London for many years.

On his return to Kingston in 1914, Garvey founded the Universal Negro Improvement Association and African Communities League, of which he became the 'President and Travelling Commissioner'. His campaign to provide education for poor Blacks was supported by the Roman Catholic bishop and Presbyterian leaders; the government was less enthusiastic about this apostle of African nationalism and Black consciousness. According to the Afro-American writer, Kelly Miller:

> The chief achievement of Marcus Garvey consists in his quickening the sense of race consciousness and self-dignity on the part of the common people among Black folk all over the world. The intelligentsia among Negroes have never been able to penetrate below a certain level of social grade. But Garvey arouses the zeal of millions of the lowliest to the frenzy of a crusade . . .

Although an unstable and rather shady character, Garvey was a genuine visionary whose influence spread from the Caribbean to the USA and West Africa. He took his crusade to America in 1916 and it is part of Rasta mythology that before leaving Jamaica he proclaimed: "Look to Africa for the crowning of a Black King, he shall be the Redeemer."

In America, as John Henrik Clarke has noted, 'His manner of dealing with those who had disagreed with him seemed to have been designed to create adversaries, of which there were many . . . Opposition to his teaching came from many quarters, including the Caribbean community in the US . . . but opposition by the black working class was practically non-existent.' America's Black and mulatto middle class resented the Garvey doctrine that 'The White race can best help the negro by telling him the truth, and not by flattering him into believing that he is as good as any white man.' Garvey condemned miscegenation – 'We of the UNIA believe in a pure Black race, just as now all self-respecting whites believe in a pure white race as far as that can be . . . The negro has at least a social, cultural and political destiny of his own and any attempt to make a white man of him is bound to fail in the end . . . The negro should not remain in the countries of the whites, to aspire for and to positions which they will never get under the rule of the majority group upon their merely asking for or demanding such positions by an accidental Constitutional right . . .' In 1924 Dr W.E.B. Du Bois, mulatto leader of the National Association for the Advancement of Coloured People, described Garvey as 'the most dangerous enemy of the negro race in America or the world . . . either a lunatic or a traitor'.

By 1927 Kelly Miller was describing the 'Garvey Movement' as 'a spent force' (in the *Contemporary Review*), yet three years later it became one of the main fertilising agents of Rastafarianism. The poor of Jamaica were not interested in Garvey's spectacular failures as a Black businessman in the USA. But many of them were very interested in his self-help gospel – 'the negro must build on his own basis apart from the white man's foundation, if he ever hopes to be a master-builder.'

In 1930, the year of Haile Selassie's coronation, the Jamaican poor were demoralised, hopeless and deeply resentful of the White colonial Fat Cats who ran their island – then suffering severly not only from the Great Depression but from the after-effects of a major hurricane. At that point Rastafarianism took off in Kingston, almost by spontaneous combustion, as a hope-giving cult that presented the Black man not as an inferior 'cheap edition' of the White man but as something separate and special. Following the Black Emperor's coronation, Revelations 5:2–5 and 19:16, Daniel 7:9 and Psalm 68:4 proved to the satisfaction of many that Haile Selassie was indeed God (the 'Redeemer' prophesied fourteen years previously by Garvey).

The actual founders of Rastafarianism were four obscure Jamaicans of whom little is known: Leonard Howell, Joseph Hibbert, Archibald Dunkley and Robert Hinds. Howell became leader of the cult and ingeniously fundraised by selling some 5000 photographs of the Black Emperor for one shilling each – as 'passports to Ethiopia'. Within a few years he was preaching six principles which greatly alarmed the authorities: 1) Hatred of Whites; 2) the undeniable superiority of the Black race, in every respect; 3) The duty to take revenge on Whites for their wickedness; 4) The duty to frustrate, persecute and humiliate the government and courts of Jamaica; 5) The need to prepare for a return to Africa; 6) The recognition of the Emperor Haile Selassie as the Supreme Being and only legitimate ruler of Black people.

On 5 January 1934 Howell was arrested and sentenced to two years' imprisonment for sedition. Soon after, his three lieutenants were also gaoled and the movement went underground – where it flourished. On Howell's release he led a large group of Rastas into the hills above Kingston and by 1940 the Pinnacle commune was well established. (Estimates of its membership vary from 500 to 1600.) Howell appointed himself Chief and acquired, simultaneously, thirteen wives. Pinnacle was accessible only on foot and the authorities were unaware of its existence; the Rastas maintained themselves by growing cash crops – including ganja, which they regularly smoked as part of their religious ritual. Then they became more ambitious and antagonised their rural neighbours by demanding that taxes should be paid to them, as representatives of Haile Selassie, rather than to the colonial government. When the police were informed of the commune's existence, in July 1941, they raided Pinnacle and arrested seventy Rastas, twenty-eight of whom were sentenced for 'acts of violence and growing a dangerous drug'. On that occasion Howell evaded arrest; his escape was widely seen as a miracle and gained the cult many new recruits.

In the early 1950s the Pinnacle commune regrouped, this time stationing fierce guard-dogs all around the periphery of its land; and now dreadlocks were first grown, symbolising African warrior status. In 1954 the dogs failed to prevent another raid, during which 163 Rastas, including Howell, were arrested. However, the authorities had realised that for every Rasta gaoled, many more deprived Jamaicans joined the movement; so all the accused were termed 'nuisances' and acquitted. As the police had annihilated Pinnacle the Rastas were released into Kingston's slums where they survived by 'skuffling' – doing odd jobs, living hand-to-mouth. Howell was by then an old man and when he completely lost his marbles, and began to claim that *he* was God, all his followers abandoned him. He is believed to have died in Kingston Mental Hospital soon after being committed in 1960.

According to a team of three professors from the University of the West Indies, who reported to the government on Rastafarianism in 1960:

> Pinnacle seems to have been rather more like an old maroon settlement than a part of Jamaica. Its internal administration was Howell's business, not Government's. It is therefore understandable that the unit could have persisted as a state within a state for several years without the people or government of Jamaica being aware of it.*

The destruction of Pinnacle – the Rastas' 'Africa substitute' – strengthened their militant wing and caused the 'Babylon' label to be fixed on the hated Establishment, of which the most hated pillar was the police force that had obliterated Pinnacle. Between 1954 and 1959 Howell's disciples launched several evangelising missions which combined religious and political revolutionary fervour. Leonard E. Barrett, himself a Jamaican, has vividly described this phase:

> Rastafarians with their dreadlocks roamed the streets like madmen calling down fire and brimstone on Babylon, using the most profane language to shock the conservative establishment. Their wild behaviour attracted large audiences and their Rastafarian rhetoric of defiance made their presence felt in Kingston. Although many were shocked by their behaviour and appearance, hundreds of the dispossessed began to receive their message and soon several small camps had sprouted in Shanty Town.†

On I March 1958 the Rastas began their first month-long *Grounation* or *Nyabingi* – a Universal Convention. Every night, in the Kingston slums, hundreds gathered around bonfires of old tyres to drum, dance, smoke the holy herb and loudly abuse the police. Among the items on the Convention agenda was 'the decapitation of a police officer as a peace offering'. When the police refused to be drawn into a confrontation, some 300 militants decided to capture the city of Kingston in the name of Haile Selassie. That was the first of a two-year series of battles with the police, during which scores of Rastas were arrested, charged with 'possession and use of ganja' and forcibly shaved. Leonard Barrett commented:

---

* M.G. Smith, Roy Augier, Rex M. Nettleford, *Social and Economic Studies* (1960)
† Leonard E. Barrett, *The Rastafarians*, Heinemann (1977)

> The sustained activity of the police against the cultists, after Pinnacle, was to create a boldness in the cultists which finally led to serious reactions. Instead of a flight to the mountains, they now decided to stand up and fight.

And he quotes the *Daily Gleaner*: 'If the problem of the Rastas is not faced now, it is liable to get so big that no one can deal with it . . .'

During the following year – 1959 – I and millions of others first heard of the Rastas when Jamaica's 'problem' briefly hit the global headlines. A crazy Jamaican clergyman (*not* a Rasta), named the Reverend Claudius Henry, returned to Kingston from his New York base and in February 1959 founded the African Reformed Church which immediately attracted many Rastas, thus splitting the movement. He presented himself as the 'Moses of the Blacks' and sold thousands of cards (price one shilling), guaranteeing to lead all card-holders back to the Promised Land – not at some unspecified time in the distant future, but on 5 October 1959.

On that date thousands of credulous card-holders from all over the island gathered at the headquarters of the African Reformed Church, laden with luggage and ready to leave instantly for the Promised Land. Most had sold their homes, livestock and fields – if they had any. They were shattered to discover that no arrangements had been made for transport to Africa. Next day the Rev. Henry explained to a *Daily Gleaner* reporter that of course he never meant 5 October to be *literally* the day of departure; it was merely the date on which he expected the government to reveal its detailed plans for repatriating Jamaica's African peoples.

A few days later Henry was arrested, fined £100 and bound to keep the peace for one year. But he didn't. Soon bizarre rumours were circulating; Henry and his Rasta allies were alleged to be planning a military take-over of Jamaica. When the police raided the headquarters of the African Reformed Church they found some 4000 detonators, a shotgun, a 32-calibre revolver, hundreds of machetes sharpened on both sides and sheathed, ample supplies of dynamite and several conch shells filled with ganja. The Rev. Henry was indicted for treason and gaoled for six years – whereupon his son Ronald took to the hills, as leader of a band of Rasta guerrillas armed with high-powered rifles imported from New York. A combined force of police and Royal Hampshire Regiment troops pursued the rebels, two British soldiers were killed and Ronald and his Rastas escaped. A National Emergency was declared and a manhunt proclaimed; several days later soldiers captured the guerrillas as they slept. When Ronald and four Rastas had been tried and sentenced to death, the leading Rasta brethren requested Dr Arthur Lewis, head of the University of the West Indies, to appoint a team of scholars to study Rastafrianism and advise the Premier of Jamaica on how to negotiate with the movement.

As so often happens – to the intense discomfiture of 'passive resistance' freaks like myself – this violent episode in Rasta history helped their cause by forcing the authorities to stop and think about the social conditions that had bred Rastafarianism. Jamaica's University of the West Indies was the island's most respected institution and the professors' report could not be ignored. Inevitably, hard-line conservatives resisted the notion of 'giving in' to those lawless fanatics from the slums. But many people, who hitherto had expressed only scorn for (and latterly fear of) the Rastas, did accept – if reluctantly – the professors' arguments that Rastafarianism must be taken seriously as a social reform movement. Within a decade most of the recommendations had been carried out by Norman Manley and the Rasta ideology was being seen as a legitimate strand in Jamaican life. The most important recommendations were:

> The Government of Jamaica should send a mission to Africa to arrange for immigration of Jamaicans. Representatives of Ras Tafari brethren should be included.
> The general public should recognise that the great majority of Ras Tafari brethren are peaceful citizens, willing to do an honest day's work.
> The police should complete their security enquiries rapidly, and cease to persecute peaceful Ras Tafari brethren.
> The building of low-rent houses should be accelerated, and provision made for self-help co-operative building.
> Ras Tafari brethren should be assisted to establish co-operative workshops.
> Press and radio facilities should be accorded to leading members of the movement.

As a result of the 'immigration mission' to Africa, Rasta leaders realised that 'repatriation' was not after all a very good idea and it was quietly demoted from an immediate demand to a shining ideal which might possibly become a reality in the distant future. I met a few Handsworth Rastas who several years ago bought one-way tickets to Ethiopia; after less than two months in the Promised Land they bought one-way tickets back to Birmingham. Marcus Garvey's Pan-Africa vision undoubtedly helped to restore the self-respect of many ex-slave communities, but its nurturing of escapist fantasies was destructive. To an extent it resembled the Gaelic/Celtic Revival in Ireland, which had certain short-term benefits and many long-term ill-effects.

To read John R. Lambert's *Crime, Police and Race Relations** in 1985 was a destabilising experience; it made me want to lie down and kick and scream. Mr Lambert collected his material in 1966–67 and gave advice which, if heeded, would have made Handsworth, twenty years on, a much more tranquil place. He foresaw exactly how things would be if the police didn't get their act together. Why does nobody listen when dispassionate observers make intelligent predictions?

This jargon-free book is still well worth reading, not least for its scrupulously fair presentation of the police's difficulties when suddenly they were

---

* John R. Lambert, *Crime, Police and Race Relations: A Study in Birmingham*, OUP (1970)

required to deal with thousands of immigrants whose cultures – and, often, languages – were totally unfamiliar to them. A policeman dealing with English (or Irish) people instinctively knows the score: how to approach a certain type of person in a given situation, what reactions to expect – and what reactions are expected of him. He is (or was in the 1960s) confident of being seen by most Whites as dependable, incorruptible and generally respect-worthy; someone on their side, if they were innocent, and someone from whom they could expect justice if they were guilty. However, Browns and Blacks arrived in Britain expecting policemen, in their dealings with the underprivileged, to be bullying, unjust, corrupt – their 'natural enemy'. Hence an English policeman doing his duty in an acceptable way might provoke hostility, fear, panic-reactions and abuse. Since British policemen are no less racialist than their compatriots, they rarely made allowances for the immigrants' background culture, language problems and other disadvantages. Instead they interpreted anti-police attitudes as personal insults, as symptoms of guilty consciences and as justification for treating 'niggers and Pakis' more roughly than they would treat any but the most recalcitrant Whites. Thus the original immigrants' assumptions became self-fulfilling prophecies.

In the 1960s Birmingham's Irish community was responsible (proportionately) for more crime than any other group. Although the coloured immigrants lived in areas of overall high crime-rates their involvement in crime was 'extremely low'. John Lambert noted that the Blacks, in particular, 'seek success within the general framework of values and rise above the delinquent and criminal standards prevalent in the areas in which they live.' But he realised that, if their reasonable ambitions were thwarted, 'the crime and disorder which surrounds them will contaminate their life-style and lead, in years to come, to a crime rate which matches that in their neighbourhoods'.

In a Foreword to Mr Lambert's book, Terence Morris (then of the LSE), stressed the point that the 'crucial role of the police in race relations will most certainly alter as the cycle of assimilation moves on toward the second generation'.

> Among American studies it has been shown that it is the children of the foreign born, rather than the foreign born themselves, who are more heavily involved in law infringements. The lack of respect between police and coloured migrants will, if anything, increase if the second generation suffers both from the consequence of second-class citizenship and the self-perception of it . . . If, by default, we allow race relations to deteriorate, we shall reap a bitter harvest indeed and . . . the reapers in the field will not be the politicians and local councillors, or the authors of racialist broadsheets, but the agents of order out there on the streets. It will not be of their sowing, but it will be the police who will bear the brunt of what may come.

Almost a generation later, it would sound naïve to suggest that deteriorating race relations are not, in part, 'of the police's sowing'. Yet most Whites remain unwilling to admit that 'the boys in blue' – so beloved of the popular press – are often guilty of viciously racialist behaviour. 'Good' policemen are a cherished part of the English image of England, as of the Irish image of Ireland. I remember once witnessing the Paris police pursuing students on the Left Bank for some reason now forgotten. My eight-year-old daughter was with me and as we sheltered in a café, looking out at the bloody fracas, she exclaimed. "These *can't* be police! *Police* don't behave like that!"

Britain's pro-police bias predisposes the public to excuse the inexcusable and to accept uncritically the most specious police explanations or denials. In cases of *racialist* misbehaviour, this bias is of course reinforced by the public's own racialism, which in turn encourages police racialism. Nowadays, a couple of P Cs beating up a Black in the privacy of a police station must feel that if their unlawful act were made public the majority would disapprove only mildly, if at all. Peregrine Worsthorne has written of 'the need for stengthening the State on other – law and order – fronts. Better the reaction-ary callousness that angers than the progressive compassion which demeans; better heads cracked by a policeman's truncheon that soul's swamped by society's pity.' (*Sunday Telegraph*, 12 July 1981).

In the second volume of his autobiography,* the Indian architect Prafulla Mohanti recalled arriving in England in 1960 when to him television was a novelty. 'I liked Dixon of Dock Green, which gave me a friendly image of the British policeman. He looked like the policemen I had met in the streets of London who went out of their way to help. In India we were always frightened of the police, who enforced law and order by violent means.' A quarter of a century later, Mr Mohanti finds that London policemen often go out of their way to insult Browns. After one such incident, when he was accompanying a New Delhi politician on an Oxford Street shopping-spree, the politician asked, "If the police treat educated Indians in that way in the West End, how do they behave towards uneducated Indians in other parts of London?" And Mr Mohanti wondered, 'What has happened to the friendly Dixon of Dock Green? There is a saying in my village: "If the protector becomes the oppressor, even God cannot help." '

The British police and Irish Gardai remain, despite an ominous lowering of standards, among the world's least brutal and corrupt police forces. But if this blessing is taken for granted standards will continue to decline, while the public looks the other way. Most forms of police misbehaviour, but particu-larly racialist misbehaviour, could quickly come to be regarded as benign social tumours, like drunken driving and prostitution – regrettable human weaknesses, yet forgivable 'when you think of all policemen have to put up with . . .' The malignancy of these tumours is hidden from the majority, who seem unaware of the contempt now felt for traditional 'law and order' by a large section of the *White* working class. During the grim Beirut T W A hijacking drama, sympathy for the hijackers was very strong among White

---

* Prafulla Mohanti, *Through Brown Eyes*, O U P (1985).

inner-city Brummies. Yet media comments suggested that the British, being a decent, law-abiding crowd, were united in deploring that barbarous deed. Scorn for Establishment hypocrisy was frequently expressed – for example, the lack of comment in the British media about the illegal use, by Israel in the Lebanon, of US weapons. Those Whites listened cynically to politicians deploring the crimes of hijackers and wondered why the crimes of governments go uncriticised. And they put the uncriticised crimes of police forces into the same category of institutionalised immorality.

Pace Mr Worsthorne, law and order cannot be upheld in a democracy by cracking heads with truncheons. Or by police witnesses who commit perjury to secure the conviction of innocent inner-city Whites, Blacks and Browns – easy prey, from the bottom of the pile.

A Black Pentecostalist friend – a young woman born and brought up elswhere who had recently moved to Handsworth – told me of her brother Daniel's experience as a police victim. When aged nineteen, he travelled to a Birmingham soccer match with his Youth Club, led by a White teacher from his old school who worshipped in the same Baptist church. Walking down Digbeth, Daniel fell behind to buy an ice-cream and was set upon by five White youths. The police quickly arrived, pulled the Whites off Daniel and charged *him* with causing a breach of the peace – on such occasions this is a common police reaction. In court two police witnesses contradicted each other's evidence. When Daniels's lawyer asked how the police knew who had started the fight, one P C replied, "He was the only Black there." Several solid citizens, including Black and White clergymen, testified to Daniel's good character. Yet he was fined £400 and when his appeal had been quashed he had to pay an extra £200 in costs – presumably to teach Blacks *not* to appeal.

Another young friend – Beverley, aged twenty-three and on the dole – was picked up at 10.15 one evening as he walked home from a Pentecostalist Youth Club which he helped to run. The police said he answered to the description of a young Black who had just mugged a middle-aged woman on a nearby street. Beverley (an exceptionally mild-mannered fellow) protested that it was simply ridiculous to accuse him of attacking anyone or stealing anything. When he insisted that he saw no reason why he should 'go for questioning' he was man-handled into a Panda and at Thornhill Road police station beaten up by three P Cs as punishment for 'resisting arrest' – though his resistance had been entirely verbal. Then two more P Cs arrived, accompanied by the mugger's victim who looked at Beverley and at once said, "No, that's not the man." Had she been the sort of White who can't tell one Black from another (or who regards *all* Blacks as prison-deserving muggers), Beverley might now be in Winson Green. He considered himself lucky to have escaped with no more than a dislocated shoulder and severe ear-ache.

Both these examples of police misconduct are so 'typical' that similar incidents fill pages of my journal. Beverley-type cases – verbal abuse and minor assaults, without any possibility of redress – seem to do even more damage than Daniel-type cases of headline-catching injustice. The niggling day-to-day (or night-to-night) tormenting of Blacks is what builds up the pressure in the volcano. Spectacular cases provide useful ammunition for professional agitators but, curiously enough, rouse not much general anger unless reinforced by personal experiences of harassment. Those experiences generate the enraged feeling that just because you're *Black* you're perceived as *bad* and so *your* word will never be accepted against the word of a policemen.

When so much animosity exists, certain individuals are prone to invent anti-police stories – either to inflate their own importance or because they feel an outsider might not believe how serious the situation is without first-hand evidence. Such story-tellers are easily detected, yet in Handsworth I rarely had reason to suspect that an incident was being exaggerated or invented. (I wasted no time discussing police behaviour with the militant Blacks, whose evidence would certainly have been unreliable.) Most of the younger genera-tion seemed a resentful yet resigned-to-their-Black-fate group, who saw police harassment as an inescapable fact of life. However, having noted that impression in my journal on 11 August 1985, I added, 'But resigned for how long? There's not much doubt they represent a dormant volcano that could erupt any day – and there's an awful lot of hate bubbling away inside that crater.'

The two most personally upsetting cases in my 'collection' involved young men (neither connected with the Villa Cross scene) whom I had come to know well. Both had been taken in for questioning, on separate occasions, and immediately after their releases they showed me their injuries – or those of them that could decently be shown to an elderly female. When I urged them to secure medical backing while the physical evidence was still fresh, and complain to the police authority, their reactions were identical – "You must be joking!" Their blow-by-blow accounts of what had happened, and why, cannot be published. Both made me promise not to reveal any detail that might enable the police to identify them; whether justified or not, their extreme fear of police retaliation was very real. Had they received their injuries in a brawl and been leading Whitey up the anti-fuzz garden path they need not have sworn me to silence; unless their accounts were accurate, the police could not have identified them.

Even during the summer of 1985 the sun appeared occasionally – whereupon we all ran out to look at this strange sight as though it were a total eclipse. But then it struck me, rather forcibly, that life in a foetid slum is much more agreeable without any summer heat to draw forth fumes from unofficial public lavatories and uncollected garbage.

On one of those rare sunny days – a midsummer Saturday – I decided to cheer myself up by observing Western democracy and the British police at their best. It is always refreshing to watch the police co-operating with nutty fringe groups who have notified their wish to disrupt the traffic for miles around by marching, demonstrating and making near-seditious speeches. This Saturday's nutty group was the Revolutionary Communist Party of Britain (Marxist-Leninist). All over Handsworth posters advertised that their march would start at noon from outside the DHSS offices on the Soho Road.

People find it quite hard to believe that the Soho Road – Handsworth's 'High Street' – is in Europe. It was my favourite Birmingham shopping street and at its liveliest and most colourful on Saturdays. On first walking down it I was overcome by nostalgia for the sub-continent. Countless details combine to create the authentic aura of an Indian/ Pakistani bazaar – window-wide displays of multi-coloured sweetmeats, carefully built into pyramids; lengths of richly shimmering materials and elegant saris and *shalwar-kameez* (worn by dummies with the palest of pale brown skins); toy-shops crammed with cheap plastic junk; jewellers' windows glittering with gold bracelets and anklets; tantalising curry aromas; greengrocers stocking what looked and smelt like every known fruit, vegetable and herb. I even saw bulls' hearts, for the first time since leaving Coorg – and sentimentally bought one, though this odd fruit is an acquired taste which I have never really acquired. My euphoria was such that on entering a Sikh-run pub I blurted out to an elderly White man at the bar, "This is a fabulous street! It's like being in India!" The man looked at me sourly and said, "Bloody right it is – who'd think this was Chamberlain's city?" I wondered then if perhaps there is something wrong with my territorial instinct; it would delight me to have a Soho Road equivalent in an Irish city.

It seems the Revolutionary Communist Party of Britain (Marxist-Leninist) does not have what it takes to arouse Handsworth's social reformers. At 11.50 only one adherent was in sight, a raggedly-dressed White man in his thirties holding a large red banner inscribed – ALL UNITE AGAINST THE STATE! I sat on a bench and ate cut-price squelchy black bananas while listening to a riveting exchange between him and two very deprived-looking White girls aged about ten. He claimed to have recently spent five years in jail for "telling the truth about Stalin" and he now told it again: "Stalin was a hero who defended the poor from the rich – the Red Army was *good* in 1944 but now it's *bad*, it's run by capitalists." As he spoke a police-van parked nearby; he waved his banner wildly and urged the girls – "Go spit on those fascist pigs! Go tell them keep their blood-stained hands off the youth of this country!" Not long before, the West Midlands Police had done a PR job in the local schools, apparently to good effect. Both girls looked up at the banner-bearer with pitying tolerance and one said, quietly but firmly, "The police are friends of everyone – if you're in trouble they *help*." Her friend added, "We need police to *protect* us, and they're strong and brave and always there when you look for them."

The Rev. Com. sneered – "Who gave you that crap? Yeah sure they'll help if you're a small kid and White – just try being a big kid and Black!"

At this point, frustratingly, the other Rev. Com.'s arrived – all ten of them. There were six White men, two Black men, one White girl and one beautiful and (I discovered) very articulate Sikh woman dressed in slacks and T-shirt and wearing her hair in a single waist-length braid. The men carried huge scarlet and gold banners blaming Nazis for the Brussels football stadium disaster. A turgid four-page newspaper was handed out *en route*, to anyone who would accept it, by the Sikh. It had a lot to say about democracy:

> Democracy in Britain has 'evolved' historically but concrete analysis of this shows that the rising bourgeoisie came to power with the slogans of democracy on its lips, on the basis of which it mobilised the broad masses of the people against the feudalists and against the absolute monarchy, and in this it played an historically progressive role, but that one of its first acts was to consolidate political power in its own hands and to put down the popular masses, with whom it more and more came into contradiction as the progress of capitalist industry brought forth the modern proletariat at the head of all the exploited and oppressed.

Having digested that edition of the *Workers' Weekly*, as best I could, it did not surprise me that the RCPB (M-L) fails to bring Handsworth's revolutionaries to the boil.

At 12.45 we took off, escorted by two PCs and two WPCs – one pair on foot, the other in the police van. Our leader was a Black with a megaphone who chanted non-stop – "Blame Nazis, *not* fans, for the Brussels disaster! The State should *not* support Nazis! The State does *not* protect the youths!" We walked for an hour and a half, down the Soho Road, up Grove Lane, then back to our starting point via Rookery Road. No one joined us and we attracted only the mildest interest/curiosity/amusement – with very occasionally a gesture of scorn. The strongest reaction came from the Sikh greybeards who habitually congregate at one end of the Soho Road, to sit talking for hours on concrete seats amidst asphyxiating traffic fumes – a sad substitute for tranquil sessions under the village neem tree. They registered almost comic shock/horror when a Sikh *woman* Rev. Com. paused to lecture them and offer copies of the *Workers Weekly*. One patriarch seized a copy, tore it to shreds and dropped it in the nearest litter-bin.

My enjoyment of this dotty perambulation was marred when, on our return march, we came to the junction of Grove Lane and Soho Road. The policeman in charge of our undemonstration was a tall, slim, handsome young man, blue-eyed, fair-haired, smooth-tongued and evidently fresh from a Community Relations course. He exuded *bonhomie* towards children of all races and was lavish with matey handshakes or slaps on the back (as appropriate) for Brown and Black men of the older generation. But then, at the junction traffic-lights, he forgot his party manners. As the lights changed a rusty little car, driven by a grey-haired Black man, stopped with its nose not more than one yard beyond the legal point. I was close enough to see the driver's amiable expression, characteristic of a certain sort of Black – an engaging half-smile directed at the world in general and often a sign of

Pentecostalist allegiance. I was about to pass in front of the car when PC Bonhomie, noticing its minuscule infringement, turned aside from the marchers to thump his clenched fist on the bonnet while vilely abusing the driver. Here the cliché 'his mask slipped' is unavoidable; that policeman's face was transformed, twisted with hatred and contempt. I looked then at the driver. He was still smiling: but when he glanced up at me there was an infinity of sadness and hurt in his eyes.

The whole incident can have lasted no more than a minute. Yet the emotions compressed into that brief time taught me more about police/Black relations than all the reports, books and theses through which I have diligently plodded during recent years. Seeing my friends' police-inflicted injuries had been shattering enough. But still that was at one remove; I was observing only the consequences of racialism. The tiny traffic-lights encounter – in one sense so trivial, involving no *physical* brutality – gave me my first close-up view of police racialism in action.

There is of course a counter-balancing vignette: there always is. Not long after that incident – by which time pre-riot tension was building up along the front-line – I wrote in my journal:

> Approaching the Villa Cross this evening, from Barker Street, I saw two *very* young PCs (male and female) doing their brave foot patrol up the Villa Road, past the pub and down Lozells Road. The usual Rastas (thirty or so) were sitting on the long low forecourt wall, several sharing joints. As the fuzz passed they blew ganja-smoke towards them, hissed and two-fingered and ordered huge slavering Dobermanns (the Rasta answer to police Alsatians) to rear up on their hind-legs, straining at their chains and snarling. The PCs maintained their steady slowish patrol pace, staring straight ahead, pretending not to notice. Yet they weren't quite expressionless; their faces were rigid with controlled fear. This is becoming a mini-war situation. How could these PCs – especially the male – *not* feel anti-Black? And when they make an arrest, or take part in a raid, or are otherwise in a position to be vengeful, inevitably they remember the occasions when they were taunted and outnumbered and frightened and could do nothing.

By that stage I had realised that Rasta Dobermann-owners are almost as odd a breed as their animals. Possibly there is an echo here of the Pinnacle guard-dog tradition. At all events, the Whitey-frightening potential of my neighbours' Dobermanns was felt to be an almost sacred attribute. One afternoon on the Radnor Road I met a Rasta artist, some of whose excellent paintings I had bought during the Handsworth Festival. As we were talking, two other Rastas joined us – one leading his dog – and engaged the painter in a long argument in patois. The dog was standing close beside me and seemed an outgoing and friendly fellow, though no doubt capable of being goaded to savagery. When I rubbed the roots of his ears he at once wagged what would have been a tail if he weren't a Dobermann. Then his owner noticed this exchange of courtesies and stepped back, jerking the dog away from my side. "How dare you touch the animal?" he yelled. "You keep your hands off other people's property – see? You think he's a pet? Man, he'd tear your arm off!" (Coincidentally, the Dobermann looked up at me then with one raised eyebrow.) When I had apologised humbly for giving offence, and was again alone with the painter, he said dryly, "The defiling touch of Babylon! And people pay big money for a fierce dog. So they've gotta feel cheated if it wags its arse for Whitey!"

On another and slightly more alarming occasion, a Dobermann from a nearby street escaped and was found by me having a glorious time amidst the overflowing dustbins outside No. 45. He too was of a sociable disposition and wildly elated by his freedom. Then his frantically worried owner came racing up Heathfield Road, to see this expensive device for intimidating Whitey standing on its hind-legs kissing my face. Unfortunately that Rasta was one of my Villa Cross 'enemies' and for a moment I thought he was going to attack me. Instead, he confined himself to a torrent of abusive obscenities while collaring his dog; and before leaving the tiny front garden he kicked towards me a torn plastic bag of used tampons. Nasty Rastas are *very* nasty. Luckily they are also very rare.

Even after my qualified acceptance as a regular, I found Villa Cross evenings exhausting though always fascinating. The strains were multiple, beginning with an insurmountable language barrier. Philologists have long been bickering about the status of the Creole languages – especially Jamaica Talk. May they or may they not be classified as separate languages? Some twenty-five years ago Professor Cassidy decided:

> If Jamaica folk speech is Creole, it is still English Creole, as distinct from Spanish or French Creole. As to the vocabulary there can be little doubt: it is a type of English. In its extreme form it certainly sounds like a different language . . . [and] . . . the biggest difference comes in grammatical structure. This is certainly not African and emphatically not English. The major complexities of both have been dispensed with, though minor features of both remain . . . The folk speaker who seeks to acquire standard English has the longer distance to go in respect of the grammar.*

Whatever any expert may have concluded, Jamaica Talk is certainly a separate language to the average outsider's ear. Often I sat between two Jamaicans, throughout a long conversation, without being able to pick up one word of what they were saying. Although no linguist, I could have understood *something* had they been speaking French, German, Spanish, Italian – or even Urdu or Punjabi, both of which slightly 'came back to me' in Bradford. Among the younger generation, patois is used as an anti-Babylon, White-excluding strategy and there is now a 'dialect' known as 'English Jamaica' and much influenced by 'Rasta-speak' – which is something else

---

* Frederic G. Cassidy, *Jamaica Talk*, Macmillan (1961).

again. This loyalty to Creole is understandable but greatly distresses parents who regard 'Standard English' as an essential prerequisite for job-success and a mark of social respectability. Because of it, my linguistic problems didn't always end when young Blacks condescended to speak English to me. Many of them had such a limited command of the language that serious communication was an energy-consuming challenge – particularly when attempted against a background of reggae.

Most of my worthwhile conversations with Villa Cross regulars took place elsewhere – either in flats or squats, or through chance meetings in Handsworth Park. But I soon noticed that talking to Whitey in public was against the code. Three open-air conversations ended in mid-sentence when my companion saw one of his brethren in the distance and abruptly stood up and walked away. Similarly, a young man who might have welcomed me warmly to his flat during the afternoon would look through me a few hours later on the Villa Road. So I quickly learned not to greet anyone as I crossed the front line.

Youngsters in a group and youngsters as individuals are quite different creatures; and the individual is usually more congenial than the group-member. Thus my tête-à-têtes with the younger regulars revealed areas of their thinking and feeling never exposed in the Villa Cross. (This range of contacts was of course comparatively narrow; those who spoke to me were *ipso facto* the least hostile to Babylon.) As group-members some young men habitually flaunted their ex-slave brands and shackles, as part of their Black identity and justification for their failure to achieve at school. 'This is how we are – this is how our history has made us – so why should we change?' was a common public attitude. It went with an ostentatious scorn for 'shit-jobs' and a pretence that accepting 'the system' (for instance, by going regularly to look for work at the Job Centre) was degrading. Yet in private conversation this anarchic shield was often lowered to reveal a desperate longing for a steady job of *any* kind. The Villa Cross sub-culture – the whole pseudo-Rasta life-style – was a refuge and a solace, but many would gladly have exchanged it for the humdrum routine of getting to a bus-stop with a lunch-satchel at 7.30 a.m. five days a week. On my early-morning walks I often met the 'lucky employed' (some the brothers or cousins of Villa Cross regulars), queuing for buses or walking to work. The same young men never appeared in the Villa Cross but were to be seen at weekends strolling through the Park with their partner and perhaps an infant or two, or doing the shopping down Soho Road, or painting their hall-doors or weeding their front patches. Immense bitterness is provoked by those who perversely put the cart before the horse by referring to jobless young Blacks as 'lazy layabouts'. Some are just that – and others are virtually unemployable, and doomed to remain so, for a variety of reasons. But the majority seem like lazy layabouts only because they have no alternative.

My impression was that many young Blacks who assert their willingness to die in 'the war against Babylon' are not merely striking a pose for Whitey's benefit. This attitude seems to be based on resentment of racialism plus a profound despair not peculiar to Black youths. In my experience, the single most harrowing feature of inner-city life was the number of youngsters, both Black and White, who lacked *the will to live*. The Whites were usually passive and sometimes on hard drugs; the Blacks – who despise hard drugs – were militant and ready to go down fighting. Both groups felt they had nothing to lose and in a sense they were right. Life should be precious when you are young and (more or less) healthy. But how can it be, for those born into a prison of urban degradation from which there seems no escape? It may be comforting to reflect that all Welfare State citizens are materially better off than 'the masses' were 200 years ago. Yet no number of 'benefits' can compensate for being expendable, having no role to play – no personal *significance*. Feudal serfs were better off than most youngsters in Europe's 1980s dole-queues. They had to work long hours for no pay and enjoyed few home-comforts. Society wasn't fair – very likely it never will be – and they were grossly exploited. But they were also *needed*: and they knew that they were needed.

Many of the young Blacks' handicaps are shared by their White inner-city contemporaries. Among my communication problems was the need to restrict my vocabulary in conversation with young people of all colours, for whom eleven years' schooling had done very little. I often felt as though I were talking to foreigners – with the sad difference that foreigners who speak some English are always pleased to learn new words, whereas inner-city dwellers are put on the defensive by 'posh talk'. It is too easy to forget – or never realise – that in Britain today there exists a considerable segment of the population whose ability to cope with the bureaucratic complexities of modern life (never mind to comprehend national or global issues) is severely limited by a lack of basic education. The Rampton Report noted: 'It is not, perhaps, sufficiently appreciated how important it is to learn to read at an early age. If reading is not learnt quickly, the child will inevitably have difficulty keeping pace with the demands of our educational system.' This is so obvious that the bored reader quickly turns the page. But Reports acquire a new meaning when their 'findings' are sitting beside you. One day in Handsworth Park, as I rested on a bench overlooking the muddy cricket pitch where multi-racial teams were playing between showers, a young Black friend joined me. He had a slight physical deformity and was carrying a sheaf of D H S S forms which he abruptly asked me to read aloud to him. When I had done so, he asked me to explain them – and then he said, "So they'll give me a benefit for my *body* not working right. But they don't see it's *worse* leaving school with my *mind* not working right – not able to read their stuff!"

I asked, "What about Adult Education classes?" – which are popular among Black school-leavers, especially girls.

"No," said Charley. "It's too late. That's same as a crutch from the D H S S.

It helps but it doesn't cure you. Nineteen's *too late*. I know, I've watched friends trying and they can't no way catch up. They're not stupid and after classes they read *better*. But it's big work for them, every page a big effort. I want to read all kinds of books for fun the way you do. I never will – but if I did I could get out of this Handsworth place just sitting in my flat . . ."

It seemed to me that Charley's genuine longing to be a 'reader for fun' could make him one, even starting almost from scratch at nineteen. Subsequently a social worker suggested to his friends that they should persuade him to go with them to classes and when I left Handsworth two months later he was reading Paddington Bear with as much enjoyment as I do. Many young Blacks, particularly those who have left their families (or never had families) easily lapse into hopelessness and their first need is morale-boosting. Charley's remark made me realise that if Britain's illiterates or semi-literates were equalled in number by those suffering visibly from the diseases of malnutrition there would be a nationwide uproar. But mental undernourishment and its consequences can be – at least for the moment – ignored.

Charley was one of a number of young Blacks whose private comments on the fuzz differed considerably from his 'group' comments. During that afternoon in the Park he conceded, "They're not *all* bad, see? There's even some *good* ones. Last year I fell crossing Soho road and I coulda been killed – my leg, I couldn't get up fast, see? And this one of the gang from Thornhill ran out and helped – ran out fast in front of a car the way he coulda been killed himself, see? Man, you remember that!"

A few days later I spent a long wet Sunday at the flat of a very literate ex-Rasta. Tobias was older than the average Villa Cross regular and had come to Handsworth at the age of thirteen. "I didn't know my mother then," he said, "not seen her for seven years. Every few months, all those years, she'd send snapshots so's I wouldn't forget. But photos don't keep love going. I didn't want to leave Jamaica, I was happy with my aunt – *her* kids were my family. And I was smart, I knew things were rough here – not all rosy the way people tried to make out in letters home. But my mother was crazy about 'good schooling'. She'd no schooling herself, she didn't know things were better that way at home than here. Lucky for me she couldn't save my fare till I was thirteen. I was a good reader and writer by then – good at maths and other things too. It shook me seeing how her small kids here weren't learning *basics* the way we had to – no respect for teachers, just fooling around at play stuff. I quit home and school at sixteen. Off to a squat – one squat after another, chased all over, never knew when you'd have to get out. And dirty insults from the fuzz every time they saw you. I was right deep into the Rasta bit – we all were that time – locks a yard long! And into the thieving bit too, just to show I could. Makes me guilty now, looking back, after she'd worked and saved to turn me into a scholar! But I couldn't take the shit at school – if they all reckon you're dumb you might as well play dumb. Then I got bored with the Rasta bit and a few of us went to Brixton. It went good for me, with a

steady job keeping accounts in a little factory. The owner could see I'm smart
– and honest when I'm not thieving! I saved enough to buy a car – ten years
old, but I worked and worked to make her look smart. I'd say the factory was
a sweat-shop, almost – sure wouldn't pass any inspections! But it wasn't going
too well the last few years and suddenly it got burnt down – the way places
do, sometimes, if they're not making a profit. O K for the owner, if he gets his
insurance, but not so funny for the rest of us. I hung around for a few months,
in and out of the Job Centre – nothing, even with a real good reference and
seven years' experience. I never liked Brixton, only for the work, so I'm back
here two years now. Brixton's got dangerous – Handsworth's kinda peaceful.
Down there in London it's got ugly – it's not only White women get mugged,
like they're always on about in the papers. There's a crowd there and they'd
smash you up for a one pound coin. I'm a big man and I got scared to walk
alone, day or night. I don't mind admitting it – I'm no way macho! It's all
different here, you don't get the real baddies – or only a few. And Brum has no
politicans making mischief, like that I L E A bunch getting the kids stirred up
against the police. I've no time for the fuzz, here or there. But I'm peaceful. I'd
fight the fuzz if they did an injustice on me but given a chance I'd keep away
from them. Why make *more* trouble? Those kids are just looking for trouble
anyway – and when they leave school, most of 'em they'll have nothing to do
but go *find* trouble. So what's the point showing them videos and wall-charts
to make 'em even angrier? Folk running that kinda campaign have to have a
reason – you don't spend thousands and thousands of pounds making *more*
trouble without a *reason* – right? Those Black kids down there – and all those
Asians – they've no education, they can't figure anything out for themselves.
You show 'em police beating the hell out of people, and perjuring and
torturing, and what do they feel? Just crazy to get out and have a go at the
fuzz, first chance there is! I go down sometimes, see my old landlady – she
looked after me seven years, so she got like a granny. So I go round, see folk,
have a smoke, talk – and you know how it's working? They're *losing* votes!
You say you've a daughter, so just think – someone gets your kid all worked
up to go out and look for trouble – you going to vote for them? No way! And
all being done with *your* money, on the rates! Think of it, £35,000 to make
more tension when even people with no church are praying for *less*! There's
not many in Brixton behind the fuzz but they don't want their kids in gaol.
They want civilised police, not animals around the street. And they don't see
how making kids *angrier* can make police *better*!"

Tobias was of course referring to I L E A's controversial video-cum-wall-
chart 'anti-racist kit', publicising instances of police racialism and distributed
to schools, clubs and libraries in the area. While he was speaking we had been
joined by Victor and Gloria. Victor's parents lived in Handsworth but he had
been working for the past eight years with disabled Black children in a
London borough. I had already met him twice at his parents' house; every
other weekend he came home to see Gloria, his nurse-assistant girlfriend.

"Toby's got it all wrong," Victor assured me, while accepted a drag on Tobias's joint. "You've got to warn kids what to expect from the police – they're being harassed one way or another from the day they go to primary school. And that publicity is true, if just shows what's been happening in London for years past. It's not propaganda some nut dreamed up 'cause he hated the fuzz. And if it raises the tension – well, maybe that's good. Who started the trouble? Not the Blacks! We're always hearing about how law-abiding our parents' generation was – and what result? The fuzz get this idea they can do as they please with the nig-nogs and get away with it! It's too late now to tell the kids to keep their heads down and make the best of things and turn the other cheek and the Lord will comfort them. That's just farts to them – smelly hot air. They've seen their community suffer too much from bullies and they're not mice. A lot of us in London now – just looking on, not involved with anything – we see it like this. The tension *must* get worse, and a lot worse, and maybe a few Blacks are killed and then the lid really comes off – and *then* we'll get action. But we won't get it *before* the lid comes off. Things have to get so bad people stop and look again at their precious Met., and see they've a mess there that *someone* has to clean up. And not with more Lords poncing about writing more reports – but with hundreds of police sacked and jailed for assault and perjury, so's the ones left are shit-scared to put a hand on a Black man. How many riots in America before anyone got to think seriously about Black problems? Fifty in one summer, with hundreds of millions of dollars-worth of damage! And then they *did* something . . . I know nothing about politics – I've *real* work to do. But if you're right, Toby, if there's political reasons behind that sort of campaigning – then it makes sense. Let the cosy people see where the Blacks have been pushed to – onto a battle-ground, and not because they ever wanted to be there!"

Gloria and I looked at each other. We had never met before but I felt we were thinking alike. She stretched across me to take the joint from Tobias and said, "I go along with Toby. What's the long-term benefit, for Blacks, in stirring up hate? I don't like it, whether it's against the fuzz or anyone else – that's the way I was trained up. Now we're all stuck here together in Britain we've got to live quietly together – why should Black kids be all hyped up to go out and get killed to suit a load of politicians? O K, there's mostly *bad* police, or that's how it can look if you're Black. But that doesn't make *hating* them good! And Vic's bull-shitting, talking about America. This is another sort of country – I know, I've been with my aunt in New York for a month. I was going to work there but they caught me. There's more than twenty million Blacks in the States—ten per cent of the population, uncle said. Even if hating and fighting was right, there isn't enough of us here to make enough trouble for anyone to help us. The more trouble we make the more harass-ment we'll get – and that's *all* we'll get! Talk about jailing police is fantasy stuff. They can murder us in daylight on the public street and only get twelve months suspended! What I'd like to see is lots of money spent teaching kids about their *rights* when they're picked up – or if they're tormented just walking along the road home. My sister's working on this with a church group in London and she gets mad 'cause the Council bully her. She wants to do it her own way, quietly, not *anti*-police stuff but giving kids legal information. If they knew *exactly* how they're fixed with the law when there's bother they'll react better – not so much panic. They're all swagger and tough talk – like Vic only worse! But even the big men – most of 'em wet their pants when they're picked up. Maybe they've done *nothing*, but still they're scared. They know they could be forced to make some confession, so's the fuzz needn't bother looking for who really did it. Then they lose their head and hit out and they *have* done something – assaulted an officer of the law! It's a bad scene . . ."

Victor looked at his partner with loving contempt, before turning to me. "Black women are supposed to be strong," he said, "but this one I've got, she's just a floppy toy! She knows all this – she's telling you how it is – and still she says 'No fighting! Must be nice to the fuzz!' Why? So's they can feel free to brutalise our kids even worse than they brutalize us?"

"We should complain more," said Gloria. "Like my sister says, if *all* Blacks with complaints went to the Police Authority, they'd see something was wrong – you couldn't have that many *inventing* stories!"

"Know what?" said Victor – "your sister needs a brain-transplant! Why should Blacks have to complain after being victimised? That's walking into Whitey's trap – we're not stupid, we're not going back to the fuzz to hand in a complaint and be noted down and victimised worse next time!"

"This is a two-faced country," said Tobias, returning from his tiny neat kitchen with a genteel tea-tray. "Everything always looks great on paper, like this new Act and an Independent Complaints Authority and leaflets from the Home Office saying how it all works – you'd think no one could ever have a problem again. But somehow if you're Black all this British justice doesn't happen for *you* . . ."

"Who in Brixton or Moss Side or Handsworth reads *Home Office* leaflets?" demanded Victor.

"Maybe they should," said Gloria – who was nobody's floppy toy. "Maybe we should all start listening to each other."

"Who's 'we'?" snapped Victor. "You want *me* to listen to the *Home Office*?"

"Yes," said Gloria calmly, handing round cups of tea. "I'd like everyone to listen to everyone else, just to see what might happen then."

I began to feel excited – and Tobias noticed, though I had said nothing. "Dervla's getting her White liberal tail up!" he remarked with a huge grin.

Victor scowled, sensing it was three-to-one. "I suppose she's S D P – serve up the milk and water and let's all get drunk on moderation!"

"I have no party political affiliations," I said primly and truthfully, "either in this country or my own."

"If we went back to the start," said Gloria, "and talked about where it all began to go wrong with police and Blacks . . ."

"That won't take long," interrupted Victor. "It went wrong the first day Blacks landed in this fuckin' den of racist bastards!"

Gloria leant forward and gripped him by the forearm. "You talk that way, I'm gone – see?"

Victor looked astonishingly cowed and Tobias said, "Sometimes the fuzz are scared of *us* – it's kinda two-way. If we're into listening, maybe we should start there?"

"No," said Gloria, "we should start like Vic said, with British racism – 'cause there isn't any other start . . . But *why* do they still feel that way?"

"It's no good!" exclaimed Victor. "We're wasting time – they won't even *admit* they're racist! They think it's something else when they feel it – patriotism, or something. That's why listening won't work. They're deaf, they can't *hear* a Black voice. Not unless it's saying 'Yes Sir! No Sir!' – then they love it. That's how Blacks should be, knowing their place and staying in it and not pushing for good jobs – or any jobs, now work in precious."

"But Toby's right about the way people *feel*," said Gloria. "Whatever about Brixton – I've never been there and don't want to go – Handsworth's Blacks aren't looking for more aggro. What's in it for us? Everybody hears the few loud-mouths, like Vic and his brethren in London, and the other sort of Blacks who're looking for political jobs. What about the rest of us – that's *most* of us – who don't want 'war on the streets'? Nobody hears us!"

"OK" said Victor – "so we're loud-mouths! But we're not a *few* – you talk about fantasy, that's *your* fantasy!"

"And the fuzz?" asked Tobias. "Maybe they want less aggro too – what's in it for them? I went to Brixton in '76 and the Handsworth scene was bad then – very, very bad. Seven years later I come back and it's better, even with unemployment worse. Why? First, 'cause a lot of the tough Rasta lads running round with knives in the seventies got put away and now they're cooled down. They're my crowd that I went to school with – I meet 'em today and man! they're like another kinda people! They don't want back inside . . . That's first. Second, the fuzz got themselves someway cleaned up. There's plenty vicious brutes left in Thornhill, only more under control. Like, they've stopped shoving Blacks' heads down the WC bowl. I had that when I was a kid – I'm not stupid, I haven't lost my memory, I know how it was . . . But all over the country you'll find some OK fuzz and give 'em a chance to organise things and it gets better for everyone. So it doesn't have to get worse all the time. If it can get better here it can get better in London – not the way things are there now, but if they'd OK fuzz in charge."

"More fantasy!" said Victor. "That's great news – they won't rub your curls in the shit any more – am I grateful! Look at it straight, man! Here things improve for a while but now they're getting bad again – or maybe you didn't notice? And that's how it always is, one step forward and five steps back . . .

And this is a small country. You get the Met. behaving like the SS and folks *here* react to that – they know Newman shoulda been in Germany fifty years ago – he just went astray in time and space!"

"Fine," said Gloria, "we get the message. But so what happens if we *don't* listen? Nothing ever stays the same, things get better or worse. And I still say most Blacks and most fuzz want things better, but every time the little gang of trouble-makers on both sides stir up more aggro there's less chance anyone will notice what *most* want. We're just the crowd in the background – no publicity – and still we're the ones should matter most, in a democracy."

"*Democracy!*" snorted Victor. "Who say *this* is a democracy?"

"Right,' said Gloria, "you like to try Nigeria or Uganda or somewhere else nice and Black? You wouldn't last a day making your speeches – they'd have your lungs for bag-pipes!" She looked at her watch then and stood up and beckoned Victor as though he were a naughty small boy being taken away from a party at which he had misbehaved.

When they had left Tobias grinned and said, "See? Black women *are* strong!"

I asked, "Is Victor right, about things getting bad again here? Or is this rising tension a seasonal thing?"

Tobias seemed not to hear. He took the tea-tray to the kitchen and washed up and tidied away; he was almost obsessionally tidy. When he returned he remarked, "You got a cubby-hole flat like this, you need *order*."

I thought of the shambles in my own pad across the street and said nothing.

Tobias sat down. "I answer straight, but you forget *I* said anything – right?"

"Right!" I promised.

" O K, so there's trouble coming and we all know that and Victor says it's the fuzz going five steps back. But why all this extra harassment and raids on the Cross and the Acapulco? 'Cause the fuzz are being pushed – right? So I like my smoke same as plenty do – decent law-abiding folk. But we smoke at home, or with friends like Vic and Gloria here. You ever see me with a joint at the Cross? No! And I don't buy there either. You're breaking the law, it's polite to do it *quietly* – right? You don't have to break it every day in public, unless you *want* trouble. O K it's a stupid law – but the fuzz didn't make it, they're just paid to see it's kept. Now they've the Whites and the Asians on their backs complaining – 'Blacks can get away with anything!' And there's plenty older Blacks saying the same thing. So they've no choice, they clean up round Villa Road or look silly. All those lads in the Cross have flats or squats where they can smoke day and night and the fuzz would pretend not to know. But instead they must organise a big ganja supermarket with customers coming from all over and weekends you can smell it coming up Soho Road! So who's surprised there's raids? Lots in there in the Cross are my friends – I like that pub, I like the music and the characters and old Kev prowling round sorting everyone out. But it's not going to last. They'll close it down the way they did the Beehive. Then the lads will be off looking for another base – and so it goes on . . ."

I asked, "But if the lads know that, why provoke the fuzz? Why do they *want* trouble?"

"I'll tell you what *I* think, even if you say it's stupid. *I* think they're bored. Just plain bored crazy. What you call provoking the fuzz, it's a *sport*. It's not like it was when I was a kid going around shop-lifting and so on. It was tougher than – that's why I got out to Brixton. I told you I'm not macho, I didn't like knives and beating up the fuzz – it wasn't only Blacks got beaten up . . . Maybe now it looks like a rough scene to you, but it's no way as rough as it was. The police have *tried* here. Makes Vic puke when I say it, but it's *true*. Now they're turning nasty again – they don't need too much excuse to forget all about 'community relations' – if they don't watch it they could soon be back where they were when I left in '76. But you've got to *admit* they've tried – it's sour and mean to say they haven't. That's why I reckon Gloria's right about listening. It could still work, if enough people got onto the game, both sides."

"Would legalising ganja make a difference?" I asked. "Would it be taken as a gesture of reconciliation?"

"Not the way I see it," replied Tobias. "They'd have to find another sport. There's only one thing to make a difference – *jobs*. Don't let anyone fool you that answer's 'too simple'. We get all sorts coming here – same in Brixton – *studying* the situation. And they like to make it all very, very complicated. But you have enough jobs – real jobs, not twelve months fooling around on some training scheme – you give 'em jobs and suddenly you've all the problems looking different. They wouldn't all go away, but they'd get *smaller*, see? Kids at school, with competition out there for work, they'd have a reason to settle to their books instead of feeling picked on and making aggro. And most of the lads in the Cross would give up regular smoking and thieving and come out into the ordinary world – earning and spending. All this anti-Babylon stuff wouldn't make sense any more if they'd a share of Babylon's goodies – right?"

"I'm not sure," I said. "Victor has a good secure job – better than most – but his anti-Babylon sentiments are still pretty strong!"

"Only in *talk*," Tobias pointed out. "You won't ever find him *doing* anything to annoy the fuzz – he might lose his good secure job! You don't want to take Black *talk* seriously. Never means much. It's when we *act* you need to watch out . . ."

13 · Action

On Wednesday 10 July the West Midlands Police Drug Squad raided the 'front-line' Acapulco Café, where young Blacks played pool, ate repulsively greasy chips and ganja-dealt during pub closing hours. Next morning Handsworth's Whites and Browns (and many Blacks) savoured the front page of their *Birmingham Post*. Smooth press/police co-ordination was discernible behind the lay-out. Below a box-headline – 'Operation Tijuana launched' – the report did not provide a ganja-dealing address. It was almost laconic:

> Drugs squad officers arrested seven men yesterday in a day-light raid on a Birmingham café. Eighty-six detectives and uniformed officers, including operational support unit teams, were used in the sensitive operation, codenamed Tijuana. Seven men were arrested and held for questioning at Queen's Road police station in Aston. Six were charged on drug offences while a seventh man faces a public order offence. Detectives with sniffer dogs seized cannabis resin and cannabis bush with a street value of £1,500, and a quantity of L S D tablets. Some £925 believed to have been used in drugs deals was also found. The meticulously-planned operation was similar to a raid six weeks ago when 150 police officers made nineteen arrests. Det. Chief Insp. Brian Wall, head of the West Midlands police drugs squad, said: "The operation lasted just eleven minutes and went very smoothly. There were no injuries or damage."

The first of two excellent photographs showed the police, looking cool, competent and determined, pouring out of one of their huge vans to invade the café. The second showed a small man in a Rasta hat being 'led away for questioning' by two very large policemen. This was just what respectable Handsworth needed; the boys in blue had hammered the Rastas – and that headline (Operation Tijuana *launched*) promised more of the same. Only a few readers winced at the figures quoted: 'a street value of £1,500' and '£925 believed to have been used in drugs deals'. These were as poignant a measure of local poverty as any DoE graph.

On that Wednesday evening, a few hours after the raid, the usual complement of Rastas (minus a few familiar faces) were showing the flag in the Villa Cross forecourt. But the bar was more than half-empty and trading had been frozen for the evening. The anger level was higher than I had ever felt it, with three enraged Rastas protesting that the fuzz has planted the LSD – "To make us look dangerous, see? Like we're into hard drugs, see? Fuzz know most folk don't take ganja too serious like – not nowadays. And looks a bit stupid, cops by the van-load – like a fuckin' army! – pickin' up few lads with bits bush 'n' resin. So you add LSD – makes it all look wicked, see?"

I said nothing, though twenty-five years ago I would have argued that *policemen* aren't like that . . . At one time, Tobias had told me, Handsworth was awash with amphetamines, barbiturates and 'acid' – when such things were popular. So it is hard to believe that nowadays *no* Rasta dealer would sink to those depths. Yet in the Villa Cross I had never heard or seen any indication of any substance other than ganja being traded. And by now unethical police practices have become so common that this accusation was as likely as not to be true.

One Rasta friend gave me a godfatherly lecture on 'Not Hanging About' during such police actions on or near the front line. "You think you're safe because we know you now – right? But when it all happens you won't be the nice lady who sits always in this corner and talks to everyone. You'll just be another Whitey and you could get hurt if you're the only one around and the police are out of reach. That day people won't be thinking, only *feeling*. It's all or nothing with us. When we were raided here, just before you came, it was nothing. But one day maybe quite soon it'll be *all* . . . I'm not a violent man but now, after that raid, I could carve up a policeman and go to bed happy. But I don't want Whites like you being hurt."

Another Rasta – less amiable – added, "Don't imagine you're *accepted* here. You're just tolerated for the moment. We can't take much more of this. It's OK for Whitey to rot his guts and brains with alcohol, *not* OK for us to smoke! Why not? Just 'cause Denis Thatcher prefers gin to ganja? So what? It's all in the mind. Alcohol is OK 'cause Babylon enjoys and exploits it, ganja is *not* OK 'cause the Rastaman enjoys and trades it. *I* know why you won't smoke – you're too old to adjust. *I* know you don't call it 'a Black vice'. But if the lid comes off while you're still around you'll only look like one more cigar-puffing Babylon figure that deserves all she gets. Nobody's going to kill you but if you get roughed up it'll be your own fault. And the same goes for the fuzz."

Handsworth's so-called 'International Festival' started two days later; it might unkindly but accurately be described as the non-event of the summer. This annual jamboree (Friday to Sunday) is sponsored by Ansells Brewery and the Anglian Building Society and receives a grant from the West Midlands County Council. It is supposed to create an atmosphere of community jollity – 'all having fun together' – but in practice disputes about who gets how much of the grant form a fertile seed-bed for factional animosities.

The weather remained reasonable, by '85 standards; it never actually rained (or not much), but was mostly overcast with clouds of midges swarming under the Park's handsome trees. When the sun briefly emerged on the Saturday afternoon I sat on a grassy slope facing the bandstand and listened with horrified fascination to groups named 'Exhibit Wha Pou' and 'Mystik Revelation' and 'Deciples' producing noises of incomparable awfulness. Perhaps they were awful even by addicts' standards because none of the performers was applauded. The audience of about 150, thinly scattered across the wide slope, consisted mainly of young mothers of all colours – a remarkable number with mixed-race offspring – whose partners (if any) were aimlessly kicking footballs around in separate racial groups. Two toddlers – a Vietnamese and a Mirpuri – romped happily together beside me; their mother and father, respectively, were sitting alone, staring impassively at the bandstand, ignoring each other and their young. Groups of elegantly dressed Sikh youths strolled past, looking supercilious. Occasional staid Hindu family parties, often including a grandparent, kept to the paths – observing but not participating. There were also a few professional Festival-goers – seedy, pallid young Whites who travel the country, singly or in pairs, ever on the look-out for a ganja-bargain. But most of the crowd were Black, doing their own 'sound' thing from the backs of parked lorries. This was my first experience of serious, uninhibited 'sound' and when standing on the grass, some ten yards from the source, I could feel it, literally, in my guts; the vibrations were perceptibly shaking my intestines. Finding this sensation somewhat disconcerting, I soon moved on. One wonders what exactly 'sound' does, physiologically and psychologically, to those who listen to it at this pitch day after day: or, more often, night after night.

Throughout the Festival, the uniformed police presence was discreet: pairs of young P Cs sauntering across the grass, looking relaxed, or taking time – and their helmets – off to smoke a cigarette while chatting with the dozen or so Blacks and Whites who were watching a cricket match.

Marquee No. 2 ('International Food – Served at Give-away Prices') was virtually empty most of the time. But Marquee No. 1 ('The Gospel Festival') generated some enthusiasm on the Sunday: as did a Half-Marathon, run around Handsworth's streets. One would expect some of the local Brown restaurant-owners to set up food-stalls but these were mainly Black, augmented by White junk-food from hamburger-vans. To me this Festival seemed peculiarly non-exhilarating, perhaps because it so strongly emphasised that Handsworth is not 'a community' but a disparate collection of communities exhaling a miasma of mutual suspicion, intolerance and dislike. Where the communities do merge most noticeably – among the lawless youth – that unity is seen by everyone else, with good reason, as a threat.

The last item on the programme was an ill-attended 'Fashion Show' in the Leisure Centre at 7.00 p.m.; the idea was that the crowd should disperse quietly before sunset. It was evident that the Blacks, who were thoroughly enjoying their 'sound', had no intention of dispersing but I went home at dusk and so missed the evening's unpleasantness. The *Birmingham Post* reported on the Tuesday:

> Violence marred the close of Handsworth's Festival, police confirmed yesterday. On Sunday night as crowds spilled out of the Park trouble started among about 500 teenagers. Bricks, paving stones and bottles were thrown at house windows and at police called to the scene. Three policemen were treated afterwards for minor injuries ... Chief Supt. Don Wilson blamed a small gang of "hotheads" for provoking twenty minutes of trouble which spoiled an otherwise well-organised event. He said, "They were Asians, Blacks and Whites, this was not a racial incident. They were just hotheads."

Meanwhile I had been getting conflicting versions of how the scuffle started. In the Villa Cross it was claimed that a plain-clothes Drugs-Squad officer conned a Rasta into offering him ganja and then signalled to uniformed officers – which caused scores of Black youths to converge on every policeman in sight. This version was a fabrication woven around an incident that occurred earlier but caused no trouble.

Some of my neighbours blamed rival gangs of youths – one gang leader had dared another to loot a shop. A Black pastor, who had been in the Park in his official capacity throughout the Festival, praised the police. "They stayed well in the background – no provocation. There was ganja-dealing behind every tree and they managed not to notice. You think about their job, it's not easy. That Park's a big place. You get a few bad lads want to knife a cop – they could have him and be gone forever! Those officers have courage, men *and* women. Sure they get a bit rough time to time – wouldn't you, after that mob teasing you up and down the Villa Road day and night?"

A Black woman social worker, who was present on the fringes of the fracas, saw four youths trying to loot a shop; when the Pandas arrived they disappeared into a hostile crowd of hundreds of young Blacks. In her view the temperature in the Park had then been going up for a few hours and a gang of fifty or so was determined to make trouble, somehow. "And it was *mostly* Blacks," she added. "I only saw a few Asians and Whites. But Wilson's right to say it wasn't a racial incident, it's just that most young thugs round here *are* Black. My youngest brother's one of them, that's why I stayed hanging around, hoping I wouldn't see him heaving a brick at the fuzz! I wouldn't be a Handsworth policeman for a million a year. Every day I'm dealing with those kids who're in and out of Thornhill Road like it was home. And you know what sickens me? It's mostly the CID who do dirt, but it's the ordinary bugger out on foot-patrol, or in a Panda, who gets the punishment. Life's not fair – not for any of us, Black or White!"

I spent that Monday afternoon with Mirpuri friends who live in a little street off the far end of Soho Road. Turning into Villa Road, soon after six o'clock, I at once got bad vibes. (As a resident of Heathfield Road, one's sensitivity to tension becomes hyper-acute.) I asked a Sikh shopkeeper friend what was happening. "It's happened," he said. "It's all over – thought we were going to have a riot this time. I went to the door and about fifty of those Rasta devils – no! they're worse than devils – they were attacking a few cops. I think they'd stopped a Rasta car looking for drugs. More police came and their Panda was bashed about. Someone said they arrested three and got a big bag of drugs. I'd arrest the lot and shove 'em in a labour-camp like they have in Russia! I don't waste sympathy on the police, they've made all this trouble for themselves over years past. They've got to look foolish, giving presents to Rasta clubs – *music systems!* And then starting cricket teams – all that 'community' nonsense. Now the public wants them to get tough and they're seeing how much it helps being friendly with gangsters! This shop we're standing in, it's been broken into five times in the last four months. Twice since you came here – *you* know, you've seen it the morning after, with hundreds of pounds' worth of stock gone. And what do the police do? Shrug their shoulders and tell me find a big dog – and go off to think some more about how to be nice to Rastas! You can't insure a business on the Villa Road. And you can't sell it either – who'd move into this gangland?"

Two hours later, in the Villa Cross, the Sikh's account of the afternoon's events was confirmed from a different perspective. One Rasta said, "Someone's *planning* trouble. Someone's real crazy keen to make a great big showdown or blow-up. They have to be – right? Else why you stop Rastaman car on front line middle day – with every Rasta kid hanging round? *Why?* You do that you have to be thinking, 'How can I stir things?' Where they want to push us? How much more they figure they can push? They think we're all sacred O A Ps? Man, they'll know!"

That evening my Villa Cross 'enemies' were particularly vocal and obnoxious and most of my friends were absent. I went home earlier than usual.

A Brown newsagency, where I often stopped for the *Birmingham Post* on my way home from the swimming-pool, had been one of the main targets of the Sunday night post-Festival mob. The owner despised British justice and policing methods; he had often told me so before. Now, with his wife still under sedation, as a result of a brick and broken glass landing on her pillow, his anger and contempt were molten. "You know what's wrong with the police? They're cowards! They shake if they see a Black man way down the end of the street! They should bloody beat 'em up – crack their legs with lathis like we do at home so they never walk straight again. You can't control poor areas with laws like you have in this country and it's bloody stupid to try. Even when they do catch 'em – not often – they let 'em out again on bloody bail, free to do more damage! They should be locked up in a dark cellar for ten days without food, then sentenced to twenty years and *kept* in . . . That way people like us – quiet people, wanting to do honest business – we'd have peace without being attacked in our beds!"

At that point the newsagent's brother emerged from the room behind the shop in a coruscation of gold. I have never seen any other man (and few women) so loaded with that metal – tie-pin, cuff-links, belt, enormous watch, pen in breast-pocket, rings galore. He was an engineer, home on holidays from an oil-rich Arab state. "Where I live now," he said, "they know all about law and order. A public entertainment was announced one day – State-run, in a big sandy park. Thousands came. A man was brought in chains – he'd raped a ten-year-old girl. A hole was dug in the sand while he watched and he was buried up to the elbows. Then his scalp and shoulders were cut – small cuts, with a very sharp knife. Salt was sprinkled on him and two hounds were let loose. They were very hungry. He didn't scream for long – I saw it all."

I would have been reaching for the smelling-salts, were this the 1880s. I said, rather faintly, "That *can't* be a true story!"

Brother chuckled. "Every little word is *so* true you won't have another ten-year-old raped in that city for two hundred years!"

Coincidentally (or not), while the Acapulco was being raided on 10 July a Birmingham motor mechanic (George Richardson, White, aged fifty-five) was being sentenced to eight years imprisonment at Birmingham Crown Court for acting 'as a vital and trusted link in an international drugs ring'. He had hidden cannabis worth £4.5 *million* behind a false wall in his Yardley garage and was responsible for supplying dealers throughout the West Midlands, the North of England and Scotland. When arrested at Birmingham International Railway station he was carrying two suitcases, each containing £100,000, for delivery to his employer at Euston Station. On 11 July, Handsworth's *Birmingham Post* readers could therefore turn to inside pages for an illustrated account of Mr Richardson's activities, including photographs of the ganja-store and a suitcase full of bank-notes. One headline said: 'JAIL FOR LINK IN DRUG RING'. And another: 'QUIET LIFE HID WORLD DRUGS RING'. Even my anti-Rasta Black friends were aggrieved – "Why does a Black man always get onto the front page for crime, even when a White man's crime is better news? Wouldn't you expect a £4.5 *million* story on the front page? Instead of £950 that *may* have been used in Acapulco deals!"

The Villa Cross view – 'Someone's *planning* trouble!' – was in a way correct. Police forces all over Britain were planning big trouble for drugs dealers and Birmingham then had its share of enormous advertisement hoardings depicting a debilitated young man in the last stages of heroin addiction. The pressure on my ganja-dealing neighbours was but a tiny fraction of that nationwide campaign. Yet it was a sadly significant fraction since it effectively marked the end of local community policing. Even I, a casual observer, had noticed a change in tactics during the first week of July; suddenly there were many fewer foot-patrols (the keystone of community policing) and many more cruising Pandas. Pandas instead of foot-patrols represent a more economical use of scarce manpower. But they also represent the impersonal, 'Them and Us' aspect of policing and in Handsworth the emotional ill-effects of this change were immediate and palpable. Also, the strolling PCs who used to drop into local pubs for an apparently casual gossip were ordered to do so no more; this broke 'police regulations'. Their being deprived of such valuable daily insights into community moods and opinions proved a tragic error.

Apart from a minority of Black militants, it seemed to me that 'Babylon's' honest effort to improve Black/police relations had been recognised by even the most unlikely sections of the Black community. Tobias was but one of a number of young Black men who commented to me (always of course in private) on the community policing achievements of the past seven or eight years. But those achievements were too fragile to withstand the pressure of vigorous Drug-Squad activity in the area – combined with the aggressive symbolism of more Pandas, fewer foot-patrols.

Throughout the rest of July and August tension increased week by week, though there were no further raids. In the Villa Cross quarrels became more frequent, suspicion flaring between dealers at the drop of a Rasta-cap. New customers, though always introduced by regulars, were treated with extreme caution and one Black (older than the average regular and among my 'enemies') was repeatedly fingered as a police spy. However, despite the fraught atmosphere trade was no less brisk than usual – contrary to police propaganda.

When I felt the need to *relax* over my pint (or two) of cider, I sometimes went to a small, quiet Irish-run pub in one of Handsworth's least salubrious corners. There the decibels permitted normal conversation and the regulars were an interesting mix: elderly English and Irish of both sexes (long resident in Handsworth), elderly Black men occasionally accompanied by their wives and a few Mirpuri and Bangladeshi youths who had assimilated to the extent of forgetting what Mohammed said about alcohol. Some of the Irish were summer visitors, holidaying with relatives, and their comments often caused me to choke with embarrassment over my pint. A typical remark came from a West Cork woman, addressing her fellow-Corkonian behind the bar – "How can you stick out the life here, with all them dirty wogs all over every place?" Luckily the West Cork accent is almost incomprehensible – even to many Irish ears, and certainly to Blacks, several of whom were sitting only two yards away. Verbal expressions of Irish racialism have been toned down by no Race Relations Act or anti-racist lobby. In theory the Irish sympathise with other victims of colonialism: but usually only at a distance. Among the older generation in Ireland, the traditional British view of 'coloureds' as inferior subject peoples is replaced by a view of 'savage heathens' in need of conversation to the Catholic Church. Some of my Black friends told me similar comments were often audible in public places when first they came to Britain, but are now rare. This is I suppose an advance of sorts, though it doesn't lessen the impact of racialism where it hurts most – in the educational, jobs and housing areas.

Two of the White regulars (husband and wife, both retired teachers) were active members of the local Residents' Association, then agitating to have the Villa Cross closed. They were not anti-Black, only anti-Rasta; when first I entered that pub they were deep in conversation with two of their Black neighbours. (Both widowers, I later discovered, who always spent Christmas Day with Sue and Dick.) We had a few impassioned but unproductive arguments about ganja – arguments which tended to draw others to our table (it was that sort of friendly pub) because the topic stirred deep feelings. Among the harmful confusions caused by ganja's illegality is the notion that local Black ganja-dealers and local Black criminals are invariably the same people. Few seem to understand that a ganja-dealer doesn't need to be a mugger, car-thief or burglar; he has another source of income and the last thing he wants is to attract police attention. No one believed me when I stated that apart from their trade most of the Villa Cross ganja-dealers were quiet, law-abiding young men.

One evening I was accompanied by a White social worker (Greg) from another – though no less deprived – inner-city area. He was in his mid-thirties and a devout teetotal Methodist. When I introduced him to Sue and Dick he at once launched into a 'legalise ganja' spiel (*not* pre-arranged by me) which clearly took them by surprise; such subversive talk from a cider-sodden Irish writer was only to be expected, but you look for something more responsible from a teetotal Nonconformist Brummie.

"Don't get me wrong," said Greg. "I'm against *all* drugs – cigarettes, the lot. But I work part-time with White junkies – and a few Asians – and that makes you think about the lesser of two evils. Heroin kills kids, cannabis doesn't. The police are undermanned and underfunded, then told to clean up the drugs scene. And having ganja illegal drains off resources needed to catch the real baddies. You follow me? Controlling the heroin trade is a matter of life or death. Then there's another worry. You scarcely ever see a Black junkie, they're dead against hard drugs. But with heroin so cheap and plentiful, pushers are desperate to widen the market and there's more and more spiked resin coming into Brum. So we're getting kids who'd never knowingly touch hard drugs conned into becoming junkies. Legalised cannabis, under government control, would look after that problem." Greg glanced across at me. "Some of your friends would lose their jobs – but kids would be safer. And the police could keep their sights fixed on what matters most."

Dick said, "If they'd been doing that for the past eight years, Handsworth wouldn't be the way it is now – terrorised by hoodlums!"

"But", Sue reminded him, "most of us thought community policing was a good idea when it started."

Dick stood up to buy his round. "Well," he said, "we live and learn, don't we?"

A slightly stooped, snowy-haired man had been standing beside us, leaning on his stick, listening. He suddenly exclaimed, "*No!* We'd be damn fools to give in to them!" He glared down at Greg. "I suppose you're a sociologist?"

"Not really," said Greg, "just a social worker."

"Same thing!" growled Snowy-hair. "Full of daft ideas and sob-stuff about the poor unemployed Rastas. *Unemployed!* Would you give one of those thugs a job? You'd have to be mad! And this country'd have to be mad to change good laws to pacify Black criminals – leaving Englishmen still going to jail for using other drugs! The day that happens I'm emigrating to Australia, thought I was eighty-two last week – and I wouldn't be travelling on my own . . ."

During the last week of August, I talked with a retired policeman who for several years had been involved in Handsworth's community policing experiment. "We felt quite proud in '81," he recalled rather sadly. "When Brixton and Toxteth went up trouble started but we contained it – what better proof that community policing works? And the West Midlands pioneered it . . . But lately it's been getting harder and harder to keep that show on the road. For one thing you've all the funding cuts – this year Handsworth has forty fewer police officers than in '81. *Forty* fewer! D'you wonder the public are complaining about inadequate police responses? And now there's a new iron-fisted Chief Constable, with holes in his velvet glove. He doesn't give a rotten orange for community policing – he won't *say* so, but his actions show it. And since last April there's been a new Super. at Thornhill Road. Hasn't been in Handsworth for years – he was stationed there as a sergeant – knows nothing about the way local feelings and conditions have been developing. Add to that what you've got all over Britain – tremendous pressure, from politicians, media and public, to sort out drug-pushers. That's fine, if cops had the cash to do the job properly. Brum's hard-drugs problem isn't as bad as some cities and we want to keep it that way. But in Handsworth the big danger is having all attention focused on the obvious Rasta boys, peddling a few quids' worth of ganja, while *Asians* quietly bring in the hard stuff. The Super, who started community policing resigned in '81 – he had some very odd ideas, well-meant but scatty. He kept the Drug-Squad out of Handsworth and I didn't go along with that. You can't have no-go areas, giving space to the heroin boys. His second-in-command took over then and to my mind got it about right. He let in the boys from Bournville Lane, on condition they didn't carelessly provoke the Rastas. Fact is, Handsworth's police *need* Rasta help to control the drug scene. Those opponents have the same basic aim: keep out the heroin-pushers! But you can't get that over to the poor old dears who're afraid to go shopping down the Villa Road at noon, never mind go out after dark – even to visit the next-door-neighbour. They'll be happy with the new Chief Constable and the new Super. – men not interested in walking the tightrope between ganja and heroin. If it's a drug it's a crime. Forget community policing."

"Do *you* think changing the law would make sense?" I asked.

He shrugged. "Honestly, I don't know. And that's after many years of debating with myself – and with Blacks and police colleagues and social workers and clergymen . . . I can think of a fair number of police who'd be glad to have their work simplified. But legalising would take away one of the Black motives for working, indirectly, with the fuzz against the smack boys. And you'd be left with a crowd of discontented small dealers, used to a certain life-style – not affluence, but better than the dole. The coke-merchants are trying to use the ganja network already, without much success. But the money involved in hard drugs is a huge temptation – we're talking of tens of thousand instead of hundreds. Then you look at it another way, legalising could improve Black/White relations, generally. Thousand of decent Blacks naturally resent being criminalised, when their vice is no worse than cigarettes and booze. I sympathise with them. Another thing, most Whites live nowhere near a Black area. They've no personal experience of how law-abiding most Blacks are – including the young, if you give them work. So they get this image through the media: 'Black equals ganja' – 'ganja is illegal' – 'Black equals criminal'. Yes, O K, I know that sounds so stupid it's nearly funny. But that's how prejudice is kept going. I've no doubt in *that* way legalising would help to change the White perception of the whole Black community."

Not long before, the same point had been made by a Barbadian law-student friend – Rupert – when we were talking in the Grey Dove. Rupert's father had served in the RAF during the war, then settled in England as a London Transport bus-driver. He so distrusted new educational theories that his son and daughter were sent to live with Granny in Barbados while being traditionally schooled.

Rupert opened the *Birmingham Post* (16 August) and tapped the leader-page article – 'VOICES ON THE LINE MAKE IT HOT FOR DRUG PUSHERS'. "Have you read this?" he asked. "What's it going to do for Brum's race relations?"

I had read it and thought it an example of sound, responsible journalism. It explained the importance of the Drug-Squad's new hot-line and encouraged the public to use it; and in the middle it stressed that 'West Indians, for example, if they use drugs at all, are unlikely to stray from cannabis, the least dangerous.' But the overall impact worried Rupert. He said, "This hot-line is good, and there's that sensible ref. to cannabis. But the last bit bothers me. Listen: 'As the police pull out all the stops to stem this trade, can you place your hand on your heart and swear that you know nothing to help them? If YOU know a dealer or a young person involved, you MUST telephone 021–477 0077. It's just a short message from you that could be the difference between life and death for someone else.' That's bad," said Rupert. "For some people it will devalue the whole hot-line exercise. Yourself, for instance. Where you live and where you drink you'd spend all day ringing 477 0077 if you took it seriously. But for other sorts it seems to confirm what they *want* to believe, that Blacks are endangering lives by pushing 'Dangerous Drugs'. And that association of West Indians with crime has rubbed off on us all. *I* don't look like a Villa Road character. I take trouble to look like a young lawyer, *very* dependable and conventional. But I'm Black. So when I go into any big store the staff tense up – 'You've got to watch *him!*' That's fine for me, I can take it, I was brought up to make allowances . . . But thousands of British citizens can't take it. It's too much for them – that feeling, as soon as you move out into the big White world, that you're automatically a suspect *because of the colour of your skin.* How could *any* Whites really understand what that feeling does to Blacks? It's the *reverse* of the White experience – think of all those countries where for centuries worthless Whites were looked up to *because* of the colour of their skin!"

"Let's start a new 'Legalise Ganja!' campaign," I suggested. "Look at how Handsworth is now – and getting worse every day. Any anti-drugs campaign has to heighten tension, as long as ganja and hard drugs are bracketed together."

"D'you want to end my career before it's started?" asked Rupert. "But if you run the campaign I'll send anonymous donations and free legal advice. Your first problem could be all the God-nuts on your back, the ones who think you'll go to hell if you have a half-pint of lager once a year. They'd say most Blacks want cigarettes and booze outlawed, not ganja legalised! Seriously, if I had to speak out I'd say the present law is unhealthy. When kids grow up inside a sub-culture based on breaking the law, and half the people they know are criminals *only* because they're into ganja – yet criminals all the same – there's a sense of moral confusion. Those kids are born into a state of lawlessness, with the line always blurred between right and wrong. So how can they grow up with respect for the law?"

Walking home through the Park, I wondered about that argument. Child-crime in Handsworth, as in all inner cities, is so widespread that the mere legalising of ganja would scarcely make much difference. That very evening, on my way to the Grey Dove, I had intervened to stop a typical bit of nastiness at the junction of the Villa and Hamstead Roads. Few people were around at 6.15 and three puny White boys – aged ten or eleven – were helping a Black boy of about the same age, but much taller and heftier, to beat up a small terrified Bangladeshi boy. His even smaller sister, wearing a tattered frilly party-frock, had flattened herself against the wall, arms outstretched like a crucifix, and was silently sobbing with terror. The little fellow's English was not fluent, yet quite good enough to tell me what had happened. On seeing his attackers trying to force open the ground-floor window of a nearby terrace house, he had bravely raised the alarm by ringing the next house's doorbell. When the Black boy vaulted over the low intervening garden wall and attempted to seize him he ran away and was overtaken where I came upon the incident. I escorted the children home (the little girl was so upset I had to carry her) and found that neither of their parents spoke one word of English.

A few days before, while standing at a bus-stop on Hamstead Road, I had seen a classic juvenile shop-theft when two other pre-teenage boys 'did' the

Pakistani grocery-cum-newsagency opposite the bus-stop. The White boy entered first and 'accidentally' knocked over a pile of tinned fruit at the back of the shop, luring the foolish owner away from his position behind the counter. Then the Black boy darted in – as I, in my new role as plain-clothes WPC, ran across the road. When he emerged with a plastic bag of chocolate bars, swiftly swept off the counter, I made to grab him. But he eluded me with a rugger-player's swerve and vanished around the nearby corner. Meanwhile his mate had vanished in the other direction. The shopkeeper spread his hands in a hopeless gesture and said No, he wouldn't bother informing the police – it irritated them to have to record such trivial incidents . . .

A bag of chocolate bars is of course trivial: almost engagingly so. And I'm told shop-lifting has become a popular sport among British schoolchildren of all sorts. Yet the fatalism of that obviously not prosperous Pakistani worried me. When a large proportion of any community comes to accept crime (minor and major) as inevitable, that climate of opinion must surely encourage more and more law-breaking. Which was the reasoning behind the local Residents' Association's demands for vigorous police action against drug-pushers and the closing of the Villa Cross.

On 21 August the *Birmingham Evening Mail* gave huge headlines to 'PLEA FOR ACTION TO END DRUG TRADING'. The report said:

> Residents are demanding action to stamp out illegal trading around a Birmingham public house. People living near the Villa Cross pub in Handsworth have called a public meeting on September 5 to express their anger . . . Mr Eric Faux, chairman of the Soho Hill Residents' Association, said the drugs problem was more prevalent in this area than other parts of the city . . . Mrs Denise Forsyth, secretary of the Handsworth Association, said "You can see the transactions going on outside the pub". Supt. David Love, of Thornhill Road police station, said, "The problem has been quite marked but since the raid in May and with the co-operation of the licensee and the brewery, the position is much quieter. We are not naive enough to think the drugs problem will go away as a result of a couple of raids, but I think that with sensible policing it can be reduced and limited." A spokesman for the pub owners, Ansells, said the brewery was as much concerned as anyone else with what had happened around the Villa Cross.

That evening I wrote in my journal:

> A cold wet evening so no one on the forecourt, but even allowing for that the Villa Cross unusually crowded for mid-week. Tension extreme: highest I've known. Everyone so quarrelsome and jittery drinks being spilled all over the place. I've never seen the placid-seeming Kevin look so worried. Copies of the *Evening Mail* being furiously read. Dissension about whether or not Rasta spokesmen should attend Residents' meeting. Even my good friends ignored me. Odd sensation, people talking across me as though I *weren't there*. General opinion, being violently expressed – if pub closed and Villa Cross bingo-hall not allowed to become an amusement arcade there will be *very* big trouble. One forecast: "It'll make Brixton look like a Boys' Brigade outing!" Another: "We'll put Handsworth in the history

books!" Just more Black bravado? Like Tobias said, "You don't want to take Black *talk* seriously." Yet somehow this evening it didn't *feel* like bravado. There was a new note of defiance and determination. Also two new girls, by arrangement with the 'usuals' who've gone on hard-earned hol's. One a tall, slender, ebony-skinned Rasta with spectacular dreadlocks, wearing a man's gaberdine raincoat over a shiny, skin-tight black leather suit. She strengthened my view that the female Rasta is *much* deadlier than the male. Incredibly aggressive. Enjoyed getting into other people's rows (no shortage this evening!) and banging her fists on tables. At one point she hit me hard across the head with her umbrella, for no apparent reason – except of course I'm White. Luckily I have a very thick skull; she seemed surprised I didn't drop to the floor. Her companion quite a contrast – Afro-Chinese from Guyana – very beautiful and serene and disdainfully amused by the shambles, even when someone deliberately poured a bottle of beer down her *décolletage*. Also a new consignment of Lebanese Gold on offer. Two young White men spent £30 each: told me that's their personal supply for a month. It's not an expensive form of relaxation – no more than I spend on mini-cigars. Awful thought. Must try again to give them up.

A photograph of the Villa Cross appeared on the front page of the September issue of Handsworth's freesheet, the *Soho Star*. The banner headline read: 'LICENCE FOR DRUGS? – Residents Oppose Pub Renewal'. The story was almost unbelievably irresponsible, given Handsworth's inflammable (literally) atmosphere at the end of August:

> Residents have declared war on Villa Cross drug pushers and are launching an all-out bid to have the Villa Cross pub, alleged to be a base for pushers, closed. At a public meeting on September 5 seven Residents' Associations are uniting in a campaign to have the pub's licence refused when it comes up for renewal next February. One Residents' leader warned that growing anger at pushers selling heroin and cocaine openly in Birmingham could lead to vigilante groups taking the law into their own hands . . . The meeting, to which representatives of Ansells and Davenports breweries have been invited as well as police, will be told that the landlord of the Villa Cross was powerless to prevent the trafficking in killer drugs. Seamus Collins, Chairman of the Handsworth Residents' Association, said, "The Villa Cross has become a very dangerous place. You have to be very brave indeed to throw a pusher out of the pub when he is there with several big friends. We also want plans for an amusement arcade at the Villa Cross dropped. It is exactly the kind of place which will attract the pushers because of the children who will visit it . . ." Supt. David Love said that Birmingham police recently transferred another fifteen officers to drug-squad duties and now have the second largest drug fighting unit in the country. He added, "We have our eye on several other pubs and clubs. Pushers can expect further police raids. It is too early to say whether we will oppose the renewal of the pub's licence. Since our raids the situation at the Villa Cross has improved and if it continues to improve there would be no reason to oppose the licence." A spokesman for Ansells confirmed that the pub was in line for a complete refurbishment programme in the coming year. A facelift for the Beehive, once a notorious haunt of pushers, helped solve the problem there.

I read all this dangerous nonsense with a mixture of fear, bewilderment and outrage. Fear, for obvious reasons. Bewilderment because Handsworth's police commander's tough talk suggested *either* that he hadn't been listening to his community police *or* that they had become totally ineffective as interpreters of the local mood. Threats of further police raids on several other pubs and clubs were what the district did *not* need at the beginning of September 1985.

However, my strongest feelings was outrage at the accusation that 'trafficking in killer drugs' took place in the Villa Cross. By then I had been closely watching 'the trade' for three months. At the end of July two ganja-dealers, alleged to have been pushing heroin elsewhere in Handsworth, were roughly dealt with by their fellow-dealers, who knew that police tolerance of ganja would evaporate still further if heroin came on the local scene. Not long after, an 'outsider' Black approached the pub as I was entering and I paused to watch him being forcibly thrown down the steps by four Rastas. He was an interloper from Small Heath, working for a Pakistani heroin pusher. Although not all Rastas are incorruptible concerning hard drugs, most avoid them on ethical or quasi-religious grounds. In Handsworth Park during the summer I had met several pathetic White junkies but none was on the Villa Cross scene.

Coincidentally, during that week an article in the *New Statesman* (30 August 1985), by Ian Williams, reported a similar situation in Liverpool:

> Ironically, one of the few parts of the city which has remained relatively free from the youth heroin problem is the Black ghetto of Liverpool 8 in Toxteth – allegedly a no-go area for police. Cannabis it has had. But for many people in the area smoking ganja is seen as being no different from having a quick half in the pub. During Toxteth's Carnival, a do-it-yourself 'Anti-Smack' squad broke into heroin pushers' houses and ransacked them. There was remarkable restraint in the police's formal exhortations 'not to take the law into their own hands', reflecting the widespread feeling that the youth of the community had enough problems without the addition of heroin usage . . . The Black Anti-Smack League spokesman said, "The neighbours came out and applauded when the raids were going on. These people are *loaded* and there's big muscle behind them. But we've got the whole community behind *us*!"

The *Soho Star* accusation prompted a perceptible closing of Black ranks. I had supped the week before with an elderly couple whose misfortune it was to live opposite a large Rasta squat. When I expressed doubts about the wisdom of organising a public meeting which amounted to a Whites versus Rasta confrontation, the husband's reply was forceful: "You can take good community relations too far. Why should those lads feel they can get away with anything just because they're Black? From that house over there this whole street is kept awake all night – you can hear it too from your place – you well know I'm not complaining for the sake of it. And most of us on this road are decent citizens, paying hundreds a year in rates – so's the police can be paid to give us a quiet life. Then the Rastas have stories about 'police harassment' if a Panda comes and asks them 'Turn down the volume' at 3.00 a.m.! Aren't we entitled to have our right to sleep protected? Sleep is a *very* important human right! White do-gooders accuse people like me of being 'disloyal to our own' when we complain – they invent all kinds of excuses for Blacks going to the bad. It's everybody's fault except the kids'! But we don't see Black criminals as 'our own' any more that White criminals or Asian criminals. No one else makes trouble here – *they* cause all the problems! It's time local people forced the police to get tough, even if it makes a bit of bother in the short run. I'm not interested in excuses. There's still more good young Blacks than bad – being young and Black doesn't mean you've *gotta* be bad!"

The day after the *Soho Star* appeared, I met the same Jamaican in a telephone queue. He was then feeling very strongly that the Rastas are 'our own'. "You seen the Residents figure our lads push 'killer drugs'? So they've 'declared war' on the Villa Cross! They should think more before they talk . . . So they may get war – and who suggested it? The Residents!"

All my older friends resented that *Soho Star* report. Seeing crowds of virtuously glowing and well-groomed Blacks swarming around Hand-sworth's churches, it is easy to forget that among them are the parents of many 'Front-line troops'. Unlike their misinformed White contemporaries, those Blacks know the difference between hard drugs and cannabis; and they know too that Rasta defiance stops short of pushing killer drugs. Also, they rightly scented racialism in this too-successful attempt to associate Rastas with hard drugs. By that stage it had become painfully evident that for many Whites this moral crusade was serving as a safety-valve for the release of long-pent-up anti-'*coloured*' (not just anti-Rasta) feelings. By flaunting their law-breaking the Rastas had given local Whites a legitimate grievance. But it shook me to discover how many Residents' Associations members were rejoicing at having found a good excuse – not overtly 'racist' – for 'hammer-ing the Blacks'.

Some other Whites shared my misgivings about the Residents' meeting. One Irishman – Jimjo, a Handsworth resident since 1960 – said he belonged to his local Association but wouldn't attend because "it can only make bad worse". The brewery's claim that 'a facelift for the Beehive, once a notorious haunt of pushers, helped solve the problem there' had infuriated him. "Who are they trying to con?" he demanded. "As long as hash is coming into this country and Blacks want it you can't stop the trade – only move it from place to place, making more aggro. My work gives me a good look at policing around here and for the past while we've been doing fine. Till April we'd a great fella at Thornhill Road, a Super. who knew the score – knew you *couldn't* stop the ganja trade without race relations falling to bits. Which is what's happening now. We've a new Chief Constable – a right fascist bastard he is too! – and a new Super. And themselves and the Residents are just egging each other on like there was no tomorrow. That's misfortunate. I may be an Irishman, but I'll tell you something straight. Give or take the odd fascist, England's police could teach the world. Any other country, they'd have these

Rasta lads in irons – and *that* wouldn't do any good, for there's always more leaving school! And you'd alienate every Black in Britain. Our police here, they try to *think* through it all – or they *did* . . . And it's no picnic policing Handsworth. Those Rastas, the way they hate the fuzz is just pathological!"

I couldn't disagree. The paranoid quality of that hatred had been most apparent to me in the Villa Cross on the evening of 24 August. Very early that morning an armed West Midlands policeman, raiding a burglar's house, had accidentally killed a sleeping five-year-old boy – his gun went off as he bent to look under the child's bed. The normal reaction to such tragedies is a feeling of almost equal sympathy for the victim, his family and the unfortunate killer. But the Villa Cross atmosphere – already of course in an anti-fuzz ferment – went poisonous with the most foul allegations against that wretched officer. Perhaps this mass-reaction, emanating from a group many of whom were kindly *individuals*, was yet another harbinger of disaster.

On 2 September I had my first inner-city visitor – Mary, a San Francisco friend who during the 1960s was deeply involved in America's Civil Rights Movement. We spent most of the day talking in my pad, mainly about inner-city/Black problems. As we left for a quick drink at the Villa Cross, before a Punjabi meal on the Soho Road, I said dismally, "There just doesn't seem to be *any* answer to any of it!"

Mary wouldn't have that. "Of course there's an answer! It's just Britain's twenty years behind America – all you've said takes me right back to where we were in the sixties! First the Whites have to face up to the depth and scope of prejudice and discrimination, like we did in our *Riot Commission Report* – and remember that was put together by what you'd call Establishment folk, not by Civil Rights activists. Next, you need positive discrimination and no messing – no wondering will the voters like it or won't they. And then you need millions and millions and millions of dollars – or pounds. And then some more millions, if necessary. All that doesn't solve the problem – it's just a good beginning. No way can you compare the situation of American Blacks *now* and twenty-five years ago. Not everyone likes that answer, but anyone who can see into the next decade will buy it. Pretending there's no solution – even pretending there's no *problem*, which a lot of Americans did for as long as they could – that can cost more in the sunset. Which we found out the hard way."

I had decided that we should go early to the Villa Cross, before trading-time, because of Mary's being an outsider. But it was yet another chilly and very wet day and already a score or so had gathered around the bar, including some of my 'enemies'. As we stood waiting for our drinks the vibes were powerfully hostile. We sat in my usual corner, otherwise empty, and soon were being pelted with large lumps of ice – coming from behind the high wooden partition near the door. Mary looked slightly unnerved. I said, "Don't react, seem not to notice." And after about six or seven minutes the aggro stopped, leaving a lakelet of melting ice on the floor around us.

"Is it always like this?" asked Mary.

"No," I said, "you've just coincided with a wee bit of tension in the area."

"A *wee* bit?" said Mary. "I guess you've picked up that British understatement habit!"

Half-an-hour later, as we walked down the Villa Road (more bad vibes outside the Acapulco) I told Mary something about the local scene. "Whose side are you on?" she asked.

"Everyone's!" I replied. "That's what's so emotionally exhausting about Handsworth – it's too easy to see all the points of view."

Next morning I was a dutiful hostess; having collected Mary from her hotel I took her to the city-centre open-air Bull Ring market. And when I saw her elaborate camera I didn't tease her about being 'a typical American tourist'; she is an excellent photographer – artistic rather than touristic. But even the Bull Ring was not entirely tension-free. As Mary stood near a clothing-stall at the end of an aisle, focusing on a colourful row of greengrocery stalls, a young Black man emerged from the clothing-stall, jostled her roughly and said, "You can't take photographs here – you've no right to – I pay for this stall, now you're keeping my customers away! Fuck off!"

Mary politely pointed out that she wasn't in fact photographing *his* stall, then again tried to get her special picture. Whereupon the young man became loudly abusive – and Mary moved away. I lingered to ask him *why* he felt so strongly about an obvious tourist taking an innocent picture. He glared at me sullenly, then replied, "Photos are for family times, or for people to give each other – or for police records. See?"

Mary said such Black/White 'incidents' are not uncommon in the States – where indeed I have myself experienced a few, when travelling by Greyhound Bus. Later we described the encounter to a local White friend who asked, "Can you blame them? They've put up with so much, they won't take any more. Isn't it the same thing, really, now in South Africa – only on a different scale?"

Was that too charitable a reaction? Does it help Blacks to excuse behaviour that can only increase White prejudice? Should they not be made to realise that even from their own point of view, never mind the everyday civilities, it is destructive to assert themselves in this way? I was shocked by the strength of my own angry resentment of that young man's aggression. Granted, the Handsworth atmospherics had by then made me a trifle edgy. And the fact of a guest of mine being abused perhaps partly explains what was an inwardly uncivilised reaction, concealed behind a façade of sweet reasonableness. That tiny incident was instructive. It helped me to understand why on occasions Black/White aggro gets so quickly out of hand, when uncivilised reactions are *not* concealed.

Vibes apart, Mary was enchanted by Handsworth, especially when summer at last arrived on 4 September – hot sun, a cloudless sky, no breeze, clear air, perfect photography weather. After lunch we strolled down Heathfield Road, turned right up Leonard Road and returned to the Villa Cross along Lozells Road. I knew it would be sensible to restrain Mary's camera wielding in this area but after a brief inner debate I allowed one of my worst weaknesses to conquer prudence. In such situations I am handicapped by an obstinate aversion to being intimidated, an irrational gut-feeling – This is a free country, even on the Rastas' front line, so why shouldn't an innocent American tourist photograph 'architectural curiosities'? It was unfortunate that one of those happened to be the Villa Cross bingo hall opposite the pub, a floridly impressive Moorish-flavoured edifice built as a cinema in 1912 and converted to bingo in 1970. For the previous month or so it had been rumoured that the police were using the bingo hall to spy on ganja-dealers.

We returned to my pad, where Mary had left a sack of laundry, and I then escorted her across the front line to a grotty little washeteria on the Villa Road, run by two ancient White women with the assistance of an eight-year-old Pakistani girl on whom they doted. There I abandoned Mary, being keen to hear a Radio 4 programme about Northern Ireland; I promised to collect her after the programme.

There were unusually few Rastas about that afternoon. But as I passed the Acapulco – walking on the edge of the pavement, with a parked car between me and the café – one of my Villa Cross 'enemies' was lounging in the doorway. He yelled a string of unflattering epithets and threats, which normally I would have ignored. But for some reason that I didn't understand (and still don't) it suddenly seemed important to pay attention. I paused and looked at him across the bonnet of the car and asked amiably, "Were you saying something to me?" His reply was loud but incomprehensible. Slowly I walked round the car and stood close in front of him and repeated, "Were you saying something?" His reply was a stream of graphically obscene threats – the sort of language that is in itself a strangely effective form of attack on middle-aged, middle-class women who have led comparatively sheltered lives. His accusations were that all the Rastas' problems started when I came to Handsworth, that I had been conclusively identified as a police informer, that I had been co-ordinating the Residents' Associations' campaign to close the Villa Cross, that 'my friend with the camera' was collecting evidence for the police and that it was well known I 'gave signals' to Drug-Squad spies in the bingo hall as I left the Villa Cross to go home.

"You walk up and down this road one day more – you go spying and peering and looking at the ganja scales – you bring friends to take our pictures – you won't last, see? Not one day more, see? You want a bottle on your head? And it be a long time before you wake up to tell your friends who hit you! See?" He wasn't drunk, I noticed.

I'm not all that easily scared, but as he spoke I could *feel* myself going pale with fear – not because of his threats of physical violence, which I didn't take too seriously, but because of the concentrated hatred which was being focused on me. This can only be described as a psychic attack and it was immeasurably more frightening than any bodily assault. When I explained – in a pleasant, level tone – that he was quite mistaken about my role in Handsworth, he became still more enraged. By then about a dozen express-ionless Rastas had gathered round to listen. All were Villa Cross regulars, yet it was impossible to gauge whose side they were on. Suddenly some instinct made me feel it was essential to outstare my enemy (no longer in inverted commas). Instead of continuing quietly to listen to his abuse, I moved even closer and held his gaze. The Rastas stood motionless and silent – both states unusual for them – and he too at once fell silent. It may sound unreal in cold print, but I wrote later in my journal – 'There was some strange contest involved.' After what seemed a very long moment my adversary turned his head slightly. I then strolled off through the group of Rastas, feigning insouciance but feeling extraordinarily drained of energy – and beginning to tremble all over. I went back to the washeteria instead of to my pad and belatedly told Mary to conceal her camera. We walked home to Heathfield Road a long way round, to avoid the front line, and Mary commented – "I guess it's a mistake to team up with D.M. if you need to *unwind* on vacation . . ."

Our plans for the evening had not included a drink at the Villa Cross, but after that incident it seemed essential for me to show the flag if I intended continuing as a regular: Mary endorsed this decision and as she is by profession 'a resolver of conflicts' I valued her opinion. By then she had admitted to being slightly rattled by our local vibes, so I assured her that she need not accompany me. But it is not Mary's way to back off from bad vibes and we went together.

The tension felt hyper yet oddly subdued. No aggro was directed towards us and none of the usual extrovert conversations was being shouted above reggae decibels. We had not long settled in when a Black man arrived (unknown to me but welcomed by several regulars) with his daughters aged three and four – the first Black children I had ever seen in the Villa Cross. Both wore heavy grey winter coats, despite the evening's mid-summer-like heat. When Dad had provided them with crisps the four-year-old walked sedately across to our corner and sat beside me, swinging her legs and ignoring us as she opened her packet – with some difficulty. On entering the pub she had stared at us unsmilingly, so I refrained from offering assistance. Then, before helping herself, she selected one large crisp and silently handed it to me – and one more which she leant forward to hand to Mary. Her expression remained unchanged: solemn, self-contained. This formal, ritualistic sharing moved us both intensely; in that super-charged atmosphere it felt like a sacrament of reconciliation received from the soul and hands of a tiny Black girl. When I woke next morning *that* was the dominant image in my mind – the most enduring image from the day before.

Two important events were marked in my calendar-diary for 5 September: the anti-Rasta Residents' Association meeting at 7.30 p.m. and the arrival of my daughter at New Street Station at 10.30 a.m. I had scarcely seen Rachel since January. Now, after a dissolute summer Euro-railing around the Continent, she had decided on a forty-eight-hour 'inner-city experience' before starting her last year at school on 9 September. As I walked down the Villa Road at 9.00 a.m. to catch a New Street bus, four friends (one Black, three Brown) stopped me because they had heard about the previous day's 'confrontation' – or had witnessed it from a distance. Each suggested that it might be time for me to 'study' another multi-racial area and their advice comforted me, both as evidence of neighbourly concern and as a reassurance that I had not been neurotically over-reacting to that incident.

On the bus I talked with a Black woman (forty-ish) going to work in the city centre. "Those Residents' Associations," she said, "they're all *White* folk. That's our fault. Why weren't we right in there from the start? Now they've forgotten there's thousands of *Black* residents in Handsworth! My son says the police are running them – always have, through the Council – and now using them against the Rastas. So how's that for community policing? Setting the communities at each other's throats! My lad wouldn't go near the Villa Cross – but he hears things . . . The police have another story, saying the Residents are forcing *them* to close the pub. Right now there's so many lies and rumours around, you couldn't believe your granny!"

I had long since promised my Rasta friends that when Rachel came I would introduce her to the Villa Cross; by local standards, bringing a sixteen-year-old into a pub seemed a minor infringement. As things were, a lunch-time drink seemed appropriate: my 'enemies' were rarely present at that hour. I deliberately did not discuss 'how things were' with Rachel, though my being insulted as we crossed the front line forced me to concede 'a wee bit of tension' (which had become a catch-phrase between Mary and myself). However, on that Thursday even the lunch-time vibes were such that Rachel, paling beneath her Euro-tan, asked my permission to smoke "just *one*" cigarette. Happily Ben arrived at that point (a very congenial Rasta) and joined us in 'my' corner to outline the plot of a play he was writing. I offered to type it for him and he promised to bring the MS to my pad on 10 September. Sadly, I haven't seen him since.

In my journal for 5 September I wrote:

Today's Villa Cross session was the most relaxed for some time. R.'s presence seemed to put an astonishing curb on the words and deeds of some of the more boisterously lewd young bucks. A few drifted over to admire her, but in a way that gratified Mamma; no crude insinuations, just politely paying court to a rather personable young woman. It was odd, having this sudden glimpse of another, 'gentlemanly' aspect of their characters. When Ben gravely proposed to R. the others wished him luck – jokingly, but in the most agreeable way. His proposal was a joke only because of the *age* difference. The *colour* difference would never occur to Ben, who is magnificently without hang-ups.

The Residents' Association meeting was held just off Villa Road, at the narrow, ill-lit, waste-land end of Hunters Road, in a beat-up red-brick building – Bonner's Memorial School Hall. That morning I had noticed a hand-written poster on the door: 'At This Evening's Meeting Questions Are To Be Confined to The Cross.' It was no longer in place when we arrived at 7.25, to see the Lord Mayor's enormous official limousine almost blocking the entire roadway. Police stood guard all evening over this provocative vehicle – one of the 'chariots of Babylon'. As a (sensitive) White resident muttered to me, "Anyone with an ounce of imagination would have borrowed a mini for this jaunt!" Such minute details, which may seem of huge unimportance to the outsider, can assume great and real significance in such areas on such occasions. Many Rastas and other young Blacks are motor-car worshippers; they covet a *good* car and know they will never possess *any* car . . .

The Lord Mayor – a Labour Councillor, Frank Carter – was wearing his chain of office and a red carnation. With him on the platform were the Chief of Birmingham's newly enlarged Drug-Squad; two Handsworth Superintendents (past and present), Martin Burton and David Love; a few local Councillors and Residents' Associations officials; a terrified young man representing Ansell's brewery and clearly convinced the Rastas were going to have him for supper; the Manager of Birmingham City FC, Ron Saunders, who at that time was running his own anti-drugs campaign (Save Our Society); and a Labour MP, Jeff Rooker, who tried to turn the meeting into a party political occasion. (It would have been no bad thing had he succeeded.) In the body of the hall were about 200 Residents – mostly angry verbose Whites and a few Asians who said nothing. Three Rastas represented the Villa Cross regulars. Also present in the audience was James Hunte, the Black Chairman of Birmingham's CRC, who in his public statements sometimes supported the police and sometimes the Rastas – depending on his listeners' predilections.

Sitting beside me was a local White clergyman, an influential figure who, when this meeting was first suggested, saw it as an obvious flash-point and tried to have it cancelled. But nobody would listen to him; other even more influential forces were by then at work. While recognising the Whites' grievances, he believed that a public meeting, attended by the Lord Mayor, was not the wisest outlet for White frustration and rage. The Lord Mayor was soon giving tongue in his accustomed manner – "As I've often said before, people who want to smoke this illegal stuff should go back where they came from, where it's legal!" As he sat down my clerical neighbour turned to me and whispered, "That's it! That's what I was afraid of – now we'll have the big trouble!" I then thought he was being over-pessimistic. But he has lived in Handsworth for many years and knows more than most about the local chemistry.

A Rasta stood up and asked with commendable restraint why the White fondness for alcohol and nicotine should be legal, when the Black fondness for comparatively harmless ganja is illegal. He spoke with dignity and courtesy; he was genuinely trying to start an intelligent debate on this ill-understood issue. But his perfectly reasonable question, addressed to the chairman of the meeting, was not taken seriously. In response, the Drug-Squad officer reasserted that "all illegal drugs dealers must be severely dealt with". And Superintendent Love said, "We believe children of thirteen and fourteen are being used as go-betweens because they are less likely to be stopped and searched." (As one of my Pentecostal neighbours remarked next day, "Some people believe the earth is flat! What proof does he have? When is he going to produce it?")

Also present – symbolically standing along one wall, not sitting with the rest of us – were half-a-dozen of my Heathfield Road neighbours from the austere-living and normally anti-Rasta and anti-ganja Marcus Garvey Foundation. As usual they had a lot to say about White racialism and they said it much more forcefully than the Rastas had done. An ineffective chairman allowed things to get more and more out of hand. Furious Whites retaliated by elaborating on the malicious police allegations about child couriers, and providing graphic details of the dire effects of all-night Blues parties on the neighbourhood, and condemning Blacks for driving untaxed cars, parking illegally, and generally taking over and terrorising the entire area. At one point a bizarre unanimity was briefly achieved when everyone denounced the idea of using the bingo hall as a gigantic amusement arcade where, in the general opinion, *hard-drugs* dealers would be likely to operate. But much more aggro soon followed, during which the chairman said – "Teenagers stand to get hooked on cannabis and they will be stuck into it like they have been with glue-sniffing!" A Rasta tried to point out that glue-sniffing is frequently lethal but that ganja is incapable of killing anyone. His words were ignored; this whole meeting was a nasty example of mass-resistance to inconvenient facts. Both residents and police were determined not to be deprived of their anti-Black stick by the introduction into the debate of scientific knowledge. It was a relief when the chairman ended this verbal brawl by announcing that another Residents' meeting would be held soon to discuss what had been discussed during the evening . . .

In my view the most significant event had occurred in the course of a particularly venomous Black/White exchange when the Rasta and MGF leaders stood up to shake hands publicly in the middle of the hall, while the seated audience stared at them uncomprehendingly. This gesture marking Black unity was perhaps not entirely irrelevant to the events of the following Monday night.

Next day the local press transformed Superintendent Love's hypothetical juvenile drug couriers into a menacing reality. The *Birmingham's Post*'s front page headlines screamed 'CHILDREN USED AS CITY DRUG CARRIERS'. And the *Evening Mail* was no less certain – 'CHILDREN

FERRY DRUGS: Action Call by Parents Over Crisis.' The *Post* reported that 'Angry Handsworth parents [said] trade in lethal drugs such as heroin and cocaine was rife and the problem was out of control'. The *Mail* quoted Superintendent Love: 'The effectiveness of the two recent raids in Handsworth shows that we are hitting the pushers where it hurts.' He was of course referring to the Villa Cross and Acapulco raids – not, inexplicably, to the major 1985 raid, on 20 August, when £300,000 worth of heroin was recovered from a Pakistani private house almost beside Thornhill Road police station. By that evening the anger level was rising fast among my *most* respectable Black neighbours. The majority had heard about the Lord Mayor's inflammatory comments, though neither paper had reported them. And the police effort to paint a totally false picture of the Handsworth drug scene was becoming daily more blatant.

On the afternoon of Saturday 7 September, as I was walking up Heathfield Avenue – a very short road just round the corner from my pad – a tall young Rasta overtook me, twisted my right arm violently, pushed me against the wall, trod hard on my left foot, repeated my other enemy's 'police informer' accusations and told me to get out of Handsworth. Then he raced off, round the corner into Radnor Road. That was a more painful but much less frightening episode than the first.

Twenty-four hours later I stood outside No. 45 watching the Carnival procession passing down Heathfield Road. Handsworth's annual Afro-Caribbean Carnival is perceived by many Blacks (not just Rastas) as Babylon-organised propaganda to show the outside world how well community policing has worked in Handsworth. The smallish crowd following the floats and steel bands was almost entirely Black and the occasion seemed to lack verve. A fortnight earlier I had gone to the Notting Hill Carnival with a group from the Marcus Garvey Foundation and had enjoyed eighteen hours of gaiety – including the bus journeys to and from London. It would be absurd to expect anything similar in Handsworth, yet an infusion of both Rasta and MGF high spirits could have done a lot, I felt, for the 1985 event. Observing the professionally matey community police in the procession, I wondered how they were *really* feeling... At that stage I still assumed the police must be aware of where the needle was on the tension-graph – despite Superintendent Love's evident unawareness at the Residents' meeting. On 29 August I had lunched with two senior police officers; but being a semi-trusted Villa Cross regular inhibited me from any explicit reporting of Rasta words and deeds. Had I realised how completely out of touch with local feeling the police then were, and had I been able to foresee the near future, I might have felt a duty to overcome my inhibitions. But the lack of second-sight spared me that nightmare writer's dilemma.

At about 5.10 p.m. on Monday 9 September I went out to post a letter, in which I mentioned my relief that Rachel had left Handsworth because 'things are getting rough around here'. They were in fact getting so rough that I never reached the post office. Instead, I returned to my pad at 5.40 and wrote in my journal:

Crossing the front line just now, saw three traffic-cops with motor-bikes (*not* local police) arguing with a driver who'd parked his car – and had no excise licence – on a double yellow line outside the Acapulco. Stood by the car and watched, scarcely able to credit what I was seeing. Given the atmospherics, for the fuzz to challenge – and try to arrest! – any Black today, in the heartland of Rasta territory, seemed an act of criminal stupidity. The cops soon realised their mistake and went white with fear beneath their huge helmets as about sixty Rastas crowded round, gesticulating and shouting the sort of gross insults to which I've recently become accustomed. The fuzz did *nothing* to provoke violence – apart from the initial error of trying to make an arrest at that spot! – yet within moments the first punch had been thrown and the action was on. Already the nearby shops had swiftly barred their doors and pulled down their steel shutters. Then a dozen local police arrived in Pandas, including two young women P Cs who walked into the middle of it all looking less scared than the males. At least the traffic cops were wearing heavy jackets and helmets; the locals were all in shirt-sleeves (today seems this summer's *hottest* in Brum) and looked alarmingly vulnerable as bricks and bottles flew from every direction – supplies are kept handy for such occasions – and litter-bins were torn from their moorings and used as weapons. I sheltered in the Acapulco doorway, able to watch every move in safety. For some reason one traffic cop tried to mount his machine and ride away. A Rasta rushed out and kicked him off it, sending him sprawling across the road. Groups of police and Blacks fought and several police vehicles were attacked. Inevitably there was a traffic-jam; the Villa Road carries heavy through traffic. A stupid bus-driver tried to edge forward – I suppose to try to get his vehicle out of range of flying missiles – just as a cop rolled half-under the bus in the course of a scuffle. For one ghastly moment I thought his torso was going to be squashed by the back wheels; then the driver heard a warning yell and stopped. It wasn't my impression that the Blacks deliberately pushed the cop under the bus; it simply happened that way. Only the senior officer was 'armed', with a pathetic short stick like quarter of a *lathi*. Wisely, he didn't use it, even when two cops were being rolled on the ground. Had he done so, we might have had a *real* riot. He left it to other P Cs to join in the fray, on equal fisticuff terms, and rescue their mates. Clever. I noticed again what's struck me before: the Rastas' bark is often worse than their bite. The cops were outnumbered by about five to one and could have been overwhelmed and mashed up. An interesting though not unusual feature was the violence of two Black women who joined in the swearing, punching and bottle-throwing as vigorously as any male. To an extent these confrontations seem like a game and both sides know how they're going to end. There's a ritualistic quality about the abusive language, missile throwing, kicking and vandalising police vehicles and (relatively) mildly assaulting cops. Then comes the arrest of a few Blacks (two this time) and suddenly the party's over . . . As the last Panda drove off, with two cops in the back literally sitting on an amiable (in my experience) Rasta, the brute who so frightened me last week came over and said, "Fuck off now, you dirty White c***! You've had a good time, right? Watching your bloodclot friends winning, right?" So I fucked off, to write down every detail while fresh. Writing easy today: arm much better. I feel I've long since ceased to 'study' Race Relations; now I'm just hanging in *surviving* Race Relations . . . No wonder poor R. thought

Handsworth's vibes "rather unsettling". But possibly this violence may, paradoxically, lower the tension – as *action* often does. To the Villa Cross now, to get Rasta reactions.

I didn't have to go even as far as the Villa Cross to get Rasta reactions. While writing the last few sentences I had smelt smoke but thought nothing of it; the season of garden bonfires was beginning. But when I stepped out of No. 45 at 7.25 I saw three fire-engines arriving outside the bingo hall beside the Acapulco. It was immediately apparent that this would be no routine fire-quelling operation; the atmosphere was electric, with Rastas yelling abuse at the firemen. (For some entirely inexplicable reason, firemen are regarded as allies of the police and so part of Babylon and 'legitimate targets', as the Provos would put it.) For a few moments I stood beside the engines, watching the hoses being unrolled. Then the bricks and bottles started flying and I moved, for the second time that day, to the shelter of the Acapulco doorway. This was two hours after the end of the last incident and there wasn't a policeman in sight. When a fireman was knocked unconscious by a brick one fire-engine sped him away to hospital. Another went around to Radnor Road, entered the bingo hall from the back and soon put out the small fire; no flames were ever visible from outside. As the third crew hastily rolled up its hoses the first petrol bombs were thrown from the Villa Cross forecourt. When petrol ignited on the pavement three yards away from me I reckoned it might be healthier to be behind rather than in front of the bombers. So I circled around them – they had a milk-crate full of petrol-bombs behind the wall – and entered the pub as eight unprotected police officers arrived from Thornhill Road in a Ford Transit van (also unprotected) which was at once rained with petrol bombs and other missiles and forced to withdraw to await reinforcements.

Kevin looked ashen – defeated. As he drew my pint of cider he said, "You'd better drink up quickly, we'll have to close soon." There were only three others in the bar; two Black youths still playing pool, ostentatiously ignoring the drama, and a very tall Rasta who stood by a window observing developments. The pub stands where the Villa Road ends and the Heathfield and Lozells Roads form the arms of a Y. I joined the Rasta as another police vehicle arrived; its windscreen was instantly smashed but a line of a dozen or so officers – with shields but without protective clothing – formed across the end of the Villa Road and held their ground while being petrol-bombed by about 200 Blacks.

At that point I had to accept the shocking fact that the police were *not* prepared for trouble at the Villa Cross – or even half-prepared. It later emerged in the Chief Constable's Report that at this time (8.00 p.m.) there were only *thirty-three* officers available, many of whom had to be used to prevent pedestrians or traffic from entering the riot area. However, if we are talking simply of courage, the West Midlands police covered themselves in glory that night. Their bravery was astounding. There is no other country in the world (except my own) where so few officers would be expected to face such appalling danger with such meagre equipment.

When another small group of police arrived – some protected, though inadequately – the rioters moved back slightly to the top of Lozells Road, directly opposite the Villa Cross windows. Thus they drew the fuzz into a position which left them vulnerable to being attacked also from the rear – from Barker Street. I crossed to a window overlooking this battle-site where the police were to be held, helpless, for the next two hours. Even to a sheltered non-participant, the scene was terrifying. So few policemen, so many Blacks hurling a variety of missiles – and all the time blazing bottles curving through the darkness and spurts of flame illuminating the ground around the fuzz. Very soon the unprotected officers were forced to withdraw: it would have been suicidal to do otherwise. Already a *protected* officer had been knocked to the ground by the sheer force behind one missile. I suddenly vividly remembered one Rasta friend's words, spoken in the Villa Cross on the evening of 10 July, after the raid on the Acapulco – "If the lid comes off while you're still around . . ." For three months I had been exposed to the Rastas' resentment, frustration, despair, rage and irrational hatred of the fuzz – as representing the very *essence* of Babylon. It didn't surprise me that one thrown missile could fell a policeman. I had listened often enough to verbal expressions of the energies that propelled that missile. The very tall Rasta was standing beside me as I silently surveyed the sort of scene that doesn't seem real when it's happening almost literally in your front garden. He said – quietly, but with the joy of triumph in his voice – "Man, you ain't seen nuthin' yet! Wait till we've got our mortar bombs!"

Kevin shouted at us – "For Christ's sake get away from the windows!" It was the first time I had ever heard him raising his voice or using profane language. Most of the bar lights were switched off then and the Rasta left; the oblivious pool-playing youths had already been sent home. I helped to draw heavy curtains across all the pub's windows. "Otherwise we could be a target," Kevin explained. "It wouldn't make sense, but there's no sense left out there." He wanted me to spend the night in the Villa Cross. "You can't go out now," he insisted. "It's got too bad – they're taking over." He hurried off then, to attend to a woman who had become hysterical (clinically hysterical) somewhere in the background. I gulped the rest of my pint, said good-bye to the barmaids and at 8.20 was the last customer to leave the Villa Cross before it closed – for ever.

I left through a normally unused door on the quiet Heathfield Road side and sprinted to the first turning on the right – Mayfield Road – which took me back onto Lozells Road. There I paused for a moment. About 100 yards away on my right the Blacks were still holding their position outside the pub; by now dense smoke from their heavy petrol-bombing marked the spot. Much closer, on my left, two large vans had been overturned and set alight at the Finch Road/Burbury Street junction; between that junction and the pub, the Lozells Road is mainly residential. Dozens of Blacks and a few Brown youths were racing towards the main shopping area beyond the fiercely burning vehicles. As I trotted after them two ferocious-looking but normally amiable Rastas sped past me – then recognised their regular drinking-companion and paused to shout kindly, "Get home you stupid bitch!"

I shouted back, "Thanks, but I'm on duty!" Human beings are peculiar. Where is the logic in being scared rigid when nothing is happening – as I was during the previous week – yet dead cool when everything is happening? Once the action starts the tension is over and adrenalin flows and away one dashes without a care in the world – very odd!

A fire-engine had just come onto the Lozells Road through side-streets and its crew was bravely attempting to deal with the burning vehicles; but they were savagely attacked and forced to withdraw quickly. No more fire-engines were seen anywhere in the area until about 10.30. It would have been futile for them to try to intervene without police protection.

Beyond the blazing vans I saw several other vehicles being set alight at strategic junctions. At first this looked like nothing more than anarchic destructiveness. Being rather slow-witted, I didn't realise until a little later that a looting area was thus being efficiently isolated from law-and-order interference. But by midnight my observations had convinced me that considerable pre-planning was involved.

The next ninety minutes felt so weirdly unreal I could scarcely believe it was all happening. During that extraordinary interlude I watched the Have-nots running riot, systematically looting and burning shops without any apparent risk of police intervention. Although started by Blacks, this was certainly no *race*-riot. Within a quarter of an hour many Browns and Whites had zestfully joined in the plundering, some hurrying from nearby areas when the local media news-flashed: 'RIOTING IN HANDSWORTH!' Prim and proper White women from little terrace houses off the Lozells Road – houses with sparkling windows and neatly pruned roses in their front garden patches – came rushing to load up prams, baby-buggies and wheelbarrows. Motor-vans and car boots were being frenziedly stuffed with goodies. And the Blacks were in a sharing mood. I saw many come leaping out of smashed shop windows to throw armfuls of loot on the street – or *lay* it on the street, in cases of delicate electronic equipment – while inviting all and sundry to help themselves. It was quite clear at this early stage that many looters regarded the operation as something more than a conventional criminal exercise in 'gain for me'. I have a most vivid memory of one elated Black youth, his face copper-coloured in the glow of flames, inviting a White woman to choose from his pile of shoe-boxes – while the emptied shoe-shop blazed in the background. "What do you need?" he asked her – shouting above the roar of the new fire. Has anyone seriously heeded this aspect of Handsworth's riot – '*What do you need?*' – and recognised its implications for the future?

Another memory is of laughing looters being cheered by onlookers as they pushed heaped supermarket trolleys down the middle of the road between high sheets of flame: I couldn't have believed those trolleys were capable of such speed. The atmosphere was totally free of any threat of inter-personal violence, racial or otherwise; it was not even a quarrelsome – far less a 'murderous' – night. Aggro was confined to the Rasta versus fuzz battle, still in progress outside the Villa Cross. There was of course a slight risk of injury from the combustible environment as car-engines, petrol-pumps and domestic gas-cylinders in the burning buildings exploded – and some of the buildings themselves began to collapse. Yet during those chaotic twelve hours only *seven* civilians were injured: a figure which tells more about the nature of the riot than any number of 'Reports'.

To compound the unreality one pub – the Lozells Arms – stayed open while the shops all around it were going up in flames. Outside the door stood a group of Black, White and Brown men, calmly swigging their pints and viewing the riot as though it were some form of street entertainment. Another pint of cider was just what I needed but had not, in the circumstances, expected to find. Half a dozen customers still sat in the pub; as the barman drew my pint I suggested that it might be time to clear the place. Then I joined the drinkers on the pavement.

In a bizarre way the feeling was of a perverted lunatic carnival rather than a riot. But the heat was intense; now all the multi-racial looters looked the same copper colour in the glow of towering flames. And still more shops, having been swiftly stripped of their stock, were being set alight with manic glee. Providentially the evening was windless. One felt sick with fear to think of the consequences should a breeze spring up and take the flames down the many little nearby streets of crowded houses.

At about nine o'clock I had passed Lozells Post Office; the adjacent buildings were ablaze but it seemed undamaged. Some fifteen minutes later I came running back, to get away from a burning garage, and saw it in flames. A Pakistani youth told me – "People are inside!" But I didn't believe him; by then it seemed incredible that anyone would have stayed in any building along Lozells Road.

By ten o'clock there wasn't much left of the Lozells shopping area; some £16 million worth of property was burning. In harrowing contrast to the carnival spirit of the looters was the dazed, incredulous grief of the traders – the majority Brown. Most were as yet too shocked to be angry; rage came later. At the end of Lozells Road I found a group sitting on the edge of the pavement near an expanse of wasteland, opposite their burning premises, weeping like little children. An elderly Pakistani man stood alone, slightly apart from the rest, sobbing and repeatedly mopping his tears with his shirt-sleeve. A passing Black youth – empty-handed – paused and crossed the road to put an arm around the trader's shoulder. Then he offered him a cigarette and a moment later they walked away together, round the corner into Wheeler Street – where shortly before I had seen the Midland Bank being ransacked.

I was amidst a maze of side-streets, where I saw more petrol bombs being made in the grounds of Holte School, during the first police advance – in a fully protected van – down Lozells Road. Vehicles were being overturned and set alight in the side streets by smallish gangs of youths – mainly Black, but supported by a few Browns. However, some protected police were at last visible, being sporadically attacked by yelling youths as they tried to cordon off the approaches to the main riot area. I returned circuitously to that area and reached the corner of Malthouse Gardens in time to see a phalanx of police, still under heavy attack from missiles and petrol bombs, slowly fighting their way through the by now almost intolerable heat of the Lozells Road. An elderly White couple were also watching. "They're risking their lives!" said the husband. "And what use are they now? There's not much left to loot! Why didn't they come two hours ago? They got 'phone calls by the dozen – they knew well what was going on . . . Why did they give those Black bastards *two hours* to help themselves? And do *this* to Lozells!" As he spoke his wife suddenly burst into tears – and then a policeman appeared beside us and said the area might have to be evacuated because of the risk of a massive garage explosion in nearby Berner Street.

During the rest of the night – while firemen were coping with the inferno and police were protecting firemen from rioters and residents from fire – I wandered about talking to people of all colours. In retrospect I realised that by then we were all – even those least personally affected – in a state of shock. And it was shock at two levels. To see a large part of one's neighbourhood destroyed by fire within ninety minutes would be traumatic even if the blaze were accidental. But for most the greater shock was the knowledge that it had been destroyed because the police could not (or, as many believed that night, *would not*) protect it. To the average citizen that was more profoundly frightening than the potential danger should a wind suddenly spring up before the firemen gained control.

While the riot was at its most dramatic I had been shaken to observe several elderly Blacks, whom I knew to be devout church-goers, encouraging the looting and burning – though not of course taking part in it. As I toured the side-streets during the small hours many other 'good citizen' Blacks refused to condemn the rioters, as most of their White and Brown neighbours were then doing – even some who had, a few hours earlier, taken advantage of the disorder to 'stock up'. Instead, these pillars of Pentecostalism were openly identifying with the 'activists' and sharing in the general Black euphoria. I kept in touch with these individuals and within forty-eight hours their 'un-respectable' emotions had been suppressed and law-abiding attitudes were again prevailing; most of them later attended an inter-faith two-hour service of reconciliation in a Methodist Church on the Lozells Road almost opposite the Villa Cross – a symbolic site. Yet what they revealed that night seemed to me at least as genuine as their 'respectable' aspect: and possibly more so. It felt as though a vast reservoir of repressed resentment of White racialism had suddenly burst its dam. Most 'immigrant-generation' Blacks may choose to ignore the manifold disadvantages of being Black in Britain. But that does not mean they are insensitive to their second-class-citizen status, or indifferent to the impotent anguish of the younger generation. So perhaps after all it is true to say that at the deepest level this *was* a race-riot – Blacks versus The Rest – but with multi-racial cross-currents of Have-nots versus Haves and an increasing infusion of common criminality as more and more professional criminals from other areas arrived to take advantage of this unprecedented break-down in law-and-order. I encountered no muggers or robbers during the night, but heard numerous reports of their activities. Significantly, of the first batch of rioters brought to court, forty-nine out of sixty-six did *not* come from Handsworth.

At about 7.00 a.m. I was devastated to hear that firemen had found two bodies in the Post Office. The Moledina brothers had been immensely kind and helpful to me – among the most welcoming Browns in Handsworth when I was a newcomer.

That was a most dreadful dawn, made inexpressibly more so by groups of jubilant Blacks celebrating their 'achievement' – their destruction of an area of Babylon – by singing and dancing in the streets while dazed Brown traders (many of whom live elsewhere) arrived to face the negation of decades of hard work and sobbed in each other's arms. At that stage it felt very like a Black versus Brown race-riot. One could understand why so much media instant-comment misinterpreted it as such, yet there had been many Brown looters and some of the Lozells Road's few Black business premises were also destroyed.

At 7.45 a.m. I rang my closest London friends from a Berners Street telephone kiosk. Its glass sides had half-melted in the heat, to become all opaque and wavy, yet the telephone was still working – which seemed part of the general unreality, since most Handsworth telephones do *not* work in normal times. Then I went home for a quick mug of coffee; usually breakfast is my main meal but I was too churned up to eat – a widespread reaction, I later discovered, among those involved in the night's events. The 9.00 a.m. news included a supremely fatuous police statement – "This trouble came as a complete surprise. A happy Carnival, opened by the Chief Constable, has just taken place, with police and West Indians dancing together in the streets."

In several media interviews during the next few days, and subsequently in his official Riot Report, Mr Geoffrey Dear made much of the fact that 'The riots took place on a Monday afternoon after a weekend on which a successful Carnival had been held in the streets.' Yet the minority of Blacks who help to organise a police-sponsored Carnival have no connection with that other minority who help to organise a riot. A police force that prides itself on its 'community policing' should know better than to regard the 'West Indians' as a homogeneous group. The claim that the riot 'came as a complete surprise' infuriated Handsworth's Browns. Mr Jaswant Sohal, secretary of the Handsworth Traders' Association and a member of the local police Consultative Committee, said – "Six Asian shops on the Soho Road were vandalised and looted by West Indians on Sunday night. It was no ordinary act of theft. I immediately contacted the police to warn them that this was likely to be the start of something bigger. I cannot believe it when the police say they were not prepared for something. They had been told, but they just did not heed the warning."

By 9.45 I was back on the Lozells Road, where hundreds of media people and sight-seers had gathered. Soon after, the BBC reported that Mr Hurd, the Home Secretary, was heading our way. (His Handsworth nickname can be left to my readers' imagination.) I could scarcely credit this official piling of stupidity on stupidity. Among both Blacks and Browns the Home Secretary (*any* Home Secretary) is at the best of times the *most* hated government minister – for obvious reasons. To have let Mr Hurd loose on the Lozells Road on that Tuesday afternoon seemed grotesquely irresponsible to every resident of Handsworth, whatever their other differences. We all knew beforehand exactly what would happen; by noon I had chosen which garden wall to lie behind while observing the farce. But it seems the police did *not* know. Although then present in vast numbers, up and down the Lozells Road, they had somehow failed to notice what was going on all morning, from about 8.00 a.m., as local Black militants, who wanted the rioting to be resumed at dusk, incited gangs of youths to more violence. There was nothing furtive about this rabble-rousing; the speakers stood on garden walls, only yards away from lines of policemen, while spouting revolution to increasingly emotional gatherings of Black youths. And yet the Home Secretary was allowed into that area to mingle with those youths – a novelist who invented such an implausible episode wouldn't be published. It was indeed brave of Mr Hurd to venture into the war-zone, but one can feel only modified admiration for that sort of bravery – based on total ignorance of and insensitivity to the feelings of a community. He was lucky to escape without injury (except to his dignity). But when he had been rescued by the police, and bundled rump-up into a prison-van, Handsworth was left to take the consequences of Home Office misjudgement and police obtuseness. As the rescue vehicle sped away, missiles flew thick as a flock of starlings and several journalists were attacked and burning car tanks exploded – including an overturned police van, close to my garden wall, which was looted before being set on fire. Then the disorder spread over a wide area of Handsworth and many more shops were looted and vehicles burned. Afterwards a black (no pun intended) joke circulated in police circles – "When we got him in the van we beat nine shades of stuffing out of him – just habit – before we saw who he was!" It would please me if that story were true, but I fear it isn't.

It was another hot sunny day, which seemed to emphasise the tragedy of the still smouldering Lozells Road. While sitting with Black friends – a middle-aged couple – on the doorstep of their terrace house in a nearby street, I listened to Mrs Thatcher setting the tone for Tory reaction to the riot. Having condemned it as "utterly appalling", and emphasised that it was in no way connected with unemployment or inner-city deprivation, she rejected any criticism of the police and added – "We shall need all the leaders of the local community to make sure it doesn't happen again." My friends switched off their transistor and looked at me despairingly. The husband slowly rubbed a hand to and fro across his forehead and said, "That frightens me. That's scary – specially the bit about community leaders. So this country's Prime Minister knows nothing – understands nothing – about our problems! How many more riots before she learns?" Immediately 'Utterly Appalling!' became a Handsworth catch-phrase; for days one heard it being chanted with derision up and down the back-streets.

Watching media people at work deepened my post-riot depression. They are set an impossible task on such occasions – flung into a complex crisis, without any background knowledge, yet required to deliver their 'piece' by a deadline. On that Tuesday morning various bemused-looking characters wandered up to me with pencils poised over notebooks and asked, "Do you live around here? Can you say *why* this riot happened – in just a few words?"

I gazed at them with genuine sympathy and replied, "I do live around here, but no comment – certainly not in less than ten thousand words." No wonder they produced so much drivel during the next few days, while trying to explain a riot in 'a few words'. It was disquieting to observe them being manipulated by publicity-seeking politicians, ambitious local councillors, devious so-called 'community leaders' – ninety per cent of whom are wildly unrepresentative of their communities – and eloquent Black zealots who fed them packs of lies about police aggro during the 'sparking off' incident outside the Acapulco. Much of the press coverage was as usual malicious/ hysterical/racialist. And unfortunately coverage of such an event only has to be *incompetent* to do more damage to community relations than the event itself.

Even more damaging than the press are television interviews, which make cruel demands in times of stress on people in authority. On that Tuesday morning the Chief Constable was expected to do his bit before the cameras after a sleepless night. When asked, "Do you think this trouble was Blacks against Asians?" he emphatically said "Yes". That monosyllable considerably heightened tension, in complicated ways, throughout the rest of the day. In one sense brief television interviews and cobbled-together newspaper articles are ephemeral as the dew and each media excitement seems to blot out the last riot/spy drama/earthquake/sex scandal. Yet given a Handsworth-type situation the most apparently trivial 'error in communication' can have malign long-term effects among people predisposed to misinterpret or take umbrage at any statement from those in authority.

By agreement with the police, all our local pubs remained closed on 10 September: a sensible move, though it punished the innocent as well as the

guilty. Throughout that day the atmosphere was very much nastier than it
had been during the night. Post-Hurd, rioting was resumed for a few hours –
this time on Heathfield Road. Many windows of private houses were
smashed; cars were overturned and a few set on fire; I saw several groups of
Rastas rushing around with more petrol bombs and about 150 Black youths
erected a barrier at the junction of Heathfield and Westminster Roads. Again
the police were excluded from an area for long enough to permit the looting
of most Heathfield Road shops and the burning of one set of premises. A
Pakistani greengrocer-cum-tobacconist had a flash of inspiration and put up
a notice saying – ALL GOODS FREE TODAY. Most of the looters
passed him by and when I entered in search of cigars the shop was deserted
and more or less intact. I went upstairs but Ali refused to take any money.
"Help yourself!" he said. "That notice is genuine!" As there was no other
shop open within a three-mile radius, and my frayed nerves needed nicotine, I
did help myself; but later I righted that wrong.

Heathfield Road remained so long unprotected because at this stage the
police were alarmingly over-extended. Many had to remain on the Lozells
Road, to keep the public out of the danger area of collapsing buildings. And
simultaneously gangs had gone into action just beyond Handsworth, in Perry
Barr, where there was much looting, burning, robbing at knife-point and
stoning of cars on the A34 trunk road.

When I passed Heathfield Primary School at 2.00 p.m. all gates into the
playground were locked and the staff had requested police protection for
their 300 pupils. Groups of tense parents stood about on the pavement,
debating what to do for the best. Should they take their children home, or
would they be safer in the school building? Emotions were tangled. When
large groups of Black youths raced purposefully past us, towards the barricade at the end of the road, fear of their violence was palpable – as it had not
been during the night. Yet mingled with that fear, on the faces and in the
voices of some young mothers, was admiration for their continuing defiance
of the fuzz.

"They've got the cops on the run!" exclaimed one Black woman, holding
her year-old baby tightly in her arms. "They'll take the Soho Road tonight –
there's no way anyone can stop them now!"

Her companion shivered and said, "*I* don't want no more burning! It'll be
houses next – our homes – anything – they've gone mad, they're just
criminals. What *good*'s it doing us?"

An older Black woman, red-eyed and dishevelled, had come to collect a
grandchild. She said, "We were evacuated last night – Berner Street, the
garage, it was like a war-film! I've a crippled husband, I thought he'd be burnt
in his bed – he's gone now to his sister in Coventry, anything could happen
tonight and he couldn't take no more." Then she threw back her head and
folded her arms and looked directly at me. "You think we're all savages?" she
asked rhetorically. "OK – *I* think we're savages. But maybe we have to be,

see? Remember the States? *I* remember! 'Burn, Baby, Burn!' And *then* something happened . . . It's bad when you're in the middle of it – like us, now, here, on the Heathfield Road and we don't know will it still be here tomorrow. And those kids are just gone crazy with excitement – it breaks the monotony, see? And maybe it has to be like this – like this and worse than this, all over Britain, wherever there's Blacks . . . And *then* maybe something happens, see?"

A very young White mother was listening; she had a pale, thin, drawn face – one of those heart-breaking inner-city faces that look old at twenty. Now she thrust out her hand to the Black granny. "Shake!" she said. "You're talking for us, too! Handsworth isn't having a race-riot – *no way!*"

Violence spread rapidly throughout that grim afternoon. All Handsworth's criminals, joined by scores from other areas, seemed to be on the rampage. Six Soho Road shops, including two jewellers, were looted and one petrol-bombed. Shops and offices on Rookery Road, Grove Lane and Oxhill Road were ransacked. Anyone who tried to defend property or cash was threatened – and several people were attacked – with knives acquired the night before along the Lozells Road. The police couldn't cope and terrified Brown traders were complaining that they had been abandoned to the mercilessness of the Blacks. Earlier the police had stupidly announced that they were treating the Moledina brothers' deaths as murder. Several newspapers had printed fictitious accounts – under 'BLOODLUST!' or 'KILLING!' or 'MURDER!' headlines – of the brothers having been beaten and stabbed by a Black gang who then set the post office alight and left them to roast to death. Anyone who had been near the post office at the time found these accounts incredible; the Lozells rioters were not, as the Chief Constable later admitted in his report, person-threatening. And many months later a twenty-year-old *White* man was convicted of the brothers' *manslaughter*. But post-riot the shockingly irresponsible media image of *Blacks murdering Browns* added immeasurably to the terror and despair felt by Brown traders when Black gangs invaded their premises and there wasn't a policeman in sight.

By dusk the windows of most shops, pubs, post offices, banks and offices had been boarded up and the siege atmosphere was strong. Happily several pubs along the Soho Road were accessible at that stage though not open; by knocking on a side-door, and identifying oneself, it was possible to gain admission. About 200 young Blacks gathered at the Soho Road–Villa Road junction soon after dark; a similar group at the Boulton Road junction petrol-bombed a police Traffic Control van. Gangs of youths – Black, Brown and White – were roaming the surrounding streets and I roamed too. At irregular intervals police-gang confrontations took place but I was then sufficiently familiar with Handsworth's back streets and alleyways to move from trouble spot to trouble spot without getting too involved. All this activity incidentally proved that my broken back had completely recovered; I was never reminded of it while avoiding street-battles by climbing over walls or into trees, or scrambling into outhouses full of unidentifiable objects. Only once, near the top of Soho Road, did I become marginally involved in the action when a riot-squad was chasing youths (that group ninety per cent Brown). The police were understandably on edge and one officer hit me hard on the right leg with his baton because I wasn't running fast enough. But one can hardly hold that against him; we the mob had to be kept moving – and if possible intimidated – lest the Soho Road too might go up in flames.

For a time I was joined by a nineteen-year-old Wykehamist then living in the squalor of Small Heath (which makes Handsworth seem like Hampstead) to escape the oppressive wealth of the parental home. He was an endearing youngster but being accompanied by a White male – especially one who spoke Wykehamese – made me feel very much more at risk. Soon after we had witnessed the looting of the Villa Road chemist shop, at midnight, I pretended that I was going home to bed and persuaded Robert to take a taxi out of Handsworth.

By then over 900 police officers were being deployed – 460 on loan from five other forces – yet a new Black barricade had been set up on the Villa Road and I saw five vehicles set alight on Hamstead Road. Around 1.00 a.m. things got very rough in that area and when police reinforcements arrived these were attacked simultaneously by Black *and* White gangs. I took refuge up Hall Road from the flying bricks and bottles and flailing batons; but unfortunately the street battle also moved in that direction, forcing me to lie flat behind a screen of nettles outside a derelict house.

After that it felt like time for a pint. I hurried through back streets – littered with half-bricks and broken glass – to a Soho Road pub that was being used by the national and international media as their Handsworth base-camp. At 2.15 a.m. I stumbled in, speechless (I thought) with exhaustion, my jacket reeking of human shit picked up behind the nettles. As I took it off by the door I was converged upon by five gentlemen of the press, all stylishly clad in sweaters, silk cravats, neatly pressed slacks – and all eagerly asking, "What's going on out there?"

I had then been in action almost continuously for thirty-two hours and something snapped. "You fucking lazy bastards!" I snarled. "You only have to walk fifty yards from here to find out for yourselves!" Then I turned my back and ordered my pint, feeling rather self-scandalised. This was the first time in my life I had ever used the word 'fucking', which just shows how corrupting riots are. Or perhaps it was simply the baneful cumulative effect of eight months' exposure to inner-city speech.

Next day I regretted my outburst. Many media people, particularly television camera-crews and press photographers, had been in real danger on that Tuesday and showed the sort of courage that wins medals for soldiers. I especially remember Radio 4's reporter (Diana Goodman, I think) who during the Hurd shambles dodged to and fro through a non-stop fusillade of missiles, gallantly recording as she went. Meanwhile I was safely tucked away, behind my cunningly chosen garden wall, timidly peering out at the scene through the billowing smoke of a burning police van and feeling no ambition to be a BBC reporter. Soon after Mr Hurd's departure a multi-racial gang robbed a television crew of £32,000 of equipment and several press photographs had their cameras seized. The media have so often helped police forces to identify 'wanted' men after crowd trouble that television cameramen and press photographers are all assumed to be loyal allies of the fuzz.

By the time I got home at 4.00 a.m. on 11 September my corner of Handsworth seemed quiet. Despite having been awake for forty-six hours I could sleep only briefly and restlessly and was on patrol again by 7.30. It then seemed to many of my equally wakeful neighbours that given Birmingham's youth unemployment rate, and the evident relish felt by non-Handsworth Whites and Browns for joining in our Rasta-led excitements, police/gang confrontations could go on indefinitely. However, two senior police officers had already met a group of Rastas during the small hours, to discuss police/Black co-operation in restoring the rule of law. Another meeting was held that afternoon in the local community centre and the police decided to accept an offer of help from a prominent Rasta – one of the two arrested outside the Acapulco on the previous Monday afternoon. He promised to exert his influence over the youthful mobs, in exchange for a police promise to remove their vans (full of riot-police) from the forecourt of the Villa Cross. The police then lent him two megaphones and he and a lieutenant toured the area by car, exhorting Black youths to disperse and go home. That evening Tranquillity Ruled OK throughout Handsworth. I met a few groups of disgruntled White youths who had come back for more action but could find none – there was not a Rasta in sight . . .

The police had made a correct and courageous decision. Their apparent collusion with 'the enemy' infuriated many Whites and Browns – especially Browns, who were already convinced that police pandering to Rastas was the cause of all their recent losses and suffering. Inevitably the officers concerned – Chief Superintendent Don Wilson and Superintendent Martin Burton – were accused of having conceded 'victory' to the Blacks by tacitly admitting that law and order could be restored only with their co-operation. (As was indeed the case – which fact seemed to confirm the Residents' Associations' worst suspicions.) The popular press – true to form – at once exacerbated a desperately difficult situation by twisting the facts and packing their pages with lies about 'Rasta vigilantes' taking over Handsworth. The *Daily Mail* devoted half a page to misleading headlines – 'POLICE DO A DEAL IN RIOT CITY: Officers Pulled Out . . . Rastafarians "on patrol".' According to the *Daily Mail* reporter – 'The deal, which astonished local MPs, came after Home Secretary Douglas Hurd had seemed to make it clear earlier in the day that he was not willing to see inner cities turned into 'no go' areas where mobs could roam unhindered.' Had the police been swayed by the Home Secretary and the local MPs Handsworth would undoubtedly have had a third night of widespread lawlessness. The numerous media reports that 'Officers pulled out' were iniquitous. The police did *not* pull out. On that evening, and for a month after the riot, I could not leave my pad and walk ten yards in any direction without meeting a foot patrol. What they did do, on Wednesday 11 September, was sensibly agree to move their protected riot vans from the forecourt of the Villa Cross (still an emotional Rasta flash-point, though the pub was closed for good) and instead park them nearby – for instance, around the corner from No. 45, in Heathfield Avenue, only a brick's throw from the Villa Cross/Acapulco front line yet not provocatively *on* Rasta territory. This is what 'community policing' is all about – making allowances for the strength of particular local feelings, about which neither Home Secretaries nor MPs know anything. Sadly, this standard of community policing was not maintained during my seven post-riot weeks in Handsworth.

14 · Post-Riot

Other riots, in Brixton and Tottenham, soon moved the spotlight from Handsworth. Yet as time passed I realised that the physical happenings of a riot – looting, burning, attacking police, erecting barricades – merely mark the beginning of a process. Life doesn't 'get back to normal'. Depending on official reactions, it can be better or worse – but never again the same. A whole community has been profoundly shocked; or, in this case, three communities. And the rioters themselves, apart from a few hardened criminals, suffer their own share of the trauma – even if they have not been 'picked up'. A month after that extraordinarily night on the Lozells Road, some of the youngsters involved were wondering, "What was it all about? Where did it get us?"

Post-riot, my corner of Handsworth changed utterly. By the end of September some 300 of my more ebullient neighbours were in prison – or under curfew restrictions, if on bail – which made for a much quieter, though in my view not more agreeable area. Where Rastas had been conspicuous pre-riot, the police were now conspicuous – their large white vans parked around every other corner, their foot-patrolling incessant. The Villa Cross stood deserted, all its doors and windows boarded up, and I mourned its passing. When I drifted into alternative pubs I quite often met other ex-Villa Cross regulars, also drifting, and we exchanged rueful little smiles. Many of them got hostile receptions in pub after pub and were 'requested to leave the premises'; the breweries were determined that no other pub should be taken over by Rasta ganja-dealers. And the official police 'explanation' for the riot strengthened that determination.

On Monday 15 September the *Birmingham Post* gave massive front-page headlines to – 'DESPERATE PUSHERS WERE RIOT WAR-LORDS: Drug Barons hit by Clampdown'. The report began: 'Drug barons fighting to defend enormous profits against a police crackdown were almost certainly behind the Handsworth riots, the West Midlands Chief Constable claims'. Next evening one of the 'Warlords' came to supper in my pad and we gloomily discussed this police fantasy. Sebbie had been among the main Villa Cross dealers. His profits were so 'enormous' that within eight days of the trade having been stopped by the riot he was virtually penniless. As he pointed out, "When the drug-squad find fourteen dealers with £3,200 between them in cash they get stories of 'enormous profits' into the papers. But how much is that? It's around £220 per dealer. If they arrested a truck-driver with £220 in his wallet would they say he made 'enormous profits'? And do the police think all that £220 – or £300 or £400 – is *profit*? Don't they know some of it has to be spent on the next supply? Don't they know we're like small *shopkeepers*? If a man sells you a pound of tea for £1.50 you need to be real dumb to think his *profit* is £1.50!" Sebbie picked up the newspaper and frowned again over the headlines and then read aloud from the report: " 'Mr Dear faced three hours of tough questioning at a private meeting of the West Midlands Police Committee, where at least one member condemned police as incompetent and inefficient during the rioting.' " He looked up at me and exclaimed – "Dangerous! And you know why? If Dear believes all this Drug Baron stuff, he knows nothing about the scene his men are supposed to be policing. And if he *doesn't* believe it, he's telling lies to take attention away from the mess his men made last week. All that shit about happy times at the Carnival – drumming in the Park while Handsworth prepares to burn! So which is worse, for a Chief Constable to be stupid or dishonest? Because this man has to be one or the other . . . And it's bad news, either way, for Handsworth!"

Towards the end of September I spent an evening in the Grey Dove with Dinah, one of my Black social worker friends. She picked me up from No. 45 and as we drove past the deserted Villa Cross I could feel her anxiety before she spoke. "This area gives me the shivers right now," she said. "What's to happen to all those Black kids? They were social rejects to start with, now they don't even have the Villa Cross. I know too many of them – I know where they stay and how they've never had stability, emotional or material. I'm scared which way they could turn from here. With that pub closed, their last bit of security is gone. The Acapulco's not the same. There's too many baddies run that scene. You know something? And those Rasta kids wouldn't like me to say this, but it's *true* – it was a White man, Kev in the Cross, gave them that homey secure feeling. Most of those kids aren't criminals – 'cept for what they smoke. OK, so they were during the riot and half of them are locked away right now. But they're not *natural* criminals – you get what I'm saying? And it bothers me they could turn criminal, after this – just being held in Winson Green, the way things are there since the riot, could drive anyone to criminality! They'll come back here angry – especially the innocent ones, who've had confessions beaten out of them. And they'll be angrier still when they see the way the fuzz have bust their scene – I mean the kids' scene, which wasn't to do with *dealing*. Maybe the cops thought they were right to try to nail the merchants – maybe they'd no choice, with all that outside pressure on them. But all they've done is scupper the kids' life-style, leaving most of the merchants walking around Handsworth figuring out how to get the trade going again . . . So the result could be a lot more *real* crime than Handsworth ever had before, with those embittered kids looking for revenge."

Like most of my Black friends and neighbours, Dinah wasted no time quibbling about the riot's 'spark' – the Traffic Police incident outside the Acapulco. "Sure those cops were crazy to start hassle on the Villa Road with tension so high. But traffic cops know damn all about local conditions, they're from outside. And Lozells Road was a riot waiting to happen – if it wasn't that incident it would've been something else. Anyway why shouldn't the fuzz treat Rastas like the rest of us? I'm a driver crossing the front line most days – and often in a big hurry – and I get fed up with all those cars illegally parked. It's just another two-fingers to the fuzz and never mind the general public . . ."

Throughout the autumn Handsworth was awash with allegations of wrongful arrests and police misbehaviour, as hundreds of homes were searched, van-loads of loot recovered and hundreds of young Blacks imprisoned. Two middle-aged, ultra-respectable Pentecostal couples of my acquaintance were deeply distressed and disillusioned by their personal experiences of police thuggery. In one case a nineteen-year-old son had spent the first half of September in London, staying with an aunt while looking for a job; he had four O Levels and couldn't accept that he must remain forever jobless. Soon after his return home he was arrested and accused of burglary during the night of 10/11 September. In the other case a twenty-one-year-old son was in Southampton during the week of the riot, visiting his girlfriend who worked there as a cinema-cleaner. He too was arrested on his return to Handsworth and accused of arson. Despite severe ill-treatment both youths refused to 'confess'; but neither is likely to forget his experience of 'British justice'.

A Rasta youth named Arnold Salmon was less resolute. After a few sessions with officers of the Serious Crimes Squad, he 'confessed' to having distributed petrol bombs and engaged in arson. In fact this decision to avoid further pain by 'confessing' was sensible because of his cast-iron alibi; during the riot he was undergoing surgery in Dudley Road Hospital. He was acquitted in Birmingham Crown Court in October 1986.

I found the general White reaction to rumours of police brutality no less disturbing than the rumours themselves. Tribalism reigned supreme. The Black tribe had savagely attacked the White tribe: therefore the White tribe was entitled to its revenge. Perhaps it is naïve of me to be always taken aback by such revelations of the primitive in twentieth-century *homo sapiens*.

Brown reactions to those same rumours were more complex. Most of my Brown friends asserted that no ill-treatment likely to be meted out by British police would be quarter severe enough to punish adequately the Rasta rioters – and their Brown and White accomplices. Yet they were less inclined than the Whites to think in simple tribal terms – 'All young Blacks are criminals and deserve what they get.' No doubt this was partly because over the years most of them had suffered from police racialism, in one form or another, and partly because their post-riot mood was implacably anti-police. Many were convinced that on 9 September senior police officers had deliberately taken decisions which sacrificed the mainly Brown territory of Lozells Road to looting Blacks, by way of saving White districts from destruction.

The most obvious riot fall-out was a pullulation of public meetings – usually acrimonious – organised by the Council Investigation Committee, the Police/Afro-Caribbean Consultative Committee, the Asian Traders' Association, the Community Relations Council (which disintegrated in the course of its meeting), the Black Power 'Defend Handsworth Campaign' (defend Handsworth against the police, that is), the Militant Left (addressed by Tony Benn, Tariq Ali and the local Marcus Garvey Foundation leader), the Lozells Road Traders' Committee (to organise compensation) and – oddest of all – a Trotskyite anti-everything rally in a damp and gloomy Nonconformist church basement at which the principal speakers were an American Trade Unionist and a young woman with a strong West Belfast accent. Most of those meetings were, I suppose, useful safety-valves for the convoluted emotions of an angry, frightened and mutually suspicious three-community populace.

There was however no meeting, that I heard of, to consider the problems of Handsworth's White OAPs, who seemed to me the group which had suffered most of all, psychologically, from the riot – even more than the younger and comparatively resilient Brown traders. Many of these frail old folk – especially those living alone – were terrorised by the events of 9–11 September; so terrorised that for weeks they couldn't sleep, were afraid to go shopping and trembled at the slightest unfamiliar sound, fearing a Rasta invasion of their flat or little house. They didn't doubt that Handsworth had had a *race*-riot. And they saw themselves as the most defenceless section of the population – doomed targets for their Black neighbours who had now *proved* that they could outwit the police and take over an area when they chose. In a tiny but gallant effort to counteract this after-effect of the riot, Sebbie and three friends (two White, one Black and also a 'Drug Baron') had started a shopping-service for the OAPs who lived in the streets immediately around them. It is sad that such boring details are never given two-inch headlines.

Although on 7 October Handsworth again felt tense, post-Tottenham riot, no one expected more local trouble in the immediate future. It was however grim to hear so many Blacks – and not a few young Browns and Whites – rejoicing because a policeman had been killed. These were not (I think) the sort of people who would ever themselves kill anyone. But they made no effort to disguise their feeling that justice, in their terms, had been done. A dead PC was seen as appropriate retribution for a maimed Black woman in Brixton, a dead Black woman in Tottenham (who allegedly died as a result of a 'police assault') and a dead five-year-old boy in Brum.

At lunch-time next day I met Tobias in one of Handsworth's few Black-run pubs, to which we had both transferred our allegiance since the closing of the Villa Cross. Behind the bar hung a brand-new notice: TOBACCO SMOKING *ONLY* PLEASE!

Tobias's flatlet, which he tended so carefully, had been taken apart by loot-hunting police not long after our riot. "They smashed things up just out of spite," he explained sadly. "I'm Black on the dole living near Lozells Road, so what could I do? Nothing but stand there watching them making a mess for fun . . . Man, they *enjoyed* it! Maybe I would too, if I was a cop a week after that night – right? We'll never have community policing again – not really, only on paper. You know what this country needs? A sort of military-type Special Riot Squad – nothing to do with the police. Not armed with guns, but maybe with whips or something like they have in South Africa. And maybe with vehicles like in Northern Ireland that can drive through anything. It's stupid expecting ordinary cops to fight battles!"

"*No!*" I said. "I've seen 'military-type' squads in action all over the place – in France, Peru, Turkey – and I wouldn't wish anything remotely like them on this country!"

Tobias wasn't swayed. "They'd be better than the way things are going – three riots in a month – and now we're into killing! People don't understand yet how things are. They don't realise when some Blacks talk about *war* they mean it. So you get all this crap about law-and-order and criminals, from Thatcher and that lot. They haven't begun to catch up with where it's all at. They reckon 'better police equipment' must be the answer – and longer jail sentences and so on. But what happened here and in Tottenham wasn't the sort of *crime* police were invented for – it was an uprising – a little bit of revolution. And there'll be lots more of the same, with more and more Whites and Asians joining in, 'cause no one's interested in *why* . . . O K, so they write yards and miles in papers and magazines and you'll be no better in your book. But nobody *does* anything. So I say let's have this military squad, *separate* from police forces. They wouldn't have to be out next day on foot patrol, pretending all's forgiven and forgotten when it isn't – see? I'm talking about two different things – law-and-order and *war*. We all need law-and-order so we all need cops – right? But isn't it crazy to put them into a war situation with one part of a community? They're just normal humans, so they'll have it in then for *all* that community. Next thing, they lose support even when they should be getting it, when they're against ordinary *real* crime – see? That's the way it's going round here this past month. Black people who've never said a word against the fuzz – ever! – they're getting to hate 'em . . . Why? 'Cause so many cops are so mad they're kicking the shit out of anything Black if it moves – right?"

"Right," I agreed gloomily, thinking of all my law-abiding Black friends to whom Tobias's remarks applied only too exactly. Within my own little Handsworth circle, several family rifts had been mended since the riot as parents rallied to the defence of sons unjustly accused and/or beaten up by the police.

I recalled that conversation in March 1986, when I spent a week in Handsworth soon after Mr Hurd had announced (in Handsworth!) that any Chief Constable's future requests for plastic bullets would be granted by the Home Secretary – even if local Police Authorities had refused to sanction their use. Mr Hurd argued that this would be a lesser evil then calling in the army, with live ammunition, to suppress a police-endangering riot. Not every one accepted this reasoning. Plastic bullets (police prefer the 'baton round' euphemism) may not be live ammunition, but in Northern Ireland fifteen of their victims are no longer live people; and numerous other innocent citizens have been permanently maimed by them. Of the fifteen killed as a result of police error, seven were children. At least most soliders know how to handle lethal weapons with the minimum risk to the general public; in this respect the British army has a good record in Northern Ireland. The misjudgements that would inevitably be made by less well trained policemen, under severe pressure from Black mobs, are only too easy to imagine – as are their consequences.

No one who witnessed the Lozells Road attack on the West Midlands police could fail to understand their Chief Constable's being tempted to lay in a supply of plastic bullets for future ref. Yet many responsible Handsworth Blacks regard this temptation as a trap being laid for the fuzz. It would perfectly suit the purposes of some Black militants if a Black rioter – or better still an innocent Black by-stander – were killed by a police bullet. And this *will* happen, sooner or later, if such weapons are used. The argument against plastic bullets is not based – as the Tory press habitually suggests – on wishy-washy humanitarianism or sentimentality about 'poor deprived Blacks'. It is based on a practical assessment of the dangers inherent in this policy change. Because 'nobody *does* anything', as Tobias said, there will be more riots in Britain and a minority of militant Blacks are longing for the use of plastic bullets as a signal for them to declare 'legitimate war' on the fuzz. The combination of this minority's extreme aggressiveness and Home Office approval of plastic bullets has frightened even tough young Rastas – when they think about it in the seclusion of their flats or squats. But this fear does *not* mean that the issuing of plastic bullets would deter those same young men from participating in a riot.

One articulate, anti-White, anti-Church friend of mine – Morgan – was appalled by the threat to everyone (Black, White, Brown) inherent in this Black militant/plastic bullet combination. In March 1986 he admitted having overcome his disdain for Black Pentecostal pastors and appealed to them to put the case against plastic bullets to the Home Office – "Because it's no good young Blacks like us agitating about them. We're supposed to be criminals and government ministers don't listen to criminals – which is why a lot of us might soon be real criminals. What the Home Office needs to understand is the *emotional* reaction you get in the Black community to the very *thought* of plastic bullets. Don't they know we identify with our South African brothers? We *really* do, it's not just political big-mouthing. If the fuzz fired on us – or even threatened it – we'd know then what we've suspected for years. We'd be *sure* they're trying to crush us same as with the Blacks in Soweto and all those places . . . And that'd be I T – man, can't they see the danger? Don't they *want* to understand? Why won't they listen? Why must they keep it all so simple? Only a law-and-order problem, no complications! Are they afraid if they try to understand they'll get to understand too much, and then maybe they couldn't live at peace with themselves? You know what I figured this past month? Reading all their statements about plastic bullets, and seeing 'em on the box spouting about how great the police are – it came clear to me, what the real problem is. They're all *too clever*. You know what I mean? They all have university degrees and talk beautiful language and have trained minds and think in a straight line – logical and rational and so on. That's the problem, they're blinded by *cleverness*. They reckon, 'Those stupid niggers, they can't see the difference between South Africa and Britain! They don't know when they're well off, they're so thick they'll swallow any propaganda.' Then they write us off, 'cause we're dumb or neurotic or ignorant or hysterical – and you don't waste time on people like that. So they carry on being logical and rational and they can't see the time-bomb under their feet. They don't know how dangerous it is to write people's feelings off just 'cause *you're* so smart you can work out they're not logical. But they're still real feelings. So they go on planning blindly, not seeing the whole of the situation. The illogical bit isn't real *for them* so it doesn't count. And yet it's the bit that sparks off the action . . ."

I remembered Morgan's perception of the 'real problem' when discussing plastic bullets with a London friend who at that time had a professional interest in the controversy. He believed their use would "call the Blacks' bluff – essentially they're cowards, they only take on the police because they know they're unarmed". I pointed out that a rioting mob of British Blacks, aflame with mass-recklessness, would be no more frightened of plastic bullets than South African Blacks are of real bullets. But my friend replied blandly that in Northern Ireland baton rounds had been proved by far the most effective method of crowd control; and there had been an average of only one fatal accident a year. He seemed unable to appreciate the temperamental difference between a White crowd in Northern Ireland and a Black crowd in Britain. It was impossible to convince him that inner-city violence could quickly spread, nationwide, as a result of *one* Black being killed by a police bullet, plastic or otherwise. His insistence that these weapons would be used only *in extremis* failed to reassure me. Northern Ireland's unhappy experience proves that the more often they are used the readier police commanders become to consider their use justified. On 15 November 1986 the BBC announced that during Loyalist crowd trouble outside Belfast's City Hall 'baton rounds were fired to protect adjacent shops from looters'. That is a long, long way from protecting *policemen*.

The Chief Constable produced his riot-report in October 1985. He recalled that five years previously the Police Authority had agreed to the Force's request for an additional 1042 officers, but only 175 had been recruited 'because of budgetary cuts' – hence only twelve officers were on duty in Handsworth when the riot started. He commented on the shortage of protective clothing within the Force and noted that 'there were obviously insufficient personnel carriers available' – while 'in the early stages of the riot communications were difficult because of the lack of adequate (radio) sets'. He also emphasised that the 'outbreak of disorder was pre-planned, well conceived and could not have been foreseen by the police or responsible members of the community. The attack was so ferocious and so extraordinary that the police were unable to control the large and uncivilized crowd with the number of officers deployed to police the area on a normal Monday evening.'

This insistence on describing 9 September as 'a normal Monday evening' provoked unrepeatable comments in Handsworth – as did Mr Dear's explanation that 'Community tension at that time was described by the local commander as "stable".' He went on to stress that neither the Handsworth Consultative Committee nor the local community leaders had mentioned 'any extraordinary display of hostile feeling towards authority . . . over the preceding months . . . There were no indications, therefore, to forecast the disorders of 9/10 September 1985 and none had [*sic*] been produced since.' So much for the Consultative Committees and community leaders.

Policing Handsworth must be hell. You can't please everyone and however you play it you are very likely to displease most people. Yet even some Rastas admitted that for a few years the area's community policing had been comparatively successful. Then came the virtual abandonment of that approach, plus pressure from both Central Government and the local Whites for 'tougher action against drug-pushers'. And then came the riot. Looking at that pattern, Mr Dear's theory that 'the riots were started by those whose livelihood was suffering at the hands of the Drug-Squad' seems superficially convincing. This theory was hatched within hours of the riot's being quelled and the Dear Report is essentially an effort to sell it to the Home Secretary and the public. Invaluable assistance came from the popular press who embraced the notion of 'Drug Barons to blame' with near-hysterical enthusiasm. But unfortunately it was not possible to sell the theory without distoring certain facts of Handsworth life. It became necessary to blur the distinction between cannabis and hard drugs, to exaggerate the effectiveness of the Drug-Squad raids in May and July and to maintain that 'all was normal' until suddenly the Drug Barons led the Black youth into action on 9 September.

One crucial weakness of the theory is its assumption that hundreds of young Blacks were either financially dependent on ganja-dealing (which is nonsense) or so devoted to the dealers that they were prepared to fight a battle on their behalf (which is more nonsense). In fact many of the Villa Cross dealers were at home in their flats or houses throughout the riot, wishing it weren't happening because it was *that* – the riot, not the Drug-Squad raids – that temporarily wrecked their livelihood. The issue was not anyone's material livelihood, but who controlled the Villa Cross territory. The psychological importance to those young Blacks of 'doing their own thing' (dealing or smoking) on the 'front line' can scarcely be exaggerated. This is not to suggest that they should be allowed to do their own thing on the public streets in broad daylight, thereby affronting their neighbours of all colours and creating an atmosphere of lawlessness conducive to other and more serious crimes. But there is a vast difference between the Dear image of 'threatened Drug Barons' using 'diversionary and reactionary tactics' and the reality – a deprived and frustrated sub-culture goaded to fury by what its members perceived as a threat to their 'space', as distinct from their *livelihood*. This however is a much more complicated explanation than Drug Barons; it is hard to think of appropriate punchy headlines. Drug-pushers can be seen as plain criminals, out to get rich by exploiting other people's weaknesses; thus they are the sort of antagonists policemen feel happy with – no 'ifs' or 'buts' . . . That other motive for rioting is discomfiting. *Why* should a large number of young British citizens feel such a need for their own 'space'? The search for answers to that question leads into a thorny forest of problems and it is not the business of any Chief Constable to provide those answers. Acknowledging the forest's existence, Mr Dear wrote:

> I believe that for too long society as a whole . . . has been persuaded to excuse patently criminal behaviour by groups that have wilfully set themselves apart from the consensus values of society . . . I would never seek to minimise the problems of being young, Black and unemployed in a decaying inner-city environment. Black youths suffer particularly from the effects of prejudice, unemployment and scarce resources. These and other ills cannot be ignored and deserve to be addressed by society as a whole. But they can never be taken as a retrospective justification for rioting, looting and murder. No group can legitimately justify its cause or actions by averring that some laws are inappropriate to it. By these assertions the members of such a group will surely set themselves apart from the society in which they live and forgo the right to make demands for acceptance on an equal basis.

Apart from the unwise reference to 'murder', all that seems reasonable from the pen of a policeman whose duty it is to uphold law and order. As Mr Dear points out elsewhere, with a tinge of understandable bitterness, it is too easy to let the inner cities stew – and then, when things go dreadfully wrong, blame it all on bad policing.

Yet as I read the report, and thought of all the individuals I knew who had been involved in that truly barbarous attack on the police, I found myself questioning the word 'crime'. It somehow seems inadequate for the events of

9 September. For the events of the following day and night, yes. But the riot itself was both more and less than 'crime'. More because it was, in intent and execution, a savage declaration of war. Less because it was, in inspiration and impetus, a reckless gesture of desperation. There is no excuse, in the general view, for such behaviour. But on what is that view based? On security, comfort, prospects, the esteem of our neighbours – *some* position in the world, whether cabinet minister or office cleaner. You take a different view if you have nothing and are seen to be nothing – or worse than nothing. Then 'the consensus values of society' are, quite simply, meaningless.

To make the Drug Barons theory saleable, Handsworth's Rastas had to be presented as a menace which, if not firmly dealt with during 1985, would soon inflict massive quantities of dangerous drugs on Birmingham. Mr Dear devotes a chapter to 'Drug and Law Enforcement', noting – 'The public awareness of this grave problem has become acute and has manifested itself in both a public and political re-appraisal of police priorities.' He states, 'There is evidence to show that the established networks for the trafficking of cannabis are now, in addition, being used for the distribution of heroin and cocaine' – but he does not produce any evidence. He brackets cannabis and LSD as 'hallucinogens', though it is a scientific fact that 'cannabis is not strong enough for those who wish to escape to a hallucinatory world for a time; they would turn to LSD'.* He observes that in the West Midlands 'drugs such as heroin and cannabis remain freely available'. He does not explain that cannabis is non-addictive, as numerous commissions and com-mittees – for example, the USA Academy of Medicine – have reported over the years. Mr Dear must be aware of those differences between cannabis and hard drugs which caused the Wootton Commission to declare that 'the legal association of cannabis with heroin is entirely inappropriate, the effects of the use of cannabis being intrinsically different from those of other drugs'. Yet he repeatedly refers to 'heroin and cannabis' in a way which can only perpetuate confusion on this issue. Even his diagram illustrating 'Persons Proceeded Against for Drug Ofference – 1981–1984' uses *syringes* with their sinister connotations (doubly sinister since the advent of AIDS). Yet 79.3 per cent of the West Midland's 1117 drug arrests in 1984 were for use of *cannabis*. And in 60 per cent of cases that cannabis was a small amount for personal use.

It is an important part of Mr Dear's argument that the 22 May raid at the Villa Cross 'dealt a positive blow to the drug-dealing fraternity and effectively curtailed the activities of a number of prominent local dealers'. This may be true of a few individual dealers, but the raid most certainly did not curtail the trade. When I arrived at the end of May it was obvious, though subdued. Everyone was slightly on edge, constantly looking out for the fuzz, and outdoor sales took place only after dark – very late, at that season. As the weeks passed, trading increased and became bolder; watching-for-police

* Michael Schofield, *The Strange Case of Pot*, Pelican (1971).

tension went down and the amounts and varieties of ganja on offer went up conspicuously. For three months I spent an hour or two, three or four evenings a week, watching resin and bush being cut and weighed and sold and smoked all around me; sometimes I had to take my glass off the table to make room for busy resin-cutters. This was not a 'drug-dealing fraternity' to whom anyone had recently dealt 'a positive blow'.

Mr Dear records that in 1984 there were seventeen warrants for drugs executed in Handsworth and up to September 1985 twelve warrants. The 1985 pre-riot difference was in the *style* rather than effectiveness of policing; the new style was High Profile – when *Black* dealers were involved.

The Dear Report's most disquieting passage comes on pages 51–52. It is disquieting because as a calculated exercise in 'disinformation' it casts doubt on the document's overall accuracy. In it Mr Dear seeks to explain away the discrepancy in the publicity organised by the police for cannabis and heroin raids. He writes:

> The execution of drugs warrants at the Villa Cross public house and the Acapulco café were highly successful operations which received considerable media coverage . . . It was reported by the media that public blame for the drug traffic in the area was being wrongly apportioned but it is worthy of note that West Midlands Police had not attempted to apportion blame in any way and each operation was planned, executed and reported on its merits. Certain sections of the community have argued that the responsibility for the introduction of hard drugs into the area lies with the Asian community. It is further suggested that whilst the execution of the warrants at the Villa Cross and the Acapulco received heavy publicity, others received little or none. Significantly, it is argued by a black faction that the arrest of members of the Asian community for the supply of heroin received no publicity. It is a fact that the warrants resulting in black arrests were executed at places of public resort, required the use of many officers and *presumably these were the reasons why media attention was attracted*. Those resulting in the arrests of Asians were at private dwellings with little or no street activity and little media attention [My italics]

A riot 'attracts media attention'. But an eleven-minute surprise Drug-Squad raid, which goes 'very smoothly', receives media attention *only* if the police organise it. No one can be expected to believe that a *Birmingham Post* photographer just happened to be standing outside the Acapulco at the precise moment on 20 July when a top-secret Drug-Squad raid began – with his camera all primed to take first-class split-second action shots of the police tackling Rastas. Moreover, he knew which plain-clothes Drug-Squad officer needed to have his face blanked out before that picture was printed . . .

Why did the police not also have a press photographer in position on 20 August, to record their triumph in finding £300,000 worth of *heroin* in a private house near the police station? And to show the *Birmingham Post* readers four Pakistanis being arrested? In terms of protecting the West Midlands from dangerous drugs, this was an incomparably more important and newsworthy victory for the police than the finding of £1,500 worth of cannabis in the Acapulco. The first brief local press reports of this spectacular haul did not specify that it had been found in a Pakistani house and were so worded that most people assumed this raid to have been part of the 'crack-down on Black drug-dealers'. No wonder 'a black faction' accused the police of campaigning to present Handsworth's Rastas as the chief villains on Birmingham's drug scene.

The term 'institutionalised racism' irritates many. Too often it is used as a thought-stopper, to 'explain' complex issues like Black pupils' under-achievement, or to rally support for unhelpfully aggressive demos, or simply to condemn any group or situation that anti-racists have deemed 'unfair' to Blacks or Browns. Yet it is no figment of the anti-racist imagination. In Britain it forms one of the highest barriers between Blacks and the sort of advances made by Afro-Americans within the past generation. It manifests itself variously and the Dear Report illustrates its subterranean, and no doubt subconscious, workings. To the Average Reader – if such reports have any average readers – its calm, lucid, precise description of the riot (before, during and after) must seem admirably fair-minded and non-racialist. But institutionalised racism – like personal racialism – is at its deadliest when least apparent. In these pages a powerful institution uses its influence, resources, political backing, access to a biased media and massive public sympathy to smear a section of the Black community incapable of defending itself. The slick Drug Barons theory, since re-echoed in other areas (e.g. Bristol) after Black-inspired disorders, appeals equally to a blinkered government and an ignorant public. It will remain an eminently saleable 'explanation' for riots until Whites have been educated about the difference between cannabis/ganja and hard drugs.

Handsworth received the Dear Report with a deserved mixture of anger, cynicism and contempt – but no surprise. To counteract it, the West Midlands County Council scraped together £10,000 and commissioned a panel of six Black and Brown anti-racists – chaired by Herman Ousley, Assistant Chief Executive, London Borough of Lambeth – to produce *A Different Reality*: 'An account of Black people's experiences and their grievances before and after the Handsworth Rebellions of September 1985'. The panel interviewed sixty-seven of Handsworth's Black and Brown organisations (many of them splinter groups) and numerous individuals. Its report is valuable as a record of the discrimination and deprivation that contributed to the 'Rebellions' and it effectively demolishes the Drug Barons theory. But overall it is scarcely less tendentious than the Chief Constable's.

On 10 September, while closely observing the media at work, I heard on seven separate occasions Black spokesmen giving a totally false account of the riot's 'sparking off' incident outside the Acapulco. Already that false account had been completely accepted by Handsworth's Blacks and it was soon to become 'official' Black history throughout Britain. Part One asserted that when a Rasta was attacked by a traffic cop a Black woman came to his defence and was herself attacked. Part Two asserted that in the mêlée a Black man was deliberately pushed under a moving bus by a traffic cop. Later (perhaps as a result of the Mrs Groce and Mrs Jarret tragedies), Part Two seems to have faded from the public consciousness and emotional indignation has been concentrated on the 'brutal police attack on a Black woman'.

I was standing within three or four feet of the traffic cops at the time. They were then talking quietly (even politely) to a Rasta; they were not attacking anyone, or threatening to do so. What I then saw was a young Black woman, who had just approached from the Heathfield Road, striking one traffic cop on the shoulder with her clenched fist. Neither he nor any other police officer retaliated. Fortunately I at once recorded every detail of that Villa Road confrontation in my journal, before the riot proper; otherwise I might now suspect myself of hallucinating, so many people have claimed – with passionate conviction – that what happened was the exact reverse of what I saw happening.

A Different Reality deals disingenuously with this myth:

> There is one point in particular which was raised by a number of those we spoke to and which the review panel believes to be of primary importance in the analysis of the rebellion. We were told repeatedly that the trigger events from which the initial eruptions arose involved a street confrontation between a Black woman and the police. She had apparently intervened on behalf of a Black man who was being abused by officers. The story, which is not mentioned in the police report of the sequence of events, was and probably is still held to be the authentic version of the rebellion's origins by many of the people of Handsworth. This brutal encounter between police and a black woman is an important link between events in Handsworth and the disorders in Brixton and Tottenham, precipitated by the shooting of Cherry Groce and the death of Cynthia Jarret during a police raid on her home. The Review Panel made extensive enquiries but were unable to locate the woman involved in this incident in order to obtain her own verifiable account of her conflict with the police. Nevertheless the primary issue is not who the woman was or even the particular circumstances in which conflict between her and the local police developed. It is rather that large numbers of the people of Handsworth have a view of the police which accepts that the assault and intimidation of Black women is consistent with general police practice. The story ... is as significant for its symbolic as for its actual value. This was the imagery in which the residents of the area expressed their anger and represented their moral outrage against patterns of policing which are experienced at a day to day level as oppression. [page 66] ... it was generally accepted that the final spark to the weeks of tension and police harassment was the attack on a Black woman. As one young woman put it: "It could have been anyone's mother" ... As with the subsequent events in Brixton and Tottenham, Black women bear the brunt of the attacks on the Black community [page 72].

By the time the Review Panel got to Handsworth the young woman in the original version of the 'street confrontation' myth had aged prematurely and 'could have been anyone's mother ...' Having failed to locate her, at least some members of the Panel obviously felt reservations about this myth. Yet instead of seeking the truth they chose to emphasise the alleged incident's 'symbolic' value, apparently not realising how such anti-police propaganda-packs boomerang. Every time Blacks are seen to be unreliable witnesses, or to have fabricated false evidence, they make it easier for a racialist society always to give the benefit of the doubt to police evidence.

Some White non-racialists found *A Different Reality* fundamentally dishonest in several respects but refrained from criticising it in public. Is this wise? Should we say, 'This is how Blacks perceived a situation, and though we know their account it objectively untrue we must respect it as *their* perception'? The Dear Report's unproven allegations and deft distortions have been loudly deplored, so why not equally loudly deplore the distortions within *A Different Reality*? It seems insulting to imply that our standards of honesty cannot be applied to Blacks on matters of factual accuracy – 'They can't be objective – they get *so* carried away! – therefore we must indulge them. Let them have their "significant symbolism" and their "imagery", let them perceive things *their* way.'

That surely betrays either ingrained racialism or an unhealthy fear of provoking Black anger and accusations of 'racism'.

Many concerned Whites recognised that *A Different Reality* is an important document, reflecting how Blacks see life in Handsworth. And, as Morgan so forcefully reminded me, Blacks act and react according to their own perceptions, not according to the facts as given in any report or by any White witness. However, if those in the myth-making and myth-spreading industry are allowed to feel that White non-racialists are afraid to challenge them, because it is seen as 'racist' to accuse any Black of telling lies, than such manipulations of the emotions of angry young Blacks will inevitably lead to more and bloodier 'rebellions'. It needs to be said, by people *not* on the Right, that some anti-racists provoke inner-city aggro by exaggerating police misbehaviour. This campaign to justify hatred of the fuzz may suit the Far Left but it does nothing for Britain's multi-racial deprived.

In its last chapter – 'What Now? Where To?' – *A Different Reality* exposes the central muddle in current Black anti-racist thinking:

> Black British, born and bred and educated (or miseducated) in Britain . . . will not tolerate being pushed around as non-status people. In 1986 Black people in Birmingham are saying that they are not alien, not part of an undesirable chunk of surplus labour to be eradicated . . . They will not accept anything less than equal treatment, justice and control of their own destiny . . . Some argue that the government must develop and lead a major anti-racist strategy to rid the country of racial discrimination . . . [This] would have to ensure that Government at central and local levels stopped deciding what was best for Black people and allowed them self-determination, self-esteem, self-pride and self-development.

The recurring emphasis, throughout this Report, on coloured communities being 'Black British' and 'not alien' is contradicted by the demand for 'control of their own destiny' and 'self-determination'. If (unimaginably) some British government did lead a successful anti-racialist campaign, Black Britons would not need 'self-determination' because all British citizens would then receive equal treatment. To the extent that this muddle (claiming to be 'Black British' while demanding 'self-determination') is a result of White racialism, it should afflict Blacks and Browns equally. Yet it does not. So far most Browns seem content to think of themselves as *Brown in Britain* rather than *Brown Britons*. And in general they have managed to preserve their 'self-esteem' and achieve a considerable degree of 'self-determination' and 'self-development'.

A Different Reality well illustrates the confusion caused by the anti-racist usage of 'Black' to include Browns. Several of my Brown friends were indignant about this. Juju – a dynamic Sikh businesswoman, the mother of three university students – said vehemently, "That report could damage the Asian communities, among people who know nothing about us. It says the educational system is failing Black kids – but it's not failing *our* kids, they do as well and better than Whites. Whichever gang of London Blacks got on the Panel, they were just trying to drag us all down to their own level. Who made the petrol bombs that night in September? And who used them? Did anyone see Asian kids attacking the police? I know some looted, when the looting started – but not many, when you think there are more Asian than Black kids in Handsworth."

Juju's brother was then (March 1986) on holiday in Handsworth from New Delhi and had been following the plastic bullet debate with incredulity. He pointed to a headline in the *Birmingham Post* – 'POLICE COMMITTEE REJECT PLASTIC BULLETS' – and said, "I thought, when I saw that, they must be looking for *real* bullets. But no – they don't want any bullets! I can't understand you people. Riots here and riots there and still you won't admit policemen need guns – and orders to use them when they see the first petrol bomb. What sort of country is this? You let packs of savages burn down your cities because you're afraid to hurt them! Why are West Indian thugs more important than decent hard-working Asians? Those Blacks need to live in India. They wouldn't dare attack *our* police – they'd know their place and they'd stay in it . . . ."

"But guns don't *solve* anything,' I pointed out wetly. "And anyone can get hold of them nowadays – d'you want full-scale guerrilla-war in Britain's inner cities?"

Kushi stamped his foot impatiently. "Dammit! I tell you I don't understand this country! These people, these Blacks, they've been given too much freedom here – filled up with ideas about equality – and they can't cope with it. There's too much liberty in this country and not enough discipline!"

"He's right," said Juju. "*Discipline* – that's a key word. Everyone knows West Indians have problems we don't have and mostly they start as family problems – or maybe no-family problems. They know nothing about making a stable home. And they don't seem to be interested, much, in what happens to their kids. But they won't face up to what's wrong, everything's blamed on 'racism'. *We* know all about racism. This family has had it from the police, schools, the Health Service, the Housing Authority and Immigration. You could write a book just about *our* battles against racism! But if you want a home in Britain you've got to learn to live with it – not burn out your neighbours because you're feeling got at."

"Perhaps", I suggested, "it's easier to learn to live with it if you're educated, middle class and prosperous. And perhaps the *quality* of racism you come up against isn't quite the same as what poor Blacks come up against."

"Now you're talking about something else," said Kushi quickly. "You're talking about *class* disadvantages, not racism."

"Anyway you're wrong," said Juju. "There are thousands and thousands of *very* poor Asians in Birmingham and they make good, secure, loving homes for their kids – *and* keep them under control, usually. Don't try to tell me they come up against less or different racism than the Blacks. A lot of them are *more* disadvantaged, because they can't speak English – or hardly. Still you don't get them organising 'rebellions' – I notice that's the new Black-speak for a riot!"

From that Sikh household, in a leafy, quiet cul-de-sac off Church Lane, I went to see Gerry and Irving in their cramped, damp flat on an un-enveloped street. Irving was one of the Blacks who had given 'personal opinions' to some members of the Review Panel.

"Maybe they were a bit too inflammatory", he said, "in their approach to the Rastas. Sometimes it was nearly like they were encouraging them to riot again soon. But they did a good job on what's wrong in Handsworth. Is there anyone honestly wants to find out how to stop another riot? If there is, they've only to read that little book and go on from there. But looks like there *isn't* anyone really cares. Nothing's changed in six months, except for the worst, with Hurd mad keen to get plastic bullets shaving off dreadlocks . . . And for every *one* Black against the police last August, there's ten against them now – after hundreds of innocent lads being locked up for months. That was pure revenge on a whole community – forget the justice bit!" He stretched behind his chair and took *A Different Reality* from the top of the bookshelf and put on his spectacles. "D'you remember this? I'll read it – 'Violent resistance is now permanently on the agenda while the oppression and the denial of rights and resources continues.' That's true, and everyone in Handsworth knows it's true whether they like the idea or not. But you listen next time and you'll hear it all again – you'll think you're listening to a record! 'Utterly appalling!' 'No excuse!' 'Senseless violence!' 'Unforgivable!' 'Mindless tribalism!' Except there will be one difference, if the fuzz have plastic bullets – 'cause then what will the lads have? Something more than petrol bombs . . . If a few police are killed I'll be sorry–I don't like killing, ever. But the Home Office will be to blame. There are Black voices now calling out the warning from all over Britain. And there's nobody listening. Nobody *ever* listens to Black voices – not unless they've trained 'em first to make noises like White voices."

Epilogue

While writing this book I began to look at old (English) friends with new eyes, trying to discern which, if any, might be described as 'racialist'. Scrutinised from this angle, it became apparent that most firmly believe in British superiority, while being too 'nicely brought up' to say so out loud. The 'ethnic minority problem' is largely a result of this tendency to view foreigners (*any* foreigners) only in relation to the English way of life and to measure their worth by their adaptability to it. The implications of this insular failure of the imagination are disquieting. A foreigner is the product of another culture, whether French or Ibo or Mexican or Hindu, and to detach him from his own culture, dismissing it as inferior because non-British, and see him as in-adequate if he is disinclined or unable to adapt to another culture, seems both stupid and cruel.

This peculiar *British* form of racialism is easier to understand if we remember that not long ago many of England's Eminent Persons were justifying the conquest or elimination of other races by emphasising their 'undeveloped' condition. Consider these statements, chosen from scores of similar pronouncements collected by Peter Fryer in his magnificent history of Black people in Britain:*

> I am apt to suspect the negroes, and in general all the other species of men . . . to be naturally inferior to the whites. There never was a civilized nation of any other complexion than white, nor even any individual eminent either in action or speculation.
>
> DAVID HUME, 1753

> The negro becomes more humanized when in his natural subordination to the European than in any other circumstance.
>
> JAMES HUNT founder of the
> Anthropoligical Society of
> London, 1864

---

* Peter Fryer, *Staying Power*, Pluto Press (1984)

The negroes are made on purpose to serve the whites, just as the black ants are made on purpose to serve the red.

WILLIAM RATHBONE GREG,
essayist, 1865

The lower work of the world will tend in the long run to be done by the lower breeds of men. This much we of the ruling colour will no doubt accept as obvious.

GILBERT MURRAY, 1900

Many Victorian moulders of British public opinion (men whose influence is still, alas! with us) were harbingers of Nazism, openly eager to implement Final Solutions all over the Empire. That illustrious man of God, Charles Kingsley (chaplain to Queen Victoria), commented on the American Indians:

One tribe exterminated, if need be, to save a whole continent. "Sacrifice of human life?" Prove that it is *human* life! It is beast-life.

Charles Dilke, MP for the Forest of Dean, wrote:

The English are more than a match for the remaining nations of the earth . . . the Saxon is the only extirpating race on earth.

John Arthur Roebuck, MP for Sheffield, said in the House of Commons:

In New Zealand the Englishmen will destroy the Maori, and the sooner the Maori are destroyed the better.

Professor Karl Pearson FRS advised Queen Victoria:

We can fill up with men of our own kith and kin the waste lands of the earth, even at the expense of the inferior races of inhabitants.

Peter Fryer reminds us that such statements were 'for real' –

Darwin's theories were distorted and adapted to provide an ideological prop for empire-building – a self-justification for a 'great power' that was expanding aggressively at the expense of 'primitive' and 'inferior' peoples. It should be borne in mind that racial extinction was not just a matter of theory. The black people of Tasmania did not long survive the invasion of their island by the dominant race. They were hunted down without mercy. The last of them died in 1869. And racist ideology justified genocide.

The Victorian exterminators cannot be excused on the grounds that it is unfair to judge them by late-twentieth-century standards. Genocide was not something other than genocide 100 or 150 years ago. And men like Carlyle, Dickens, Ruskin, Tennyson, Kingsley and Matthew Arnold, who gave it their full support, were quite intelligent enough to be held morally responsible for publicly condoning it. If the New Right ever gained control of Britain, and the ideological descendants of Kingsley & Co. were in power, how safe would Britain's Blacks and Browns be? A preposterous question! Or is it? Who would have thought, before the 1930s, that the murder of millions of 'inferior' people was about to be organised by a Western European government?

Some anti-racists see public confessions of White responsibility for the Third World's problems as an important antidote to British racialism. They argue that if English people could be made to recognise how ruthlessly their colonising ancestor misbehaved, the national prejudice-level would fall as the guilt-level rose. To me it seems more likely that the reverse would happen; guilt is often converted into hostility towards those wronged. However, Britain's Whites do need to be informed about the realities of the past they share with Browns and Blacks. They need to understand that the exploitation of other people's resources and the dismantling of their cultures cannot be justified by complacent references to roads, railways, canals, hospitals, schools or any of the material benefits incidentally conferred on Asia, Africa or the Americas. We Whites were not and are not alone in our inter-racial villainy. But, being technologically more advanced and administratively better organised than any other race, we have been far more successful as villains.

There can be no neat-and-tidy ending to a book of this sort. (In fact there may well be *no* ending, for the author. After writing *A Place Apart* I became more involved in the problems of Northern Ireland than I ever was while collecting my material.) At the end of a travel book you pick up the atlas and think about the next journey. At the end of a book about people's unhappiness, the feeling is very different. You cannot put down your pen and walk away from it all. There is nothing much to be *done*. But you still want to hang in there, with the friends you've made.